FEAR IN THE BLOOD

FEAR IN THE BLOOD

*Tales from the Dark
Lineages of the Weird*

Edited by
MIKE ASHLEY

This edition published 2024 by
The British Library
96 Euston Road
London NW1 2DB

Selection, introduction and notes © 2024 Mike Ashley
Volume copyright © 2024 The British Library Board

"Silent Snow, Secret Snow" © 1932, 1959 Conrad Aiken. Used by permission of Brandt and Hochman Literary Agents, Inc. All rights reserved.
The Estate of Conrad Aiken.

"The Pipe-Smoker" © 1932 The Estate of Martin Armstrong. Reprinted by permission of Peters Fraser & Dunlop (www.petersfraserdunlop.com) on behalf of the Estate of Martin Armstrong.

"Wogglebeast" © 1964 The Estate of Edgar Pangborn.

"To Reach the Sea" © 1965 The Estate of Monica Dickens. Reprinted by permission of Peters Fraser & Dunlop (www.petersfraserdunlop.com) on behalf of the Estate of Monica Dickens.

"The Secret Ones" © 1972 Mary Danby.

"Old Fillikin" © 1982 Joan Aiken.

"My Name is Samantha" © 1983 The Estate of Mary C. Pangborn.

"Fran Nan's Story" © 2016 Sarah LeFanu.

Every effort has been made to trace copyright holders and to obtain their permission for the use of copyright material. The publisher apologises for any errors or omissions and would be pleased to be notified of any corrections to be incorporated in reprints or future editions.

Cataloguing in Publication Data
A catalogue record for this publication is available from the British Library

ISBN 978 0 7123 5565 0

e-ISBN 978 0 7123 6832 2

Frontispiece illustration by Sandra Gómez
Cover design by Mauricio Villamayor with illustration by Sandra Gómez
Text design and typesetting by Tetragon, London
Printed in England by CPI Group (UK) Ltd, Croydon, CR0 4YY

CONTENTS

INTRODUCTION: BLOODLINES	7
A NOTE FROM THE PUBLISHER	11

THE MARRYAT FAMILY

Krantz's Narrative	FREDERICK MARRYAT	15
The Haunted Nursery	FLORENCE MARRYAT	43

THE SHERIDAN AND LE FANU FAMILIES

The Watcher	JOSEPH SHERIDAN LE FANU	67
What It Meant	RHODA BROUGHTON	115
Fran Nan's Story	SARAH LEFANU	135

THE HAWTHORNE FAMILY

Young Goodman Brown	NATHANIEL HAWTHORNE	149
The Mysterious Case of My Friend Browne	JULIAN HAWTHORNE	167
Unawares	HILDEGARDE HAWTHORNE	189

THE DICKENS FAMILY

A Child's Dream of a Star	CHARLES DICKENS	199
My Fellow Travellers	MARY ANGELA DICKENS	205
To Reach the Sea	MONICA DICKENS	221
The Secret Ones	MARY DANBY	227

THE PANGBORN FAMILY

The Substitute GEORGIA WOOD PANGBORN	239
Wogglebeast EDGAR PANGBORN	253
My Name Is Samantha MARY C. PANGBORN	265

THE AIKEN FAMILY

Silent Snow, Secret Snow CONRAD AIKEN	283
The Pipe-Smoker MARTIN ARMSTRONG	307
Old Fillikin JOAN AIKEN	319
STORY SOURCES	333

INTRODUCTION

Bloodlines

It is no surprise to learn that quite often trades or skills pass down through the generations in many families. There are wine-making and glass-making firms in France and Italy that have been in the same family for around one thousand years. Near where I live in Kent there's a construction company that has stayed in the same family since 1591.

The same is true of writers but perhaps not over such extensive periods. I know of no living descendants of Geoffrey Chaucer, for example, let alone any who were poets. There are, though, many direct descendants of the fourteenth-century poet Dante Alighieri, who wrote the *Divine Comedy*, and though the present generation includes astrophysicist Sperello di Serego Alighieri, who has written many scientific papers, I haven't traced many poets or authors in the generations between.*

There are, though, families where the writing gene seems to pass to descendants, of which probably the best known are those of Charles Dickens. Amongst his bloodline are the writers Mary Angela Dickens, Monica Dickens and Mary Danby, all represented here. Dickens also provides us with an opportunity to explore our specialist subject, because not only Dickens but several of his descendants turned their hand to tales of the supernatural.

Which is the theme of this volume. I have selected six literary families and chosen stories from different generations to show how

---

* But it's a big family tree. I could have missed someone!

an interest in dark tales has passed down the bloodline. The families include some of the more obvious—the Le Fanu and Sheridan families, whose literary connections spread far and wide, and the Hawthornes, whose ancestry takes us back to the notorious Salem witch trials. Then there are the Pangborns and the mystery of why the children never spoke about their mother, despite her literary skills.

There are, of course, many other such literary families. Had space allowed I might have included Louisa Baldwin, the aunt of Rudyard Kipling, who between her and her sisters had many literary and artistic connections. Then there are the Kingsleys—the well-known Charles Kingsley, of *The Water Babies* fame, along with his dark-horse brother Henry, his sister Charlotte Chanter, author of several sensational gothic novels, and his daughter Mary, who wrote as Lucas Malet. And who can forget the Waugh family: Arthur, his sons Alec and Evelyn and his grandson Auberon. Coming up to date we have Stephen King, his wife Tabitha and their sons Owen and Joseph—who writes as Joe Hill. Enough to show that writing and the weird flow in the blood of many literary families.

In this volume I trace the contributions to the weird made by six families who alone have left a considerable literary legacy. I've also explored whether any family traits or experiences may have appeared in the stories. I'll highlight a few in my story introductions, but the more you get to know about each family, the more revelatory the stories become. The supernatural proved a canny way to disguise family secrets.

MIKE ASHLEY

INTRODUCTION

ACKNOWLEDGEMENTS

Most of the research for this volume comes from my own books and papers, but I must acknowledge the help of several people and certain specific books. I must also acknowledge having drawn upon data researched through the family-tree website ancestry.com. Firstly, my thanks to Douglas A. Anderson and Johnny Mains for feedback on all manner of queries, to Curt Phillips for helping with American military history and to Catherine Pope for her comments regarding Florence Marryat's work. In addition to biographies mentioned in the story introductions I found the following of considerable help.

Helena Kelly, *The Life & Lies of Charles Dickens* (Icon Books, 2023).
Catherine Pope, *Florence Marryat* (EER Publishers, 2020).
Jessica Amanda Salmonson, "Introduction" to Hildegarde Hawthorne, *Faded Garden: The Collected Ghost Stories of Hildegarde Hawthorne* (The Strange Company, 1985).
Jessica Amanda Salmonson, "Gothic Magician: The Life and Supernatural Tales of Julian Hawthorne", introduction to Julian Hawthorne, *The Rose of Death* (Ash-Tree Press, 1997).
Jessica Amanda Salmonson, "The Uncanny Stories of Georgia Wood Pangborn", introduction to Georgia Wood Pangborn, *The Wind at Midnight* (Ash-Tree Press, 1999).
Marilyn Wood, *Rhoda Broughton: Profile of a Novelist* (Paul Watkins, 1993).

A NOTE FROM THE PUBLISHER

The original short stories reprinted in the British Library Tales of the Weird series were written and published in a period ranging across the nineteenth and twentieth centuries. There are many elements of these stories which continue to entertain modern readers; however, in some cases there are also uses of language, instances of stereotyping and some attitudes expressed by narrators or characters which may not be endorsed by the publishing standards of today. We acknowledge therefore that some elements in the stories selected for reprinting may continue to make uncomfortable reading for some of our audience. With this series British Library Publishing aims to offer a new readership a chance to read some of the rare material of the British Library's collections in an affordable paperback format, to enjoy their merits and to look back into the worlds of the past two centuries as portrayed by their writers. It is not possible to separate these stories from the history of their writing and as such the following stories are presented as they were originally published with minor edits only, made for consistency of style and sense. We welcome feedback from our readers, which can be sent to the following address:

> British Library Publishing
> The British Library
> 96 Euston Road
> London, NW1 2DB
> United Kingdom

The Marryat Family

According to Florence Marryat in *The Life and Letters of Captain Frederick Marryat* (1872), the family can trace its roots back to the Norman Conquest when three brothers served with Duke William and, after their success at the Battle of Hastings, were granted lands in Yorkshire, Leicestershire and Kent.

Amongst their descendants was John de Maryat, who held lands in Suffolk, and "had the honour of dancing in a masque before the virgin Queen..." He was sent to France to assist the Protestant Huguenots in their resistance against the French authorities. Maryat joined forces with the French Admiral, Gaspard de Coligny, but Coligny's murder in 1572 led to the St Bartholomew's Day massacre. Over 200,000 Huguenots fled France, with some 50,000 coming to England. Maryat accompanied them and from him descended several generations of non-conformist ministers, including Obadiah Marryat (1651–1699) and his son Zephaniah (1684–1754). Both wrote and printed scores of sermons which may be where the writing gene began.

Zephaniah's son, Thomas (1730–1792), also served as a minister but trained as a physician and was known for providing free medical help for the poor. Perhaps it was with him that the more fanciful literary gene entered the family. In his youth he had been one of a circle of writers who met weekly at a hostelry in London and spent half the night reciting poetry and trading wit. Thomas's humour was often biting, for which he became famous, but over time it lost him friends who tired of his insults. Aside from his medical notes, he used his wit and imagination in *Medical Aphorisms* (1757) and *Sentimental Fables* (1771), the latter in the style of Aesop. Unfortunately, his benevolence led to his own poverty whilst his acerbic wit alienated his friends. There is a record of him sitting in a coffee-house with a note displayed in the window asking if anyone remembered him!

The family fortunes were restored by his son Joseph (1757–1824), though it pains me to say that this was chiefly through slavery. He had migrated to the West Indies in the mid-1780s where he established a lucrative sugar trade to London and America. It was in America that he met his future wife, Charlotte, whom he married in 1790. He already had a two-year-old daughter, Ann, fathered upon one of his slaves. He returned home in 1791 and remained as a merchant in London. He became a Member of Parliament in 1808 having already petitioned parliament against the abolition of slavery.

Joseph had fifteen children, ten of whom survived to adulthood. As Florence recorded, "a passion for literature seems to have pervaded the family" and at least four of the children turned their hand to writing, but the one who interests us is Frederick.

1839

KRANTZ'S NARRATIVE

Frederick Marryat

Before he was ten Frederick Marryat (1792–1848) had experienced loss. Three of his younger siblings had died, and two more followed over the next decade. That sense of loss permeates the following story. Frederick was a rebellious child, often attempting to run away to sea. His father conceded and in 1806, secured Frederick a place on the frigate HMS Impérieuse, *which was renowned for harrying French and Spanish ships in the years after the victory of Trafalgar when Britain "ruled the waves". Marryat was involved in many naval campaigns. He rose through the ranks, becoming a captain in 1825. He was posted to St Helena in 1820 to guard the exiled Napoleon Bonaparte. From 1823 he served in the East Indies, taking an active role in the Anglo-Burmese War of 1824.*

It was while there that he had a supernatural experience. He had written to his brother, Samuel, but had no reply. A few months later he was lying in his bed, when Samuel entered his cabin and said, "Fred, I am come to tell you that I am dead." Marryat leapt from his bed but the vision had vanished. He noted the exact date and when back in England he learned his brother had died at the same time as his vision.

Marryat was awarded the Companion of the Order of Bath, second only to a knighthood, for his gallantry during the Burmese War. He also received a medallion from the Royal Humane Society for saving lives at sea. He resigned in November 1830 saying it was for personal reasons, but he had created enemies with his opposition to impressment, when men were forced into military or naval service. This irritated the future king William IV and thereafter Marryat was no longer welcome at court. He remained outspoken and, despite his father having been a slave owner, stated his detestation of slavery.

Marryat threw himself into writing and his reputation grew with novels of adventure, many based upon his experiences, notably The Naval Officer *(1829),* Peter Simple *(1834) and* Mr Midshipman Easy *(1836). Amongst books for younger readers were* Masterman Ready *(1841) and* The Children of the New Forest *(1847). He had married in 1819 and had eleven children. Three of his daughters became novelists, including Florence.*

Marryat's only venture into the supernatural was The Phantom Ship *(1839). It drew upon the legend of the* Flying Dutchman, *first recounted in the 1790s. The ship and its crew is doomed to sail the ocean around the Cape of Good Hope forever after the captain, Vanderdecken, defied the Almighty in his determination to round the Cape. In Marryat's novel we meet Vanderdecken's son, Philip, who learned of the* Flying Dutchman *from his mother and discovers that only he can save his father if he can find him and present him with a relic of the True Cross. He experiences several strange episodes in his attempts to find the ship and there is much tragedy, including the fate of Philip's beautiful wife, Amine. Within the novel is a separate story told by Krantz, one of Philip's fellow seamen, about his father and the fate of his siblings. The story stands well on its own and has the distinction of being, apparently, the first story about a were-wolf written in English.*

"I take it for granted, that you have heard people speak of the Hartz Mountains," observed Krantz.

"I have never heard people speak of them that I can recollect," replied Philip; "but I have read of them in some book, and of the strange things which have occurred there."

"It is indeed a wild region," rejoined Krantz, "and many strange tales are told of it; but, strange as they are, I have good reason for believing them to be true. I have told you, Philip, that I fully believe in your communion with the other world—that I credit the history of your father, and the lawfulness of your mission; for that we are surrounded, impelled, and worked upon by beings different in their nature from ourselves, I have had full evidence, as you will acknowledge, when I state what has occurred in my own family. Why such malevolent beings as I am about to speak of should be permitted to interfere with us, and punish, I may say, comparatively unoffending mortals, is beyond my comprehension; but that they are so permitted is most certain."

"The great principle of all evil fulfils his work of evil; why, then, not the other minor spirits of the same class?" inquired Philip. "What matters it to us, whether we are tried by, and have to suffer from, the enmity of our fellow-mortals, or whether we are persecuted by beings more powerful and more malevolent than ourselves? We know that we have to work out our salvation, and that we shall be judged according to our strength; if then there be evil spirits who delight to oppress man, there surely must be, as Amine asserts, good spirits, whose delight is to do him service. Whether, then, we have to struggle against our passions only, or whether we have to struggle not only against our passions, but also the dire influence of unseen enemies, we ever struggle with the same odds in our favour, as the good are stronger than the evil which we combat. In either case we are on the 'vantage ground, whether, as in the first, we fight the good cause single-handed, or as in the second, although opposed, we have the host of Heaven ranged on our side. Thus are the scales of Divine Justice evenly balanced, and man is still a free agent, as his own virtuous or vicious propensities must ever decide whether he shall gain or lose the victory."

"Most true," replied Krantz, "and now to my history.

"My father was not born, or originally a resident, in the Hartz Mountains; he was the serf of an Hungarian nobleman, of great possessions, in Transylvania; but, although a serf, he was not by any means a poor or illiterate man. In fact, he was rich, and his intelligence and respectability were such, that he had been raised by his lord to the stewardship; but, whoever may happen to be born a serf, a serf must he remain, even though he become a wealthy man; such was the condition of my father. My father had been married for about five years; and, by his marriage, had three children—my eldest brother Caesar, myself (Hermann), and a sister named Marcella. You know, Philip, that Latin is still the language spoken in that country; and that will account for our high sounding names. My mother was a very beautiful woman, unfortunately more beautiful than virtuous: she was seen and admired by the lord of the soil; my father was sent away upon some mission; and, during his absence, my mother, flattered by the attentions, and won by the assiduities, of this nobleman, yielded to his wishes. It so happened that my father returned very unexpectedly, and discovered the intrigue. The evidence of my mother's shame was positive: he surprised her in the company of her seducer! Carried away by the impetuosity of his feelings, he watched the opportunity of a meeting taking place between them, and murdered both his wife and her seducer. Conscious that, as a serf, not even the provocation which he had received would be allowed as a justification of his conduct, he hastily collected together what money he could lay his hands upon, and, as we were then in the depth of winter, he put his horses to the sleigh, and taking his children with him, he set off in the middle of the night, and was far away before the tragical circumstance had transpired. Aware that he would be pursued, and that he had no chance of escape if he remained in any portion of his native country (in which the authorities could lay hold of him), he continued his flight without intermission until he had buried himself in the intricacies and seclusion of the Hartz Mountains. Of course, all that I have now told you I learned afterwards. My oldest recollections are knit to a rude, yet comfortable cottage, in which I lived with my father, brother, and sister. It was on the confines of one of those vast forests which cover the northern part of Germany; around it were a few acres of ground, which, during the summer months, my father cultivated, and which, though they yielded a doubtful harvest, were sufficient for our support. In the winter we remained much in doors, for, as my father followed the chase, we were left alone, and the wolves, during that season, incessantly prowled about. My father had purchased the cottage, and land about it, of one of the rude foresters, who gain their livelihood partly by hunting, and partly by burning charcoal, for the purpose of smelting the ore from the neighbouring mines; it was distant about two miles from any other habitation. I can call to mind the whole landscape now: the tall pines which rose up on the mountain above us, and the wide expanse of forest beneath, on the topmost boughs and heads of whose trees we looked down from our cottage, as the mountain below us rapidly descended into the distant valley. In summertime the prospect was beautiful; but during the severe winter, a more desolate scene could not well be imagined.

"I said that, in the winter, my father occupied himself with the chase; every day he left us, and often would he lock the door, that we might not leave the cottage. He had no one to assist him, or to take care of us—indeed, it was not easy to find a female servant who would live in such a solitude; but, could he have found one, my father would not have received her, for he had imbibed a horror of the sex, as the difference of his conduct towards us, his two boys, and my poor little sister, Marcella, evidently proved. You may suppose we were sadly neglected; indeed, we suffered much, for my father, fearful that we might come to some harm, would not allow us fuel, when he left the cottage; and we were obliged, therefore, to creep under the heaps of bears'-skins, and there to keep ourselves as warm as we could until he returned in the evening, when a blazing fire was our delight. That my father chose this restless sort of life may appear strange, but the fact was that he could not remain quiet; whether from remorse for having committed murder, or from the misery consequent on his change of situation, or from both combined, he was never happy unless he was in a state of activity. Children, however, when left much to themselves, acquire a thoughtfulness not common to their age. So it was with us; and during the short cold days of winter we would sit silent, longing for the happy hours when the snow would melt, and the leaves burst out, and the birds begin their songs, and when we should again be set at liberty.

"Such was our peculiar and savage sort of life until my brother Caesar was nine, myself seven, and my sister five, years old, when the circumstances occurred on which is based the extraordinary narrative which I am about to relate.

"One evening my father returned home rather later than usual; he had been unsuccessful, and, as the weather was very severe, and many feet of snow were upon the ground, he was not only very cold, but in a very bad humour. He had brought in wood, and we were all three of us gladly assisting each other in blowing on the embers to create the blaze, when he caught poor little Marcella by the arm and threw her aside; the child fell, struck her mouth, and bled very much. My brother ran to raise her up. Accustomed to ill usage, and afraid of my father, she did not dare to cry, but looked up in his face very piteously. My father drew his stool nearer to the hearth, muttered something in abuse of women, and busied himself with the fire, which both my brother and I had deserted when our sister was so unkindly treated. A cheerful blaze was soon the result of his exertions; but we did not, as usual, crowd round it. Marcella, still bleeding, retired to a corner, and my brother and I took our seats beside her, while my father hung over the fire gloomily and alone. Such had been our position for about half-an-hour, when the howl of a wolf, close under the window of the cottage, fell on our ears. My father started up, and seized his gun: the howl was repeated, he examined the priming, and then hastily left the cottage, shutting the door after him. We all waited (anxiously listening), for we thought that if he succeeded in shooting the wolf, he would return in a better humour; and although he was harsh to all of us, and particularly so to our little sister, still we loved our father, and loved to see him cheerful and happy, for what else had we to look up to? And I may here observe, that perhaps there never were three children who were fonder of each other; we did not, like other children, fight and dispute together; and if, by chance, any disagreement did arise between my elder brother and me, little Marcella would run to us, and kissing us both, seal, through her entreaties, the peace between us. Marcella was a lovely, amiable child; I can recall her beautiful features even now—Alas! poor little Marcella."

"She is dead then?" observed Philip.

"Dead! yes, dead!—but how did she die?—But I must not anticipate, Philip; let me tell my story.

"We waited for some time, but the report of the gun did not reach us, and my elder brother then said, 'Our father has followed the wolf, and will not be back for some time. Marcella, let us wash the blood from your mouth, and then we will leave this corner, and go to the fire and warm ourselves.'

"We did so, and remained there until near midnight, every minute wondering, as it grew later, why our father did not return. We had no idea that he was in any danger, but we thought that he must have chased the wolf for a very long time. 'I will look out and see if father is coming,' said my brother Caesar, going to the door. 'Take care,' said Marcella, 'the wolves must be about now, and we cannot kill them, brother.' My brother opened the door very cautiously, and but a few inches; he peeped out.—'I see nothing,' said he, after a time, and once more he joined us at the fire. 'We have had no supper,' said I, for my father usually cooked the meat as soon as he came home; and during his absence we had nothing but the fragments of the preceding day.

"'And if our father comes home after his hunt, Caesar,' said Marcella, 'he will be pleased to have some supper; let us cook it for him and for ourselves.' Caesar climbed upon the stool, and reached down some meat—I forget now whether it was venison or bear's meat; but we cut off the usual quantity, and proceeded to dress it, as we used to do under our father's superintendence. We were all busied putting it into the platters before the fire, to await his coming, when we heard the sound of a horn. We listened—there was a noise outside, and a minute afterwards my father entered, ushering in a young female, and a large dark man in a hunter's dress.

"Perhaps I had better now relate, what was only known to me many years afterwards. When my father had left the cottage, he perceived a large white wolf about thirty yards from him; as soon as the animal saw my father, it retreated slowly, growling and snarling. My father followed; the animal did not run, but always kept at some distance; and my father did not like to fire until he was pretty certain that his ball would take effect: thus they went on for some time, the wolf now leaving my father far behind, and then stopping and snarling defiance at him, and then again, on his approach, setting off at speed.

"Anxious to shoot the animal (for the white wolf is very rare), my father continued the pursuit for several hours, during which he continually ascended the mountain.

"You must know, Philip, that there are peculiar spots on those mountains which are supposed, and, as my story will prove, truly supposed, to be inhabited by the evil influences; they are well known to the huntsmen, who invariably avoid them. Now, one of these spots, an open space in the pine forests above us, had been pointed out to my father as dangerous on that account. But, whether he disbelieved these wild stories, or whether, in his eager pursuit of the chase, he disregarded them, I know not; certain, however, it is, that he was decoyed by the white wolf to this open space, when the animal appeared to slacken her speed. My father approached, came close up to her, raised his gun to his shoulder, and was about to fire; when the wolf suddenly disappeared. He thought that the snow on the ground must have dazzled his sight, and he let down his gun to look for the beast—but she was gone; how she could have escaped over the clearance, without his seeing her, was beyond his comprehension. Mortified at the ill success of his chase, he was about to retrace his steps, when he heard the distant sound of a horn. Astonishment at such a sound—at such an hour—in such a wilderness, made him forget for the moment his disappointment, and he remained riveted to the spot. In a minute the horn was blown a second time, and at no great distance; my father stood still, and listened: a third time it was blown. I forget the term used to express it, but it was the signal which, my father well knew, implied that the party was lost in the woods. In a few minutes more my father beheld a man on horseback, with a female seated on the crupper, enter the cleared space, and ride up to him. At first, my father called to mind the strange stories which he had heard of the supernatural beings who were said to frequent these mountains; but the nearer approach of the parties satisfied him that they were mortals like himself. As soon as they came up to him, the man who guided the horse accosted him. 'Friend Hunter, you are out late, the better fortune for us: we have ridden far, and are in fear of our lives, which are eagerly sought after. These mountains have enabled us to elude our pursuers; but if we find not shelter and refreshment, that will avail us little, as we must perish from hunger and the inclemency of the night. My daughter, who rides behind me, is now more dead than alive,—say, can you assist us in our difficulty?'

"'My cottage is some few miles distant,' replied my father, 'but I have little to offer you besides a shelter from the weather; to the little I have you are welcome. May I ask whence you come?'

"'Yes, friend, it is no secret now; we have escaped from Transylvania, where my daughter's honour and my life were equally in jeopardy!'

"This information was quite enough to raise an interest in my father's heart. He remembered his own escape: he remembered the loss of his wife's honour, and the tragedy by which it was wound up. He immediately, and warmly, offered all the assistance which he could afford them.

"'There is no time to be lost, then, good sir,' observed the horseman; 'my daughter is chilled with the frost, and cannot hold out much longer against the severity of the weather.'

"'Follow me,' replied my father, leading the way towards his home.

"'I was lured away in pursuit of a large white wolf,' observed my father; 'it came to the very window of my hut, or I should not have been out at this time of night.'

"'The creature passed by us just as we came out of the wood,' said the female in a silvery tone.

"'I was nearly discharging my piece at it,' observed the hunter; 'but since it did us such good service, I am glad that I allowed it to escape.'

"In about an hour and a half, during which my father walked at a rapid pace, the party arrived at the cottage, and, as I said before, came in.

"'We are in good time, apparently,' observed the dark hunter, catching the smell of the roasted meat, as he walked to the fire and surveyed my brother and sister, and myself. 'You have young cooks here, Mynheer.' 'I am glad that we shall not have to wait,' replied my father. 'Come, mistress, seat yourself by the fire; you require warmth after your cold ride.' 'And where can I put up my horse, Mynheer?' observed the huntsman.' 'I will take care of him,' replied my father, going out of the cottage door.

"The female must, however, be particularly described. She was young, and apparently twenty years of age. She was dressed in a travelling dress, deeply bordered with white fur, and wore a cap of white ermine on her head. Her features were very beautiful, at least I thought so, and so my father has since declared. Her hair was flaxen, glossy and shining, and bright as a mirror; and her mouth, although somewhat large when it was open, showed the most brilliant teeth I have ever beheld. But there was something about her eyes, bright as they were, which made us children afraid; they were so restless, so furtive; I could not at that time tell why, but I felt as if there was cruelty in her eye; and when she beckoned us to come to her, we approached her with fear and trembling. Still she was beautiful, very beautiful. She spoke kindly to my brother and myself, patted our heads, and caressed us; but Marcella would not come near her; on the contrary, she slunk away, and hid herself in the bed, and would not wait for the supper, which half an hour before she had been so anxious for.

"My father, having put the horse into a close shed, soon returned, and supper was placed upon the table. When it was over, my father requested that the young lady would take possession of his bed, and he would remain at the fire, and sit up with her father. After some hesitation on her part, this arrangement was agreed to, and I and my brother crept into the other bed with Marcella, for we had as yet always slept together.

"But we could not sleep; there was something so unusual, not only in seeing strange people, but in having those people sleep at the cottage, that we were bewildered. As for poor little Marcella, she was quiet, but I perceived that she trembled during the whole night, and sometimes I thought that she was checking a sob. My father had brought out some spirits, which he rarely used, and he and the strange hunter remained drinking and talking before the fire. Our ears were ready to catch the slightest whisper—so much was our curiosity excited.

"'You said you came from Transylvania?' observed my father.

"'Even so, Mynheer,' replied the hunter. 'I was a serf to the noble house of ——; my master would insist upon my surrendering up my fair girl to his wishes; it ended in my giving him a few inches of my hunting-knife.'

"'We are countrymen, and brothers in misfortune,' replied my father, taking the huntsman's hand, and pressing it warmly.

"'Indeed! Are you, then, from that country?'

"'Yes; and I too have fled for my life. But mine is a melancholy tale.'

"'Your name?' inquired the hunter.

"'Krantz.'

"'What! Krantz of —— I have heard your tale; you need not renew your grief by repeating it now. Welcome, most welcome, Mynheer, and, I may say, my worthy kinsman. I am your second cousin, Wilfred of Barnsdorf,' cried the hunter, rising up and embracing my father.

"They filled their horn mugs to the brim, and drank to one another, after the German fashion. The conversation was then carried on in a low tone; all that we could collect from it was, that our new relative and his daughter were to take up their abode in our cottage, at least for the present. In about an hour they both fell back in their chairs, and appeared to sleep.

"'Marcella, dear, did you hear?' said my brother in a low tone.

"'Yes,' replied Marcella, in a whisper; 'I heard all. Oh! brother, I cannot bear to look upon that woman—I feel so frightened.'

"My brother made no reply, and shortly afterwards we were all three fast asleep.

"When we awoke the next morning, we found that the hunter's daughter had risen before us. I thought she looked more beautiful than ever. She came up to little Marcella and caressed her; the child burst into tears, and sobbed as if her heart would break.

"But, not to detain you with too long a story, the huntsman and his daughter were accommodated in the cottage. My father and he went out hunting daily, leaving Christina with us. She performed all the household duties; was very kind to us children; and, gradually, the dislike even of little Marcella wore away. But a great change took place in my father; he appeared to have conquered his aversion to the sex, and was most attentive to Christina. Often, after her father and we were in bed, would he sit up with her, conversing in a low tone by the fire. I ought to have mentioned, that my father and the huntsman Wilfred, slept in another portion of the cottage, and that the bed which he formerly occupied, and which was in the same room as ours, had been given up to the use of Christina. These visitors had been about three weeks at the cottage, when, one night, after we children had been sent to bed, a consultation was held. My father had asked Christina in marriage, and had obtained both her own consent and that of Wilfred; after this a conversation took place, which was, as nearly as I can recollect, as follows:—

"'You may take my child, Mynheer Krantz, and my blessing with her, and I shall then leave you and seek some other habitation—it matters little where.'

"'Why not remain here, Wilfred?'

"'No, no, I am called elsewhere; let that suffice, and ask no more questions. You have my child.'

"'I thank you for her, and will duly value her; but there is one difficulty.'

"'I know what you would say; there is no priest here in this wild country: true; neither is there any law to bind; still must some ceremony pass between you, to satisfy a father. Will you consent to marry her after my fashion? if so, I will marry you directly.'

"'I will,' replied my father.

"'Then take her by the hand. Now, Mynheer, swear.'

"'I swear,' repeated my father.

"'By all the spirits of the Hartz Mountains—'

"'Nay, why not by Heaven?' interrupted my father.

"'Because it is not my humour,' rejoined Wilfred; 'if I prefer that oath, less binding perhaps, than another, surely you will not thwart me.'

"'Well, be it so then; have your humour. Will you make me swear by that in which I do not believe?'

"'Yet many do so, who in outward appearance are Christians,' rejoined Wilfred; 'say, will you be married, or shall I take my daughter away with me?'

"'Proceed,' replied my father, impatiently.

"'I swear by all the spirits of the Hartz Mountains, by all their power for good or for evil, that I take Christina for my wedded wife; that I will ever protect her, cherish her, and love her; that my hand shall never be raised against her to harm her.'

"My father repeated the words after Wilfred.

"'And if I fail in this my vow, may all the vengeance of the spirits fall upon me and upon my children; may they perish by the vulture, by the wolf, or other beasts of the forest; may their flesh be torn from their limbs, and their bones blanch in the wilderness; all this I swear.'

"My father hesitated, as he repeated the last words; little Marcella could not restrain herself, and as my father repeated the last sentence, she burst into tears. This sudden interruption appeared to discompose the party, particularly my father; he spoke harshly to the child, who controlled her sobs, burying her face under the bedclothes.

"Such was the second marriage of my father. The next morning, the hunter Wilfred mounted his horse, and rode away.

"My father resumed his bed, which was in the same room as ours; and things went on much as before the marriage, except that our new mother-in-law did not show any kindness towards us; indeed, during my father's absence, she would often beat us, particularly little Marcella, and her eyes would flash fire, as she looked eagerly upon the fair and lovely child.

"One night, my sister awoke me and my brother.

"'What is the matter?' said Caesar.

"'She has gone out,' whispered Marcella.

"'Gone out!'

"'Yes, gone out at the door, in her night-clothes,' replied the child; 'I saw her get out of bed, look at my father to see if he slept, and then she went out at the door.'

"What could induce her to leave her bed, and all undressed to go out, in such bitter wintry weather, with the snow deep on the ground, was to us incomprehensible; we lay awake, and in about an hour we heard the growl of a wolf, close under the window.

"'There is a wolf,' said Caesar; 'she will be torn to pieces.'

"'Oh, no!' cried Marcella.

"In a few minutes afterwards our mother-in-law appeared; she was in her night-dress, as Marcella had stated. She let down the latch of the door, so as to make no noise, went to a pail of water, and washed her face and hands, and then slipped into the bed where my father lay.

"We all three trembled, we hardly knew why, but we resolved to watch the next night: we did so—and not only on the ensuing night, but on many others, and always at about the same hour, would our mother-in-law rise from her bed, and leave the cottage—and after she was gone, we invariably heard the growl of a wolf under our window, and always saw her, on her return, wash herself before she retired to bed. We observed, also, that she seldom sat down to meals, and that when she did, she appeared to eat with dislike; but when the meat was taken down, to be prepared for dinner, she would often furtively put a raw piece into her mouth.

"My brother Caesar was a courageous boy; he did not like to speak to my father until he knew more. He resolved that he would follow her out, and ascertain what she did. Marcella and I endeavoured to dissuade him from this project; but he would not be controlled, and, the very next night he lay down in his clothes, and as soon as our mother-in-law had left the cottage, he jumped up, took down my father's gun, and followed her.

"You may imagine in what a state of suspense Marcella and I remained, during his absence. After a few minutes, we heard the report of a gun. It did not awaken my father, and we lay trembling with anxiety. In a minute afterwards we saw our mother-in-law enter the cottage—her dress was bloody. I put my hand to Marcella's mouth to prevent her crying out, although I was myself in great alarm. Our mother-in-law approached my father's bed, looked to see if he was asleep, and then went to the chimney, and blew up the embers into a blaze.

"'Who is there?' said my father, waking up.

"'Lie still, dearest,' replied my mother-in-law, 'it is only me; I have lighted the fire to warm some water; I am not quite well.'

"My father turned round and was soon asleep; but we watched our mother-in-law. She changed her linen, and threw the garments she had worn into the fire; and we then perceived that her right leg was bleeding profusely, as if from a gun-shot wound. She bandaged it up, and then dressing herself, remained before the fire until the break of day.

"Poor little Marcella, her heart beat quick as she pressed me to her side—so indeed did mine. Where was our brother, Caesar? How did my mother-in-law receive the wound unless from his gun? At last my father rose, and then, for the first time I spoke, saying, 'Father, where is my brother, Caesar?'

"'Your brother!' exclaimed he, 'why, where can he be?'

"'Merciful Heaven! I thought as I lay very restless last night,' observed our mother-in-law, 'that I heard somebody open the latch of the door; and, dear me, husband, what has become of your gun?'

"My father cast his eyes up above the chimney, and perceived that his gun was missing. For a moment he looked perplexed, then seizing a broad axe, he went out of the cottage without saying another word.

"He did not remain away from us long: in a few minutes he returned, bearing in his arms the mangled body of my poor brother; he laid it down, and covered up his face.

"My mother-in-law rose up, and looked at the body, while Marcella and I threw ourselves by its side wailing and sobbing bitterly.

"'Go to bed again, children,' said she sharply. 'Husband,' continued she, 'your boy must have taken the gun down to shoot a wolf, and the animal has been too powerful for him. Poor boy! he has paid dearly for his rashness.'

"My father made no reply; I wished to speak—to tell all—but Marcella, who perceived my intention, held me by the arm, and looked at me so imploringly, that I desisted.

"My father, therefore, was left in his error; but Marcella and I, although we could not comprehend it, were conscious that our mother-in-law was in some way connected with my brother's death.

"That day my father went out and dug a grave, and when he laid the body in the earth, he piled up stones over it, so that the wolves should not be able to dig it up. The shock of this catastrophe was to my poor father very severe; for several days he never went to the chase, although at times he would utter bitter anathemas and vengeance against the wolves.

"But during this time of mourning on his part, my mother-in-law's nocturnal wanderings continued with the same regularity as before.

"At last, my father took down his gun, to repair to the forest; but he soon returned, and appeared much annoyed.

"'Would you believe it, Christina, that the wolves—perdition to the whole race—have actually contrived to dig up the body of my poor boy, and now there is nothing left of him but his bones?'

"'Indeed!' replied my mother-in-law. Marcella looked at me, and I saw in her intelligent eye all she would have uttered.

"'A wolf growls under our window every night, father,' said I.

"'Aye, indeed?—why did you not tell me, boy?—wake me the next time you hear it.'

"I saw my mother-in-law turn away; her eyes flashed fire, and she gnashed her teeth.

"My father went out again, and covered up with a larger pile of stones the little remnants of my poor brother which the wolves had spared. Such was the first act of the tragedy.

"The spring now came on: the snow disappeared, and we were permitted to leave the cottage; but never would I quit, for one moment, my dear little sister, to whom, since the death of my brother, I was more ardently attached than ever; indeed I was afraid to leave her alone with my mother-in-law, who appeared to have a particular pleasure in ill-treating the child. My father was now employed upon his little farm, and I was able to render him some assistance.

"Marcella used to sit by us while we were at work, leaving my mother-in-law alone in the cottage. I ought to observe that, as the spring advanced, so did my mother-in-law decrease her nocturnal rambles, and that we never heard the growl of the wolf under the window after I had spoken of it to my father.

"One day, when my father and I were in the field, Marcella being with us, my mother-in-law came out, saying that she was going into the forest, to collect some herbs my father wanted, and that Marcella must go to the cottage and watch the dinner. Marcella went, and my mother-in-law soon disappeared in the forest, taking a direction quite contrary to that in which the cottage stood, and leaving my father and I, as it were, between her and Marcella.

"About an hour afterwards we were startled by shrieks from the cottage, evidently the shrieks of little Marcella. 'Marcella has burnt herself, father,' said I, throwing down my spade. My father threw down his, and we both hastened to the cottage. Before we could gain the door, out darted a large white wolf, which fled with the utmost celerity. My father had no weapon; he rushed into the cottage, and there saw poor little Marcella expiring: her body was dreadfully mangled, and the blood pouring from it had formed a large pool on the cottage floor. My father's first intention had been to seize his gun and pursue, but he was checked by this horrid spectacle; he knelt down by his dying child, and burst into tears: Marcella could just look kindly on us for a few seconds, and then her eyes were closed in death.

"My father and I were still hanging over my poor sister's body, when my mother-in-law came in. At the dreadful sight she expressed much concern, but she did not appear to recoil from the sight of blood, as most women do.

"'Poor child!' said she, 'it must have been that great white wolf which passed me just now, and frightened me so—she's quite dead, Krantz.'

"'I know it—I know it!' cried my father in agony.

"I thought my father would never recover from the effects of this second tragedy: he mourned bitterly over the body of his sweet child, and for several days would not consign it to its grave, although frequently requested by my mother-in-law to do so. At last he yielded, and dug a grave for her close by that of my poor brother, and took every precaution that the wolves should not violate her remains.

"I was now really miserable, as I lay alone in the bed which I had formerly shared with my brother and sister. I could not help thinking that my mother-in-law was implicated in both their deaths, although I could not account for the manner; but I no longer felt afraid of her: my little heart was full of hatred and revenge.

"The night after my sister had been buried, as I lay awake, I perceived my mother-in-law get up and go out of the cottage. I waited some time, then dressed myself, and looked out through the door, which I half opened. The moon shone bright, and I could see the spot where my brother and my sister had been buried; and what was my horror, when I perceived my mother-in-law busily removing the stones from Marcella's grave.

"She was in her white night-dress, and the moon shone full upon her. She was digging with her hands, and throwing away the stones behind her with all the ferocity of a wild beast. It was some time before I could collect my senses and decide what I should do. At last, I perceived that she had arrived at the body, and raised it up to the side of the grave. I could bear it no longer; I ran to my father and awoke him.

"'Father! father!' cried I, 'dress yourself, and get your gun.'

"'What!' cried my father, 'the wolves are there, are they?'

"He jumped out of bed, threw on his clothes, and in his anxiety did not appear to perceive the absence of his wife. As soon as he was ready, I opened the door, he went out, and I followed him.

"Imagine his horror, when (unprepared as he was for such a sight) he beheld, as he advanced towards the grave, not a wolf, but his wife, in her night-dress, on her hands and knees, crouching by the body of my sister, and tearing off large pieces of the flesh, and devouring them with all the avidity of a wolf. She was too busy to be aware of our approach. My father dropped his gun, his hair stood on end; so did mine; he breathed heavily, and then his breath for a time stopped. I picked up the gun and put it into his hand. Suddenly he appeared as if concentrated rage had restored him to double vigour; he levelled his piece, fired, and with a loud shriek, down fell the wretch whom he had fostered in his bosom.

"'God of Heaven!' cried my father, sinking down upon the earth in a swoon, as soon as he had discharged his gun.

"I remained some time by his side before he recovered. 'Where am I?' said he, 'what has happened?—Oh!—yes, yes! I recollect now. Heaven forgive me!'

"He rose and we walked up to the grave; what again was our astonishment and horror to find that instead of the dead body of my mother-in-law, as we expected, there was lying over the remains of my poor sister, a large, white she wolf.

"'The white wolf!' exclaimed my father, 'the white wolf which decoyed me into the forest—I see it all now—I have dealt with the spirits of the Hartz Mountains.'

"For some time my father remained in silence and deep thought. He then carefully lifted up the body of my sister, replaced it in the grave, and covered it over as before, having struck the head of the dead animal with the heel of his boot, and raving like a madman. He walked back to the cottage, shut the door, and threw himself on the bed; I did the same, for I was in a stupor of amazement.

"Early in the morning we were both roused by a loud knocking at the door, and in rushed the hunter Wilfred.

"'My daughter!—man—my daughter!—where is my daughter!' cried he in a rage.

"'Where the wretch, the fiend, should be, I trust,' replied my father, starting up and displaying equal choler; 'where she should be—in hell!—Leave this cottage or you may fare worse.'

"'Ha—ha!' replied the hunter, 'would you harm a potent spirit of the Hartz Mountains. Poor mortal, who must needs wed a weir wolf.'

"'Out demon! I defy thee and thy power.'

"'Yet shall you feel it; remember your oath—your solemn oath—never to raise your hand against her to harm her.'

"'I made no compact with evil spirits.'

"'You did; and if you failed in your vow, you were to meet the vengeance of the spirits. Your children were to perish by the vulture, the wolf—'

"'Out, out, demon!'

"'And their bones blanch in the wilderness. Ha!—ha!'

"My father, frantic with rage, seized his axe, and raised it over Wilfred's head to strike.

"'All this I swear,' continued the huntsman, mockingly.

"The axe descended; but it passed through the form of the hunter, and my father lost his balance, and fell heavily on the floor.

"'Mortal!' said the hunter, striding over my father's body, 'we have power over those only who have committed murder. You have been guilty of a double murder—you shall pay the penalty attached to your marriage vow. Two of your children are gone; the third is yet to follow—and follow them he will, for your oath is registered. Go—it were kindness to kill thee—your punishment is—that you live!'

"With these words the spirit disappeared. My father rose from the floor, embraced me tenderly, and knelt down in prayer.

"The next morning he quitted the cottage for ever. He took me with him and bent his steps to Holland, where we safely arrived. He had some little money with him; but he had not been many days in Amsterdam before he was seized with a brain fever, and died raving mad. I was put into the Asylum, and afterwards was sent to sea before the mast. You now know all my history. The question is, whether I am to pay the penalty of my father's oath? I am myself perfectly convinced that, in some way or another, I shall."

On the twenty-second day the high land of the south of Sumatra was in view; as there were no vessels in sight, they resolved to keep their course through the Straits, and run for Pulo Penang, which they expected, as their vessel laid so close to the wind, to reach in seven or eight days. By constant exposure, Philip and Krantz were now so bronzed, that with their long beards and Mussulman dresses, they might easily have passed off for natives. They had steered during the whole of the days exposed to a burning sun; they had lain down and slept in the dew of night, but their health had not suffered. But for several days, since he had confided the history of his family to Philip, Krantz had become silent and melancholy; his usual flow of spirits had vanished, and Philip had often questioned him as to the cause. As they entered the Straits, Philip talked of what they should do upon their arrival at Goa. When Krantz gravely replied, "For some days, Philip, I have had a presentiment that I shall never see that city."

"You are out of health, Krantz," replied Philip.

"No; I am in sound health, body and mind. I have endeavoured to shake off the presentiment, but in vain; there is a warning voice that continually tells me that I shall not be long with you. Philip, will you oblige me by making me content on one point: I have gold about my person which may be useful to you; oblige me by taking it, and securing it on your own."

"What nonsense, Krantz."

"It is no nonsense, Philip. Have you not had your warnings? Why should I not have mine? You know that I have little fear in my composition, and that I care not about death; but I feel the presentiment which I speak of more strongly every hour. It is some kind spirit who would warn me to prepare for another world. Be it so. I have lived long enough in this world to leave it without regret; although to part with you and Amine, the only two now dear to me, is painful, I acknowledge."

"May not this arise from over-exertion and fatigue, Krantz? consider how much excitement you have laboured under within these last four months. Is not that enough to create a corresponding depression? Depend upon it, my dear friend, such is the fact."

"I wish it were—but I feel otherwise, and there is a feeling of gladness connected with the idea that I am to leave this world, arising from another presentiment, which equally occupies my mind."

"Which is?"

"I hardly can tell you; but Amine and you are connected with it. In my dreams I have seen you meet again; but it has appeared to me, as if a portion of your trial was purposely shut from my sight in dark clouds; and I have asked, 'May not I see what is there concealed?'—and an invisible has answered, 'No! 'twould make you wretched. Before these trials take place, you will be summoned away'—and then I have thanked Heaven, and felt resigned."

"These are the imaginings of a disturbed brain, Krantz; that I am destined to suffering may be true; but why Amine should suffer, or why you, young, in full health and vigour, should not pass your days in peace, and live to a good old age, there is no cause for believing. You will be better tomorrow."

"Perhaps so," replied Krantz;—"but still you must yield to my whim, and take the gold. If I am wrong, and we do arrive safe, you know, Philip, you can let me have it back," observed Krantz, with a faint smile—"but you forget, our water is nearly out, and we must look out for a rill on the coast to obtain a fresh supply."

"I was thinking of that when you commenced this unwelcome topic. We had better look out for the water before dark, and as soon as we have replenished our jars, we will make sail again."

At the time that this conversation took place, they were on the eastern side of the Strait, about forty miles to the northward. The interior of the coast was rocky and mountainous, but it slowly descended to low land of alternate forest and jungles, which continued to the beach: the country appeared to be uninhabited. Keeping close in to the shore, they discovered, after two hours' run, a fresh stream which burst in a cascade from the mountains, and swept its devious course through the jungle, until it poured its tribute into the waters of the Strait.

They ran close in to the mouth of the stream, lowered the sails, and pulled the peroqua against the current, until they had advanced far enough to assure them that the water was quite fresh. The jars were soon filled, and they were again thinking of pushing off; when, enticed by the beauty of the spot, the coolness of the fresh water, and wearied with their long confinement on board of the peroqua, they proposed to bathe—a luxury hardly to be appreciated by those who have not been in a similar situation. They threw off their Mussulman dresses, and plunged into the stream, where they remained for some time. Krantz was the first to get out; he complained of feeling chilled, and he walked on to the banks where their clothes had been laid. Philip also approached nearer to the beach, intending to follow him.

"And now, Philip," said Krantz, "this will be a good opportunity for me to give you the money. I will open my sash, and pour it out, and you can put it into your own before you put it on."

Philip was standing in the water, which was about level with his waist.

"Well, Krantz," said he, "I suppose if it must be so, it must; but it appears to me an idea so ridiculous—however, you shall have your own way."

Philip quitted the run, and sat down by Krantz, who was already busy in shaking the doubloons out of the folds of his sash; at last he said—

"I believe, Philip, you have got them all, now?—I feel satisfied."

"What danger there can be to you, which I am not equally exposed to, I cannot conceive," replied Philip; "however—"

Hardly had he said these words, when there was a tremendous roar—a rush like a mighty wind through the air—a blow which threw him on his back—a loud cry—and a contention. Philip recovered himself, and perceived the naked form of Krantz carried off with the speed of an arrow by an enormous tiger through the jungle. He watched with distended eyeballs; in a few seconds the animal and Krantz had disappeared!

"God of Heaven! would that Thou hadst spared me this," cried Philip, throwing himself down in agony on his face. "Oh! Krantz, my friend—my brother—too sure was your presentiment. Merciful God! have pity—but Thy will be done;" and Philip burst into a flood of tears.

For more than an hour did he remain fixed upon the spot, careless and indifferent to the danger by which he was surrounded. At last, somewhat recovered, he rose, dressed himself, and then again sat down—his eyes fixed upon the clothes of Krantz, and the gold which still lay on the sand.

"He would give me that gold. He foretold his doom. Yes! yes! it was his destiny, and it has been fulfilled. *His bones will bleach in the wilderness*, and the spirit-hunter and his wolfish daughter are avenged."

1886

THE HAUNTED NURSERY

Florence Marryat

Florence (1833–1899) was Frederick's ninth child. Frederick, now retired from the Navy, was determined to help with the education of his children. Alas, with his and Catherine's separation in 1839, the six-year-old Florence spent her time alternating between her father in Norfolk and her mother in London. Catherine does not seem to have been the most devoted mother. Charles Dickens noted that "she had no interest whatever in the children." Years later when The Idler *magazine asked novelists whether childhood was "the happiest or the most miserable period of one's existence?" Florence responded that it was "decidedly the most miserable." She went so far as to say that not a hundredth of "the men and women who marry are fit to become fathers and mothers."*

Florence may have held that view partly because of her own life. In 1854, after her father's death and finding it difficult coping with her mother, she married a family friend whom she barely knew, Thomas Church, of the 12th Madras Staff Corps. She toured India with him, but they were ill-matched, as Church was a strict disciplinarian. She returned to England in 1860 with her three children and a fourth imminent, who alas died after ten days. Church remained in India, though returned to England from time to time to claim his conjugal rights. By the early 1870s they had separated and Church, now a Major, returned to India. Florence had become a successful author and Church tried to lay claim on her wealth. During this acrimonious period Florence moved in with Francis Lean, a retired lieutenant-colonel. Church sued for divorce. A week after the final decree was signed at the end of May 1879, Florence and Lean married. Alas, this turned out to be almost as horrendous a marriage as the first. They separated within two years.

Throughout this difficult life Florence continued to write. She published 68 novels, plus plays, non-fiction and short stories. She also turned to acting and for three years edited the magazine London Society. *Her first book,* Love's Conflict *(1865), and many that followed, notably* Too Good for Him *(1865) and* The Prey of the Gods *(1871), dealt with marital cruelty, adultery and prostitution. Florence earned a reputation for "dangerously inflammatory" fiction.*

Her interest in the supernatural grew after she attended a séance in 1873 and purportedly made contact with both her brother, Frank, who had died in 1855, and daughter (also called Florence), who had died at ten days old in 1860, but who had continued to grow in the spirit world. Marryat wrote about these experiences in There Is No Death *(1891) and* The Spirit World *(1894). Her views inspired several novels, including* The Dead Man's Message *(1894),* The Strange Transfiguration of Hannah Stubbs *(1896) and* The Blood of the Vampire *(1897). This last appeared in the same year as Bram Stoker's* Dracula, *but was very different, being a psychological study of a young woman who fears she may have inherited vampirism from her mixed-race parents. Most of her weird tales were collected in* The Ghost of Charlotte Cray *(1883) but others remain to be discovered. The following has not been published in book form since it first appeared in 1886. Its connections to her first marriage and her spiritualistic beliefs are all too apparent.*

It was very delightful, of course, to come home again after that charming month in Italy, when Charlie seemed to belong so much to me and nobody else in the wide world, and to settle down amongst my friends as a married woman; but it was provoking not to be able to go to our own house. However, it wasn't ready for us, so it was no use thinking about it.

Our marriage had been so sudden—so indelicately sudden, as Aunt Ellen said (but then the poor old thing had never had an offer in her life, so how could she be a judge!) that there was really no time to get ready.

Lord Erskine—that's my Charlie you know—had only come in Woodfern Abbey about a month before he met me, and he said it would not be fit for us to go into until it had been done up and refurnished from top to bottom.

Aunt Ellen suggested that the wedding should be postponed until it was ready, but Charlie wouldn't hear of it; men are so ridiculously impatient. The whole affair was, certainly, very sudden, though I hope it wasn't indelicate; but I really could scarcely believe, when it was all over, that I was actually married. It seemed to take place like a flash of lightning; but then Charlie is not like other men. The first time he was introduced to me—it was at Mrs Sutton's ball, I felt as if I had seen him some where before, and when we had danced together for ten minutes I was talking to him as if we had known each other all our lives. But Charlie has such a way about him. He is not a bit shy, and puts one much at one's ease.

The very next day he called on Aunt Ellen, and as she was too cross and tired after the ball to see visitors, I had to go downstairs and receive him, and he stayed quite an hour and a half by the clock; and after that I don't think he ever let a day pass without calling on me.

He had always some good excuse, of course. Sometimes he brought flowers or music, or he wanted to enquire after Aunt Ellen's neuralgia, or to return an umbrella which he had taken in mistake for his own.

Aunt Ellen said she didn't believe in any of his excuses, but she was obliged to receive him all the same, and I knew, oh, long before it came to pass! that he was going to ask me to be his wife.

And so he did about a month after we first met, and a month after that we were married. Then came the question of Woodfern Abbey, which couldn't be ready for us under three months.

Aunt Ellen, as I have said before, wanted to put off the wedding all that time; but Charlie wouldn't hear of it, and as she was very anxious to get me off her hands, I suppose she concluded it would be better not to offend him. The only difficulty was about a house for us to return to after the honeymoon, but Charlie soon settled that. He told an agent exactly what we wanted, and there it was, ready for us a whole week before we came back from Genoa. No. 37 Abergeldie Terrace, furnished from attic to basement with everything we could possibly require; and when the servants had been sent on from Woodfern Abbey to London we had nothing to do but to walk in and take possession.

It was on a gloomy day in March that we returned from our continent trip, and Abergeldie Terrace, which was built of smoke-coloured stucco, looked more dignified than cheerful under a wintry sky. But I was very much pleased with the interior of the house. The stairs were carpeted with velvet pile of a deep claret colour, and velvet curtains of the same shade draped the landings and the doors. The drawing-room walls were hung with dark oil paintings in velvet frames of the prevailing colour, and the brightest piece of furniture in it was a table, inlaid with marble and set in ormolu.

"What a dismal looking place," exclaimed Charlie, as he entered it. "Why, it feels like a vault! Lily, my darling, if you don't like it, we'll turn out tomorrow and find another house that suits us better."

"But Charlie, dear, I do like it," I replied. "I think it is so stately and warm looking. Just what a London house should be. Besides, you won't know the room when it has lace curtains at the windows, and a few flowers on the table."

"Oh, yes, of course!" he said. "It's the lace curtains that I miss. What were the servants about, not to put them up before you arrived? If your Aunt Ellen were not such a cantankerous old individual, she would have seen to such things for you."

"I would much rather see to them myself, Charlie. But this is a very big house, dear. What are two little people to do in it all alone?"

"We won't be alone for long, Lily. We'll ask your sister Cissy to come and stay with us, and my brother Jack, and anybody else you may take a fancy to, and make the house cheerful with music, and dancing. I am sure it wants something to brighten it up."

I was delighted at my husband's proposal. Of course, he was all the world to me, and always would be. Still, I loved my sister dearly, and knew how pleased she would be to get out of Aunt Ellen's clutches, were it only for a little while. With a light heart I ran up to inspect the bedrooms, and found them on quite as palatial a scale as the other apartments.

Above the drawing-room were four rooms dedicated to Charlie and myself; above them again four guest chambers, and over the servants' offices and attic.

As I stood in my bedroom, changing my dress for dinner, my maid told me that a woman wished to speak to me. I went to the door, where I encountered a respectable-looking person, clad in black, who introduced herself to my notice as the caretaker whom the agent had put into the house to await the arrival of the servants from the Abbey.

"Which I cleaned from top to bottom, my lady," she said, in conclusion, "and terribly dirty it was, and I hope as I've given satisfaction and left all as it should be."

"I have no doubt you have," I answered; "and you had better go to the housekeeper for your money. She will pay you what is due."

"Thank you, my lady. And if you please, my lady, I was going to make so bold as to ask if this belonged to you." She took her hand from under her shawl as she spoke, and produced a child's toy, half broken, but gay with colouring.

"To me!" I exclaimed. "No! Certainly not. Where did you find it?"

"In one of the top rooms, my lady, as I was cleaning of it, and I thought," continued the caretaker in a whining voice, "that if so be no one wanted it, I had a little boy at home as would set great store by such a thing, and—"

"Oh, no, you mustn't take it home," I interrupted, decidedly. "Everything in this house belongs to the owners of it, and we shall have to restore it in the same condition in which it was found. Please give me the toy, and I will put it back into its place."

The woman muttered something about its never being missed, but gave it to me nevertheless, and I returned with it to the bedroom.

It was a curious toy, and evidently not of English manufacture. It represented a sort of pagoda and several people driving cows, all of them painted in the most brilliant colours and varnished like glass. Charlie told me afterwards that it came from Bombay, where toys of the same sort were manufactured by the natives. I put it on my mantelpiece, however, and thought no more about it.

I had to get ready for our first dinner in a house of our own, and when I ran down in a lovely aesthetic terra-cotta coloured dress, with a Vandyke collar round my throat and a row of Venetian beads, Charlie said he should never think the house dull again whilst he had such a gay-looking butterfly sporting about it.

That was a happy evening, as everyone may well imagine, and so was the next day when I inspected my new domains. As I ascended to the upper storey, accompanied by the housekeeper, I encountered at the head of the stairs a gate, latched and bolted.

"What is this for?" I exclaimed, in my ignorance of children and their requirements.

"Why, sure, my lady, it was to prevent the little ones from falling downstairs. The room to the right was the nursery, my lady, as anyone can see by entering…"

Then I remembered the painted toy on my mantelpiece. Surely it must have belonged to this room.

"Go downstairs," I said to the housekeeper, "and fetch a child's toy from my bedroom. The caretaker brought it to me from the nursery."

The woman left me and I entered the room alone. It was a bright and cheerful apartment, as all good nurseries are. It looked out upon the front of the house, had a warm carpet on the floor, and a gay paper on the walls, which were covered with coloured pictures. In one corner of the room stood a little iron crib, in another a rocking-horse. This had evidently been the abode of our landlord's children, and I wondered how many little pairs of feet had pattered about that floor.

Though it was such a cheerful-looking room I felt melancholy whilst standing in it—all seemed so silent and so still. I went over and examined the crib—it was quite a small one, not more than three, feet long, and I was speculating if a little boy or a little girl had slept there, when I was startled from my reverie by an exclamation from the housekeeper.

"Lord save us!" she said suddenly, as she appeared on the threshold.

"What's the matter?" I enquired, turning round.

"Oh, it's nothing, my lady; it was foolish of me to call out, but I thought as I came into the room, that I caught sight of something at your side."

"At my side!" I repeated; looking down; "How could there be? The room is empty."

"Oh, yes, my lady, of course, and it was all my fancy, I daresay, but here's the toy, my lady, if this is what you mean."

She held out the Indian toy as she spoke, and I placed it in the crib.

"It must have been forgotten in the hurry of departure," I said. "See that it is not touched again."

But to my amazement I found that the housekeeper had taken French leave and left me to my own devices; so, thinking she had mistaken my orders, I followed her downstairs.

I believe it was about three days after this occurrence that I was waked one night by the sound of a whimpering or whining, which seemed to come from outside my bedroom door. I thought at first it was some little dog shut out from its rightful home, and I was further persuaded in the idea by hearing the pattering of soft little feet on the polished oak planking that ran on each side of the stair carpet. I am very fond of animals, and I pitied the poor little beast that was evidently in distress.

"Charlie, Charlie," I exclaimed, as I pinched my lord and master to make him wake. But Charlie had been to the theatre two nights running, and was very sleepy.

"What is it all about, Lily?" he said, in a muffled voice.

"Don't you hear that noise, Charlie—like a little dog whining outside the bedroom door? Do get up and see what it is."

"Can't be a dog," replied Charlie, lazily, "there isn't one in the house."

"Perhaps it belongs to the servants," I suggested, "or has been shut in the house by mistake. Anyway, I'm sure it's in pain by the way it's crying."

Charlie had waked by this time and heard the noise.

"It isn't a dog at all," he said. "It's a child!"

"Oh, no! How could a child be on the stairs?"

"It isn't on the stairs, my darling; it's next door. You don't know how thin the walls of these London houses are. You can hear everything your neighbours do or say."

"Charlie, that sound comes from our staircase. It is not next door at all."

"I see you won't be satisfied until you've turned me out of bed to solve the mystery," he said, good-naturedly, as he jumped up and opened the bedroom door; but there was nothing there. Charlie whistled, and coaxed, and called, but no dog or cat answered his invitation, and after a minute or two he returned to his own quarters.

"I told you it was nothing, Lily," he said; "but I tell you what is rather funny. As I opened the door I saw in the darkness before me such a beautiful star, not large, but so bright and glittering! It seemed to float right down the staircase into the hall."

"Oh, Charlie, you are more fanciful than I am!" I said, laughing, and we had soon forgotten our little adventure in sleep.

But not long afterwards it was brought to my remembrance. I was waiting one evening for Charlie to come back from the station, where he had gone to meet my sister Cissy. I had dressed myself very carefully in a dark-blue velvet dress, never before worn, that I might show my sister how well I looked as Lady Erskine, and I had descended to the drawing-room to attend her arrival.

When I reached it I found the gas still unlit. There was a good fire in the grate, but the room was in semi darkness. I walked across it, stopped to arrange a few ornaments on the centre table, and then went toward the bell to ring for lights.

As I stooped to reach it I felt someone pull my dress from behind. I fancied I had caught the train in something, and I turned to disengage it. But the folds were perfectly free, and I returned to my original design of ringing the bell.

Again was my dress pulled from behind, and this time in a very decided manner. I had rung the bell, but I turned again to ascertain the cause, when I saw distinctly in the darkness of the doorway a star such as Charlie had described to me, but small, and very bright and clear, which seemed to dance before my eyes for a few moments, and then flicker away upon the staircase. I was still staring at the spot where it had disappeared, and asking myself whether I was asleep or awake, when the servant entered in answer to my summons and lit the gas.

My first impulse was to examine my dress. Yes! There on the new velvet was the distinct impress of a little hand where the material had been grasped and pulled, just about on a level with my knees. There is no material that shows the marks of pressure so plainly as a blue velvet. A few minutes afterwards, however, the carriage arrived with Charlie and Cissy, and I could think of nothing but my sister for the remainder of the evening.

And when I told the circumstances I have related to my husband, he laughed at me so heartily as almost to kill my belief in my own understanding. And he had out the blue velvet dress by day light, and showed me a dozen places where it had been marked and creased in the packing, until I had lost faith in my eyesight as well. And, certainly, the marks of which I had told him were not to be seen at the time, though I looked for them everywhere. They had totally disappeared, although I could have sworn I had seen them plainly when I saw them alone.

Charlie declared it was all the effects of a highly-strung organization, but if so, it seemed to run in the family, for the next person who suffered from it was Cissy herself. I thought she looked very pale and tired a week after she had come to us, and I told her so.

"We shall have to stop the theatres and evening parties. Cissy, if they affect you like this," I said, laughing. "You look as yellow as Aunt Ellen this morning."

"Well, the fact is," replied Cissy, with little hesitation, "I haven't slept very well lately, Lily. The child disturbs me so."

"The child! What child?" I demanded in amazement.

My sister looked puzzled. "Don't you know of it?" she asked. "Don't you know that one of your servants has a child to sleep in the house? I wouldn't mind if it did sleep, but it moans and frets half the night, and patters about the room, and I can't sleep through it."

"About which room?" I said.

"The one over mine."

"No one sleeps there," I replied. "It used to be the nursery, but it is empty now."

Cissy looked incredulous.

"I don't want you to make a disturbance on my account, Lily dear, but I assure you, someone does sleep there, for I have lain awake for hours and hours, listening to the noises that go on."

"I will take care you are not disturbed again," I said, as I rang the bell for the housemaid, to enquire into the reason why my sister's rest was broken. The servant first stared at my story, then looked frightened, finally denying, with evident confusion, that she knew anything of a child being in the house.

"Don't dare to tell me a story!" I said, angrily. "You mean to say Miss Carew can be mistaken? She says she hears a baby crying: and running about every night. Some of you must know about it."

"I don't, then, my lady, nor any others as I know of," replied the woman, firmly.

"Have you ever heard the noises yourself?" I asked.

"Yes, my lady. I have; and so have Jane and Mrs Stephens."

"Do they come from next door?"

"I don't think they do, my lady."

"You don't *think*? What do you mean? I insist upon your speaking plainly to me."

Thereupon the housemaid advanced closer to my side and lowered her voice—

"If you please, my lady, me and Jane and Mrs Stephens have all heard the noises, and we don't think they're nothing natural, and we're all praying for the day when, we shall go back to the Abbey, where there ain't no speerits, thank God, nor nothing of the sort," she added with a blanched cheek.

Cissy, sitting close by, broke into a peal of laughter.

"Spirits!" she cried. "Why, you don't mean to say that you believe it is the ghost of a baby? No, no. The crying I hear is much too real for anything but flesh and blood, and you must tell that story to somebody less sensible than Lady Erskine."

But I, remembering the voice and footsteps I had heard outside my bedroom door, and the little hand that had pulled at my velvet-dress, did not feel inclined to join in my sister's ridicule at the housemaid's fears.

"Whatever it may be," I said, trying to speak lightly, "I cannot have you disturbed any longer, Cissy, and so you must occupy the next room to my own in future. Please see that Miss Carew's things are moved down before tonight, and don't let this silly story get wind more than is absolutely necessary. I shall be angry if I hear anything about it again."

The servant left my presence, still white and trembling. Cissy asked me if I intended to let the matter rest there.

"I believe, from her manner, Lily, that she is the culprit, else why should she grow so confused? Depend upon it, she has got some of her relations in the house. There was no mistaking the sounds I heard."

"Never mind," I answered, carelessly, "so long as they do not annoy you again. I don't like to seem too harsh with the servants at first. We shall soon be down at the Abbey, and they will have no opportunity of playing tricks upon us there."

"Well, I think you are far too lenient," said my sister, in a dissatisfied tone.

I should have thought so myself, if what I had already heard and seen had not commenced to prey upon my spirits. In a short time, however, our family party was increased by the arrival of Charlie's brother and two or three other young men, and in the all-absorbing amusement of flirtation, Cissy seemed to forget the nuisance, real or imagined, to which she had been subjected.

One day, however, I heard the voice of Mrs Stephens, the housekeeper, most unnecessarily raised in anger, and on enquiring the cause, I found that the Bombay toy I had placed in the little crib had disappeared.

"And when you told me particular it wasn't to be touched, my lady, and I said the same to them all, but someone's been and took it away, and I can't find it nowhere."

"Well, it wasn't me," pleaded Jane, who was the supposed offender Mrs Stephens had pitched upon.

"Whoever it was, it must be found again," I interposed; "mind that, Mrs Stephens. The owners of the house are sure to miss it on their return, and it would be most unpleasant to be unable to produce it. It must be found!" I added determinedly.

"It shall be found, my lady," echoed the housekeeper, fiercely; "if I have to rip up everyone in the house before I come to it."

But at this bloodthirsty resolution I fled, lest Mrs Stephens, in ill zeal and outraged honour, should commence upon me.

That very evening Charlie and Jack and their friends went off to some bachelor's haunt together, and Cissy and I were left in the house to amuse each other, the consequence of which was that by 10 o'clock we were quite ready to part company and go to bed. I had an interesting book in hand, and when I had dismissed my maid I sat down before the fire in my dressing-room and prepared to read until my husband's return.

Of how long I had sat there I had no idea, for time never passes so quickly as when in the company of an entertaining author, but I knew that it must be growing late, for I had heard the servants one after another creep up the stairs to bed, and knew that only the sleepy footman was left dozing below until such time as his master should return and need his services.

My fire had burned low, but I did not trouble myself to replenish it, for the spring was coming on fast now, and the nights began to be warm, and the big house was very quiet—so quiet that when a coal dropped from the grate to the fender it made me jump.

But, suddenly, as I sat there with my eyes fixed upon my book, I became aware—I don't know how—that I was not alone, and half expectant, half afraid, I looked up to see who shared my room with me.

Had I been asked to guess who stood upon the threshold I should have said Cissy, or Charlie, or my maid, and yet it would have been a foolish venture, for I had heard no sound of the opening or shutting of the door. But what I did see inspired me at first with no alarm.

I looked up, and there, between my chair and the doorway, stood the loveliest little figure of a child I had ever seen.

Excepting for a cambric garment trimmed with lace his little limbs appeared to be bare; but his large blue eyes, wet with tears, were wide open, and his rosebud mouth was drawn down pathetically at the corners, as though he was just about to cry.

Forgetting the sounds I had heard and the stories I had been told, and believing that I saw a living child before me, I sprang from my chair and advanced to the little figure, which retreated before me.

"You little darling!" I exclaimed. "Don't be afraid of me. I will not hurt you. Tell me your name, dear, and why you have come here!"

But all the answer the child made by fixing his frightened, weeping eyes upon me, whilst he backed towards the door, exclaiming in a plaintive whisper—

"Let me go—let me go!"

"Where do you want to go to, dear?" I answered—"to your mother? Is your mother here, baby? Do you wish to go to her, dear?"

But the golden-curled little head was shaken sadly, as the child, still backing towards the door, held out towards me the Bombay toy, and, passing through the panels, disappeared.

Then, in a moment, I understood it all. I know what I had seen; I knew to whom he had belonged; I knew that he had been one of the children of the house, and that I had looked upon the face of the risen dead. When Charlie rushed into the room a few minutes afterwards he found me in a dead faint on the floor.

After that incident, and when he heard why it had occurred, Lord Erskine was very anxious that we should give up No. 37 Abergeldie Terrace, and go into another house. He did not believe that I had seen a ghost, or that I had seen anything at all, but he considered the house too dull and gloomy for me, and he thought that my surroundings had had a bad effect upon my imagination, and that a more cheerful residence would cure my fears.

But I would not hear of going away. What! Was I to confess myself a prey to supernatural terrors just as I had become a happy wife, or let Aunt Ellen's sarcastic tongue jeer at me for being fanciful and full of whims? No, if I had died for it, I resolved to remain at Abergeldie Terrace, and to remain silent, also, on the subject of the apparition. So no one, not even Cissy, heard of what I had seen.

I was not very well for a few days afterward, and lay about on the sofas in the dining-room, while Cissy, like a dear, fond sister as she was, tried to amuse me and make the time pass quicker by reading aloud.

There was one thing, however, which I had insisted upon Charlie finding out and telling to me, and that was the names of the owners of the house we occupied, and the reason that they had vacated it.

Then the truth came out. They were a Mr and Mrs Duncan, people of great wealth and position in the mercantile world, who had come back from India to settle in England, with an only child, who had died of some malignant disorder shortly after their arrival, and the parents, heartbroken at their loss, had been unable to remain in the place where it had occurred.

Charlie looked very grave when he told me this story.

"I blame the agents very much for not having informed me of this before letting the house," he said. "Suppose it was typhus or scarlet-fever the child died of, and I have risked your health in bringing you here."

"You need not be afraid," I answered. "If it had been any infectious disorder, and I had caught it, it would have developed itself before now. But the poor parents and their only little child, Charlie. They are what I think of most. No wonder they could not bear to remain in the house where he died!"

Cissy brought a new novel to read to me this morning, but my mind was so full of what I had heard, I did not seem to care for stories.

"Read me some poetry, dear," I said languidly. "I like to hear your sweet voice, falling and swelling in the rhythm of some tender verse."

So Cissy fetched her book of latest extracts, and fell to repeating sundry bits of poetry which she had collected from books and newspapers, and amongst others she came to this of Moir's. It was called "Mother and Her Dead Child."

> With ceaseless sorrow uncontrolled, the mother mourned her lot,
> She wept and would not be consoled, because her child was not.
> She gazed upon its nursery floor, but there it did not play;
> The toys it loved, the clothes it wore, all void and vacant lay.
> Her house, her heart, were dark and drear without their wonted light.
> Her little star had left its sphere that there had shone so bright.
> Her tears at each returning thought felt like the frequent rain;
> Time on its wings no healing brought, and Wisdom spoke in vain.

"Oh, isn't that like poor Mrs Duncan?" I exclaimed, suddenly.

"Who is Mrs Duncan?" asked Cissy.

"Never mind—never mind! Go on with the next verse. I am so deeply interested in your poem."

She went on—

> Even in the middle hour of night she sought no soft relief;
> But, by the taper's misty light, sat nourishing her grief,
> 'Twas then a sight of solemn awe rose near her like a cloud—
> The image of her child she saw, wrapped in its little shroud!
> It sat within its favourite chair—it sat and seemed to sigh,
> And turned upon its mother there a meek, imploring eye.

"Just as it did on me," I exclaimed breathlessly, "and it kept on saying, 'Let me go! let me go!'"

"Lily, you are mad," cried my sister.

"No, no, dear, I will tell you all in a minute, but I must hear the end of the verses first—I feel what is coming, but I must hear it, all the same."

"I shall begin to think you have really seen a ghost if you go on in this extraordinary way," said Cissy, as she returned to her book.

> "Oh, child! what brings that breathless form back from its place of rest?
> For well I know no life can warm again that livid breast;
> The grave is now your bed my child! Go, slumber there in peace!"
> "I cannot go," it answered mild, "until your sorrows cease.
> I've tried to rest in that dark bed, but rest I cannot get,
> For always, with the tears you shed, my winding-sheet is wet.
> The drops, dear mother, trickle still into my coffin deep:
> It feels so comfortless—so chill—I cannot go to sleep."
> "Oh, child! those words, that touching look, my fortitude restore;
> I feel and own the fond rebuke, and weep thy loss no more."
> She spoke and dried her tears the while, and as her passion fell,
> The vision wore an angel smile, and looked a fond farewell.

When my sister had concluded reading—ah! and long before that—my face was wet with tears.

"I see it all now," I said, "and understand why the poor, little darling has disturbed us so much. Oh! how I wish I could tell his mother my story and read her those verses just as you read them to me! But listen, Cissy, and you shall hear what has upset me so much the last few days."

Cissy settled herself to listen, but was not destined to hear the tale just then, for at that moment the footman threw open the door and announced "Mrs Duncan."

I jumped off the sofa with such alacrity as to astonish my sister, and advanced promptly to meet my visitor. It seemed as if my wish had been granted by magic.

Mrs Duncan was a young woman of about thirty, very pale, very thin, and very haggard in appearance. Her eyes had dark hollows beneath them that looked as if she nearly cried herself blind, and her crape-covered robes and funeral veil added to the melancholy picture.

"Lady Erskine," she commenced, in a harsh, unnatural voice, "I have to apologize for intruding upon you without a personal introduction; but I am in town only for a few days, and I thought that under the circumstances—"

"Don't apologize," I said, interrupting her, "for it is quite unnecessary. Is there anything I can do for you?"

She glanced round the room with a sort of scared looked, and then resumed: "As we have been moving about the continent for some time, I took the liberty of directing a small parcel to be sent to me here, and as it is of some importance, I thought I would call for it."

"I have not heard of any parcel for you," I said, "but I will ring and ask the servants."

On enquiry it proved that such a parcel had been received and taken charge of by the butler. It was brought to her on a salver—a small book-packet, with "Photographs only" printed above the name.

Mrs Duncan received it with a shudder, and held it in her hand as if it were something dead that chilled her. After a pause, she said in a low trembling voice: "There was another request I wished to make you, Lady Erskine. I left behind me a toy—a worthless, painted thing from Bombay. I dare say it has been lost or stolen, but if not—"

"No, no, it is not lost!" I cried. "I have taken especial care of it. It is in the nursery. I will go and fetch it for you."

But as I turned to leave the room she cast eyes of wild entreaty on me.

"May I go with you?" she said imploringly.

"What a question to ask in your own house, Mrs Duncan! Why, of course you may, if you care to take the trouble."

She followed me up the stairs, bent almost double with emotion, and I heard her moaning at each step as if she had been in bodily pain. When we reached the nursery we found the windows open and the bright sun streaming in upon the carpet, yet Mrs Duncan sank upon the nearest chair, and shivered as if she had been in a vault.

I knew her feelings. I was not a mother, but I was a woman, and one woman always understands another. I knelt down by her side and laid my two hands upon hers.

"Dear Mrs Duncan," I said, "I have heard of your loss, and I sympathize so truly with your grief."

She turned her sorrow-laden eyes to me, and ejaculated—"Thank you. But no one knows—no one can understand—what it was to lose him except myself!"

Then she pulled, with feverish hands, at the twine that held the packet together.

"You shall see what he was like," she said, "I lost his portrait. I wanted another copy of it, and told them to send it here."

She tore away the envelope and the protecting cardboard, and turned the picture's face upwards for me to see. What did I behold? Not a laughing baby in frock or knickerbockers, but the representation of a naked cherub borne aloft by angels. Mrs Duncan stared at it for a moment—turned it about curiously, and burst into tears.

"It is a mistake!" she cried; "but oh! if I could only think of him like this, instead of mouldering in his grave, I might—someday—be able to remember my darling, and thank Heaven that he was gone."

"Dear Mrs Duncan," I replied, "try and believe that that is his true portrait, and be comforted. Nay, do not sob so violently, but lay your hands in mine and let me tell you what I have seen."

So, grasping each other as if we had been friends for years, I told the bereaved mother how her child had come to me, and how the beautiful poem I had heard seemed to have revealed to my mind that it was her uncontrolled regret that kept him from rising with the angels to a higher sphere.

She listened with wide-open, horror-stricken eyes, as if she felt that she had been guilty of a crime.

"My little one," she moaned, "my poor little one. Kept out of glory for my ingratitude and discontent. But it shall be so no more. I will pray, night and day, until I learn the bitter lesson of resignation to Heaven's will."

"See!" I exclaimed, as I glanced towards the empty cot. "He is there! He is rising already! Your first desire for his welfare, irrespective of your own, has been answered by himself!"

And as we gazed together—awestruck as in the presence of an angel—we saw a shadowy infant form float smiling upward until it was lost to view in the radiance of the sun.

When I looked round at Mrs Duncan for the interpretation of the vision, I found that she had sunk upon her knees in prayer.

It is years and years since those events took place, and Mrs Duncan and myself are still fast friends. She has several children now, and so have I, but neither of us have forgotten the spirit child that was imprisoned for a while in Abergeldie Terrace.

Only the other day his mother told me that she could never find out how that photograph came into her hands. The photographers denied all knowledge of its being sent. Yet there it was. It is one of those mysteries which it seems futile to attempt to unravel. But it taught her a lesson not to hold the blessings of life with a loose hand, and to believe that though hidden maybe from sight, they never can be lost to us, until time and eternity have come to an end.

The Sheridan and Le Fanu Families

The Le Fanu and Sheridan families are so concentrated with literary talent that I shall have to be selective otherwise I'd fill this entire book.* Like the Marryats, the Le Fanus can trace their origins to Normandy in France but not so far back as the Norman Conquest. The furthest takes us to Michel Le Fanu (d. 1576), a lawyer from Caen, who was also something of a poet, so the literary gene goes back at least 450 years. The Le Fanus were Protestants, known as Huguenots in France, who would eventually fall foul of the revocation of the Edict of Nantes in 1685, which had hitherto allowed religious tolerance. This led to considerable unrest and the Huguenots fled France, many to Holland, England and Ireland. Michel's great-great grandson, Philippe (1681–1743) settled in Dublin in 1710 and it was from him that the Irish Le Fanus are descended.

Philippe's grandson, Joseph (1743–1825) married, as his second wife, Alicia Sheridan, sister of the playwright Richard Brinsley Sheridan (1751–1816), who is best remembered for his plays *The Rivals* (1775) and *The School for Scandal* (1777)—both clever comedies of manners. Sheridan shared with Thomas Marryat a biting wit which

---

* To discover the scale and diversity of the Le Fanu family tree visit the family's website at www.lefanus-online.org

alienated both friends and enemies and, despite the success of his plays, he also ended up a pauper, because of his gambling and profligacy. He was not the first literary member of the family. He almost certainly inherited his wit from his grandfather, Thomas (1687–1738), who was a schoolmaster in Dublin. Jonathan Swift, author of *Gulliver's Travels* (1726), despite being twenty years Sheridan's senior, became close friends and Sheridan taught Swift Greek. It is likely that Swift's own delight in wordplay came from Sheridan.

The Sheridans can trace their ancestry back to the Earls of Tyrone in the sixteenth century but let's stay with the playwright Richard Brinsley Sheridan and his sister Alicia who married Joseph Le Fanu. Through his son, the Reverend Thomas Le Fanu (1784–1845), Joseph was the grandfather of Joseph Sheridan Le Fanu who was thus the grand-nephew of the playwright. What's more the playwright's own writing table somehow passed down the generations to Sheridan Le Fanu, to whom we now turn.

1847

THE WATCHER

Joseph Sheridan Le Fanu

Sheridan Le Fanu (1814–1873) was two before he could speak and as a child was educated at home, benefitting from access to his father's extensive library. It clearly worked, because he became renowned for his debating skills when he attended Trinity College, Dublin. He trained as a lawyer but never practised, being drawn towards journalism and literature. He contributed to the Dublin University Magazine, *of which he would later become proprietor. His first story was "The Ghost and the Bone-Setter" (January 1838), the start of a series related by the parish priest Father Purcell. There are often feelings of guilt that pervade his stories as in "The Fortunes of Sir Robert Ardagh" (1838) and especially the story reprinted here, regarded by many as his best. That influence may be from within the family as in "Passage in the Secret History of an Irish Countess" (1838) which formed the basis for his best-known novel,* Uncle Silas *(1864).*

Le Fanu's earliest novels had historical settings. He drew upon his own family history in The Fortunes of Colonel Torlogh O'Brien *(1847). He rarely ventured into the supernatural at novel length, though he created a marked gothic atmosphere in* The House by the Churchyard *(1863) and* Wylder's Hand *(1864). It was in his shorter works that he established his reputation as a pioneer of the weird tale that gave the ghost story a pedigree and a status. Many were collected in* Ghost Stories and Tales of Mystery *(1851),* Chronicles of Golden Friars *(1871),* In a Glass Darkly *(1872), which includes the classic vampire novella "Carmilla", and* The Purcell

Papers *(1880)*. M. R. James rated Le Fanu as *"one of the best storytellers of the nineteenth century"* and compiled a volume of his hitherto uncollected stories as Madam Crowl's Ghost *(1923)*.

Le Fanu had married Susanna Bennett in 1844 and was devoted to her. They had four children, but her health and mental state deteriorated and she died in 1858 aged only 35. Le Fanu was distraught and compensated by throwing himself into his work. His health suffered and he became increasingly reclusive. He died of a heart attack on 10 February 1873 aged only 58.

It is now more than fifty years since the occurrences which I am about to relate caused a strange sensation in the gay society of Dublin. The fashionable world, however, is no recorder of traditions; the memory of selfishness seldom reaches far; and the events which occasionally disturb the polite monotony of its pleasant and heartless progress, however stamped with the characters of misery and horror, scarcely outlive the gossip of a season, and (except, perhaps, in the remembrance of a few more directly interested in the consequences of the catastrophe) are in a little time lost to the recollection of all. The appetite for scandal, or for horror, has been sated; the incident can yield no more of interest or novelty; curiosity, frustrated by impenetrable mystery, gives over the pursuit in despair; the tale has ceased to be new, grows stale and flat; and so, in a few years, inquiry subsides into indifference.

Somewhere about the year 1794, the younger brother of a certain baronet, whom I shall call Sir James Barton, returned to Dublin. He had served in the navy with some distinction, having commanded one of his Majesty's frigates during the greater part of the American war. Captain Barton was now apparently some two or three-and-forty years of age. He was an intelligent and agreeable companion, when he chose it, though generally reserved, and occasionally even moody. In society, however, he deported himself as a man of the world and a gentleman. He had not contracted any of the noisy brusqueness sometimes acquired at sea; on the contrary, his manners were remarkably easy, quiet, and even polished. He was in person about the middle size, and somewhat strongly formed; his countenance was marked with the lines of thought, and on the whole wore an expression of gravity and even of melancholy. Being, however, as we have said, a man of perfect breeding, as well as of affluent circumstances and good family, he had, of course, ready access to the best society of the metropolis, without the necessity of any other credentials. In his personal habits Captain Barton was economical. He occupied lodgings in one of the then fashionable streets in the south side of the town, kept but one horse and one servant, and though a reputed freethinker, he lived an orderly and moral life, indulging neither in gaming, drinking, nor any other vicious pursuit, living very much to himself, without forming any intimacies, or choosing any companions, and appearing to mix in gay society rather for the sake of its bustle and distraction, than for any opportunities which it offered of interchanging either thoughts or feelings with its votaries. Barton was therefore pronounced a saving, prudent, unsocial sort of a fellow, who bid fair to maintain his celibacy alike against stratagem and assault, and was likely to live to a good old age, die rich and leave his money to a hospital.

It was soon apparent, however, that the nature of Captain Barton's plans had been totally misconceived. A young lady, whom we shall call Miss Montague, was at this time introduced into the fashionable world of Dublin by her aunt, the Dowager Lady Rochdale. Miss Montague was decidedly pretty and accomplished, and having some natural cleverness, and a great deal of gaiety, became for a while the reigning toast. Her popularity, however, gained her, for a time, nothing more than that unsubstantial admiration which, however pleasant as an incense to vanity, is by no means necessarily antecedent to matrimony, for, unhappily for the young lady in question, it was an understood thing, that, beyond her personal attractions, she had no kind of earthly provision. Such being the state of affairs, it will readily be believed that no little surprise was consequent upon the appearance of Captain Barton as the avowed lover of the penniless Miss Montague.

His suit prospered, as might have been expected, and in a short time it was confidentially communicated by old Lady Rochdale to each of her hundred and fifty particular friends in succession, that Captain Barton had actually tendered proposals of marriage, with her approbation, to her niece, Miss Montague, who had, moreover, accepted the offer of his hand, conditionally upon the consent of her father, who was then upon his homeward voyage from India, and expected in two or three months at furthest. About his consent there could be no doubt. The delay, therefore, was one merely of form; they were looked upon as absolutely engaged, and Lady Rochdale, with a vigour of old-fashioned decorum with which her niece would, no doubt, gladly have dispensed, withdrew her thenceforward from all further participation in the gaieties of the town. Captain Barton was a constant visitor as well as a frequent guest at the house, and was permitted all the privileges and intimacy which a betrothed suitor is usually accorded. Such was the relation of parties, when the mysterious circumstances which darken this narrative with inexplicable melancholy first began to unfold themselves.

Lady Rochdale resided in a handsome mansion at the north side of Dublin, and Captain Barton's lodgings, as we have already said, were situated at the south. The distance intervening was considerable, and it was Captain Barton's habit generally to walk home without an attendant, as often as he passed the evening with the old lady and her fair charge. His shortest way in such nocturnal walks lay, for a considerable space, through a line of streets which had as yet been merely laid out, and little more than the foundations of the houses constructed. One night, shortly after his engagement with Miss Montague had commenced, he happened to remain unusually late, in company only with her and Lady Rochdale. The conversation had turned upon the evidences of revelation, which he had disputed with the callous scepticism of a confirmed infidel. What were called "French principles" had, in those days, found their way a good deal into fashionable society, especially that portion of it which professed allegiance to Whiggism, and neither the old lady nor her charge was so perfectly free from the taint as to look upon Captain Barton's views as any serious objection to the proposed union. The discussion had degenerated into one upon the supernatural and the marvellous, in which he had pursued precisely the same line of argument and ridicule. In all this, it is but true to state, Captain Barton was guilty of no affectation; the doctrines upon which he insisted were, in reality, but too truly the basis of his own fixed belief, if so it might be called; and perhaps not the least strange of the many strange circumstances connected with this narrative, was the fact that the subject of the fearful influences we are about to describe was himself, from the deliberate conviction of years, an utter disbeliever in what are usually termed preternatural agencies.

It was considerably past midnight when Mr Barton took his leave, and set out upon his solitary walk homeward. He rapidly reached the lonely road, with its unfinished dwarf walls tracing the foundations of the projected rows of houses on either side. The moon was shining mistily, and its imperfect light made the road he trod but additionally dreary; that utter silence, which has in it something indefinably exciting, reigned there, and made the sound of his steps, which alone broke it, unnaturally loud and distinct. He had proceeded thus some way, when on a sudden he heard other footsteps, pattering at a measured pace, and, as it seemed, about two score steps behind him. The suspicion of being dogged is at all times unpleasant; it is, however, especially so in a spot so desolate and lonely: and this suspicion became so strong in the mind of Captain Barton, that he abruptly turned about to confront his pursuers, but, though there was quite sufficient moonlight to disclose any object upon the road he had traversed, no form of any kind was visible.

The steps he had heard could not have been the reverberation of his own, for he stamped his foot upon the ground, and walked briskly up and down, in the vain attempt to wake an echo. Though by no means a fanciful person, he was at last compelled to charge the sounds upon his imagination, and treat them as an illusion. Thus satisfying himself, he resumed his walk, and before he had proceeded a dozen paces, the mysterious footfalls were again audible from behind, and this time, as if with the special design of showing that the sounds were not the responses of an echo, the steps sometimes slackened nearly to a halt, and sometimes hurried for six or eight strides to a run, and again abated to a walk.

Captain Barton, as before, turned suddenly round, and with the same result; no object was visible above the deserted level of the road. He walked back over the same ground, determined that, whatever might have been the cause of the sounds which had so disconcerted him, it should not escape his search; the endeavour, however, was unrewarded. In spite of all his scepticism, he felt something like a superstitious fear stealing fast upon him, and, with these unwonted and uncomfortable sensations, he once more turned and pursued his way. There was no repetition of these haunting sounds, until he had reached the point where he had last stopped to retrace his steps. Here they were resumed, and with sudden starts of running, which threatened to bring the unseen pursuer close up to the alarmed pedestrian. Captain Barton arrested his course as formerly; the unaccountable nature of the occurrence filled him with vague and almost horrible sensations, and, yielding to the excitement he felt gaining upon him, he shouted, sternly, "Who goes there?"

The sound of one's own voice, thus exerted, in utter solitude, and followed by total silence, has in it something unpleasantly exciting, and he felt a degree of nervousness which, perhaps, from no cause had he ever known before. To the very end of this solitary street the steps pursued him, and it required a strong effort of stubborn pride on his part to resist the impulse that prompted him every moment to run for safety at the top of his speed. It was not until he had reached his lodging, and sat by his own fireside, that he felt sufficiently reassured to arrange and reconsider in his own mind the occurrences which had so discomposed him: so little a matter, after all, is sufficient to upset the pride of scepticism, and vindicate the old simple laws of nature within us.

Mr Barton was next morning sitting at a late breakfast, reflecting upon the incidents of the previous night, with more of inquisitiveness than awe—so speedily do gloomy impressions upon the fancy disappear under the cheerful influences of day—when a letter just delivered by the postman was placed upon the table before him. There was nothing remarkable in the address of this missive, except that it was written in a hand which he did not know—perhaps it was disguised—for the tall narrow characters were sloped backward; and with the self-inflicted suspense which we so often see practised in such cases, he puzzled over the inscription for a full minute before he broke the seal. When he did so, he read the following words, written in the same hand:—

> "Mr Barton, late Captain of the *Dolphin*, is warned of *danger*. He will do wisely to avoid —— Street—(here the locality of his last

night's adventure was named)—if he walks there as usual, he will meet with something bad. Let him take warning, once for all, for he has good reason to dread

"THE WATCHER."

Captain Barton read and re-read this strange effusion; in every light and in every direction he turned it over and over. He examined the paper on which it was written, and closely scrutinized the handwriting. Defeated here, he turned to the seal; it was nothing but a patch of wax, upon which the accidental impression of a coarse thumb was imperfectly visible. There was not the slightest mark, no clue or indication of any kind, to lead him to even a guess as to its possible origin. The writer's object seemed a friendly one, and yet he subscribed himself as one whom he had "good reason to dread." Altogether, the letter, its author, and its real purpose, were to him an inexplicable puzzle, and one, moreover, unpleasantly suggestive, in his mind, of associations connected with the last night's adventure.

In obedience to some feeling—perhaps of pride—Mr Barton did not communicate, even to his intended bride, the occurrences which we have just detailed. Trifling as they might appear, they had in reality most disagreeably affected his imagination, and he cared not to disclose, even to the young lady in question, what she might possibly look upon as evidences of weakness. The letter might very well be but a hoax, and the mysterious footfall but a delusion of his fancy. But although he affected to treat the whole affair as unworthy of a thought, it yet haunted him pertinaciously, tormenting him with perplexing doubts, and depressing him with undefined apprehensions. Certain it is, that for a considerable time afterwards he carefully avoided the street indicated in the letter as the scene of danger.

It was not until about a week after the receipt of the letter which I have transcribed, that anything further occurred to remind Captain Barton of its contents, or to counteract the gradual disappearance from his mind of the disagreeable impressions which he had then received. He was returning one night, after the interval I have stated, from the theatre, which was then situated in Crow Street, and having there handed Miss Montague and Lady Rochdale into their carriage, he loitered for some time with two or three acquaintances. With these, however, he parted close to the College, and pursued his way alone. It was now about one o'clock, and the streets were quite deserted. During the whole of his walk with the companions from whom he had just parted, he had been at times painfully aware of the sound of steps, as it seemed, dogging them on their way. Once or twice he had looked back, in the uneasy anticipation that he was again about to experience the same mysterious annoyances which had so much disconcerted him a week before, and earnestly hoping that he might *see* some form from whom the sounds might naturally proceed. But the street was deserted; no form was visible. Proceeding now quite alone upon his homeward way, he grew really nervous and uncomfortable, as he became sensible, with increased distinctness, of the well-known and now absolutely dreaded sounds.

By the side of the dead wall which bounded the College Park, the sounds followed, recommencing almost simultaneously with his own steps. The same unequal pace, sometimes slow, sometimes, for a score yards or so, quickened to a run, was audible from behind him. Again and again he turned, quickly and stealthily he glanced over his shoulder almost at every half-dozen steps; but no one was visible. The horrors of this intangible and unseen persecution became gradually all but intolerable; and when at last he reached his home his nerves were strung to such a pitch of excitement that he could not rest, and did not attempt even to lie down until after the daylight had broken.

He was awakened by a knock at his chamber-door, and his servant entering, handed him several letters which had just been received by the early post. One among them instantly arrested his attention; a single glance at the direction aroused him thoroughly. He at once recognized its character, and read as follows:—

> "You may as well think, Captain Barton, to escape from your own shadow as from me; do what you may, I will see you as often as I please, and you shall see me, for I do not want to hide myself, as you fancy. Do not let it trouble your rest, Captain Barton; for, with a *good conscience*, what need you fear from the eye of
>
> "THE WATCHER?"

It is scarcely necessary to dwell upon the feelings elicited by a perusal of this strange communication. Captain Barton was observed to be unusually absent and out of spirits for several days afterwards; but no one divined the cause. Whatever he might think as to the phantom steps which followed him, there could be no possible illusion about the letters he had received; and, to say the least of it, their immediate sequence upon the mysterious sounds which had haunted him was an odd coincidence. The whole circumstance, in his own mind, was vaguely and instinctively connected with certain passages in his past life, which, of all others, he hated to remember.

It so happened that just about this time, in addition to his approaching nuptials, Captain Barton had fortunately, perhaps, for himself, some business of an engrossing kind connected with the adjustment of a large and long-litigated claim upon certain properties. The hurry and excitement of business had its natural effect in gradually dispelling the marked gloom which had for a time occasionally oppressed him, and in a little while his spirits had entirely resumed their accustomed tone.

During all this period, however, he was occasionally dismayed by indistinct and half-heard repetitions of the same annoyance, and that in lonely places, in the daytime as well as after nightfall. These renewals of the strange impressions from which he had suffered so much were, however, desultory and faint, insomuch that often he really could not, to his own satisfaction, distinguish between them and the mere suggestions of an excited imagination. One evening he walked down to the House of Commons with a Mr Norcott, a Member. As they walked down together he was observed to become absent and silent, and to a degree so marked as scarcely to consist with good breeding; and this, in one who was obviously in all his habits so perfectly a gentleman, seemed to argue the pressure of some urgent and absorbing anxiety. It was afterwards known that, during the whole of that walk, he had heard the well-known footsteps dogging him as he proceeded. This, however, was the last time he suffered from this phase of the persecution of which he was already the anxious victim. A new and a very different one was about to be presented.

Of the new series of impressions which were afterwards gradually to work out his destiny, that evening disclosed the first; and but for its relation to the train of events which followed, the incident would scarcely have been remembered by any one. As they were walking in at the passage, a man (of whom his friend could afterwards remember only that he was short in stature, looked like a foreigner, and wore a kind of travelling-cap) walked very rapidly, and, as if under some fierce excitement, directly towards them, muttering to himself fast and vehemently the while. This odd-looking person proceeded straight toward Barton, who was foremost, and halted, regarding him for a moment or two with a look of menace and fury almost maniacal; and then turning about as abruptly, he walked before them at the same agitated pace, and disappeared by a side passage. Norcott distinctly remembered being a good deal shocked at the countenance and bearing of this man, which indeed irresistibly impressed him with an undefined sense of danger, such as he never felt before or since from the presence of anything human; but these sensations were far from amounting to anything so disconcerting as to flurry or excite him—he had seen only a singularly evil countenance, agitated, as it seemed, with the excitement of madness. He was absolutely astonished, however, at the effect of this apparition upon Captain Barton. He knew him to be a man of proved courage and coolness in real danger, a circumstance which made his conduct upon this occasion the more conspicuously odd. He recoiled a step or two as the stranger advanced, and clutched his companion's arm in silence, with a spasm of agony or terror; and then, as the figure disappeared, shoving him roughly back, he followed it for a few paces, stopped in great disorder, and sat down upon a form. A countenance more ghastly and haggard it was impossible to fancy.

"For God's sake, Barton, what is the matter?" said Norcott, really alarmed at his friend's appearance. "You're not hurt, are you? nor unwell? What is it?"

"What did he say? I did not hear it. What was it?" asked Barton, wholly disregarding the question.

"Tut, tut, nonsense!" said Norcott, greatly surprised; "who cares what the fellow said? You are unwell, Barton, decidedly unwell; let me call a coach."

"Unwell! Yes, no, not exactly unwell," he said, evidently making an effort to recover his self-possession; "but, to say the truth, I am fatigued, a little overworked, and perhaps over anxious. You know

I have been in Chancery, and the winding up of a suit is always a nervous affair. I have felt uncomfortable all this evening; but I am better now. Come, come, shall we go on?"

"No, no. Take my advice, Barton, and go home; you really do need rest; you are looking absolutely ill. I really do insist on your allowing me to see you home," replied his companion.

It was obvious that Barton was not himself disinclined to be persuaded. He accordingly took his leave, politely declining his friend's offered escort. Notwithstanding the few commonplace regrets which Norcott had expressed, it was plain that he was just as little deceived as Barton himself by the extempore plea of illness with which he had accounted for the strange exhibition, and that he even then suspected some lurking mystery in the matter.

Norcott called next day at Barton's lodgings, to inquire for him, and learned from the servant that he had not left his room since his return the night before; but that he was not seriously indisposed, and hoped to be out again in a few days. That evening he sent for Doctor Richards, then in large and fashionable practice in Dublin, and their interview was, it is said, an odd one.

He entered into a detail of his own symptoms in an abstracted and desultory kind of way, which seemed to argue a strange want of interest in his own cure, and, at all events, made it manifest that there was some topic engaging his mind of more engrossing importance than his present ailment. He complained of occasional palpitations, and headache. Doctor Richards asked him, among other questions, whether there was any irritating circumstance or anxiety to account for it. This he denied quickly and peevishly; and the physician thereupon declared his opinion, that there was nothing amiss except some slight derangement of the digestion, for which he accordingly wrote a prescription, and was about to withdraw, when Mr Barton, with the air of a man who suddenly recollects a topic which had nearly escaped him, recalled him.

"I beg your pardon, doctor, but I had really almost forgot; will you permit me to ask you two or three medical questions?—rather odd ones, perhaps, but as a wager depends upon their solution, you will, I hope, excuse my unreasonableness."

The physician readily undertook to satisfy the inquirer.

Barton seemed to have some difficulty about opening the proposed interrogatories, for he was silent for a minute, then walked to his book-case and returned as he had gone; at last he sat down, and said,—

"You'll think them very childish questions, but I can't recover my wager without a decision; so I must put them. I want to know first about lock-jaw. If a man actually has had that complaint, and appears to have died of it—so that in fact a physician of average skill pronounces him actually dead—may he, after all, recover?"

Doctor Richards smiled, and shook his head.

"But—but a blunder may be made," resumed Barton. "Suppose an ignorant pretender to medical skill; may *he* be so deceived by any stage of the complaint, as to mistake what is only a part of the progress of the disease, for death itself?"

"No one who had ever seen death," answered he, "could mistake it in the case of lock-jaw."

Barton mused for a few minutes. "I am going to ask you a question, perhaps still more childish; but first tell me, are not the regulations of foreign hospitals, such as those of, let us say, Lisbon, very lax and bungling? May not all kinds of blunders and slips occur in their entries of names, and so forth?"

Doctor Richards professed his inability to answer that query.

"Well, then, doctor, here is the last of my questions. You will probably laugh at it; but it must out nevertheless. Is there any disease, in all the range of human maladies, which would have the effect of perceptibly contracting the stature, and the whole frame—causing the man to shrink in all his proportions, and yet to preserve his exact resemblance to himself in every particular—with the one exception, his height and bulk; *any* disease, mark, no matter how rare, how little believed in, generally, which could possibly result in producing such an effect?"

The physician replied with a smile, and a very decided negative.

"Tell me, then," said Barton, abruptly, "if a man be in reasonable fear of assault from a lunatic who is at large, can he not procure a warrant for his arrest and detention?"

"Really, that is more a lawyer's question than one in my way," replied Doctor Richards; "but I believe, on applying to a magistrate, such a course would be directed."

The physician then took his leave; but, just as he reached the hall-door, remembered that he had left his cane upstairs, and returned. His reappearance was awkward, for a piece of paper, which he recognized as his own prescription, was slowly burning upon the fire, and Barton sitting close by with an expression of settled gloom and dismay. Doctor Richards had too much tact to appear to observe what presented itself; but he had seen quite enough to assure him that the mind, and not the body, of Captain Barton was in reality the seat of his sufferings.

A few days afterwards, the following advertisement appeared in the Dublin newspapers:—

"If Sylvester Yelland, formerly a foremast man on board his Majesty's frigate *Dolphin*, or his nearest of kin, will apply to Mr Robery Smith, solicitor, at his office, Dame Street, he or they may hear of something greatly to his or their advantage. Admission may be had at any hour up to twelve o'clock at night for the next fortnight, should parties desire to avoid observation; and the strictest secrecy, as to all communications intended to be confidential, shall be honourably observed."

The *Dolphin*, as we have mentioned, was the vessel which Captain Barton had commanded; and this circumstance, connected with the extraordinary exertions made by the circulation of hand-bills, etc., as well as by repeated advertisements, to secure for this strange notice the utmost possible publicity, suggested to Doctor Richards the idea that Captain Barton's extreme uneasiness was somehow connected with the individual to whom the advertisement was addressed, and he himself the author of it. This, however, it is needless to add, was no more than a conjecture. No information whatsoever, as to the real purpose of the advertisement itself, was divulged by the agent, nor yet any hint as to who his employer might be.

Mr Barton, although he had latterly begun to earn for himself the character of a hypochondriac, was yet very far from deserving it. Though by no means lively, he had yet, naturally, what are termed "even spirits," and was not subject to continual depressions. He soon, therefore, began to return to his former habits; and one of the earliest symptoms of this healthier tone of spirits was his appearing at a grand dinner of the Freemasons, of which worthy fraternity he was himself a brother. Barton, who had been at first gloomy and abstracted, drank much more freely than was his wont—possibly with the purpose of dispelling his own secret anxieties—and under the influence of good wine, and pleasant company, became gradually (unlike his usual self) talkative, and even noisy. It was under this unwonted excitement that he left his company at about half-past ten o'clock; and as conviviality is a strong incentive to gallantry, it occurred to him to proceed forthwith to Lady Rochdale's, and pass the remainder of the evening with her and his destined bride.

Accordingly, he was soon at —— Street, and chatting gaily with the ladies. It is not to be supposed that Captain Barton had exceeded the limits which propriety prescribes to good fellowship; he had merely taken enough of wine to raise his spirits, without, however, in the least degree unsteadying his mind, or affecting his manners. With this undue elevation of spirits had supervened an entire oblivion or contempt of those undefined apprehensions which had for so long weighed upon his mind, and to a certain extent estranged him from society; but as the night wore away, and his artificial gaiety began to flag, these painful feelings gradually intruded themselves again, and he grew abstracted and anxious as heretofore. He took his leave at length, with an unpleasant foreboding of some coming mischief, and with a mind haunted with a thousand mysterious apprehensions, such as, even while he acutely felt their pressure, he, nevertheless, inwardly strove, or affected to contemn.

It was his proud defiance of what he considered to be his own weakness which prompted him up on this occasion to the course which brought about the adventure which we are now about to relate. Mr Barton might have easily called a coach, but he was conscious that his strong inclination to do so proceeded from no cause other than what he desperately persisted in representing to himself to be his own superstitious tremors. He might also have returned home by a route different from that against which he had been warned by his mysterious correspondent; but for the same reason he dismissed this idea also, and with a dogged and half desperate resolution to force matters to a crisis of some kind, to see if there were any reality in the causes of his former suffering, and if not, satisfactorily to bring their delusiveness to the proof, he determined to follow precisely the course which he had trodden upon the night so painfully memorable in his own mind as that on which his strange persecution had commenced. Though, sooth to say, the pilot who for the first time steers his vessel under the muzzles of a hostile battery never felt his resolution more severely tasked than did Captain Barton, as he breathlessly pursued this solitary path; a path which, spite of every effort of scepticism and reason, he felt to be, as respected *him*, infested by a malignant influence.

He pursued his way steadily and rapidly, scarcely breathing from intensity of suspense; he, however, was troubled by no renewal of the dreaded footsteps, and was beginning to feel a return of confidence, as, more than three-fourths of the way being accomplished with impunity, he approached the long line of twinkling oil lamps which indicated the frequented streets. This feeling of self-congratulation was, however, but momentary. The report of a musket at some two hundred yards behind him, and the whistle of a bullet close to his head, disagreeably and startlingly dispelled it. His first impulse was to retrace his steps in pursuit of the assassin; but the road on either side was, as we have said, embarrassed by the foundations of a street, beyond which extended waste fields, full of rubbish and neglected lime and brick kilns, and all now as utterly silent as though no sound had ever disturbed their dark and unsightly solitude. The futility of attempting, single-handed, under such circumstances, a search for the murderer, was apparent, especially as no further sound whatever was audible to direct his pursuit.

With the tumultuous sensations of one whose life had just been exposed to a murderous attempt, and whose escape has been the narrowest possible, Captain Barton turned, and without, however, quickening his pace actually to a run, hurriedly pursued his way. He had turned, as we have said, after a pause of a few seconds, and had just commenced his rapid retreat, when on a sudden he met the well-remembered little man in the fur cap. The encounter was but momentary. The figure was walking at the same exaggerated pace, and with the same strange air of menace as before; and as it passed him, he thought he heard it say, in a furious whisper, "Still alive, still alive!"

The state of Mr Barton's spirits began now to work a corresponding alteration in his health and looks, and to such a degree that it was impossible that the change should escape general remark. For some reasons, known but to himself, he took no step whatsoever to bring the attempt upon his life, which he had so narrowly escaped, under the notice of the authorities; on the contrary, he kept it jealously to himself; and it was not for many weeks after the occurrence that he mentioned it, and then in strict confidence to a gentleman, the torments of his mind at last compelled him to consult a friend.

Spite of his blue devils, however, poor Barton, having no satisfactory reason to render to the public for any undue remissness in the attentions which his relation to Miss Montague required, was obliged to exert himself, and present to the world a confident and cheerful bearing. The true source of his sufferings, and every circumstance connected with them, he guarded with a reserve so jealous, that it seemed dictated by at least a suspicion that the origin of his strange persecution was known to himself, and that it was of a nature which, upon his own account, he could not or dare not disclose.

The mind thus turned in upon itself, and constantly occupied with a haunting anxiety which it dared not reveal, or confide to any human breast, became daily more excited; and, of course, more vividly impressible, by a system of attack which operated through the nervous system; and in this state he was destined to sustain, with increasing frequency, the stealthy visitations of that apparition, which from the first had seemed to possess so unearthly and terrible a hold upon his imagination.

*

It was about this time that Captain Barton called upon the then celebrated preacher, Doctor Macklin, with whom he had a slight acquaintance; and an extraordinary conversation ensued. The divine was seated in his chambers in college, surrounded with works upon his favourite pursuit and deep in theology, when Barton was announced. There was something at once embarrassed and excited in his manner, which, along with his wan and haggard countenance, impressed the student with the unpleasant consciousness that his visitor must have recently suffered terribly indeed to account for an alteration so striking, so shocking.

After the usual interchange of polite greeting, and a few commonplace remarks, Captain Barton, who obviously perceived the surprise which his visit had excited, and which Doctor Macklin was unable wholly to conceal, interrupted a brief pause by remarking,—

"This is a strange call, Doctor Macklin, perhaps scarcely warranted by an acquaintance so slight as mine with you. I should not, under ordinary circumstances, have ventured to disturb you, but my visit is neither an idle nor impertinent intrusion. I am sure you will not so account it, when—"

Doctor Macklin interrupted him with assurances, such as good breeding suggested, and Barton resumed,—

"I am come to task your patience by asking your advice. When I say your patience, I might, indeed, say more; I might have said your humanity, your compassion; for I have been, and am a great sufferer."

"My dear sir," replied the churchman, "it will, indeed, afford me infinite gratification if I can give you comfort in any distress of mind, but—but—"

"I know what you would say," resumed Barton, quickly. "I am an unbeliever, and, therefore, incapable of deriving help from religion, but don't take that for granted. At least you must not assume that, however unsettled my convictions may be, I do not feel a deep, a very deep, interest in the subject. Circumstances have lately forced it upon my attention in such a way as to compel me to review the whole question in a more candid and teachable spirit, I believe, than I ever studied it in before."

"Your difficulties, I take it for granted, refer to the evidences of revelation," suggested the clergyman.

"Why—no—yes; in fact I am ashamed to say I have not considered even my objections sufficiently to state them connectedly; but—but there is one subject on which I feel a peculiar interest."

He paused again, and Doctor Macklin pressed him to proceed.

"The fact is," said Barton, "whatever may be my uncertainty as to the authenticity of what we are taught to call revelation, of one fact I am deeply and horribly convinced: that there does exist beyond this a spiritual world—a system whose workings are generally in mercy hidden from us—a system which may be, and which is sometimes, partially and terribly revealed. I am sure, I know," continued Barton, with increasing excitement, "there is a God—a dreadful God—and that retribution follows guilt. In ways, the most mysterious and stupendous; by agencies, the most inexplicable and terrific; there is a spiritual system—great Heavens, how frightfully I have been convinced!—a system malignant, and inexorable, and omnipotent, under whose persecutions I am, and have been, suffering the torments of the damned!—yes, sir—yes—the fires and frenzy of hell!"

As Barton continued, his agitation became so vehement that the divine was shocked and even alarmed. The wild and excited rapidity with which he spoke, and, above all, the indefinable horror which stamped his features, afforded a contrast to his ordinary cool and unimpassioned self-possession, striking and painful in the last degree.

"My dear sir," said Doctor Macklin, after a brief pause, "I fear you have been suffering much, indeed; but I venture to predict that the depression under which you labour will be found to originate in purely physical causes, and that with a change of air and the aid of a few tonics, your spirits will return, and the tone of your mind be once more cheerful and tranquil as heretofore. There was, after all, more truth than we are quite willing to admit in the classic theories which assigned the undue predominance of any one affection of the mind to the undue action or torpidity of one or other of our bodily organs. Believe me, that a little attention to diet, exercise, and the other essentials of health, under competent direction, will make you as much yourself as you can wish."

"Doctor Macklin," said Barton, with something like a shudder, "I *cannot* delude myself with such a hope. I have no hope to cling to but one, and that is, that by some other spiritual agency more potent than that which tortures me, *it* may be combated, and I delivered. If this may not be, I am lost—now and for ever lost."

"But, Mr Barton, you must remember," urged his companion, "that others have suffered as you have done, and—"

"No, no, no," interrupted he with irritability; "no, sir, I am not a credulous—far from a superstitious man. I have been, perhaps, too much the reverse—too sceptical, too slow of belief; but unless I were one whom no amount of evidence could convince, unless I were to contemn the repeated, the *perpetual* evidence of my own senses, I am now—now at last constrained to believe I have no escape from the conviction, the overwhelming certainty, that I am haunted and dogged, go where I may, by—by a Demon."

There was an almost preternatural energy of horror in Barton's face, as, with its damp and deathlike lineaments turned towards his companion, he thus delivered himself.

"God help you, my poor friend!" said Doctor Macklin, much shocked. "God help you; for, indeed, you *are* a sufferer, however your sufferings may have been caused."

"Ay, ay, God help me," echoed Barton sternly; "but *will* He help me? will He help me?"

"Pray to Him; pray in an humble and trusting spirit," said he.

"Pray, pray," echoed he again; "I can't pray; I could as easily move a mountain by an effort of my will. I have not belief enough to pray; there is something within me that will not pray. You prescribe impossibilities—literal impossibilities."

"You will not find it so, if you will but try," said Doctor Macklin.

"Try! I *have* tried, and the attempt only fills me with confusion and terror. I have tried in vain, and more than in vain. The awful, unutterable idea of eternity and infinity oppresses and maddens my brain, whenever my mind approaches the contemplation of the Creator; I recoil from the effort, scared, confounded, terrified. I tell you, Doctor Macklin, if I am to be saved, it must be by other means. The idea of the Creator is to me intolerable; my mind cannot support it."

"Say, then, my dear sir," urged he, "say how you would have me serve you. What you would learn of me. What can I do or say to relieve you?"

"Listen to me first," replied Captain Barton, with a subdued air, and an evident effort to suppress his excitement; "listen to me while I detail the circumstances of the terrible persecution under which my life has become all but intolerable—a persecution which has made me fear *death* and the world beyond the grave as much as I have grown to hate existence."

Barton then proceeded to relate the circumstances which we have already detailed, and then continued,—

"This has now become habitual—an accustomed thing. I do not mean the actual seeing him in the flesh; thank God, *that* at least is not permitted daily. Thank God, from the unutterable horrors of that visitation I have been mercifully allowed intervals of repose, though none of security; but from the consciousness that a malignant spirit is following and watching me wherever I go, I have never, for a single instant, a temporary respite: I am pursued with blasphemies, cries of despair, and appalling hatred; I hear those dreadful sounds called after me as I turn the corners of streets; they come in the night-time while I sit in my chamber alone; they haunt me everywhere, charging me with hideous crimes, and—great God!—threatening me with coming vengeance and eternal misery! Hush! do you hear *that*?" he cried, with a horrible smile of triumph. "There—there, will that convince you?"

The clergyman felt the chillness of horror irresistibly steal over him, while, during the wail of a sudden gust of wind, he heard, or fancied he heard, the half articulate sounds of rage and derision mingling in their sough.

"Well, what do you think of *that*?" at length Barton cried, drawing a long breath through his teeth.

"I heard the wind," said Doctor Macklin; "what should I think of it? What is there remarkable about it?"

"The prince of the powers of the air," muttered Barton, with a shudder.

"Tut, tut! my dear sir!" said the student, with an effort to reassure himself; for though it was broad daylight, there was nevertheless something disagreeably contagious in the nervous excitement under which his visitor so obviously suffered. "You must not give way to those wild fancies: you must resist those impulses of the imagination."

"Ay, ay; 'resist the devil, and he will flee from thee,'" said Barton, in the same tone; "but *how* resist him? Ay, there it is: there is the rub. What—*what* am I to do? What *can* I do?"

"My dear sir, this is fancy," said the man of folios; "you are your own tormentor."

"No, no, sir; fancy has no part in it," answered Barton, somewhat sternly. "Fancy, forsooth! Was it that made *you*, as well as me, hear, but this moment, those appalling accents of hell? Fancy, indeed! No, no."

"But you have seen this person frequently," said the ecclesiastic; "why have you not accosted or secured him? Is it not somewhat precipitate, to say no more, to assume, as you have done, the existence of preternatural agency, when, after all, everything may be easily accountable, if only proper means were taken to sift the matter."

"There are circumstances connected with this—this *appearance*," said Barton, "which it were needless to disclose, but which to *me* are proofs of its horrible and unearthly nature. I know that the being who haunts me is not *man*. I say I *know* this; I could prove it to your own conviction." He paused for a minute, and then added, "And as to accosting it, I dare not—I could not! When I see it I am powerless; I stand in the gaze of death, in the triumphant presence of preterhuman power and malignity; my strength, and faculties, and memory all forsake me. Oh, God! I fear, sir, you know not what you speak of. Mercy, mercy! heaven have pity on me!"

He leaned his elbow on the table, and passed his hand across his eyes, as if to exclude some image of horror, muttering the last words of the sentence he had just concluded, again and again.

"Dr Macklin," he said, abruptly raising himself, and looking full upon the clergyman with an imploring eye, "I know you will do for me whatever may be done. You know now fully the circumstances and the nature of the mysterious agency of which I am the victim. I tell you I cannot help myself; I cannot hope to escape; I am utterly passive. I conjure you, then, to weigh my case well, and if anything may be done for me by vicarious supplication, by the intercession of the good, or by any aid or influence whatsoever, I implore of you, I adjure you in the name of the Most High, give me the benefit of that influence, deliver me from the body of this death! Strive for me; pity me! I know you will; you cannot refuse this; it is the purpose and object of my visit. Send me away with some hope, however little—some faint hope of ultimate deliverance, and I will nerve myself to endure, from hour to hour, the hideous dream into which my existence is transformed."

Doctor Macklin assured him that all he could do was to pray earnestly for him, and that so much he would not fail to do. They parted with a hurried and melancholy valediction. Barton hastened to the carriage which awaited him at the door, drew the blinds, and drove away, while Dr Macklin returned to his chamber, to ruminate at leisure upon the strange interview which had just interrupted his studies.

It was not to be expected that Captain Barton's changed and eccentric habits should long escape remark and discussion. Various were the theories suggested to account for it. Some attributed the alteration to the pressure of secret pecuniary embarrassments; others to a repugnance to fulfil an engagement into which he was presumed to have too precipitately entered; and others, again, to the supposed incipiency of mental disease, which latter, indeed, was the most plausible, as well as the most generally received, of the hypotheses circulated in the gossip of the day.

From the very commencement of this change, at first so gradual in its advances, Miss Montague had, of course, been aware of it. The intimacy involved in their peculiar relation, as well as the near interest which it inspired, afforded, in her case, alike opportunity and motive for the successful exercise of that keen and penetrating observation peculiar to the sex. His visits became, at length, so interrupted, and his manner, while they lasted, so abstracted, strange, and agitated, that Lady Rochdale, after hinting her anxiety and her suspicions more than once, at length distinctly stated her anxiety, and pressed for an explanation. The explanation was given, and although its nature at first relieved the worst solicitudes of the old lady and her niece, yet the circumstances which attended it, and the really dreadful consequences which it obviously threatened as regarded the spirits, and, indeed, the reason, of the now wretched man who made the strange declaration, were enough, upon a little reflection, to fill their minds with perturbation and alarm.

General Montague, the young lady's father, at length arrived. He had himself slightly known Barton, some ten or twelve years previously, and being aware of his fortune and connections, was disposed to regard him as an unexceptionable and indeed a most desirable match for his daughter. He laughed at the story of Barton's supernatural visitations, and lost not a moment in calling upon his intended son-in-law.

"My dear Barton," he continued gaily, after a little conversation, "my sister tells me that you are a victim to blue devils in quite a new and original shape."

Barton changed countenance, and sighed profoundly.

"Come, come; I protest this will never do," continued the General; "you are more like a man on his way to the gallows than to the altar. These devils have made quite a saint of you."

Barton made an effort to change the conversation.

"No, no, it won't do," said his visitor, laughing; "I am resolved to say out what I have to say about this magnificent mock mystery of yours. Come, you must not be angry; but, really, it is too bad to see you, at your time of life, absolutely frightened into good behaviour, like a naughty child, by a bugaboo, and, as far as I can learn, a very particularly contemptible one. Seriously, though, my dear Barton, I have been a good deal annoyed at what they tell me; but, at the same time, thoroughly convinced that there is nothing in the matter that may not be cleared up, with just a little attention and management, within a week at furthest."

"Ah, General, you do not know—" he began.

"Yes, but I do know quite enough to warrant my confidence," interrupted the soldier. "I know that all your annoyance proceeds from the occasional appearance of a certain little man in a cap and greatcoat, with a red vest and bad countenance, who follows you about, and pops upon you at the corners of lanes, and throws you into ague fits. Now, my dear fellow, I'll make it my business to *catch* this mischievous little mountebank, and either beat him into a jelly with my own hands, or have him whipped through the town at the cart's tail."

"If *you* knew what I know," said Barton, with gloomy agitation, "you would speak very differently. Don't imagine that I am so weak and foolish as to assume, without proof the most overwhelming, the conclusion to which I have been forced. The proofs are here, locked up here." As he spoke, he tapped upon his breast, and with an anxious sigh continued to walk up and down the room.

"Well, well, Barton," said his visitor, "I'll wager a rump and a dozen I collar the ghost, and convince yourself before many days are over."

He was running on in the same strain when he was suddenly arrested, and not a little shocked, by observing Barton, who had approached the window, stagger slowly back, like one who had received a stunning blow—his arm feebly extended towards the street, his face and his very lips white as ashes—while he uttered, "There—there—there!"

General Montague started mechanically to his feet, and, from the window of the drawing-room, saw a figure corresponding, as well as his hurry would permit him to discern, with the description of the person whose appearance so constantly and dreadfully disturbed the repose of his friend. The figure was just turning from the rails of the area upon which it had been leaning, and without waiting to see more, the old gentleman snatched his cane and hat, and rushed down the stairs and into the street, in the furious hope of securing the person, and punishing the audacity of the mysterious stranger. He looked around him, but in vain, for any trace of the form he had himself distinctly beheld. He ran breathlessly to the nearest corner, expecting to see from thence the retreating figure, but no such form was visible. Back and forward, from crossing to crossing, he ran at fault, and it was not until the curious gaze and laughing countenances of the passers-by reminded him of the absurdity of his pursuit, that he checked his hurried pace, lowered his walking-cane from the menacing altitude which he had mechanically given it, adjusted his hat, and walked composedly back again, inwardly vexed and flurried. He found Barton pale and trembling in every joint; they both remained silent, though under emotions very different. At last Barton whispered, "You saw it?"

"It!—him—someone—you mean—to be sure I did," replied Montague, testily. "But where is the good or the harm of seeing him? The fellow runs like a lamplighter. I wanted to *catch* him, but he had stolen away before I could reach the hall door. However, it is no great matter; next time, I dare say, I'll do better; and, egad, if I once come within reach of him, I'll introduce his shoulders to the weight of my cane, in a way to make him cry *peccavi*."

Notwithstanding General Montague's undertakings and exhortations, however, Barton continued to suffer from the self-same unexplained cause. Go how, when, or where he would, he was still constantly dogged or confronted by the hateful being who had established over him so dreadful and mysterious an influence; nowhere, and at no time, was he secure against the odious appearance which haunted him with such diabolical perseverance. His depression, misery, and excitement became more settled and alarming every day, and the mental agonies that ceaselessly preyed upon him began at last so sensibly to affect his general health, that Lady Rochdale and General Montague succeeded (without, indeed, much difficulty) in persuading him to try a short tour on the Continent, in the hope that an entire change of scene would, at all events, have the effect of breaking through the influences of local association, which the more sceptical of his friends assumed to be by no means inoperative in suggesting and perpetuating what they conceived to be a mere form of nervous illusion. General Montague, moreover, was persuaded that the figure which haunted his intended son-in-law was by no means the creation of his own imagination, but, on the contrary, a substantial form of flesh and blood, animated by a spiteful and obstinate resolution, perhaps with some murderous object in perspective, to watch and follow the unfortunate gentleman. Even this hypothesis was not a very pleasant one; yet it was plain that if Barton could once be convinced that there was nothing preternatural in the phenomenon, which he had hitherto regarded in that light, the affair would lose all its terrors in his eyes, and wholly cease to exercise upon his health and spirits the baneful influence which it had hitherto done. He therefore reasoned, that if the annoyance were actually escaped from by mere change of scene, it obviously could not have originated in any supernatural agency.

Yielding to their persuasions, Barton left Dublin for England, accompanied by General Montague. They posted rapidly to London, and thence to Dover, whence they took the packet with a fair wind for Calais. The General's confidence in the result of the expedition on Barton's spirits had risen day by day since their departure from the shores of Ireland; for, to the inexpressible relief and delight of the latter, he had not, since then, so much as even once fancied a repetition of those impressions which had, when at home, drawn him gradually down to the very abyss of horror and despair. This exemption from what he had begun to regard as the inevitable condition of his existence, and the sense of security which began to pervade his mind, were inexpressibly delightful; and in the exultation of what he considered his deliverance, he indulged in a thousand happy anticipations for a future into which so lately he had hardly dared to look. In short, both he and his companion secretly congratulated themselves upon the termination of that persecution which had been to its immediate victim a source of such unspeakable agony.

It was a beautiful day, and a crowd of idlers stood upon the jetty to receive the packet, and enjoy the bustle of the new arrivals. Montague walked a few paces in advance of his friend, and as he made his way through the crowd, a little man touched his arm, and said to him, in a broad provincial *patois*,—

"Monsieur is walking too fast; he will lose his sick comrade in the throng, for, by my faith, the poor gentleman seems to be fainting."

Montague turned quickly, and observed that Barton did indeed look deadly pale. He hastened to his side.

"My poor fellow, are you ill?" he asked anxiously.

The question was unheeded, and twice repeated, ere Barton stammered,—

"I saw him—by ——, I saw him!"

"*Him!*—who?—where?—when did you see him?—where is he?" cried Montague, looking around him.

"I saw him—but he is gone," repeated Barton, faintly.

"But where—where? For God's sake, speak," urged Montague, vehemently.

"It is but this moment—*here*," said he.

"But what did he look like?—what had he on?—what did he wear?—quick, quick," urged his excited companion, ready to dart among the crowd, and collar the delinquent on the spot.

"He touched your arm—he spoke to you—he pointed to me. God be merciful to me, there is no escape!" said Barton, in the low, subdued tones of intense despair.

Montague had already bustled away in all the flurry of mingled hope and indignation; but though the singular *personnel* of the stranger who had accosted him was vividly and perfectly impressed upon his recollection, he failed to discover among the crowd even the slightest resemblance to him. After a fruitless search, in which he enlisted the services of several of the bystanders, who aided all the more zealously as they believed he had been robbed, he at length, out of breath and baffled, gave over the attempt.

"Ah, my friend, it won't do," said Barton, with the faint voice and bewildered, ghastly look of one who has been stunned by some mortal shock; "there is no use in contending with it; whatever it is, the dreadful association between me and it is now established; I shall never escape—never, never!"

"Nonsense, nonsense, my dear fellow; don't talk so," said Montague, with something at once of irritation and dismay; "you must not; never mind, I say—never mind, we'll jockey the scoundrel yet."

It was, however, but lost labour to endeavour henceforward to inspire Barton with one ray of hope; he became utterly desponding.

This intangible and, as it seemed, utterly inadequate influence was fast destroying his energies of intellect, character, and health. His first object was now to return to Ireland, there, as he believed, and now almost hoped, speedily to die.

To Ireland, accordingly, he came, and one of the first faces he saw upon the shore was again that of his implacable and dreaded persecutor. Barton seemed at last to have lost not only all enjoyment and every hope in existence, but all independence of will besides. He now submitted himself passively to the management of the friends most nearly interested in his welfare. With the apathy of entire despair, he implicitly assented to whatever measures they suggested and advised; and, as a last resource, it was determined to remove him to a house of Lady Rochdale's in the neighbourhood of Clontarf, where, with the advice of his medical attendant (who persisted in his opinion that the whole train of impressions resulted merely from some nervous derangement) it was resolved that he was to confine himself strictly to the house, and to make use only of those apartments which commanded a view of an enclosed yard, the gates of which were to be kept jealously locked. These precautions would at least secure him against the casual appearance of any living form which his excited imagination might possibly confound with the spectre which, as it was contended, his fancy recognized in every figure that bore even a distant or general resemblance to the traits with which he had at first invested it. A month or six weeks' absolute seclusion under these conditions, it was hoped, might, by interrupting the series of these terrible impressions, gradually dispel the predisposing apprehension, and effectually break up the associations which had confirmed the supposed disease, and rendered recovery hopeless. Cheerful society and that of his friends was to be constantly supplied, and on the whole, very sanguine expectations were indulged in, that under this treatment the obstinate hypochondria of the patient might at length give way.

Accompanied, therefore, by Lady Rochdale, General Montague, and his daughter—his own affianced bride—poor Barton, himself never daring to cherish a hope of his ultimate emancipation from the strange horrors under which his life was literally wasting away, took possession of the apartments whose situation protected him against the dreadful intrusions from which he shrank with such unutterable terror.

After a little time, a steady persistence in this system began to manifest its results in a very marked though gradual improvement alike in the health and spirits of the invalid. Not, indeed, that anything at all approaching to complete recovery was yet discernible. On the contrary, to those who had not seen him since the commencement of his strange sufferings, such an alteration would have been apparent as might well have shocked them. The improvement, however, such as it was, was welcomed with gratitude and delight, especially by the poor young lady, whom her attachment to him, as well as her now singularly painful position, consequent on his mysterious and protracted illness, rendered an object of pity scarcely one degree less to be commiserated than himself.

A week passed—a fortnight—a month—and yet no recurrence of the hated visitation had agitated and terrified him as before. The treatment had, so far, been followed by complete success. The chain of association had been broken. The constant pressure upon the overtasked spirits had been removed, and, under these comparatively favourable circumstances, the sense of social community with the world about him, and something of human interest, if not of enjoyment, began to reanimate his mind.

It was about this time that Lady Rochdale, who, like most old ladies of the day, was deep in family receipts, and a great pretender to medical science, being engaged in the concoction of certain unpalatable mixtures of marvellous virtue, despatched her own maid to the kitchen garden with a list of herbs which were there to be carefully culled and brought back to her for the purpose stated. The handmaiden, however, returned with her task scarce half-completed, and a good deal flurried and alarmed. Her mode of accounting for her precipitate retreat and evident agitation was odd, and to the old lady unpleasantly startling.

It appeared that she had repaired to the kitchen garden, pursuant to her mistress's directions, and had there begun to make the specified selection among the rank and neglected herbs which crowded one corner of the enclosure, and while engaged in this pleasant labour she carelessly sang a fragment of an old song, as she said, "to keep herself company." She was, however, interrupted by a sort of mocking echo of the air she was singing; and looking up, she saw through the old thorn hedge, which surrounded the garden, a singularly ill-looking, little man, whose countenance wore the stamp of menace and malignity, standing close to her at the other side of the hawthorn screen. She described herself as utterly unable to move or speak, while he charged her with a message for Captain Barton, the substance of which she distinctly remembered to have been to the effect that he, Captain Barton, must come abroad as usual, and show himself to his friends out of doors, or else prepare for a visit in his own chamber. On concluding this brief message, the stranger had, with a threatening air, got down into the outer ditch, and seizing the hawthorn stems in his hands, seemed on the point of climbing through the fence, a feat which might have been accomplished without much difficulty. Without, of course, awaiting this result, the girl, throwing down her treasures of thyme and rosemary, had turned and run, with the swiftness of terror, to the house. Lady Rochdale commanded her, on pain of instant dismissal, to observe an absolute silence respecting all that portion of the incident which related to Captain Barton; and, at the same time, directed instant search to be made by her men in the garden and fields adjacent. This measure, however, was attended with the usual unsuccess, and filled with fearful and indefinable misgivings, Lady Rochdale communicated the incident to her brother. The story, however, until long afterwards, went no further, and of course it was jealously guarded from Barton, who continued to mend, though slowly and imperfectly.

Barton now began to walk occasionally in the courtyard which we have mentioned, and which, being surrounded by a high wall, commanded no view beyond its own extent. Here he, therefore, considered himself perfectly secure; and, but for a careless violation of orders by one of the grooms, he might have enjoyed, at least for some time longer, his much-prized immunity. Opening upon the public road, this yard was entered by a wooden gate, with a wicket in it, which was further defended by an iron gate upon the outside. Strict orders had been given to keep them carefully locked; but, in spite of these, it had happened that one day, as Barton was slowly pacing this narrow enclosure, in his accustomed walk, and reaching the further extremity, was turning to retrace his steps, he saw the boarded wicket ajar, and the face of his tormentor immovably looking at him through the iron bars. For a few seconds he stood riveted to the earth, breathless and bloodless, in the fascination of that dreaded gaze, and then fell helplessly upon the pavement.

There was he found a few minutes afterwards, and conveyed to his room, the apartment which he was never afterwards to leave alive. Henceforward, a marked and unaccountable change was observable in the tone of his mind. Captain Barton was now no longer the excited and despairing man he had been before; a strange alteration had passed upon him, an unearthly tranquillity reigned in his mind; it was the anticipated stillness of the grave.

"Montague, my friend, this struggle is nearly ended now," he said, tranquilly, but with a look of fixed and fearful awe. "I have, at last, some comfort from that world of spirits, from which my *punishment* has come. I know now that my sufferings will be soon over."

Montague pressed him to speak on.

"Yes," said he, in a softened voice, "my punishment is nearly ended. From sorrow perhaps I shall never, in time or eternity, escape; but my *agony* is almost over. Comfort has been revealed to me, and what remains of my allotted struggle I will bear with submission, even with hope."

"I am glad to hear you speak so tranquilly, my dear fellow," said Montague; "peace and cheerfulness of mind are all you need to make you what you were."

"No, no, I never can be that," said he, mournfully. "I am no longer fit for life. I am soon to die: I do not shrink from death as I did. I am to see *him* but once again, and then all is ended."

"He said so, then?" suggested Montague.

"*He?* No, no; good tidings could scarcely come through him; and these were good and welcome; and they came so solemnly and sweetly, with unutterable love and melancholy, such as I could not, without saying more than is needful or fitting, of other long-past scenes and persons, fully explain to you." As Barton said this he shed tears.

"Come, come," said Montague, mistaking the source of his emotions, "you must not give way. What is it, after all, but a pack of dreams and nonsense; or, at worst, the practices of a scheming rascal that enjoys his power of playing upon your nerves, and loves to exert it; a sneaking vagabond that owes you a grudge, and pays it off this way, not daring to try a more manly one."

"A grudge, indeed, he owes me; you say rightly," said Barton, with a sullen shudder; "a grudge as you call it. Oh, God! when the justice of heaven permits the Evil One to carry out a scheme of vengeance, when its execution is committed to the lost and frightful victim of sin, who owes his own ruin to the man, the very man, whom he is commissioned to pursue; then, indeed, the torments and terrors of hell are anticipated on earth. But heaven has dealt mercifully with me: hope has opened to me at last; and if death could come without the dreadful sight I am doomed to see, I would gladly close my eyes this moment upon the world. But though death is welcome, I shrink with an agony you cannot understand; a maddening agony, an actual frenzy of terror, from the last encounter with that—that DEMON, who has drawn me thus to the verge of the chasm, and who is himself to plunge me down. I am to see him again, once more, but under circumstances unutterably more terrific than ever."

As Barton thus spoke, he trembled so violently that Montague was really alarmed at the extremity of his sudden agitation, and hastened to lead him back to the topic which had before seemed to exert so tranquillizing an effect upon his mind.

"It was not a dream," he said, after a time; "I was in a different state, I felt differently and strangely; and yet it was all as real, as clear and vivid, as what I now see and hear; it was a reality."

"And what *did* you see and hear?" urged his companion.

"When I awakened from the swoon I fell into on seeing *him*," said Barton, continuing, as if he had not heard the question, "it was slowly, very slowly; I was reclining by the margin of a broad lake, surrounded by misty hills, and a soft, melancholy, rose-coloured light illuminated it all. It was indescribably sad and lonely, and yet more beautiful than any earthly scene. My head was leaning on the lap of a girl, and she was singing a strange and wondrous song, that told, I know not how, whether by words or harmony, of all my life, all that is past, and all that is still to come. And with the song the old feelings that I thought had perished within me came back, and tears flowed from my eyes, partly for the song and its mysterious beauty, and partly for the unearthly sweetness of her voice; yet I know the voice, oh! how well; and I was spellbound as I listened and looked at the strange and solitary scene, without stirring, almost without breathing, and, alas! alas! without turning my eyes toward the face that I knew was near me, so sweetly powerful was the enchantment that held me. And so, slowly and softly, the song and scene grew fainter, and ever fainter, to my senses, till all was dark and still again. And then I wakened to this world, as you saw, comforted, for I knew that I was forgiven much." Barton wept again long and bitterly.

From this time, as we have said, the prevailing tone of his mind was one of profound and tranquil melancholy. This, however, was not without its interruptions. He was thoroughly impressed with the conviction that he was to experience another and a final visitation, illimitably transcending in horror all he had before experienced. From this anticipated and unknown agony he often shrunk in such paroxysms of abject terror and distraction, as filled the whole household with dismay and superstitious panic. Even those among them who affected to discredit the supposition of preternatural agency in the matter, were often in their secret souls visited during the darkness and solitude of night with qualms and apprehensions which they would not have readily confessed; and none of them attempted to dissuade Barton from the resolution on which he now systematically acted, of shutting himself up in his own apartment. The window-blinds of this room were kept jealously down; and his own man was seldom out of his presence, day or night, his bed being placed in the same chamber.

This man was an attached and respectable servant; and his duties, in addition to those ordinarily imposed upon *valets*, but which Barton's independent habits generally dispensed with, were to attend carefully to the simple precautions by means of which his master hoped to exclude the dreaded intrusion of the "Watcher," as the strange letter he had at first received had designated his persecutor. And, in addition to attending to these arrangements, which consisted merely in anticipating the possibility of his master's being, through any unscreened window or opened door, exposed to the dreaded influence, the valet was never to suffer him to be for one moment alone: total solitude, even for a minute, had become to him now almost as intolerable as the idea of going abroad into the public ways; it was an instinctive anticipation of what was coming.

It is needless to say, that, under these mysterious and horrible circumstances, no steps were taken toward the fulfilment of that engagement into which he had entered. There was quite disparity enough in point of years, and indeed of habits, between the young lady and Captain Barton, to have precluded anything like very vehement or romantic attachment on her part. Though grieved and anxious, therefore, she was very far from being heartbroken; a circumstance which, for the sentimental purposes of our tale, is much to be deplored. But truth must be told, especially in a narrative whose chief, if not only, pretensions to interest consist in a rigid adherence to facts, or what are so reported to have been.

Miss Montague, nevertheless, devoted much of her time to a patient but fruitless attempt to cheer the unhappy invalid. She read for him, and conversed with him; but it was apparent that whatever exertions he made, the endeavour to escape from the one constant and ever-present fear that preyed upon him was utterly and miserably unavailing.

Young ladies, as all the world knows, are much given to the cultivation of pets; and among those who shared the favour of Miss Montague was a fine old owl, which the gardener, who caught him napping among the ivy of a ruined stable, had dutifully presented to that young lady.

The caprice which regulates such preferences was manifested in the extravagant favour with which this grim and ill-favoured bird was at once distinguished by his mistress; and, trifling as this whimsical circumstance may seem, I am forced to mention it, inasmuch as it is connected, oddly enough, with the concluding scene of the story. Barton, so far from sharing in this liking for the new favourite, regarded it from the first with an antipathy as violent as it was utterly unaccountable. Its very vicinity was insupportable to him. He seemed to hate and dread it with a vehemence absolutely laughable, and to those who have never witnessed the exhibition of antipathies of this kind, his dread would seem all but incredible.

With these few words of preliminary explanation, I shall proceed to state the particulars of the last scene in this strange series of incidents. It was almost two o'clock one winter's night, and Barton was, as usual at that hour, in his bed; the servant we have mentioned occupied a smaller bed in the same room, and a candle was burning. The man was on a sudden aroused by his master, who said,—

"I can't get it out of my head that that accursed bird has escaped somehow, and is lurking in some corner of the room. I have been dreaming of him. Get up, Smith, and look about; search for him. Such hateful dreams!"

The servant rose, and examined the chamber, and while engaged in so doing, he heard the well-known sound, more like a long-drawn gasp than a hiss, with which these birds from their secret haunts affright the quiet of the night. This ghostly indication of its proximity, for the sound proceeded from the passage upon which Barton's chamber-door opened, determined the search of the servant, who, opening the door, proceeded a step or two forward for the purpose of driving the bird away. He had, however, hardly entered the lobby, when the door behind him slowly swung to under the impulse, as it seemed, of some gentle current of air; but as immediately over the door there was a kind of window, intended in the daytime to aid in lighting the passage, and through which the rays of the candle were then issuing, the valet could see quite enough for his purpose. As he advanced he heard his master (who, lying in a well-curtained bed had not, as it seemed, perceived his exit from the room) call him by name, and direct him to place the candle on the table by his bed. The servant, who was now some way in the long passage, did not like to raise his voice for the purpose of replying, lest he should startle the sleeping inmates of the house, began to walk hurriedly and softly back again, when, to his amazement, he heard a voice in the interior of the chamber answering calmly, and the man actually saw, through the window which over-topped the door, that the light was slowly shifting, as if carried across the chamber in answer to his master's call. Palsied by a feeling akin to terror, yet not unmingled with a horrible curiosity, he stood breathless and listening at the threshold, unable to summon resolution to push open the door and enter. Then came a rustling of the curtains, and a sound like that of one who in a low voice hushes a child to rest, in the midst of which he heard Barton say, in a tone of stifled horror—"Oh, God—oh, my God!" and repeat the same exclamation several times. Then ensued a silence, which again was broken by the same strange soothing sound; and at last there burst forth, in one swelling peal, a yell of agony so appalling and hideous, that, under some impulse of ungovernable horror, the man rushed to the door, and with his whole strength strove to force it open. Whether it was that, in his agitation, he had himself but imperfectly turned the handle, or that the door was really secured upon the inside, he failed to effect an entrance; and as he tugged and pushed, yell after yell rang louder and wilder through the chamber, accompanied all the while by the same hushing sounds. Actually freezing with terror, and scarce knowing what he did, the man turned and ran down the passage, wringing his hands in the extremity of horror and irresolution. At the stair-head he was encountered by General Montague, scared and eager, and just as they met the fearful sounds had ceased.

"What is it?—who—where is your master?" said Montague, with the incoherence of extreme agitation. "Has anything—for God's sake, is anything wrong?"

"Lord have mercy on us, it's all over," said the man, staring wildly towards his master's chamber. "He's dead, sir; I'm sure he's dead."

Without waiting for inquiry or explanation, Montague, closely followed by the servant, hurried to the chamber-door, turned the handle, and pushed it open. As the door yielded to his pressure, the ill-omened bird of which the servant had been in search, uttering its spectral warning, started suddenly from the far side of the bed, and flying through the doorway close over their heads, and extinguishing, in its passage, the candle which Montague carried, crashed through the skylight that overlooked the lobby, and sailed away into the darkness of the outer space.

"There it is, God bless us!" whispered the man, after a breathless pause.

"Curse that bird!" muttered the general, startled by the suddenness of the apparition, and unable to conceal his discomposure.

"The candle was moved," said the man, after another breathless pause; "see, they put it by the bed!"

"Draw the curtains, fellow, and don't stand gaping there," whispered Montague, sternly.

The man hesitated.

"Hold this, then," said Montague, impatiently, thrusting the candlestick into the servant's hand; and himself advancing to the bedside, he drew the curtains apart. The light of the candle, which was still burning at the bedside, fell upon a figure huddled together, and half upright, at the head of the bed. It seemed as though it had shrunk back as far as the solid panelling would allow, and the hands were still clutched in the bedclothes.

"Barton, Barton, Barton!" cried the general, with a strange mixture of awe and vehemence.

He took the candle, and held it so that it shone full upon his face. The features were fixed, stern and white; the jaw was fallen, and the sightless eyes, still open, gazed vacantly forward toward the front of the bed.

"God Almighty, he's dead!" muttered the general, as he looked upon this fearful spectacle. They both continued to gaze upon it in silence for a minute or more. "And cold, too," said Montague, withdrawing his hand from that of the dead man.

"And see, see; may I never have life, sir," added the man, after another pause, with a shudder, "but there was something else on the bed with him! Look there—look there; see that, sir!"

As the man thus spoke, he pointed to a deep indenture, as if caused by a heavy pressure, near the foot of the bed.

Montague was silent.

"Come, sir, come away, for God's sake!" whispered the man, drawing close up to him, and holding fast by his arm, while he glanced fearfully round; "what good can be done here now?—come away, for God's sake!"

At this moment they heard the steps of more than one approaching, and Montague, hastily desiring the servant to arrest their progress, endeavoured to loose the rigid grip with which the fingers of the dead man were clutched in the bedclothes, and drew, as well as he was able, the awful figure into a reclining posture. Then closing the curtains carefully upon it, he hastened himself to meet those who were approaching.

It is needless to follow the personages so slightly connected with this narrative into the events of their after lives; it is enough for us to remark that no clue to the solution of these mysterious occurrences was ever afterwards discovered; and so long an interval having now passed, it is scarcely to be expected that time can throw any new light upon their inexplicable obscurity. Until the secrets of the earth shall be no longer hidden these transactions must remain shrouded in mystery.

The only occurrence in Captain Barton's former life to which reference was ever made, as having any possible connection with the sufferings with which his existence closed, and which he himself seemed to regard as working out a retribution for some grievous sin of his past life, was a circumstance which not for several years after his death was brought to light. The nature of this disclosure was painful to his relatives and discreditable to his memory.

It appeared, then, that some eight years before Captain Barton's final return to Dublin, he had formed, in the town of Plymouth, a guilty attachment, the object of which was the daughter of one of the ship's crew under his command. The father had visited the frailty of his unhappy child with extreme harshness, and even brutality, and it was said that she had died heartbroken. Presuming upon Barton's implication in her guilt, this man had conducted himself towards him with marked insolence, and Barton resented this—and what he resented with still more exasperated bitterness, his treatment of the unfortunate girl—by a systematic exercise of those terrible and arbitrary severities with which the regulations of the navy arm those who are responsible for its discipline. The man had at length made his escape, while the vessel was in port at Lisbon, but died, as it was said, in an hospital in that town, of the wounds inflicted in one of his recent and sanguinary punishments.

Whether these circumstances in reality bear or not upon the occurrences of Barton's after-life, it is of course impossible to say. It seems, however, more than probable that they were, at least in his own mind, closely associated with them. But however the truth may be as to the origin and motives of this mysterious persecution, there can be no doubt that, with respect to the agencies by which it was accomplished, absolute and impenetrable mystery is like to prevail until the day of doom.

1881

WHAT IT MEANT

Rhoda Broughton

Rhoda Broughton (1840–1920) was the niece of Sheridan Le Fanu's wife Susanna—the daughter of her sister, Jane Bennett, who had married the Reverend Delves Broughton. Although she was born in Wales her family, the Broughtons, was long established in Staffordshire and can trace its ancestry back to the fourteenth century. The family home was at Broughton Hall which had seen violent action during the English Civil War, resulting in the legend of a family ghost. Even though she was not a Le Fanu she owed her literary career to her uncle.

When Rhoda's father died in 1863, she went to live with one of her sisters who soon moved to Wales. Le Fanu visited them there the following year. Rhoda was by then 24 and had already written drafts of a couple of novels. They must have discussed her writing because Le Fanu invited her to visit him in Dublin and bring along the manuscripts. When they met again she had completed the first, Not Wisely But Too Well. *He recommended that she send it to his London publisher and also arranged for it to be serialized in the* Dublin University Magazine, *which he now both owned and edited. It appeared there from August 1865 to July 1866, and was immediately followed by her second novel,* Cometh Up as a Flower. *The success of these first two books allowed her to support herself by writing, which she did ceaselessly over the next forty years producing what might be described as romantic tragedies with strong female characters. But Broughton disliked having to pad out books to fit the three-decker novels then in vogue for the circulating libraries and turned to writing shorter works, including ghost stories. These began with "The Truth, the Whole Truth, and Nothing but the Truth" (1868), included in the Tales of the Weird volume* Into the London Fog. *There was soon sufficient for a collection,* Tales for Christmas Eve *(1872) followed by the lesser-known* Betty's Visions and Mrs Smith of Longmains *(1886).*

Several of Broughton's stories explore dreams and visions, including the following, which was not included in any of her early collections. It may be that she was inspired by a dream of her aunt Susanna's, Le Fanu's wife. Her father had died in 1863 and this long preyed on her mind, and one night she dreamed that her father visited her at her bedside. She told this to her husband who made a note of it and may well have used it in "The Vision of Tom Chuff" (1870), but it's an idea that Broughton used time and again.

I had the last look. I shall always maintain that. Alice thought that she had got the better of me by going round to the other side of the cab and teasing him to kiss her through the window, though she was all smouched with tears—a thing he never liked, and he was hunting for his flask which he had mislaid; but I was even with her. I jumped in at the last moment and drove down with him to the gate. We did not say anything at all, but he let me hold his hand all the way, and at the very last, when I was actually on the step getting out, he said, "God bless you!"

Alice will not believe it, but he did. He, so undemonstrative, who never in his life be-dear-ed or be-darling-ed us, he said, "God bless you!" I am so glad that I did not annoy him with tears. I think that that was his way of paying me. I told Alice so, which made her very angry, as she had cried like a pump; but after all, perhaps it distracted us a little to brawl over it, as we did intermittently for the rest of the day. If we had not quarrelled, I cannot think how we should have got through the day at all. It was at least an occupation, and the only one which was not rendered intolerable by being inextricably entangled with his memory. Ever since he came home on sick leave, five months earlier, our life had been so built upon him and his convenience, that now that the keystone was withdrawn, our bridge seemed to collapse. For five months our every action had had some reference to him. Now that he was gone, all action seemed useless. This parting was, as we both agreed, worse, far worse, than any former one. They had all been bad enough, but when he was at school there were at least the long Midsummer and the short Christmas to look to; there was jam to send him, and the penny post to bring letters only twelve hours old. Even when he first went out to join his regiment in India, his own buoyant gladness in the prospect, his confidence that the climate would suit him—(did not hot weather here always suit him? the hotter the better)—had imparted to us, too, some faint ray of courage. But now that we knew certainly that that young confidence had been misplaced, now that there was burnt in upon our memories the look of him sent back to us as he had been last autumn—faint, deathly, bleached and emaciated almost past recognition—is it any wonder that our pulses beat low as we gave him back trembling to that feverish soil that is ever being new-paved with British graves?

And though he would not for a moment have suffered us to indulge, nor indeed would we have plagued him with, any morbid forebodings, yet we agreed, Alice and I, that his own dear heart seemed to grow heavy as the time for parting drew nigh. Not so heavy though as ours which he left behind. On that black first day, house and garden were equally bitter to us; the house where in the hall still stood the invalid couch on which, for weeks after his return, he languidly lay stretched; the garden where in his later better time, during the two or three days of premature summer that had thrust themselves among February's harsh cold troop, he had swung a hammock for us. There it still hung between the ilex that the hard winter had pinched, and the cedar that no stress of frost or storm could change from its unaltered green. I stood with my hand on the hammock ropes. "Only sons should not be sent on foreign service!" I said with sententious sadness; my eyes absently fixed on the solid red brick Georgian house that seemed to share the sullenness of the low slate-coloured sky.

"Only sons' sisters should be sent on foreign service with them!" answered Alice, bettering my sentiment; "oh, if" (with a profound sigh) "we were all three steaming down to Folkestone together!"

"How pleased the regiment would be to see us!" rejoined I drily, and we both laughed. We were surprised and shocked the moment that we had done it, but we did laugh. Yes, he had not been gone three hours when we laughed! At luncheon we were quite upset again by Figaro the black poodle going unasked through all the tricks that Dick had taught him. Usually it required entreaties, threats, and unlimited Albert biscuits to induce him to execute one; but today, just when he knew they would be too much for us, he volunteered them all! In the evening—the evening latterly dedicated to our rubber—that happy muff-rubber which in its qualities of levity and clamour much more nearly resembled a round game—in the evening, I say, we all lay strewn about, limp and tearful in our armchairs, leaving sacredly empty his, and gazing at it wistfully till the clock struck ten, and the day was mercifully at an end. The next day was a shade better, we cried less and ate more; the next a shade better again; and the next a shade better again than that. In fine, by the end of the week we had plucked up our spirits so far as to teach Figaro half a new trick, and our armchairs being limited—and our dear boy's empty one patently far the most comfortable one—we had, reluctantly at first, but with ever-growing callousness, abandoned the idea of its consecration to emptiness and memory. Indeed Alice and I had wrangled a good deal over our respective claims to its possession. By-and-by came his letters, the first from Paris, to say that he had had a rough passage, and that everybody on board, except himself, had been sick, but that he had walked about and enjoyed it; that he was going to the play at the Variétés; and that he hoped we would not forget to send him the sporting papers. The next letter was from Brindisi; the third from

Aden, and so on. Very soon father and mother began to drop into their old way of showing his letters about: taking them with them to exhibit when they paid visits, and bringing them forth to read, in whole or in part, when any one called. It was a plan that Alice and I had always deprecated, and that no one would have disliked more than Dick himself, could he have known it. Alice and I had often noticed the stifled yawns of indifferent guests during these readings, and had still oftener observed the hurried excuses and regrets for being unable to stay longer as soon as there was any talk of the Indian letters being produced. And so, in time, he reached India, and was welcomed back as one from the dead by his fellow-soldiers, who hardly knew him again, so hale, and brown, and strong on his legs. And as to us, we fell into our old tame and tranquil ways—our main events, the Indian mail days; our twin bugbears, cholera and war. We had returned to our evening rubber; mother, who never could tell one card from another, and hated them all, being mercilessly compelled by us to take a hand.

As the season advanced, and the air warmed, and the buds swelled, we spent more and more of our time lying in his hammock in the garden, where the cedar let fall its uncapricious dark shade on us, and even the shrivelled ilex put out some new leaves. When May came, there was scarce a moment of the day when it was not occupied by one or other of us, and we quarrelled over the right to occupy it as sharply as we had quarrelled over the possession of his armchair, and of the old torn gloves too worthless to take with him, that he had left lying—petulantly pulled off and rejected—on the hall table.

May had now just gone, and June's first splendid days were holding high holiday in earth and sky. The lilacs were over; they had been exceptionally profuse this year, even the thorns were on the wane, and the hot sun gave them the *coup de grâce*; and though the pink horse-chestnut still held up its stiff and stately spikes, yet a little tell-tale flushed carpet at its foot betrayed that it too was departing. But to make up to us for what we lost, the white pinks spread their spicy mats everywhere about the borders; the roses were only waiting for one lightest shower, to rush forth, one and all, and the cloying syringa made the air languid. It was not only the syringa, however. The day had been weighted with excess of unwonted heat, and even oncoming night had brought but little freshness. We had stayed on the parched lawn and under the unstirred trees in vain search of a reviving breath, listening to the owl and the harsh but summer-voiced corncrake. We stayed till bedtime had come and passed—since our dear lad went, the day had seemed long enough, yes over-long by ten—and the clocks with one consent were telling the hour of eleven. So we turned homewards, and limply climbed the stairs to bed. My room was in the roof, and on that roof, all through the immense June day, the sun had been mightily striking, so that, though all my three windows were set open to their fullest extent, the atmosphere was as of an engine-room.

    I undressed dejectedly and lay down beneath the one sheet, which on that night seemed to have the weight and consistency of five good blankets. With small hope of sleep I lay down; my eyes, widely open, staring out at the tennis-ground and the hammock, and the pink horse-chestnut tree, not pink any longer now, but (all distinctions of colour lost in one grave gloom) of the same hue as the cedar and the ilex and the elm. I had small hope of sleep; and yet, by-and-by, sleep came. It must have come rather soon too, as I have no recollection of having heard the clocks strike again. I was awaked or, at least I seemed to be awaked, not with a start, but gradually by a voice. I found myself sitting up in bed and listening. I have no recollection of any panic fear, of any loud heart-beating, or paralysing of tongue or limbs, of any cold sweat of terror at this unexplained sound that was breaking the intense stillness of the night. I was only sitting up and listening. I could not tell whence the voice came, not even from what direction it seemed to issue. I had no slightest clue as to whom or what it could belong to. It was accompanied by no rustling of any earthly garment, by no most cautious stirring of any human foot. It was only a voice. I caught myself pondering as to whose voice it could be. To what voice that I knew had it any likeness? I could find none. Yet there was nothing dreadful, nothing threatening or fear-inspiring in its quality. It was simply a voice, and it was saying most slowly, most solemnly and most sadly, with a light pause between each two words, "Your brother!—your brother!—your brother!"

Then there was silence again. I listened intensely, poignantly, still unaccountably without fear; but there was nothing more. There was no sound of any one breathing near me, and no form intervened between me and the casement square. I do not know for how long I listened; it might have been minutes, or only half a minute. Then I spoke. I can hardly believe now that I dared to do it; were such a voice to come to me again—which God avert!—I am very sure that I should have no power to unclose my lips or utter intelligible speech. But then I did. I said, still sitting up in bed, and staring strainingly out into the dim but not dark room, and I can still recall the odd sound of my own voice as it broke upon the dumbness round me. "My brother! what about my brother?" There was another pause, during which you might, perhaps, have counted ten rather slowly; and then the voice came again, exactly the same as before; as slow, as solemn, as profoundly sad, and as impossible to trace whence it came—"Go into the garden and you will find a yellow lily striped with brown, and then you will know!" That was all. I listened, listened, listened, but there was nothing more. The words that I had heard kept ringing and echoing in my head, without my attaching any meaning to them at first; but then all at once they grew clear. "Go into the garden and you will find a yellow lily striped with brown, and then you will know!" How could I go into the garden now—the clocks were just striking one—alone—(for the idea of waking anybody never occurred to me)? The doors would be locked and bolted. I doubted if I should be able to draw the heavy bolts. Go into the garden in dressing-gown and bare feet at one o'clock in the morning! I had never done such a thing in my life! And a yellow lily striped with brown?—there was no such lily in the garden I was sure. It was not so large in extent that I could not have an intimate acquaintance with each blossom; and I recollected no such flower. In what border could it be? I ran over in my head our lilies. There were turncap lilies, but they were some red and some yellow. There were Mary lilies; but they were white, and as yet only in green bud. There were irises indeed so curiously and whimsically painted and streaked that there might be among them a yellow one striped with brown, but then irises are not lilies. Seized by a hot and biting curiosity, I slipped out of bed and—still inexplicably free from fear—walked barefoot to the window. There lay the garden—not precisely dark, for I could still see the tennis nets and the hammock, but overspread with so dusky a veil, that a hundred strange lilies might be hiding in its beds without my being able to distinguish or detect them. There was nothing for it but to go down and search. I could not resist the apparently senseless impulse. Go I must. I put on dressing-gown and slippers, and not lighting any candle, trusting to the lenity of the summer night and the bright planets, I opened my door and ran along the passages and down the stairs, whose every step I knew so well as to be able safely to race blind-fold down them. I had recollected that the garden door locked less stiffly than the others, and had no bolts. In effect, I opened it without more noise than the slight unavoidable click that any key makes in turning, and stood on the sward outside. How strangely strange the familiar garden looked! Could this really be the tennis-ground, worn bare by our feet—this solemn silent space? Could this be the pink horse-chestnut at whose rosy foot I had left my book lying last evening—this towering mass of darkness? How in this universal gloom that spread one colourless shade over all, could I distinguish the tint of one flower from another? I walked alongside the borders, stooping as I went to peer at the faces of the blossoms, both those that thriftily close at advancing night, nor waste their beauty on the unperceiving darkness, and those that still hold up their chalices to the stars. It was perfectly useless. I was stepping hopelessly across the grass, to a large oval bed of mixed shrubs and herbaceous plants which occupied the space immediately in front of the drawing-room windows, and of which I well knew, as I thought, every inmate, and was convinced that among them grew no such flower as I sought, when suddenly the moon, who tonight rose late, looked over the belt of girdling forest trees that hedged us in. At once, directly before me, as plainly as if it were in the very eye of noon, I saw—I can see it now—a large tall yellow lily, with lines of brown streaking its petals. That there had been no such lily there, when last—late on the previous evening—I had visited the parterre (by which old-fashioned name we always called this part of the pleasure grounds) I was thoroughly convinced. Growing there straight and stately, unlike also any of our lilies, it was absolutely impossible that I could have overlooked it. It was still more absolutely impossible that it could have sprung up in its strength and beauty in the course of the night. Was it an optical delusion? Could I be suffering from some strange hallucination? I bent down low and touched it; put my fingers about its vigorous stem, and peered into the great orange-stamened vase of its expanded flower. For, like other lilies, it was as widely open as if it were the noon of day, instead of the noon of night. Into their pure cups the constellations look as freely as does the sun. It was certainly real, and as I stood in complete bewilderment, the words that the voice had uttered echoed back in my mind: "Go into the garden, and you will find a yellow lily striped with brown, and then you will know!" But I had gone into the garden and found the lily, and I knew no more than before. No ray of enlightenment pierced my darkness. The moon had sailed up above our elms, and was raining down her white and dreamful radiance. I gazed long and earnestly at the mystic blossom, eagerly trying to wile its secret from it, but it was in vain. The answer to the riddle, the key of the puzzle, escaped me. After long or what seemed long and hopeless waiting, I had to turn away baffled, and retrace my steps across the ghostly white open spaces, and through the ghostly black shadows to the house. Up the dark stairs I climbed to my room. It was exactly as I had left it, only lighter, silent and empty. The shadow of the window-frames lay in a cross-bar pattern, black and white upon the floor. There was even a patch of wan radiance upon the bed-quilt. I looked out of the window, trying if at this distance and by the aid of the now powerful moon, I could distinguish the strange new lily, but it was too far off. So at last, I unwillingly threw off my dressing-gown, and again lay down, meaning to await in bewildered wakefulness the coming of the morning, when I could correct by the help of daylight the errors and delusions of the night. But strange to say, almost before my head was well laid on the pillow, I was asleep again. For how long, who shall say? There is nothing more difficult to measure than the periods of sleep. I had been too preoccupied to ascertain at what hour I had returned to the house, nor at my waking did it even occur to me to think of the length of my slumber. For I awoke again, precisely as I had done before, without start or jump or heart-throbbing; woke to find myself once more sitting up in bed and listening, listening to the same voice, monotonously mournful, that had spoken to me before, and that was now a second time addressing me in precisely the same words: "Your brother!—your brother!—your brother!"

The room, which before had not been really dark, was now almost quite light. Besides the moon, which still sailed high, the dawn was breaking—in June, there is virtually no night—and had there been any person, any form or apparition of any kind in the room, I must have perceived it. But in this case hearing drew no aid from sight. It was quite as impossible as before for me to decide whence the sound came. It was neither from above nor below, nor did it seem to proceed from any one point of the compass more than another. It was a voice, that was all. It was neither loud nor low, it was neither soft nor harsh. It was a voice and it was sorrowful. That was all you could certainly say of it. It repeated the words as before, three times: "Your brother!—your brother!—your brother!" And I as before, still strangely stout-hearted, but in a passion of haste and eagerness, answered without any such interval as I had let elapse on the former occasion, staring out the while vaguely, for I did not know in which direction to look into the still and vacant chamber, where the two lights—the one that must wax and the one that must wane—were contending: "My brother! what about my brother?" Again there was a little pause, as there had been before, and then the voice sounded again, vague and sad through the room: "Go to your wardrobe, and you will find a yellow ribbon striped with brown, and then you will know!"

I am not sure that I had not expected a repetition of the former words—to be again bidden to go and seek the lily; but at this new injunction, I remained for a few moments awed and still, waiting perhaps for something more to follow. But nothing came. "A yellow ribbon striped with brown!" It flashed upon me that I had no such ribbon in my possession. I ran over in my head my simple and limited stock of personal adornments. I could remember among them none such. I was perfectly convinced that I owned no such ribbon. But then, on the other hand, I had been as firmly convinced that there was no such lily in the garden as the one that I had not only seen with my own eyes, but also touched and smelt there. I sprang out of bed and ran to my wardrobe. It was composed of a hanging press for gowns on one side, and drawers on the other. With feverish haste I pulled out every drawer, beginning at the bottom. To reach the higher ones I had to mount upon a chair. I had pulled them all out except one, and had eagerly turned over and rummaged their contents, without finding anything that I did not already know to be there. Only one more drawer remained to be examined! The probabilities were twenty to one that it also would be found to be empty of what I sought, or rather of what I anxiously sought not to find. I drew a heavy breath of relief at the thought that this time the voice had spoken falsely, and that therefore even if I heard it again and yet again repeat its melancholy message, I might dismiss it from my thoughts as some curious form of aural delusion. I hurriedly drew out the top drawer, and the first thing that met my eye, lying above everything else, and unrolled so as to stretch across almost the whole width of the drawer, lay a ribbon—a yellow ribbon striped with brown, a ribbon that I had assuredly never been possessed of, or even seen before! There could be no mistake as to its colours. Momently the morning was broadening across the world, and the two tints were so distinct, the stripes so clearly marked, that error was impossible. I took it out and let it fall across my fingers. No! I had never seen it before. As to how it came there, or whence it came, I could hazard no conjecture. "Go to your wardrobe, and you will find a yellow ribbon striped with brown, and then you will know!" But I had gone to my wardrobe; I held the ribbon in my hand, and still I knew not. The message of the ribbon was as dark to me as had been that of the flower. As I so stood, in even more hopeless bewilderment than I had stood in the garden, painfully striving to find the moral of this twice-repeated enigma, a bird—some little finch—struck up the first few notes of his sleepy dawn song. I listened eagerly to him, thinking that perhaps he might give me the key to the riddle. But in his little song there was nothing but joy—joy at the coming of another day; joy at being alive; joy at being a little garden finch. He could not help me. Neither could the widening morning red, nor the awakening flowers. None of them could help me. By-and-by I laid down the ribbon in despair, carefully replacing it exactly as I had found it. I closed the drawer, got down from the chair, shut the wardrobe, and went back to bed. This time I was resolved that sleep should not again overtake nor expose me to the possibility of being again aroused by that tormenting riddle-speaking voice. And indeed, so vividly, agitatedly wakeful was I, that it seemed most unlikely that I should again lapse into slumber. And yet as before, scarce had my head touched the pillow, before I was sound asleep again.

Next time that I woke, the June sun was blazing aloft; for the one sleepy finch, a score of blackbirds and thrushes and linnets were making their heavenly din, and my maid was offering me my morning tea. I took it drowsily, but before I had tasted it—the act of sitting up having fully aroused me—the incidents of the night rushed back on my mind. Hastily thrusting aside the tray, I jumped out of bed, and running to the wardrobe, opened it, climbed up on a chair, and pulled out the top drawer, in which I had so plainly seen the ribbon lying; not only seen but touched and handled it. There was no brown-and-yellow ribbon there. Then I pulled out hastily all the others. Neither in any of them was there such a ribbon; nor, although I clearly recollected having overturned and displaced their contents, was there any least trace of such overturning and displacing. Everything lay neat and orderly as was its wont. I was feverishly exploring the bottom drawer, when my maid in a voice, through which her astonishment at my unwonted procedure plainly pierced, asked me—"What I was looking for." I answered. "Nothing, or at least," re-closing the wardrobe as I spoke, "nothing that I was likely to find." I dressed in feverish haste—usually I was of a lazy habit; lay long and was hard to rouse—and in half an hour from the time at which I was called, I was racing across the sward to the bed that had held the mystic flower. What a different garden it was to the midnight one! holding no secrets in its frank and sunny breast, and sung to by what sweet and practised minstrels! I reached the bed, but I could see no lily. In the night, as I remembered, it was the very first object that had struck my sight.

It was impossible to overlook it, even in that comparatively faint light; but now, even with strong daylight helping me, I could find no trace of it. I searched through the whole large bed, pushing even between the Gueldres rose and mock-orange bushes, but it was not there. There were peonies—huge red ones, pale pink ones—that seemed as if they were trying to be mistaken for great roses; there was weigelia, delicate as apple-blossom; there were irises; there were Canterbury-bells; there were lupins—but there was no yellow lily striped with brown. As I still—though now convinced that it was in vain—peered and pushed aside leaves and blossoms, the voice of Alice, who had come suddenly up behind, startled me:

"What are you looking for?"

"Nothing," I answered hurriedly, stepping back on to the grass again.

"Have you lost a ring or a glove?" inquired she, looking at me with some attention, for I suppose I appeared flurried and disordered.

"No," I replied, "I have lost nothing; at least"—casting one more fruitless glance around—"nothing that I am likely to find."

Neither flower nor ribbon! Must it then have been only a dream? At first I rejected scornfully this explanation. Had ever dream such consistency? Did ever dream move with such apparent coherence from its beginning to its close? In it had been none of the strange starts and freaks that are always occurring in the dream-world. In it there had been nothing *décousu*; no leaps from the probable to the entirely impossible; no metamorphosis of myself into some one else; no unexplained transition from here to there, from now to then, such as have abounded in every dream—even the most vivid and life-like ones—that I have ever previously had. And yet, as the day wore on, the suspicion deepened, changed at last into a conviction, that it was a dream. I had never awakened really. I had never trodden the midnight garden, or opened my wardrobe doors. All the time that I imagined I had been so doing, I had been in point of fact resting quietly on my bed; possibly some awkward way of lying, some uneasiness of posture, had produced the phenomena that I have described. I spoke of my dream, if it was a dream, to no one, not even to Alice. Some strange reluctance tied my tongue. But I went heavily and ill at ease all through the day. It was never out of my head. I puzzled over its enigma from early morning until night again fell, and bedtime returned. The heat had moderated and the air was fresher. Tired and yet excited, I lay down. I closed my eyes, dreading a repetition of the vision (though, indeed, that is a misnomer as there was nothing to be seen), and yet nervously hoping for some continuation of it that might give me the clue to guide me through its labyrinth—that might give me a reassuring solution of its riddle. But none such came. I had difficulty in falling asleep at all at first, so hopelessly alert and at work seemed my brain; but gradually lassitude got the better of my excitement, and I slept. But no trace of any dream disturbed or varied my deep slumber. Nor on any of the succeeding nights did I hear any repetition of that strange and melancholy voice. It seemed to have had leave to speak but that once. And as the days and hours passed by, time's influence, invariably numbing, deadened the impression that at first had been so keen. After a while I tried to avoid thinking of it, as of something painful, unnerving, and yet meaningless, nor did I mention it to any living soul. To relate it would have seemed to give it added importance.

And so a week of our placid and uniform life slipped away. The weather was cool again, and we played tennis from morning to night. At first the same sentiment which had made us leave Dick's chair vacant, prevented us from supplying his place in the game; but as this principle could not be carried out through life, that whatever he had done must henceforth, until his return, be left undone, we by-and-by associated to ourselves, as occasion offered, a neighbouring curate, or squire, and so, all day long, the balls flew, and the grass waxed ever barer, balder, and more worn, where our persevering feet continually trampled it. But still, of course, the Indian mail remained the event of our lives. We were so much behind the time and lived so deep-sunk in the country, that we had no second post, nor would my father take any steps to obtain one, as he said that once a day was quite enough to be pestered with letters, and that, for his part, if it were once a week instead, he could very well put up with it. But it was by the second post that the Indian letters came to our post town, and on the mail day it was an invariable custom that some of us should drive in to fetch them. To send a servant for them would have balked our impatience and would besides have seemed a disrespect to them.

So, whether it shone or rained, Alice and I, as surely as the post day came, might be seen whipping up our old pony into unwonted and unwilling speed along the road to ——.

On that day it shone; shone so strongly that Alice, who drove, asked me for a share of my large sunshade; and beneath it we trotted along in happy expectancy. The air blew heavily sweet from the bean field (until that day I loved the smell of a blossoming bean field), and the birds sang—oh, *how* they sang!

> For there was none of them that feigned
> To sing, for each of them him pained
> To find out merry crafty notes,
> They ne spared not their throats.

When we reached the post office, the letters were still being sorted, so we had to wait a few moments. But we were rewarded for our waiting. A letter in the beloved handwriting, and with the usual postmark, was soon put into our eager hands. We waited to open it till we were out of the little town, and off the cobble stones, so that we might comfortably enjoy it, the one who read without raising her voice, and the one who listened without straining her ears. It was addressed to Alice, though of course, like all his letters, meant for the benefit of the whole family. We were always glad when the letters were to either of us, as they were usually of a lighter and more conversational type than those directed to our parents—less about the customs and habits of the natives, the resources of the country, &c., and more about the gossip of the station, the picnics, the quarrels of the regimental ladies, the flirtations. This was a particularly good specimen of our favourite kind, and as we passed along, the old pony dropped unrebuked into a leisurely rolling amble, the reins fell loose on his back while Alice and I together stooped our heads over the page in the vain effort to decipher an illegible but obviously important word on which the point of a whole sentence turned. We were so absorbed that we did not perceive a telegraph boy who was marching along the dusty road in the same direction as ourselves, until recognizing our pony chaise, he made signs to us to stop, holding out, as he did so, one of those familiar orange missives that alternately order dinners and announce deaths. I took it, though with no particular misgiving: people employ the telegraph wires for such harmless trifles nowadays. It was addressed—not to any of us—but to

"MRS. GRAINGER,
"Housekeeper at —— Hall."

Mrs Grainger was one of those servants who—rail, and justly rail as one may at the class of domestic servants in general—are yet so numerous that one can scarcely ever take up a *Times* without reading the lamented death of one of those chronicled in its obituary. She had nursed us all three lovingly: Dick first, and most lovingly, and was now almost as well known to our friends—to some even of Dick's friends, notably to his *alter ego*, Major ——, who not long before our boy's departure had been paying us a visit—as we ourselves.

"It is for Na Na!" I said (we still called her by that infantile name). "I hope that it is not bad news for her, she was rather frightened by the last accounts of her consumptive niece."

"You had better open it, at all events," answered Alice, "it may require an answer."

So I opened it, she looking over my shoulder.

"From MAJOR ——,   *to*   Mrs GRAINGER,
"——, India.   "Housekeeper at —— Hall,
                                       "——shire.

"Mr —— attacked by tiger, out shooting. Killed on the spot. Break it to his family. Have written."

I read it through at first without any comprehension, so totally unexpectant was I, so prepossessed with the idea that the telegram did not concern us at all, but contained ill news for Na Na; and when comprehension did come, there came with it utter incredulity. It was nonsense! Why, it was not two minutes since we had been reading his letter, laughing over his account of the misadventures that had happened at the picnic he had been at; puzzling over the ill-written word! How *could* he write letters and be dead?

I snatched up the letter, and frantically turned back to the date on the first page. It was a month ago! The telegram was not twenty-four hours old!

Then I believe I gave a dreadful yelling laugh, and then God had pity on me—indeed I needed it—and I remember no more.

But that was what my dream meant, I suppose. The yellow lily striped with brown; the yellow ribbon striped with brown. They were figures and foreshadowings of the cruel striped beast that tore our boy.

* * *

The singular dream and its solution related above are true. Only the dressing-up is fictitious.

2016

FRAN NAN'S STORY

Sarah LeFanu

Sarah LeFanu (b. 1953)—notice how the surname has contracted—is Sheridan Le Fanu's fifth cousin, three times removed (if I've calculated it properly). In other words, her 4xgreat-grandfather was Sheridan Le Fanu's great-grandfather. What's more, her 5xgreat grandfather was the Reverend Dr Thomas Sheridan who had taught Jonathan Swift Greek, so she also shares the Sheridan bloodline.

Sarah is a Scottish academic who has championed the cause of women's science fiction chiefly through her role as editor at the Women's Press in the 1980s and 1990s, but also with her anthology, Despatches from the Frontiers of the Female Mind *(1985), compiled with Jen Green, and her study* In the Chinks of the World Machine: Feminism and Science Fiction *(1988). A guide for aspiring writers is* Writing Fantasy Fiction *(1996). Sarah has perhaps become best known for her biographies including* Rose Macaulay *(2003) and that of Samora Machel and Mozambique's independence* S is for Samora *(2012). She has also written personal studies of how she has been affected by her research such as* Dreaming of Rose *(2012) and* Talking to the Dead *(2023), which explores the journals she made while researching Rudyard Kipling, Charles Kingsley and Arthur Conan Doyle's activities during the Anglo-Boer War for the book* Something of Themselves *(2020).*

Her research and writing leaves little time for short fiction but on those rare occasions when she does, the weird tale is not far away.

Fran, one of the two juniors we have working in the salon, leads my new client to the washbasins at the rear of the room, and seats her down in one of the reclining chairs. The foil highlighting packages that I put in half an hour ago are ready to be unwrapped. Fran carefully lifts up the lady's hair, drapes a towel around her shoulders, and tucks it into the neck of the brown robe she's wearing. Then with the tips of her fingers Fran guides her head backwards so that it rests in the washbasin's recessed curve. Fran's seventeen, and she's been working for me for five months now.

She's good with her hands, gentle but firm, not too soft; but, oh dear, she does talk. Some of the clients don't mind, but others come here hoping for a bit of peace and quiet, a spot of relaxation while they're having their hair done, and they don't always get that from Fran.

I have to remind her every so often about keeping her mouth buttoned up—unless the client wants to talk, of course—but I fear it's water off a duck's back, or down the basin plughole, more like. Still, she's a nice girl and the clients mostly seem to like her. The tips she gets are often generous.

I used to work in a salon in the centre of town, but when I set up my own place I did so out here in Thornsea. We're not far from the motorway, and I draw clientele from all the surrounding area. Today we're short-staffed, and as I've got to send off a big order to our new stockists, I sit myself behind the reception desk and make up the order while Fran washes the new client's hair.

FRAN NAN'S STORY

This new client, Alison Mildmay, has recently moved out of town to the village of Brackenbury on the far side of the moor. She's in her mid-thirties, I guess, and she's wearing a dark skirt, black tights, ankle boots. I noticed her coat was cashmere. Currently she has blonde highlights streaked through the natural soft brown of her hair. Her nails are neatly manicured and glossed, and her eyebrows shaped into smooth curves. Subtle make-up, with a touch of blusher on the cheekbones.

In other words, smart-looking. Knows what kind of impression she wants to make. While I was putting in her foils she told me that she's some kind of a marketing consultant. Travels all over. She may not tolerate Fran's gabbiness. We'll see.

Fran has already elicited from her where she's living, and has confided in her that her nan lives in the same village.

"I drove here over the moor," says Alison Mildmay, "rather than coming round by the main road, because it looks like a short cut, but the road's so narrow that I had to keep stopping and reversing to find a place where cars could pass me, so in the end it was no quicker."

I'm familiar with the road she's talking about. It's built up from the soil dredged from the rhynes—that's what we call the ditches round here—which have been draining the moor for centuries, since it was first taken from the sea for pasture. The road slices across the moor in a series of straight lines with sharp right-angled turns. It's no more than a narrow metalled track between two deep rhynes, a couple of feet above the level of the surrounding fields, which is just as well in a wet winter when the rhynes fill up and overflow and it looks as if the sea has crept back to cover the land once more.

"You want to be careful of them rhynes," I hear Fran say. "My nan could tell you a story or two about them."

"Mmm?" says Alison Mildmay.

Semi-encouraging, I judge.

Fran unpicks the last remaining foil package and rinses out the ends of Alison Mildmay's hair.

"Not just old stories, neither," she adds. With the back of her hand she tests the temperature of the water gushing from the shower head, and directs the flow from the ends of Alison's hair up to her scalp.

"Is the water all right? Not too hot for you?"

"It's fine, thanks."

"This happened some years ago," begins Fran, "during the foot-and-mouth, on one of the farms on the edge of the moor. An old farmer, a widower, lived there in the farmhouse with his son and his son's wife and their two children. He were called Billy, and his son were called Billy, too. Old Billy and Young Billy they were. Young Billy's wife, Mary, were a dinner lady at the primary school where their kids went. My nan were a dinner lady there too. The two of them got quite close.

"Old Billy had the arthritis in his back and walked with a stick. He had a dog called Jess, a border collie, who'd lost a leg when she were young. She'd ran out into the lane and were hit by a speeding car. You have to be careful in them lanes. But although she only had three legs she was nimble as any of the other dogs, and ace with the sheep. But now she were getting old too, and a bit slow. She had her bed in the kitchen next to the range—the other dogs was in their kennels in the yard—and she were always up early and ready to be out with the old man when he come down of a morning. The two of them, Jess and the old man, hobbling around the yard together, were a right sight."

Fran squirts a ball of shampoo into the palm of her hand and starts to work it into Alison's hair.

"It were some weeks into the foot-and-mouth and no-one could move any animals—they weren't allowed—and they were slaughtering even healthy ones that was next door to infected stock. I were only little then but I remember piles, or pyres you call them, with things poking out like sticks of wood. It were the legs of the dead sheep and cows, all in a heap. Young Billy had sheep out on the moor, right next to sheep belonging to other farmers that had the grazing out there too.

"The old man said they should bring the animals back to an empty field next to the farm where the grass was green and lush and they'd be safe away from the neighbour's sheep. Lots of the farmers were moving their stock. They couldn't use their trailers, but you'd see saloon cars whizzing along the lanes with a great big heap of something under a blanket on the back seat.

"Sometimes you'd see it moving and you'd think, ay up, what's that the farmer's got all muffled up on the back seat of his car? Well, it ain't his old mum, I don't think. They were moving the sheep two and three at a time, looking out all the while for the men from the ministry.

"Young Billy said no, he thought it were too risky. But the old man must've thought otherwise. He decided he'd herd the sheep back to the farm along one of the old drovers' roads, them's the dirt tracks that criss-cross the moor, in the dead of night when no-one was around to see. And if anyone noticed in the next few days or weeks that an empty field suddenly had sheep in, well, he could act stone deaf and stupid when he wanted.

"What I'm telling you now, Young Billy and his Mary discovered from the old man when he told them the next day what had happened. Late that night, when all the family were abed, he had set off soft-like with Jess. It were a clear night, with a half-moon just bright enough to throw a little bit of shadow, and the two of them rounded up the sheep—twenty-five of them—and set off back along the drovers' road. They were trotting along, well, the sheep were, and the old man was hobbling as fast as he could go at the front, and Jess was worrying at their heels behind, when suddenly a fox leaped out onto the path from a thick tangle of thorn. It must've been a vixen, and they were too close to her lair, and maybe she had cubs in there, otherwise she'd just have laid low or slipped away quiet into the shadows. But she stood her ground and she barked. The sheep panicked. They're stupid beasts. Some went one way and some went another, for'ard, backward, sideways."

Fran rinses off the first shampoo, and applies a second dose. Mrs Mildmay's eyes remain closed.

"Jess had shot off after those silly sheep, said the old man, dashing up and down the track to gather them in, rounding up one and then another. Then they all hurried on. At last the farm buildings rose up dark in front, and the old man turned down towards the field and counted the sheep in at the open gate while Jess lay panting by the wall. He counted in twenty-two, twenty-three, twenty-four. That were it. He looked at Jess. Her sides were heaving. 'There be one missing,' he said. She whined, and didn't move.

"But a sheep's a sheep and worth money in the market place—well, not during the foot-and-mouth, they weren't worth nothing, but who knew how long that would last, and anyway the ministry'd promised compensation. 'Go seek,' he ordered Jess.

"Off Jess ran on her three legs, back the way they'd come, and the old man followed after with his flashlight, slowly, and leaning on his stick. He passed the tangle of thorn and briars where the vixen had jumped out and scattered the flock, and ahead of him he heard splashing and scrabbling and Jess's little high-pitched yelps. The stupid sheep had fallen into a rhyne, of course; its front legs were up on the bank but it couldn't get a purchase with its back ones, and the old man saw that the weight of its wet wool was dragging it back down into the water. He sat on the bank and leaned over to hook the crook of his stick behind one of the animal's legs, as high up as he could so as not to break it, and told Jess to harry the sheep from behind. Jess was running up and down the bank, yipping and yelping, and, as the sheep's back legs came scrabbling up the muddy slope, Jess dashed down to get behind them. The animal must've found a purchase for its hooves, for suddenly in a great flurry it came whooshing up the bank and knocked the old man over. All were turned upside down, flashlight trampled and broken. Where was his stick? The old man groped for it and slowly pulled himself up.

"He whistled for Jess. She didn't come. He called. The only sound was the sheep tearing at a clump of rough grass off to the side of the track. He laid himself down on the churned earth, and dipped his crook into the dark water. Nothing. He staggered up, and called again. Then the dawn wind came gusting over the moor. He had to get that last sheep back before anyone else was astir."

Fran breaks off her story to rinse away the second shampoo. She turns to the shelves behind her and picks out a conditioner, squeezes a blob of it into her palms, rubs them together and strokes them through the damp hair. She begins to massage Alison's scalp.

"Well, the old man hobbled back to the farm with the one sheep. He let the other dogs out their kennels and sent them away across the moor to look for Jess. Then he went into the kitchen and put kettle on, and Mary and Young Billy came downstairs and Mary fussed over him and made him put on dry clothes and didn't say a word about the mud and wet and weeds on the kitchen floor though she were usually ever so particular. She were fond of the old fellow. Young

Billy went out to see after the yard dogs, and found them all back in their kennels, crouched low on their bellies, noses on paws. They knew Jess weren't a-coming home to them.

"When the littl'uns—Amy and Joe—come down for breakfast they asked where was Jess. She were always there at breakfast, waiting for one of them to slip her a little bit of buttered toast or somesuch under the table and they were dreadful upset to hear she were lost. I remember that day. We were living with my nan back then and I went to the same school as them. I were in year one with Amy—Joe were in reception. Well, I remember Amy crying, but maybe that were another day."

I lift my head from the catalogues and look across at the basins. Fran stares into space.

She's holding Alison Mildmay's head between her hands, but her hands aren't moving.

"Fran!" I say, sharpish, and she blinks, looks down, and starts again to move her fingers rhythmically across Alison's scalp, kneading and pushing.

Alison Mildmay's getting an extra-long massage, I realize. I hope she's enjoying it. She's not fidgeting, her eyes are closed, she appears relaxed.

"Four or five men went out later that morning with poles, and a net, but they didn't find Jess. Sometimes there be currents deep down in the rhynes that you can't see on the surface, and things turn up on the far side of moor. But there was no trace of her, not that day nor in the days that followed."

Fran picks up a comb and combs out the massage tangles in Alison Mildmay's hair before she sluices it clean with a final rinse. Then she pats it dry with a fresh towel.

"I'd better turban you up," she says, but Alison raises a hand.

FRAN NAN'S STORY

"Hang on," Alison says. "What happened then?"

Fran looks up at me and I nod a "yes", and gesture to her to cover Alison's hair with another fresh towel, so that her damp head doesn't get cold. Fran goes on:

"There were a gloom settled over the farm then. 'Cause of the foot-and-mouth the dogs weren't getting their usual exercise, and moped in their kennels or quarrelled in the yard. One evening the family were sat at their tea when the old man banged down his knife and fork and says, 'Hark to that dog barking out on moor!' 'What? I don't hear nothing,' says Mary. 'She sounds like my old Jess.' Little Joe started to cry. 'Shush, dad,' says Young Billy. 'See what you've done now. You're upsetting the littl'uns.' But Old Billy just turned away and stared out the window at the dusk gathering outside.

"One night soon after Mary was woken by the noise of the back door being opened and shut. She went down to the kitchen—it were two o'clock in the morning—and found the old man there. 'Look at you, all wet and muddy. What you doing?' she asked. 'I've bin out,' he said. 'I heard Jess barking for me again.' 'You silly old man,' she said. 'It were another dog. Those dogs over at Grove Farm are always fussing and barking.' 'No,' he said. 'I seen her. I seen a dog with three legs. She were standing there on the old drovers' track. I knows it were my Jess. She were a-calling me. But when I got to where she were, she warn't there no more.'

"Billy and Mary thought perhaps the old man was losing his marbles, and they tried to make him see a doctor, but he was stubborn, and said there were nothing wrong with him, and them two just wanted to get their hands on the farm. And it all got a bit nasty. Well, they backed down, but Mary asked him to please not talk about the dog any more because it were frightening the children, and he said okay. He might even have said he were sorry. I don't know.

"And they said that the pretty red collie bitch over at Grove Farm had just had a litter of six, and perhaps it was time to get a new pup, and would the old man like to choose one? No, he wouldn't, and he didn't care that Amy and Joe wanted one, and he told them to shut up and leave him be. Anyway by then they had other things to think about. The foot-and-mouth was coming nearer. A sick cow was found on the same farm that had its sheep out on moor. Just one animal—that was all that was needed, and you lost all of them. The ministry vets was coming round testing the whole area.

"Old Billy and Young Billy hardly spoke for the few days beforehand. Mary tried to be cheerful for the kids but it were hard going. In the pub there were talk of farmers that had lost their stock, and had gone out into their barns and hanged theirselves. But it were okay—they tested clear.

"After that it were quiet for a week or two, until the moon were growing past its half again, and then early one morning Amy, the little girl, comes down to the kitchen to get herself a drink of water and finds the back door wide open, and out in the yard the dogs whining in their kennels. She runs up the stairs to get her mum and dad, and they look in the old man's room and finds it empty. They go out and call for him all around, but they find not sight nor sound of him, so they call the neighbours again, and soon after that, the police. The police call out the fire brigade because it's them that've got the equipment.

"Well, later that morning they found the old man's body in the rhyne, along with Jess's body too, not far from where the old drovers' road crosses it and where they'd struggled together over that stray sheep. They were all tangled up together, him and his three-legged dog, with his arms around her. There weren't much left of Jess; she'd been in that rhyne for a good month, mind."

FRAN NAN'S STORY

While Fran's been talking, someone—Kay, or Hannah perhaps, I didn't notice—has turned down the volume on the iPod shuffle. Now the snick of Kay's scissors sounds loud in the silence. Fran twists up Alison's damp hair into a towel turban and leads her back to the mirror station. I put away my order books and wheel the haircutting trolley over to them, and ask Fran to turn up the volume on the iPod. Fran meets Alison Mildmay's eyes in the mirror.

"And this were the odd thing. The old man were the same."

I can't stop myself. I blurt out, "What do you mean?"

"My nan says it were all hushed up, but the old man—well, his body were in the same state as Jess's. They could barely tell it were him."

Alison turns round in the swivel chair and looks up directly at Fran.

"Yes," says Fran. "They said he must've been in rhyne a month at least."

The Hawthorne Family

There is a family legend about the ancestors of Nathaniel Hawthorne that far back in the mists of time an innkeeper in the village of Bray in Berkshire travelled to London and learned from a man, who had had a dream, that there was a treasure buried on Hawthorn Hill near the innkeeper's home. The innkeeper promptly returned home and in the middle of the night climbed the hill, dug deep and found a pot of gold. Reading an inscription on the pot he returned to the hill and found another pot of gold. The family, then known by the name Hothorne, became rich and used the money to benefit the community. Whether true or not, these ancestors enter the public record in the fifteenth and sixteenth centuries as well-to-do citizens. William Hathorne (*c.* 1607–1681) as the name had now become, sailed to America in 1633 with his wife Anne and established himself as one of the leading officials in the town of Salem, Massachusetts. Hathorne was a Puritan, one of those extreme Protestants who wished to rid England of Catholic practices, many of whom left England for fear of reprisals under King Charles I.

Salem would become notorious for its extremist Puritan views that led to the hysteria of the infamous Salem Witch Trials of 1692 and 1693. Prominent amongst the prosecutors of the alleged witches was William's son, John Hathorne (1641–1717). The trials resulted in over two hundred women, men and children being accused with twenty being executed. Five others, including two children, died in prison.

The witch trials cast a dark cloud over Salem and it continued to haunt the family down through the generations. John Hathorne's great-great grandson, Nathaniel Hawthorne (a changed surname again) referred to the period as that "hideous epoch" and the trials themselves as that "terrible delusion" in *The House of the Seven Gables* (1851), a novel which seeks to atone, at least to some degree, the guilt of the past.

1835

YOUNG GOODMAN BROWN

Nathaniel Hawthorne

It has been suggested that Nathaniel Hawthorne (1804–1864) added the "w" to his surname to distance himself from the family history, though as the Hathornes had been resident in Salem for over 170 years, it seems a rather futile gesture and one that clearly did not work, because Salem haunts many of Hawthorne's stories. After his marriage, Hawthorne moved from Salem to Concord, Massachusetts, settling in The Old Manse that lent its name to his story collection Mosses from an Old Manse *(1846). Hawthorne's first novel,* Fanshawe *(1828) appeared soon after he had finished at college and although it was published anonymously, he later disowned it. His most celebrated novels drew upon his life experiences and family history, notably* The Scarlet Letter *(1850), where a young girl is humiliated in her punishment for having had a child out of wedlock, and particularly* The House of the Seven Gables *(1851) set in a house whose occupants trace their ancestors back to the witch trials.*

There is a sense in many of Hawthorne's stories that he is seeking perfection, or at least to eradicate past blemishes, but that this is doomed to failure. His early story "Dr Heidegger's Experiment" (1837) is about the search for the elixir of life. In "The Birthmark" (1843) a scientist tries to remove a birthmark from his wife's face with fatal results, whilst in "The Artist of the Beautiful" (1844) a scientist attempts to create the perfect automaton butterfly. Perhaps his best known story, "Rappaccini's Daughter" (1844), has a scientist trying to protect his child from the evils of the world. Hawthorne even joined a utopian transcendental commune, Brook Farm, near Boston, in 1841, partly in the hope of making a profit from his time spent there but perhaps also to impress the young lady he hoped to marry, Sophia Peabody, which to some degree worked, as they were married the following year. His experiences formed the basis for his novel, The Blithedale Romance *(1852) which explores how personal desires may clash with communal ideals. No matter where you turn in Hawthorne's fiction there is the need for redemption, the hope of preserving the good and defeating the bad, even though no matter what is tried, perfection proves elusive.*

Young Goodman Brown came forth at sunset, into the street of Salem village, but put his head back, after crossing the threshold, to exchange a parting kiss with his young wife. And Faith, as the wife was aptly named, thrust her own pretty head into the street, letting the wind play with the pink ribbons of her cap, while she called to Goodman Brown.

"Dearest heart," whispered she, softly and rather sadly, when her lips were close to his ear, "pr'ythee, put off your journey until sunrise, and sleep in your own bed tonight. A lone woman is troubled with such dreams and such thoughts, that she's afeard of herself, sometimes. Pray, tarry with me this night, dear husband, of all nights in the year!"

"My love and my Faith," replied young Goodman Brown, "of all nights in the year, this one night must I tarry away from thee. My journey, as thou callest it, forth and back again, must needs be done 'twixt now and sunrise. What, my sweet, pretty wife, dost thou doubt me already, and we but three months married!"

"Then God bless you!" said Faith, with the pink ribbons, "and may you find all well, when you come back."

"Amen!" cried Goodman Brown. "Say thy prayers, dear Faith, and go to bed at dusk, and no harm will come to thee."

So they parted; and the young man pursued his way, until, being about to turn the corner by the meeting-house, he looked back and saw the head of Faith still peeping after him, with a melancholy air, in spite of her pink ribbons.

"Poor little Faith!" thought he, for his heart smote him. "What a wretch am I, to leave her on such an errand! She talks of dreams, too. Methought, as she spoke, there was trouble in her face, as if a dream had warned her what work is to be done tonight. But, no, no! 't would kill her to think it. Well; she's a blessed angel on earth; and after this one night, I'll cling to her skirts and follow her to Heaven."

With this excellent resolve for the future, Goodman Brown felt himself justified in making more haste on his present evil purpose. He had taken a dreary road, darkened by all the gloomiest trees of the forest, which barely stood aside to let the narrow path creep through, and closed immediately behind. It was all as lonely as could be; and there is this peculiarity in such a solitude, that the traveller knows not who may be concealed by the innumerable trunks and the thick boughs overhead; so that, with lonely footsteps, he may yet be passing through an unseen multitude.

"There may be a devilish Indian behind every tree," said Goodman Brown to himself; and he glanced fearfully behind him, as he added, "What if the devil himself should be at my very elbow!"

His head being turned back, he passed a crook of the road, and looking forward again, beheld the figure of a man, in grave and decent attire, seated at the foot of an old tree. He arose, at Goodman Brown's approach, and walked onward, side by side with him.

"You are late, Goodman Brown," said he. "The clock of the Old South was striking, as I came through Boston; and that is full fifteen minutes agone."

"Faith kept me back awhile," replied the young man, with a tremor in his voice, caused by the sudden appearance of his companion, though not wholly unexpected.

It was now deep dusk in the forest, and deepest in that part of it where these two were journeying. As nearly as could be discerned, the second traveller was about fifty years old, apparently in the same rank of life as Goodman Brown, and bearing a considerable resemblance to him, though perhaps more in expression than features. Still, they might have been taken for father and son. And yet, though the elder person was as simply clad as the younger, and as simple in manner too, he had an indescribable air of one who knew the world, and would not have felt abashed at the governor's dinner-table, or in King William's court, were it possible that his affairs should call him thither. But the only thing about him, that could be fixed upon as remarkable, was his staff, which bore the likeness of a great black snake, so curiously wrought, that it might almost be seen to twist and wriggle itself like a living serpent. This, of course, must have been an ocular deception, assisted by the uncertain light.

"Come, Goodman Brown!" cried his fellow-traveller, "this is a dull pace for the beginning of a journey. Take my staff, if you are so soon weary."

"Friend," said the other, exchanging his slow pace for a full stop, "having kept covenant by meeting thee here, it is my purpose now to return whence I came. I have scruples, touching the matter thou wot'st of."

"Sayest thou so?" replied he of the serpent, smiling apart. "Let us walk on, nevertheless, reasoning as we go, and if I convince thee not, thou shalt turn back. We are but a little way in the forest, yet."

"Too far, too far!" exclaimed the goodman, unconsciously resuming his walk. "My father never went into the woods on such an errand, nor his father before him. We have been a race of honest men and good Christians, since the days of the martyrs. And shall I be the first of the name of Brown, that ever took this path and kept"—

"Such company, thou wouldst say," observed the elder person, interrupting his pause. "Well said, Goodman Brown! I have been as well acquainted with your family as with ever a one among the Puritans; and that's no trifle to say. I helped your grandfather, the constable, when he lashed the Quaker woman so smartly through the streets of Salem. And it was I that brought your father a pitch-pine knot, kindled at my own hearth, to set fire to an Indian village, in king Philip's war. They were my good friends, both; and many a pleasant walk have we had along this path, and returned merrily after midnight. I would fain be friends with you, for their sake."

"If it be as thou sayest," replied Goodman Brown, "I marvel they never spoke of these matters. Or, verily, I marvel not, seeing that the least rumor of the sort would have driven them from New England. We are a people of prayer, and good works to boot, and abide no such wickedness."

"Wickedness or not," said the traveller with the twisted staff, "I have a very general acquaintance here in New England. The deacons of many a church have drunk the communion wine with me; the selectmen, of divers towns, make me their chairman; and a majority of the Great and General Court are firm supporters of my interest. The governor and I, too—but these are state-secrets."

"Can this be so!" cried Goodman Brown, with a stare of amazement at his undisturbed companion. "Howbeit, I have nothing to do with the governor and council; they have their own ways, and are no rule for a simple husbandman like me. But, were I to go on with thee, how should I meet the eye of that good old man, our minister, at Salem village? Oh, his voice would make me tremble, both Sabbath-day and lecture-day!"

Thus far, the elder traveller had listened with due gravity, but now burst into a fit of irrepressible mirth, shaking himself so violently, that his snake-like staff actually seemed to wriggle in sympathy.

"Ha! ha! ha!" shouted he, again and again; then composing

himself, "Well, go on, Goodman Brown, go on; but, prithee, don't kill me with laughing!"

"Well, then, to end the matter at once," said Goodman Brown, considerably nettled, "there is my wife, Faith. It would break her dear little heart; and I'd rather break my own!"

"Nay, if that be the case," answered the other, "e'en go thy ways, Goodman Brown. I would not, for twenty old women like the one hobbling before us, that Faith should come to any harm."

As he spoke, he pointed his staff at a female figure on the path, in whom Goodman Brown recognized a very pious and exemplary dame, who had taught him his catechism in youth, and was still his moral and spiritual adviser, jointly with the minister and Deacon Gookin.

"A marvel, truly, that Goody Cloyse should be so far in the wilderness, at nightfall!" said he. "But, with your leave, friend, I shall take a cut through the woods, until we have left this Christian woman behind. Being a stranger to you, she might ask whom I was consorting with, and whither I was going."

"Be it so," said his fellow-traveller. "Betake you to the woods, and let me keep the path."

Accordingly, the young man turned aside, but took care to watch his companion, who advanced softly along the road, until he had come within a staff's length of the old dame. She, meanwhile, was making the best of her way, with singular speed for so aged a woman, and mumbling some indistinct words, a prayer, doubtless, as she went. The traveller put forth his staff, and touched her withered neck with what seemed the serpent's tail.

"The devil!" screamed the pious old lady.

"Then Goody Cloyse knows her old friend?" observed the traveller, confronting her, and leaning on his writhing stick.

"Ah, forsooth, and is it your worship, indeed?" cried the good dame. "Yea, truly is it, and in the very image of my old gossip, Goodman Brown, the grandfather of the silly fellow that now is. But, would your worship believe it? my broomstick hath strangely disappeared, stolen, as I suspect, by that unhanged witch, Goody Cory, and that, too, when I was all anointed with the juice of smallage and cinque-foil and wolf's-bane"—

"Mingled with fine wheat and the fat of a new-born babe," said the shape of old Goodman Brown.

"Ah, your worship knows the recipe," cried the old lady, cackling aloud. "So, as I was saying, being all ready for the meeting, and no horse to ride on, I made up my mind to foot it; for they tell me, there is a nice young man to be taken into communion tonight. But now your good worship will lend me your arm, and we shall be there in a twinkling."

"That can hardly be," answered her friend. "I may not spare you my arm, Goody Cloyse, but here is my staff, if you will."

So saying, he threw it down at her feet, where, perhaps, it assumed life, being one of the rods which its owner had formerly lent to the Egyptian Magi. Of this fact, however, Goodman Brown could not take cognizance. He had cast up his eyes in astonishment, and looking down again, beheld neither Goody Cloyse nor the serpentine staff, but his fellow-traveller alone, who waited for him as calmly as if nothing had happened.

"That old woman taught me my catechism!" said the young man; and there was a world of meaning in this simple comment.

They continued to walk onward, while the elder traveller exhorted his companion to make good speed and persevere in the path, discoursing so aptly, that his arguments seemed rather to spring up in the bosom of his auditor, than to be suggested by himself. As they went, he plucked a branch of maple, to serve for a walking-stick, and began to strip it of the twigs and little boughs, which were wet with evening dew. The moment his fingers touched them, they became strangely withered and dried up, as with a week's sunshine. Thus the pair proceeded, at a good free pace, until suddenly, in a gloomy hollow of the road, Goodman Brown sat himself down on the stump of a tree, and refused to go any farther.

"Friend," said he, stubbornly, "my mind is made up. Not another step will I budge on this errand. What if a wretched old woman do choose to go to the devil, when I thought she was going to Heaven! Is that any reason why I should quit my dear Faith, and go after her?"

"You will think better of this by-and-by," said his acquaintance, composedly. "Sit here and rest yourself awhile; and when you feel like moving again, there is my staff to help you along."

Without more words, he threw his companion the maple stick, and was as speedily out of sight as if he had vanished into the deepening gloom. The young man sat a few moments by the road-side, applauding himself greatly, and thinking with how clear a conscience he should meet the minister, in his morning-walk, nor shrink from the eye of good old Deacon Gookin. And what calm sleep would be his, that very night, which was to have been spent so wickedly, but purely and sweetly now, in the arms of Faith! Amidst these pleasant and praiseworthy meditations, Goodman Brown heard the tramp of horses along the road, and deemed it advisable to conceal himself within the verge of the forest, conscious of the guilty purpose that had brought him thither, though now so happily turned from it.

On came the hoof-tramps and the voices of the riders, two grave old voices, conversing soberly as they drew near. These mingled sounds appeared to pass along the road, within a few yards of the young man's hiding-place; but owing, doubtless, to the depth of the gloom, at that particular spot, neither the travellers nor their steeds were visible. Though their figures brushed the small boughs by the way-side, it could not be seen that they intercepted, even for a moment, the faint gleam from the strip of bright sky, athwart which they must have passed. Goodman Brown alternately crouched and stood on tip-toe, pulling aside the branches, and thrusting forth his head as far as he durst, without discerning so much as a shadow. It vexed him the more, because he could have sworn, were such a thing possible, that he recognized the voices of the minister and Deacon Gookin, jogging along quietly, as they were wont to do, when bound to some ordination or ecclesiastical council. While yet within hearing, one of the riders stopped to pluck a switch.

"Of the two, reverend Sir," said the voice like the deacon's, "I had rather miss an ordination-dinner than tonight's meeting. They tell me that some of our community are to be here from Falmouth and beyond, and others from Connecticut and Rhode Island; besides several of the Indian powows, who, after their fashion, know almost as much deviltry as the best of us. Moreover, there is a goodly young woman to be taken into communion."

"Mighty well, Deacon Gookin!" replied the solemn old tones of the minister. "Spur up, or we shall be late. Nothing can be done, you know, until I get on the ground."

The hoofs clattered again, and the voices, talking so strangely in the empty air, passed on through the forest, where no church had ever been gathered, nor solitary Christian prayed. Whither, then, could these holy men be journeying, so deep into the heathen wilderness? Young Goodman Brown caught hold of a tree, for support, being ready to sink down on the ground, faint and over-burthened with the heavy sickness of his heart. He looked up to the sky, doubting whether there really was a Heaven above him. Yet, there was the blue arch, and the stars brightening in it.

"With Heaven above, and Faith below, I will yet stand firm against the devil!" cried Goodman Brown.

While he still gazed upward, into the deep arch of the firmament, and had lifted his hands to pray, a cloud, though no wind was stirring, hurried across the zenith, and hid the brightening stars. The blue sky was still visible, except directly overhead, where this black mass of cloud was sweeping swiftly northward. Aloft in the air, as if from the depths of the cloud, came a confused and doubtful sound of voices. Once, the listener fancied that he could distinguish the accents of town's-people of his own, men and women, both pious and ungodly, many of whom he had met at the communion-table, and had seen others rioting at the tavern. The next moment, so indistinct were the sounds, he doubted whether he had heard aught but the murmur of the old forest, whispering without a wind. Then came a stronger swell of those familiar tones, heard daily in the sunshine, at Salem village, but never, until now, from a cloud of night. There was one voice, of a young woman, uttering lamentations, yet with an uncertain sorrow, and entreating for some favor, which, perhaps, it would grieve her to obtain. And all the unseen multitude, both saints and sinners, seemed to encourage her onward.

"Faith!" shouted Goodman Brown, in a voice of agony and desperation; and the echoes of the forest mocked him, crying—"Faith! Faith!" as if bewildered wretches were seeking her, all through the wilderness.

The cry of grief, rage, and terror, was yet piercing the night, when the unhappy husband held his breath for a response. There was a scream, drowned immediately in a louder murmur of voices, fading into far-off laughter, as the dark cloud swept away, leaving the clear and silent sky above Goodman Brown. But something fluttered lightly down through the air, and caught on the branch of a tree. The young man seized it, and beheld a pink ribbon.

"My Faith is gone!" cried he, after one stupefied moment. "There is no good on earth; and sin is but a name. Come, devil! for to thee is this world given."

And maddened with despair, so that he laughed loud and long, did Goodman Brown grasp his staff and set forth again, at such a rate, that he seemed to fly along the forest-path, rather than to walk or run. The road grew wilder and drearier, and more faintly traced, and vanished at length, leaving him in the heart of the dark wilderness, still rushing onward, with the instinct that guides mortal man to evil. The whole forest was peopled with frightful sounds; the creaking of the trees, the howling of wild beasts, and the yell of Indians; while, sometimes the wind tolled like a distant church-bell, and sometimes gave a broad roar around the traveller, as if all Nature were laughing him to scorn. But he was himself the chief horror of the scene, and shrank not from its other horrors.

"Ha! ha! ha!" roared Goodman Brown, when the wind laughed at him. "Let us hear which will laugh loudest! Think not to frighten me with your deviltry! Come witch, come wizard, come Indian powow, come devil himself! and here comes Goodman Brown. You may as well fear him as he fear you!"

In truth, all through the haunted forest, there could be nothing more frightful than the figure of Goodman Brown. On he flew, among the black pines, brandishing his staff with frenzied gestures, now giving vent to an inspiration of horrid blasphemy, and now shouting forth such laughter, as set all the echoes of the forest laughing like demons around him. The fiend in his own shape is less hideous, than when he rages in the breast of man. Thus sped the demoniac on his course, until, quivering among the trees, he saw a red light before him, as when the felled trunks and branches of a clearing have been set on fire, and throw up their lurid blaze against the sky, at the hour of midnight. He paused, in a lull of the tempest that had driven him onward, and heard the swell of what seemed a hymn, rolling solemnly from a distance, with the weight of many voices. He knew the tune; It was a familiar one in the choir of the village meeting-house. The verse died heavily away, and was lengthened by a chorus, not of human voices, but of all the sounds of the benighted wilderness, pealing in awful harmony together. Goodman Brown cried out; and his cry was lost to his own ear, by its unison with the cry of the desert.

In the interval of silence, he stole forward, until the light glared full upon his eyes. At one extremity of an open space, hemmed in by the dark wall of the forest, arose a rock, bearing some rude, natural resemblance either to an altar or a pulpit, and surrounded by four blazing pines, their tops a flame, their stems untouched, like candles at an evening meeting. The mass of foliage, that had overgrown the summit of the rock, was all on fire, blazing high into the night, and fitfully illuminating the whole field. Each pendant twig and leafy festoon was in a blaze. As the red light arose and fell, a numerous congregation alternately shone forth, then disappeared in shadow, and again grew, as it were, out of the darkness, peopling the heart of the solitary woods at once.

"A grave and dark-clad company!" quoth Goodman Brown.

In truth, they were such. Among them, quivering to-and-fro, between gloom and splendor, appeared faces that would be seen, next day, at the council-board of the province, and others which, Sabbath after Sabbath, looked devoutly heavenward, and benignantly over the crowded pews, from the holiest pulpits in the land. Some affirm, that the lady of the governor was there. At least, there were high dames well known to her, and wives of honored husbands, and widows, a great multitude, and ancient maidens, all of excellent repute, and fair young girls, who trembled lest their mothers should espy them. Either the sudden gleams of light, flashing over the obscure field, bedazzled Goodman Brown, or he recognized a score of the church-members of Salem village, famous for their especial sanctity. Good old Deacon Gookin had arrived, and waited at the skirts of that venerable saint, his reverend pastor. But, irreverently consorting with these grave, reputable, and pious people, these elders of the church, these chaste dames and dewy virgins, there were men of dissolute lives and women of spotted fame, wretches given over to all mean and filthy vice, and suspected even of horrid crimes. It was strange to see, that the good shrank not from the wicked, nor were the sinners abashed by the saints. Scattered, also, among their pale-faced enemies, were the Indian priests, or powows, who had often scared their native forest with more hideous incantations than any known to English witchcraft.

"But, where is Faith?" thought Goodman Brown; and, as hope came into his heart, he trembled.

Another verse of the hymn arose, a slow and mournful strain, such as the pious love, but joined to words which expressed all that our nature can conceive of sin, and darkly hinted at far more. Unfathomable to mere mortals is the lore of fiends. Verse after verse was sung, and still the chorus of the desert swelled between, like the deepest tone of a mighty organ. And, with the final peal of that dreadful anthem, there came a sound, as if the roaring wind, the rushing streams, the howling beasts, and every other voice of the unconverted wilderness, were mingling and according with the voice of guilty man, in homage to the prince of all. The four blazing pines threw up a loftier flame, and obscurely discovered shapes and visages of horror on the smoke-wreaths, above the impious assembly. At the same moment, the fire on the rock shot redly forth, and formed a glowing arch above its base, where now appeared a figure. With reverence be it spoken, the apparition bore no slight similitude, both in garb and manner, to some grave divine of the New England churches.

"Bring forth the converts!" cried a voice, that echoed through the field and rolled into the forest.

At the word, Goodman Brown stepped forth from the shadow of the trees, and approached the congregation, with whom he felt a loathful brotherhood, by the sympathy of all that was wicked in his heart. He could have well nigh sworn, that the shape of his own dead father beckoned him to advance, looking downward from a smoke-wreath, while a woman, with dim features of despair, threw out her hand to warn him back. Was it his mother? But he had no power to retreat one step, nor to resist, even in thought, when the minister and good old Deacon Gookin seized his arms, and led him to the blazing rock. Thither came also the slender form of a veiled female, led between Goody Cloyse, that pious teacher of the catechism, and Martha Carrier, who had received the devil's promise to be queen of hell. A rampant hag was she! And there stood the proselytes, beneath the canopy of fire.

"Welcome, my children," said the dark figure, "to the communion of your race! Ye have found, thus young, your nature and your destiny. My children, look behind you!"

They turned; and flashing forth, as it were, in a sheet of flame, the fiend-worshippers were seen; the smile of welcome gleamed darkly on every visage.

"There," resumed the sable form, "are all whom ye have reverenced from youth. Ye deemed them holier than yourselves, and shrank from your own sin, contrasting it with their lives of righteousness, and prayerful aspirations heavenward. Yet, here are they all, in my worshipping assembly! This night it shall be granted you to know their secret deeds; how hoary-bearded elders of the church have whispered wanton words to the young maids of their households; how many a woman, eager for widow's weeds, has given her husband a drink at bedtime, and let him sleep his last sleep in her bosom; how beardless youths have made haste to inherit their father's wealth; and how fair damsels—blush not, sweet ones!—have dug little graves in the garden, and bidden me, the sole guest, to an infant's funeral. By the sympathy of your human hearts for sin, ye shall scent out all the places—whether in church, bed-chamber, street, field, or forest—where crime has been committed, and shall exult to behold the whole earth one stain of guilt, one mighty blood-spot. Far more than this! It shall be yours to penetrate, in every bosom, the deep mystery of sin, the fountain of all wicked arts, and which inexhaustibly supplies more evil impulses than human power—than my power, at its utmost!—can make manifest in deeds. And now, my children, look upon each other."

They did so; and, by the blaze of the hell-kindled torches, the wretched man beheld his Faith, and the wife her husband, trembling before that unhallowed altar.

"Lo! there ye stand, my children," said the figure, in a deep and solemn tone, almost sad, with its despairing awfulness, as if his once angelic nature could yet mourn for our miserable race. "Depending upon one another's hearts, ye had still hoped that virtue were not all a dream! Now are ye undeceived!—Evil is the nature of mankind. Evil must be your only happiness. Welcome, again, my children, to the communion of your race!"

"Welcome!" repeated the fiend-worshippers, in one cry of despair and triumph.

And there they stood, the only pair, as it seemed, who were yet hesitating on the verge of wickedness, in this dark world. A basin was hollowed, naturally, in the rock. Did it contain water, reddened by the lurid light? or was it blood? or, perchance, a liquid flame? Herein did the Shape of Evil dip his hand, and prepare to lay the mark of baptism upon their foreheads, that they might be partakers of the mystery of sin, more conscious of the secret guilt of others, both in deed and thought, than they could now be of their own. The husband cast one look at his pale wife, and Faith at him. What polluted wretches would the next glance show them to each other, shuddering alike at what they disclosed and what they saw!

"Faith! Faith!" cried the husband. "Look up to Heaven, and resist the Wicked One!"

Whether Faith obeyed, he knew not. Hardly had he spoken, when he found himself amid calm night and solitude, listening to a roar of the wind, which died heavily away through the forest. He staggered against the rock, and felt it chill and damp, while a hanging twig, that had been all on fire, besprinkled his cheek with the coldest dew.

The next morning, young Goodman Brown came slowly into the street of Salem village, staring around him like a bewildered man. The good old minister was taking a walk along the graveyard, to get an appetite for breakfast and meditate his sermon, and bestowed a blessing, as he passed, on Goodman Brown. He shrank from the venerable saint, as if to avoid an anathema. Old Deacon Gookin was at domestic worship, and the holy words of his prayer were heard through the open window. "What God doth the wizard pray to?" quoth Goodman Brown. Goody Cloyse, that excellent old Christian, stood in the early sunshine, at her own lattice, catechizing a little girl, who had brought her a pint of morning's milk. Goodman Brown snatched away the child, as from the grasp of the fiend himself.

Turning the corner by the meeting-house, he spied the head of Faith, with the pink ribbons, gazing anxiously forth, and bursting into such joy at sight of him, that she skipt along the street, and almost kissed her husband before the whole village. But Goodman Brown looked sternly and sadly into her face, and passed on without a greeting.

Had Goodman Brown fallen asleep in the forest, and only dreamed a wild dream of a witch-meeting?

Be it so, if you will. But, alas! it was a dream of evil omen for young Goodman Brown. A stern, a sad, a darkly meditative, a distrustful, if not a desperate man, did he become, from the night of that fearful dream. On the Sabbath-day, when the congregation were singing a holy psalm, he could not listen, because an anthem of sin rushed loudly upon his ear, and drowned all the blessed strain. When the minister spoke from the pulpit, with power and fervid eloquence, and with his hand on the open bible, of the sacred truths of our religion, and of saint-like lives and triumphant deaths, and of future bliss or misery unutterable, then did Goodman Brown turn pale, dreading lest the roof should thunder down upon the grey blasphemer and his hearers. Often, awaking suddenly at midnight, he shrank from the bosom of Faith, and at morning or eventide, when the family knelt down at prayer, he scowled, and muttered to himself, and gazed sternly at his wife, and turned away. And when he had lived long, and was borne to his grave, a hoary corpse, followed by Faith, an aged woman, and children and grandchildren, a goodly procession, besides neighbors, not a few, they carved no hopeful verse upon his tombstone; for his dying hour was gloom.

1872

THE MYSTERIOUS CASE OF MY FRIEND BROWNE

Julian Hawthorne

Julian Hawthorne (1846–1934) may have inherited the dark legacy of Salem and its "witches"—indeed, towards the end of his life he wrote a series featuring an occult sensitive, Martha Klemm, who claimed to be the reincarnation of a witch hanged in the Salem witch trials—but he inherited from his mother, Sophia, an interest in the occult. She collected various esoteric volumes and studied transcendentalism. Amongst her friends was Ada Shepard, governess to young Julian and his two sisters, who had the talent as a medium. At one session, held in Florence, Ada began to write messages purporting to be from a spirit once known as Mary Rondel. Years later, when looking through his father's library, Julian found a copy of Philip Sydney's Arcadia, *which had belonged to his grandfather Daniel (1731–1796), where Daniel had highlighted verses to attract a young lady—Mary Rondel!*

Julian was a healthy, active boy—at college he excelled at sports—but he failed academically. He trained as an engineer and, while studying in Germany in 1869, met his future wife May (or Minne). Back in the United States, he tried to hold down an engineering job but turned to writing, a vocation he much preferred. He sold his first story in 1870 and had some moderate success with his early novels, in the gothic mystery mode, but sales did not pay the bills and he could only continue to write thanks to his wife, who supported him through her own work. Over time his short fiction proved popular, especially in England where he and Minne lived from 1874 to 1882. Many of his short stories were supernatural or fantasy, including fairy tales for children. Collections include The Laughing Mill *(1879)*, Ellice Quentin and Other Stories *(1880) and* David Poindexter's Disappearance *(1888)*.

He tried various endeavours to raise money, even farming in Jamaica, but seldom with much success. His wife became exhausted through supporting him and they separated in the mid-1890s. Yet just at this time he won first prize in a $10,000 novel contest run by the New York Herald Tribune *with* A Fool of Nature *(1896). It allowed him to indulge in various literary pursuits, including compiling the ten-volume* Lock and Key Library *(1909) of mysteries and ghost stories from around the world. Unfortunately, Hawthorne also fell foul of a scam. He was asked to invite people to invest in what proved to be a non-existent mining venture. He was tried for mail fraud in 1913 and served six months in prison. He moved to California where he spent the last twenty years of his life with the lady who became his second wife, after Minne died in 1925. Amongst his later writings were a spiritualistic science-fiction serial, "A Cosmic Courtship" (1917) and the series featuring Martha Klemm starting with "Absolute Evil" (1918). His last published story, in 1925, "A Sea Secret", also had supernatural elements.*

Julian never really emerged from the shadow of his father, but though almost forgotten, he left behind a significant body of work, much of which is weird fiction. It includes the remarkable novella about dual personalities, Archibald Malmaison *(1879), which appeared years before Robert Louis Stevenson's* Strange Case of Dr Jekyll and Mr Hyde *(1886). Some of Hawthorne's best weird tales were collected by Jessica Amanda Salmonson as* The Rose of Death and Other Mysterious Delusions *(1997)*.

How bitterly cold it was in New York on the evening of the 4th of February, 1871! I was sitting in front of a snug coal fire in my cozy little library in Washington Square. I am somewhat inclined to be what is called a bookworm: I love with my whole heart whatever is old, quaint, and musty in the way of books. They are fascinating to me in proportion as they are ancient, and possessed of that peculiar smell characteristic of antiquated bindings and worm-eaten paper. What other merits they may possess is a matter of indifference to me. To be acceptable they must be old.

On this especial evening my happiness was complete. During the day I had determined to brave the winter wind in search of some new antiquity of literature—something that should be exceptionally ragged, obscure, and aromatic. Accordingly I betook myself to my favorite resort in such emergencies—the old second-hand bookstore in Ann Street, and, after ransacking about for a while, I hit upon what seemed to be a number of old, decayed letters bound up together, and protected by a time-worn leather cover.

Here was a prize indeed! With trembling eagerness I inquired the price, and felt offended almost at being told it was ten cents! Willingly would I have given a hundred times as much, had it been asked. But I reflected that swine were always prone to trample upon pearls, and paid my ten cents in silence. Then, placing my purchase carefully in my innermost breast pocket, I hurried homeward through the biting wind.

Supper over, I ensconced myself in my big easy-chair, and prepared for a campaign into the realms of antiquity. My centre, as already hinted, was protected by a glowing fire, my right flank defended by my last half bottle of rare old port-wine, my left wing strengthened by a time-honored pipe of fragrant Latakia, and my rear brought up by a judicious arrangement of cushions and springs. Every thing being ready, I drew forth my precious budget, and the campaign began.

After a little general skirmishing and reconnoitring, in which long practice and experience had rendered me an adept, I began to gain an insight into what had at first glance appeared somewhat involved. The papers (consisting of copies of letters and extracts from a journal) contained a story of three individuals—two men and a woman—who lived about a hundred and fifty years ago. One peculiar circumstance was noticeable which considerably added to the obscurity of this tale—all the proper names had been omitted. A blank space was left for each one. Even the person (a friend, apparently, of the chief actor in the drama) who had copied and arranged the original letters and papers was as nameless as the rest. But by dint of inserting initials in these blank spaces, and noting down here an event and there a date, I gradually arrived at a comprehension of the main points of the story, which (for I shall resist the temptation to transcribe it in the original words) ran somewhat as follows:

Early in the last century a man, M——, was residing in the vicinity of what was then the flourishing town of New York. He was an enterprising and successful young farmer, who, barring the fact that he was an orphan and unmarried, wanted nothing to complete his felicity. It seems probable that the very fact of his having so little to desire put it into his head that he needed a wife—some one to take charge of his household affairs, receive him with a kiss and smile on his return from the day's work, and bear him children who should transmit his name to posterity. Such a one he believed himself to have found in the person of Miss H——, a young lady belonging to one of the best families in the neighborhood. The parents, well-to-do people, readily gave their consent to the young farmer's suit; she herself seemed to favor him and reciprocate his affection, and every thing seemed to prophesy a speedy and happy marriage.

At this point B—— made his appearance on the scene. He was at this time a lawyer of fair standing and repute—young, good-looking, and, for those days, well versed in the arts and usages of polite society. Retained as counsel by the H—— family in a lawsuit, on its termination in their favor he gradually advanced from the position of legal adviser to that of a trusty and intimate friend; and in the heart of one at least in the family he seems to have stood higher still.

One morning M—— came down to New York, went to the jeweler's, and bought a handsome gold ring, which he purposed presenting to his mistress as a pledge of their approaching union. But that union was destined never to take place. On reaching her house he found every thing in wild confusion: the young lady had eloped the night previous with the traitor B——, and no one knew whither. M—— returned to his farm, moody and sullen, and from that hour was an altered man. The ring which the falsehood of Miss H—— had defrauded of its original purpose he wore always thereafter around his neck and next his heart; and surely, if there be poison in the evil passions and unhallowed emotions of the human soul, we can almost believe them to have hardened into the gold and crystallized into the gems of that engagement-ring!

Meanwhile B—— and his wife found little difficulty in obtaining the forgiveness and favor of the H—— family; and at the decease of the old people they inherited half the estate, the remainder going to an only son, at that time absent in Europe. M——, however, kept entirely aloof from them until the time of his death; but shortly before that event he sent to B—— a letter professing forgiveness and a desire for reconciliation, and inclosing the engagement-ring as a pledge thereof. But, for whatever reason made, this pledge seems to have been insincere; for of the same date is an extract from M——'s journal containing these words:

> Being nowe sicke past hope of recoverie, I doe herebye declare my ondyinge Hatred toward B——, himselfe and his posteritie forever; and I pray God that my Revenge be fulfilled to the Uttermoste— yea, at the Perill of mine own Soule! Amen.

These words, dreadful in any case, but doubly so as coming from a dying man, closed the collection. A note, written apparently by S——, the compiler, added that M—— had been buried in Trinity Church-yard, and that the tombstone above him bore this inscription:

> In memory of —— M——,
> Who died February 6, 1771.
> Requiescat in pace.

I laid down the manuscript, poured out a glass of wine, and sipped and pondered. The omission of all the names puzzled me. What object could the papers have been collected for, unless to record a vow of vengeance, and the causes which led to and justified it? Yet, without the names, was it not void of all significance? True, the omission had probably greatly increased the chances of the manuscript's being preserved through so many years; but preservation at the expense of identification seemed objectless. On the other hand, was it likely that M——, at the moment of dissolution, would have prayed for vengeance on his enemy, even at peril of his own soul, and have caused the prayer to be written down, without any purpose whatever? Decidedly not! How he had intended or expected his revenge to be accomplished was beyond my comprehension; perhaps he deemed the ring a sort of talisman, enabling his disembodied spirit to haunt the wearer. I finished my glass of port and set it down. A little wine always makes me imaginative!

While debating whether to light a fresh pipe or my bedroom candle, a loud ring at the door-bell settled the question for me. "Who the deuce can be coming here at this time of night!" I grunted, rubbing my eyes and yawning. A knock at the door heralded the entrance of my friend Browne. I had not seen him for a week or two, but he could not have changed more in as many years. I was quite startled at his appearance.

"Good Heavens, Browne!" I exclaimed. "Why, you look as if you'd seen a ghost!"

Browne started and looked at me for a moment; then he dropped into my easy-chair (from which I had incautiously risen to give him welcome), leaned his elbows on his knees and his head on his hands, gazed gloomily into the fire for a few moments, and then said, in a low, awestruck voice, very different from his usual brisk, lively tone:

"And so I have, Simpson!"

I was completely unnerved. Until this evening I had known Browne as a rising young barrister, clever, sensible, and always in good spirits. The idea of such a man as he coming in suddenly and deliberately at that hour of the night and solemnly asserting that he had seen a ghost, was enough to unnerve any body. I was at a loss what to say, and therefore said the very last thing I meant to: I asked him to have a glass of wine!

Browne, without a word, filled my glass to the brim, drained it, filled it again, and drained that, looking all the while as if he were going to be hanged. But I began to look rather serious myself then.

"Simpson," said Browne, abstractedly, again gazing into the fire, "I shan't blame you for being incredulous. I should have been myself—if I hadn't seen it with my own eyes!"

I began to feel a little nervous, I think. Browne was a larger man than I, and if, as I believed, his mind was affected, he might become violent at any moment. I felt that the wisest course would be to humor him.

"Of course," I said, "that alters the case."

Again Browne fixed his eyes on me, and nodded silently. How pale and strange he looked! Again he took the bottle, filled the glass, and drained it. Positively it was becoming unpleasant. Wine was the worst thing for any one in his condition, and—there were not more than three glassfuls left in the bottle.

"Don't you think," I began, "that you'd better——"

"I will!" exclaimed Browne, abruptly; "and as briefly as possible: it happened in this way. You knew I was engaged to Miss Hammill. Well, I went down there the other day to give her the engagement-ring. It was a queer, old-fashioned thing, that I found in a secret drawer of a desk that had belonged to some great-great-grandfather of mine, but handsome enough, for all that. I put it on her finger, and told her how it had been in our family a hundred years for all I knew, but that she was the first who'd ever worn it. Oh, how sweet and lovely she looked as she put her hands in mine, and promised me that as long as she lived she would remain true to the giver of that ring! And yet, even as she spoke the words, it seemed to me she shuddered convulsively and turned pale; and at the same moment I felt a sudden chill and horror at my own heart. But we both shook it off, whatever it was, and parted as usual, except that when I kissed her I could not be sure whether I had really touched her lips or not."

"I must say, Browne," remarked I, for my nervousness was beginning to pass off, and I felt sleepy, and in no degree inclined to listen to a lover's rhapsodies, "I don't see any thing in all this to warrant you in—"

I did not finish my protest; I was too much engaged in watching Browne fill and drain another glass of my port. I resolved not to interrupt him again.

"When I called the next evening," continued he, "I noticed a change in her at once. I know not how to describe it. It was not so much that she was cold to me, as that she seemed chilled herself. Her affections, her emotions, appeared in a manner paralyzed. She seemed to elude my grasp, so to speak; I couldn't reach her; I felt as if some nameless, impalpable, but insurmountable barrier had grown up between us since the day before. And several times I turned around, under the impression that somebody else was in the room. Her eyes wore a kind of sad, hopeless, distant expression, as if she felt that some one or something were taking her away from me. Yet still she wore the ring on which she had sworn to be true to the giver; but I saw her look at it once, and it may have been my fancy, but I thought she shivered, and grew even paler than before."

"Nothing but a headache on her part, and indigestion on yours, depend upon it," growled I, forgetting my resolution. But Browne didn't take any wine this time. He only sighed heavily and shook his head.

"The next day—yesterday," he went on, "I resolved to call early, take her out to walk, and trust to open air and exercise to set every thing right; for I could not, would not, believe that my impressions of the day before had been any thing but a morbid fancy. I felt quite reinspirited, and walked rapidly along up Fifth Avenue toward her house. She lives, you know, corner of the avenue and Fifty-first Street. I had reached Forty-second Street, when I caught sight of her about a block ahead of me, and walking slowly in the same direction. She walked as if her life were ebbing away from her at every step; there was an indescribable droop and languor about her, so different from her usual springy step, and bright, cheerful manner. But I hardly more than noticed her; for, walking by her side, apparently talking to her, I saw, as plainly as I now see you," said Browne, raising himself to an upright position in his chair, and looking fixedly at me, "I saw—It!"

"'It'! Why, what on earth do you mean, Browne?" cried I, feeling cold chills run down my back and creep into the calves of my legs.

"The stout, burly figure of a man, with a high-crowned, broad-brimmed hat, and masses of rusty hair falling on its shoulders. It was clad in a cloak of dusky gray, and wore knee-breeches and stockings of the same color. It stalked along the pavement in clumsy high-heeled shoes, in a manner that would have been ridiculous, had I been in any mood for laughing."

"I should have felt in a mood to kick him into the street!" declared I, valiantly. But there was something in Browne's manner that made me a little doubtful whether I would have done so, after all. He continued, without heeding my interruption:

"It struck me as especially strange that, notwithstanding the great peculiarity of the figure's dress, manner, and general appearance, and though it was broad daylight and the avenue well filled, no one seemed to notice or even see It. Even Miss Hammill, I fancied, did not realize its presence, though she was certainly in some way impressed by It. She never looked at or appeared otherwise conscious of It than as hearing, or rather feeling, what It said. Occasionally she would wince or shrink, as if its words were blows or stabs; and at such times the figure would appear vastly amused, throwing back its head, raising its hands, and contorting its burly form, as if indulging in an immoderate fit of laughter.

"By this time I had gained considerably on them, but was puzzled to observe that, although I had all along kept my eyes steadily fixed on the strange figure, I could not see It as distinctly as when further off. The sun still shone brightly, and the air was as clear and cold as ever; but the outlines of the shape were blurred or undefined, as if seen out of focus through a telescope. The nearer I approached, the more indistinct and shadowy did It appear, though still I was aware that It continued to stride along by Miss Hammill's side, ever and anon breaking forth into fresh ebullitions of ugly merriment. Nearer yet I came, until not more than twenty paces separated us, and now I could distinguish nothing save a kind of gloomy shadow that seemed to hover along the pavement. In a few steps more this, too, had vanished; and when I came up with Miss Hammill, I was only conscious of a subtle influence in the air. I felt again that mysterious chill of horror at my heart; and though I was walking beside her, and her arm was in mine, she seemed immeasurable miles away."

Browne paused and drew a deep breath. As for me, I felt the cold chills worse than ever. I poured out a glass of wine with trembling hand and drank it hurriedly. It was really a very cold night!

"Under such circumstances," continued Browne, "it was not strange that our greeting was quiet, almost formal. I knew she was aware of an evil presence, as well as I. Could she have been separated from herself, she might have seen It; as it was, that was reserved for me only. But we both knew that, even at that moment, It was there—between us, around us, exerting some malignant spell over us, to separate, perhaps destroy us. And why should It have power to injure us thus? Had she not sworn on the ring to be true till death to the giver? Was not I the giver? Yet she was lost to me, and I could feel the ring upon her finger, as her hand rested in my arm; it seemed to burn and sear my flesh, as if it had been heated in hell fire.

"So we walked onward, pretty much in silence, and soon reached her house. I bade her farewell on the doorstep, for I had no heart to enter, even had she invited me. 'You have been alone all day?' I asked her, as I turned to go. 'All alone,' replied she, in a sad, far-away voice. 'I'm always alone now, except for my thoughts;' and then she shivered, and shrank into herself, as it were from a stab. I left her standing there, and turning as I reached the end of the block, she stood there still; but oh, horror! by her side stood again that gloomy, fantastic shape, with high-crowned hat and dusky cloak, tossing its arms about, and actually capering with ghastly jollity! As I gazed, horror-stricken, the door opened, and she passed in and disappeared; and the mysterious figure, turning toward me, took off its hat with a flourish, and made me a low mock obeisance; then, with a parting wave of the hand, It stalked in after her. I knew that It and I would meet again; but something in my heart told me that I had seen the last of Alice Hammill."

"But, Browne," said I, in a low, remonstrative tone (why *would* that closet door keep creaking so!), "that was only yesterday afternoon, you know. Why, man alive, you must have been dreaming, or crazy! On Fifth Avenue—yesterday—in the middle of the afternoon—a healthy, sensible young fellow like you—talk of *your* seeing a ghost! Come, now, say you were fooling, Browne, do!" entreated I, making a violent effort to laugh it off. Heaven knows I would willingly have given half a dozen bottles of my best port-wine to have seen him join in, in his usual hearty fashion, and acknowledge it was all a hoax. But as I looked at him my laugh died away into a very questionable quaver. He didn't look at all genial.

"I reasoned in the same way, Simpson," said he, "after I reached home. I found that my recollection of the weird figure, though vivid enough, seemed more like the memory of a vivid dream than of a reality. Having escaped from its immediate influence, I persuaded myself it must be some extraordinary mental or optical delusion; and I went to bed, resolved to see whether a good night's rest would not aid in dispelling it.

"I woke this morning feeling fresh and strong, and determined to see Miss Hammill at once, tell her all my fears and fancies, and prove to myself and her that it was all a wretched delusion. So, having eaten a hearty breakfast at the Fifth Avenue Hotel, I set off, and in a quarter of an hour stood on the doorstep. I rang the bell, and the servant appeared.

"'I want to see Miss Hammill. Is she in?'

"'Yes, Sir,' returned the man; 'but she's very bad with the headache, and can't see no one. The doctor says as how she's out of her head, Sir.'

"'Do you mean to say she's insane?' cried I, with a terrible throb of my heart.

"'Not just that, Sir,' replied he; 'but he says she must be kept quite quiet, Sir, for several days; and, more especially, not see any one she cared for, Sir.'

"I turned away, sick at heart, and at that moment I felt again that nameless, creeping chill, as if some unholy thing had brushed past me. Impelled by a dark foreboding, I looked down the street, and there, standing clearly defined in the crisp winter sunlight, I saw the Thing again."

"What! this very morning?" gasped I, half expecting to see the grisly phantom rise up between us. "Oh, not this very morning, Browne?" But it was no use.

"This morning," repeated Brown, "about eleven o'clock. It stood there beckoning to me impatiently, as if to follow It. It stamped its foot imperiously, and pointed down the avenue. And all at once a wild passion took possession of me. There stood the Thing that had destroyed my happiness, blighted my love, perhaps purposed to deprive me of life itself. My whole soul rose up in hatred and defiance. I burned to rush after It and grapple with It, though death should be the forfeit of the struggle. I did not care for death, if I might have revenge. And there It still stood, beckoning to me. I sprang down the steps, and then a ghastly chase began."

"Good gracious, Browne!" exclaimed I, piteously; "you don't mean to say you ran after It?" But he did not hear me—I don't think he knew I was in the room—so absorbed was he in the recollection of his dreadful adventure.

"The figure stalked on in front of me," said he, "with long, easy strides, once in a while cutting the most grotesque capers, flinging out its legs, and flourishing its arms abroad. It was always about sixty yards ahead, and I found it impossible to lessen this distance. But the faster I walked, the better pleased It seemed to be, skipping with frantic glee along the frozen pavements, and ever and anon half turning round to motion me onward still more rapidly. Stop I could not: I was drawn onward by an irresistible power that no will of mine could modify or overcome. But I had no desire to pause; my own heart drove me like a goad.

"As we kept on I noticed that no one saw the fantastic phantom, though, as It passed, men and women would shudder and turn pale, and draw their winter cloaks more closely about them. But, as our speed increased, I observed them stop and turn to look at me as I passed; and no wonder! I must have presented a strange spectacle, hurrying onward, with bloodless lips and face and fixed, straining eyes. But, so they did not stop me, it was little I cared for that.

"On we went, faster and faster! We passed directly under the windows of the Fifth Avenue Hotel, which I had left on my way up not half an hour before. I was dimly conscious of the crowd before the door, of the stage waiting for its passengers, and of the big clock standing on the sidewalk; but every thing seemed like a dream, save only the ghastly shadow that still stalked before me with ever-increasing pace.

"We crossed the square, and now we were on Broadway. The dusky shape glided forward with easy speed, holding a direct line through the hurrying crowd. Faster yet! My breath began to come hard, but still I kept on; I was under my own control no longer. Union Square was passed, and Grace Church was close at hand. Turning the corner, the figure paused a moment and looked around, and I thought I could distinguish an evil leer overspreading its pallid features; then It waved its arms, and was off again.

"The whole stretch of lower Broadway now lay before us, filled from side to side with its endless stream of human beings, and the roar and rattle of horses and carts. But I, by virtue of my ghostly companionship, felt as far removed and isolated from them as if I were beholding them from another world. All that was most commonplace and familiar seemed weird and strange, and the only reality for me was the dreadful phantom that still led me on.

"At the farther extremity of the long road I could now see the spire of Trinity Church, outlined against the clear blue morning sky. At the same moment we quickened our speed; my guide seemed to flit like a passing shadow over the crowded sidewalk. His merriment also appeared momentarily to increase; he was now in a continual convulsion of chuckling laughter. On we rushed! Canal Street was passed;

the City Hall was left behind; and at last the railing of Trinity Churchyard appeared, with the clustering groups of time-worn grave-stones behind it. And then the strain that had been drawing me onward ceased at once, like the snapping of a cord, and I realized for the first time how weak and exhausted I was. But still I staggered onward: I would see the end, though already half suspecting what it was to be.

"I reached the gate of the graveyard and looked through the bars into the inclosure; and there, sitting on a gray, crumbling headstone, leaning with its head on its hands and its elbows on its knees, I saw It for the last time. It looked at me with an awful leer; a sombre shadow fell about It, which the cheerful sunshine could not penetrate; but the eyes of the mysterious figure emitted a dusky, phosphorescent glare, illuminating its features with a pale, unnatural light. The face was that of a corpse already mouldering into its native earth, and as I looked It seemed to crumble gradually away; the shadow grew duskier, until only the phosphorescent gleam was visible; then that too faded, an icy gust of wind swept through the church-yard, and I heard the clock strike noon."

As Browne concluded he sank back in his chair, and began to shiver as if in an ague fit. At such a moment all personal considerations give way to the exigencies and impulses of the moment. I poured out the last glass of wine in the bottle, and myself forced it down his throat. Any thing was better than to see him thus; and he had said that the presence of the ghost always produced a shuddering! But I was resolved to believe my friend insane, or dying, or any thing else, in preference to putting faith in the awful vision he believed himself to have seen.

"Come, come, Browne, you're sick, and that's the whole difficulty," asserted I, stoutly. "Stay with me tonight, and if you aren't better tomorrow, we'll have the doctor here."

The wine seemed partially to have restored Browne's nerve. He sat up and gazed at me with a dead, hopeless expression in his eyes, that did not look much like improvement. He shook his head when I repeated my invitation.

"No, no," said he; "I must be off. I shall leave here next Monday, and shall never come back. Alice is dead—to me, at all events. Here," he added, handing me a card—"there's the inscription on the gravestone: I copied it down after—And here's an old piece of paper, in which I found the ring folded up. It has some writing on it, I believe, and may explain something: you're good at that sort of thing. Goodnight!" And before I could speak again he was gone, and I saw him no more. On the card was written:

> In memory of THOMAS MURRAY,
> Who died February 6, 1771.
> Requiescat in pace.

"Rather a satire on the old fellow, that *'requiescat in pace'*," commented I—"that is, if Browne *should* turn out not to be a lunatic!" The paper he had given me was old and yellow, and the writing on it appeared too illegible to puzzle out that night. So, resolving to see him the next day, and talk it all over in a sober and sensible way, I yawned and retired.

That night I had a very vivid dream, in which the marvelous story related to me by Browne was in some way mixed up with the old manuscript I had purchased in Ann Street. I imagined that all the blank spaces were filled out, and with the names of Browne, Alice Hammill, and Thomas Murray, I myself figuring as the copier and compiler of the whole.

With the first light of day I sprang out of bed, the influence of my dream still strong upon me, and rushed into my study after the manuscript. There it lay on the top shelf of my book-case, where I had placed it the night before; but a jar of some chemical liquid, which I remembered to have seen standing around ever since I was a boy, and which I had been told was an heir-loom in our family for many generations, had fallen over on it and broken, and the liquid had run out and deluged the manuscript completely. With a sigh for the sad fate of the jar, I took down the papers and opened them.

The sight that met my eyes made me feel as if the roots of my hair were alive and moving! All the blanks were filled up with names, written in a pale, reddish ink; and they were all exactly as I had dreamed they were. Thomas Murray was the young farmer whose life had been blighted by the lawyer, who was none other than Browne himself! while the lady who had caused all the trouble was Alice Hammill! And—yes! I was there too! My name was signed to the note appended to Thomas Murray's prayer for vengeance—"John Simpson" in full!

"Now how the deuce," soliloquized I, "did those names get written down there? They certainly weren't there yesterday. Ah! here's one only half written! How's that? Ah!" I exclaimed, drawing a long breath of relief, "I see now! Sympathetic writing, by George! and it was the old jar of chemicals brought it out!"

Such was the fact. One of the names, written near a corner of the paper, had partially escaped being wetted by the liquid in the jar, and that part which had escaped was invisible, while the rest presented the same pale reddish tinge as the others. In this, likewise, I saw the explanation of the existence of the jar in our family during so many years. Doubtless my old ancestor, John Simpson, when he wrote the names in sympathetic ink, had provided himself with the reagent to be used when needed; and the occasion not arising during his own life, it had passed down from one generation to another, until all remembrance of its original purpose had been lost; fortunately, however, it had not itself been so forgetful, but had sacrificed itself to duty precisely at the proper time.

This turn of affairs, though decidedly exciting, substantiated my friend Browne's story too completely to be altogether pleasant. Comparing his copy of the tombstone inscription with that in the manuscript, I found them word for word identical. I next bethought myself of the piece of paper which Browne had found with the ring. On examining it I discovered it to be neither more nor less than the original of Murray's letter to Browne, professing reconciliation! Really, things were becoming disagreeably clear.

Had it not been that I accidentally became aware, about this time, that I was nearly frozen to death, I should probably have remained pondering over my mysteries all day in the peculiarly simple attire appropriated to repose. I now commenced the operation of dressing, holding converse with my reflection in the mirror the while.

The result of my meditations was that I had better hunt up Browne, tell him all I had discovered, and consult with him on its significance and importance. The connection of the characters in the drama of a hundred years ago with those of today was fully established. The dreadful prayer for vengeance made by the dying Murray had evidently been granted—at the peril of his own soul, I could not doubt—but still granted. Only one mystery still awaited solution: why had the retribution come so late? why had it been reserved for my friend and the woman he loved to expiate the crimes of their long-buried ancestors?

Here the incident of the ring recurred to my mind. I remembered having idly speculated on the possibility of its being a talisman whereby the spirit of its owner might be enabled to persecute the wearer of it; and, looking at the matter in the new light I had obtained, it seemed not unfeasible. In his dying moments Murray had sent this ring, incrusted with the hate and passion of all the years of his blighted life, to the man who had ruined him. Doubtless he had believed that if he or any of his race were to accept and wear it, it would have power, if any thing could, to infuse into their hearts and souls some of the misery and poison which had been exhaled into it by his. Apparently it had been laid aside and forgotten until discovered by my friend; and Alice Hammill, the descendant of that family by the son mentioned as being absent in Europe, had received as a pledge of betrothal the greatest curse which it was possible to bring upon her. Acting upon her delicate and sensitive nature, the ring had distilled its morbid poison to the best advantage, paralyzing her with the ghastly shadow of the crime which had mouldered unavenged throughout a century. And Browne, by virtue of his love for her, had come in also for his share of the punishment so long deferred. Their souls had been united, and the same baleful influence that had poisoned her, had exercised its influence on him also. He had made her swear fealty to the giver of the ring; but was he the real giver? was it not rather the gift of the terrible phantom which had haunted them? and did not that oath give It the power to do so? For haunted beyond a doubt they were: whether by the actual semblance of a disembodied spirit, or by the fantasy of a diseased mind and imagination, made little difference: the effect was the same; and until we attain to a far more lucid theory for such mysteries than we possess at present, we must accept the old explanation as twice as simple and quite as probable as any other. But the question was now, what was to be the end?

I started out on my search for Browne immediately after breakfast. Not finding him at home, I thought it probable he would be at Miss Hammill's, and thither accordingly I betook myself. But he was not there: and the servant who answered the bell told me that Miss Alice had been growing gradually worse, and that the doctor gave slight hopes of her ever regaining her mind. I have often wondered since whether she still wore the ring.

So all day long I wandered over New York, searching for my friend; but night closed in, and still I had not found him. The following afternoon, however, I got upon his track, and followed him from one point to another till at last I traced him to the Hudson River dépôt. Just before I reached there the eight p.m. express had left, carrying him a passenger in the sleeping-car. I heard the whistle of the engine as it rushed away, carrying many a soul on a longer journey than they had ever before undertaken: all the world has heard of the disaster of New Hamburg! Living or dead, I never saw my friend again, nor was his body ever, so far as I know, recovered. Doubtless it was better so: he never could have found life sweet on earth again. But often, in the evenings, as I sit before my fire, I think of him and of the gray, crumbling tombstone in Trinity Church-yard, and marvel that life should seem so simple and commonplace.

1908

UNAWARES

Hildegarde Hawthorne

Hildegarde Hawthorne (1871–1952) was something of a rebellious child, attributed by some to the fact that she had no settled home, as her parents travelled so much—Germany, England, Jamaica—but it raised in her a spirit of freedom and of a wild world. "We all live in a fairy tale far more than in what we are pleased to call the real world," she wrote in an essay in 1905 and that sums up the enchantment she saw in everything. Her passion for nature and the outdoor life is evident in The Lure of the Garden *(1911) which traces the history of gardens and their social benefit. She earned a reputation as a poet, her love of words conjuring up images of beauty and enchantment.*

She also became known as a biographer and in all her studies of people she looked for that escapist spirit. Her biography of her grandfather, Nathaniel, was called Romantic Rebel *(1932), whilst the pioneer naturalist Henry David Thoreau she called* Concord's Happy Rebel *(1940). Escapism is the key to* Girls in Bookland *(1917) where two sisters are whisked away by a fairy friend into the world of different books.*

There is no doubt that Hildegarde was the product of creative grandparents and restless parents. When her first story, "A Legend of Sonora" (1891) was published, the Anglo-American Times *remarked that she "had the family inheritance". It was a very short ghost story, less than 700 words, yet* Harper's Monthly *paid $50, some seven cents a word, which would have impressed her father. Soon after she won a $100 prize for the best story about the World's Fair. Tucked away amongst her writings are a few other ghost stories, such as the following from 1908.*

"It's going to be a real, old-fashioned Christmas Eve, Selina," said her husband, looking out into the gray afternoon, fluttering with snowflakes. "It makes me think of the days when I used to drag you about in the little red sled with black horses painted on it—it's up in the garret now, Selina, isn't it? Well, well, that was a long while ago."

"A long while ago," answered the little white-haired lady, knitting by the wood fire. "A long while ago, Silas. The years between have been happy—and have been sad, too! But I'd willingly live them all over again, if it weren't for just one thing." And she gave a sigh, quickly followed by a smile as her husband turned towards her.

"Yes, dear?" he said, half inquiringly, half wistfully.

"If we'd had the little child, Silas. A child to cherish, to guide, to—Oh, Silas, a little one to play about us, to love us, to grow up and have a little one of its own, that should gleam about our old age as the sunlight flickers and glows about the old oaks at our door. What a Christmas Eve we should have, getting the pretty toys and candy, lighting the tree, seeing the big blue eyes dance with happiness, hearing the sweet voice crying joyfully, 'Grandpapa, grandmamma.'" She stopped, with a sudden movement of her hands to her throat. "Silas, *dearie*, don't mind me—" she turned away to hide the tears in her eyes.

But Silas understood, and sitting beside her drew her close, their white hairs mingling together, while the firelight shone in kindly wise on their sweet old faces, wrinkled and worn, perhaps, but expressing in every line their gentle natures.

"We have had much, dear," he whispered. "What a life, what a world would this have been for me without you—without you? Why, it is inconceivable!"

She laughed a tearful laugh and patted his hand.

"I couldn't realize life without you any more than I could realize not being born at all," she murmured.

For a while they sat silent, looking at the fire that danced and played on the hearth, even as the child they desired might have danced and played about the chamber.

"I knew I wanted too much for Earth," went on Selina, presently, "but I have longed, dear, yes, and wept. You never knew, I would not tell even you. I know it is wrong, when the Lord has given me such happiness, such peace. But I—oh, just to clasp it close, just once to make a Christmas for it. First it was our own little child, now it is our own little grandchild I want—I wanted."

"I knew, beloved wife. I knew. I too have not spoken, not told even you. I too have longed to see you as a mother—to bless our child."

They drew closer, with a sigh at once sad and happy. Selina looked up at last.

"I am content, dear," she said, "we have had much—more than many, than most. We are old—perhaps this is our last Christmas Eve. Give me a kiss, dear husband. The Lord knows best, and I am content."

They kissed each other, solemnly, smilingly.

"Isn't some one knocking?" replied Silas, going towards the door. Just as he reached it a decided knock made him throw it open, crying, "Come in, neighbor," in his hearty old voice, full of friendly welcome.

On the threshold, blown by the wind, powdered by the snow, stood a little girl, smiling out of big blue eyes, her cheeks rosy as the dawn, her hair yellow as the ripened wheat.

"Why, come in, darling," said the old man, drawing her inside and closing the door. "Whose little girl are you, out in such a stormy afternoon?"

The child shook off the snow laughingly, clasping one of his fingers in her little hand.

"Where's your mother?" asked Silas, and then—"Look here, Selina, here's a little girl come to see us."

The laughing child ran eagerly across the room, throwing herself into Selina's lap and putting up her rosy face for a kiss.

"Kiss me, G'anmamma," she cried, "kiss little Désirée."

Selina turned pale and clasped the little one close—close.

"Little Désirée," she whispered. "Little Désirée. But *I'm* not your grandmamma, dearie. Who are you? Where do you belong?"

The baby drew back, shaking her head and smiling.

"Is it *nearly* Ch'istmas?" she asked, eagerly. "Shall I soon have my sled and my dolly and my candies—dear g'anpapa, is it *nearly* Ch'istmas?"

Silas and Selina exchanged a look.

"She's not one of the neighbor's children, Silas," said the old lady, presently, her eyes following the child, that had now seated itself on the hearthrug, and was holding out its little hands to the blaze. "I never saw her before—it is very strange."

"Some one visiting over Christmas," replied Silas. "I will go around among the neighbors presently and inquire. But in the mean time let us make the little creature at home—she shall have a Christmas here, too, Selina. I will get the little sled out of the garret—" Silas's eyes lighted up, and he smiled eagerly at his wife—"and perhaps they will let us keep her a while—she came here so—" he stopped, and bending over the little head, kissed the clustering hair. "So like an angel," he ended.

"Dear g'anpapa," murmured the child, putting up a hand to stroke his cheek.

"Take off Désirée's coat," she added, struggling up.

Selina began slipping off her things. Such a pretty fur-trimmed coat, so white and warm and soft.

"You look like a transfigured snowflake yourself, pet," she said, as the child, freed from her outer garments, danced in the flickering shadows thrown by the leaping flames. Her dress was as white and soft as her coat, and she fluttered back and forth like a bird, too light and free to stay on the dull earth while such a medium of pure air existed to float or fly in.

"Ch'istmas is coming, Ch'istmas is coming," she chanted, and suddenly clambered to Selina's lap. "Tell me a story," she implored, snuggling down and laying her sweet face against Selina's gentle breast. "Tell me a story, g'anmamma."

Silas stood looking at the group a moment, and then, with a smile like the singing of birds in spring, sat down beside them.

"A story, precious? G'anmother hasn't told many stories to little girls, but perhaps—perhaps—" she paused, looking dreamily into the fire.

The child lay warm against her, its fair curls spread over her arm, its soft breathing perceptible to her ear, its clasping hands on her wrists. So holding it, her mind drifted back to the golden days of her young womanhood, her young wifehood. The dreams, the fancies, the hope—never alas, fulfilled—of that time transmuted themselves into words, and fell quietly, gently, on the listening ears of the two. As Selina sat there, talking out the long-hidden desire of her heart, her husband occasionally whispered a word of love. She seemed not to hear him. Her words came with a sort of rhythm, it was as though they moved to unheard music. All the pent-up mother love of her heart expressed itself nobly, exquisitely, self forgetting, earth forgetting, inspired by the heavenly regions of her soul. Finally she stopped, still looking at the fire, now fallen into a smouldering glow, still clasping the child to her heart. Then she bent and kissed her.

"Precious darling," she murmured, "mother's own dearest."

The child threw its little arms about her neck, in a quick, enchanting embrace. Then slipping to the floor—

"See, mamma, papa has a sled for me," she cried, clapping her hands. "A red sled for little Désirée."

Selina laughed gayly, and presently Silas joined in, and soon the three of them were shouting together, while the rafters of the unaccustomed room fairly quivered in sympathy.

"How young you look, dear Silas," observed his wife, smiling at him rather roguishly. "And why don't you bring little Désirée the pretty dolly we have for her, and the Christmas candies?"

"If I look young, you look beautiful, Selina," replied Silas, with his gentle smile—"Doesn't mother look beautiful?" he asked the baby, laughingly, catching her up in his arms. "Come, kiss papa for the red sled and the Christmas candies, that are hidden there in the cupboard all ready for our little Désirée."

And Désirée kissed him and kissed Selina, and crowed over the candy. Then Selina brought out a doll with rosy cheeks and golden hair, even like Désirée's own. And they threw fresh wood on the fire, and put apples to roast. And Désirée played on the hearthrug, while the couple sat hand in hand, smiling and watching her.

"Isn't she pretty?" said Selina. "See, she seems to throw a light of her own as she moves. Silas dear, how absurd we've been, thinking we were old and worn out. *You* old, beloved!" She laid her hand over his, gazing up at him. "I never saw you look so well before."

"Old, sweetheart? The child would be enough to keep us young, even without our immortal love to safeguard us."

Again the child, tired of play, climbed into Selina's lap. The light faded outdoors, the snow still fell, whitening all the land. Inside the room the long shadows drew together, but the fire still leaped about the huge logs, cheery as a laugh.

"You must go to bed soon, baby," said Selina. "Soon mother must tuck you in, to wake up and play with your red sled in the snow on Christmas Day."

"Let her stay with us a little longer, sweetheart," pleaded Silas. "Christmas Eve comes so seldom, and we are so happy, we three."

"So happy," murmured his wife, leaning towards him, gathering the sleeping child close. "So happy."

"Hold the horse a moment, Sally," said her lover, "and I'll just run in with the basket and wish Silas and Selina a Merry Christmas—dear old people." He vanished within the house, but the next moment came back again.

"Sally," he called, gravely, "come here—something has happened."

Before the cold hearth the old couple were sitting, hand in hand, their white heads close together, a tender smile on their faces.

For a little while Sally regarded them, the tears filling her eyes, then turning to her lover, she whispered, "It must have been a happy death. See, dear, how beautiful they look."

The Dickens Family

You might imagine that Charles Dickens, seen by many as England's greatest novelist, would be descended from some illustrious literary family. But no. In fact, it's not easy to trace his ancestors back much beyond his grandfather, William Dickens (1719–1785), who was a butler in the household of Cheshire MP John Crewe. Some records identify William's mother as having the wonderful name of Temperance Chisholm (1670–1735) which suggests that her parents were of Puritan stock, like the Hathornes. William Dickens's wife, Elizabeth (1745–1824), the housekeeper at Crewe Hall, was remembered by her children and grandchildren as an "inimitable storyteller", so she may be the source of Charles's literary gene.

Dickens's father, John (1785–1851), was a clerk in the navy pay office and was based at Portsmouth when Charles was born, the second of eight children. The Dickens family moved around several of the naval dockyards in his childhood including Chatham in Kent where he first became acquainted with neighbouring Rochester which features in several of his novels. Charles's childhood, though, was difficult, especially after his father was imprisoned for debt in 1824. He was only in prison for a few months but it was enough for young Charles to seek work to support himself since such money as the family had, had been invested in his sister Fanny who was training as a pianist. As Charles told his later biographer, John Forster, he found work in a boot-blacking factory run by his maternal uncle, but more recent research by Helena Kelly in *The Life & Lies of Charles Dickens* (2023) suggests that young Charles, still only twelve years old, did not do any blacking of boots, as he liked to suggest, but probably worked in the office doing paperwork and writing copy. If so, then this introduced him to writing for a living. He was always a voracious reader and also enjoyed the theatre and when his father embarked on a new career as a journalist, young Charles thought he could follow suit. He had worked briefly as a solicitor's clerk but now became a journalist and parliamentary reporter. By 1833 he had placed his first story "A Dinner at Poplar Walk"—"placed" rather than sold as the magazine in which it appeared offered no payment. But Charles's literary career had begun.

1850

A CHILD'S DREAM OF A STAR

Charles Dickens

Mention the name of Charles Dickens (1812–1870), and all manner of books and characters flood into our communal memories—Oliver Twist, Nicholas Nickleby, David Copperfield—and, inevitably, Ebenezer Scrooge. Scrooge is, need I remind anyone, the miserly curmudgeon in A Christmas Carol *(1843), the first of Dickens's Christmas stories which pretty much started the vogue of a ghost story at Christmas. But it wasn't Dickens's first ghost story. He had attracted the public's attention with a series of short stories and anecdotes which appeared under the alias Boz and which were collected as* Sketches by Boz *(1836). These included the macabre story "The Black Veil", but his first true weird tale was "The Story of the Goblins who Stole a Sexton", published as a standalone story in* The Posthumous Papers of the Pickwick Club *(1837), better known as* The Pickwick Papers. *Dickens would rework the basic theme of this story, where a miserable old gravedigger has a series of visions which change his character, as* A Christmas Carol. *It was* The Pickwick Papers *that made Dickens's name, and the series contains other ghost stories, including "The Bagman's Story", "The Ghosts of the Mail" and "The Lawyer and the Ghost".*

Dickens's fascination for ghost stories was instilled in him when he was only five years old. His nursemaid, Mary Weller, would tell him stories that left him terrified, but he would still plead for more. He retold some as "Nurse's Stories" in The Uncommercial Traveller *(1860), which included "Captain Murderer" and "The Rat That Could Speak". Dickens became closely associated with the ghost story. Amongst the twenty or so that he wrote is one of the best of all Victorian ghost stories, "The Signalman". It was one of a series of stories by various contributors under the heading "Mugby Junction" for the Christmas 1866 issue of Dickens's magazine* All the Year Round. *Also in that issue were ghost stories by Charles Allston Collins, who married Dickens's daughter Kate, and Amelia B. Edwards. Dickens encouraged others to write ghost stories including Mrs Gaskell, George Augustus Sala and Hesba Stretton.*

The following story, though, had a different origin and emphasizes Dickens's devotion to family. When Dickens was only two his younger brother Arthur died, aged only six months. Dickens may not have been too aware, but it left a mark on his parents. When Dickens was fifteen his sister Harriet died, just before her eighth birthday, and when he was 36, and at the height of his fame, his eldest sister Fanny died of consumption. Dickens was distraught, fearful that the disease might affect his own children. Fanny, the talented musician, had a disabled son, Harry, who was probably the model for Tiny Tim in A Christmas Carol. *He died just four months after his mother, aged only nine. As a way of channelling his grief Dickens wrote "A Child's Dream of a Star" for his new magazine* Household Words *in 1850. Just a year after that story was published, Dickens's daughter Dora died, not quite nine months old, and just two weeks after his father had died. For Dickens, the grief continued.*

There was once a child, and he strolled about a good deal, and thought of a number of things. He had a sister, who was a child too, and his constant companion. These two used to wonder all day long. They wondered at the beauty of the flowers; they wondered at the height and blueness of the sky; they wondered at the depth of the bright water; they wondered at the goodness and the power of GOD who made the lovely world.

They used to say to one another, sometimes, Supposing all the children upon earth were to die, would the flowers, and the water, and the sky, be sorry? They believed they would be sorry. For, said they, the buds are the children of the flowers, and the little playful streams that gambol down the hill-sides are the children of the water; and the smallest bright specks, playing at hide and seek in the sky all night, must surely be the children of the stars; and they would all be grieved to see their playmates, the children of men, no more.

There was one clear shining star that used to come out in the sky before the rest, near the church spire, above the graves. It was larger and more beautiful, they thought, than all the others, and every night they watched for it, standing hand in hand at a window. Whoever saw it first, cried out, "I see the star!" And often they cried out both together, knowing so well when it would rise, and where. So they grew to be such friends with it, that, before lying down in their beds, they always looked out once again, to bid it good night; and when they were turning round to sleep, they used to say, "God bless the star!"

But while she was still very young, oh very very young, the sister drooped, and came to be so weak that she could no longer stand in the window at night; and then the child looked sadly out by himself, and when he saw the star, turned round and said to the patient pale face on the bed, "I see the star!" and then a smile would come upon the face, and a little weak voice used to say, "God bless my brother and the star!"

And so the time came, all too soon! when the child looked out alone, and when there was no face on the bed; and when there was a little grave among the graves, not there before; and when the star made long rays down towards him, as he saw it through his tears.

Now, these rays were so bright, and they seemed to make such a shining way from earth to Heaven, that when the child went to his solitary bed, he dreamed about the star; and dreamed that, lying where he was, he saw a train of people taken up that sparkling road by angels. And the star, opening, showed him a great world of light, where many more such angels waited to receive them.

All these angels, who were waiting, turned their beaming eyes upon the people who were carried up into the star; and some came out from the long rows in which they stood, and fell upon the people's necks, and kissed them tenderly, and went away with them down avenues of light, and were so happy in their company, that lying in his bed he wept for joy.

But, there were many angels who did not go with them, and among them one he knew. The patient face that once had lain upon the bed was glorified and radiant, but his heart found out his sister among all the host.

His sister's angel lingered near the entrance of the star, and said to the leader among those who had brought the people thither:

"Is my brother come?"

And he said "No."

She was turning hopefully away, when the child stretched out his arms, and cried "O, sister, I am here! Take me!" and then she turned her beaming eyes upon him, and it was night; and the star was shining into the room, making long rays down towards him as he saw it through his tears.

From that hour forth, the child looked out upon the star as on the Home he was to go to, when his time should come; and he thought that he did not belong to the earth alone, but to the star too, because of his sister's angel gone before.

There was a baby born to be a brother to the child; and while he was so little that he never yet had spoken word, he stretched his tiny form out on his bed, and died.

Again the child dreamed of the opened star, and of the company of angels, and the train of people, and the rows of angels with their beaming eyes all turned upon those people's faces.

Said his sister's angel to the leader:

"Is my brother come?"

And he said "Not that one, but another."

As the child beheld his brother's angel in her arms, he cried, "O, sister, I am here! Take me!" And she turned and smiled upon him, and the star was shining.

He grew to be a young man, and was busy at his books, when an old servant came to him, and said:

"Thy mother is no more. I bring her blessing on her darling son!"

Again at night he saw the star, and all that former company. Said his sister's angel to the leader:

"Is my brother come?"

And he said, "Thy mother!"

A mighty cry of joy went forth through all the star, because the mother was reunited to her two children. And he stretched out his arms and cried, "O, mother, sister, and brother, I am here! Take me!" And they answered him "Not yet," and the star was shining.

He grew to be a man, whose hair was turning grey, and he was sitting in his chair by the fireside, heavy with grief, and with his face bedewed with tears, when the star opened once again.

Said his sister's angel to the leader, "Is my brother come?"

And he said, "Nay, but his maiden daughter."

And the man who had been the child saw his daughter, newly lost to him, a celestial creature among those three, and he said "My daughter's head is on my sister's bosom, and her arm is round my mother's neck, and at her feet there is the baby of old time, and I can bear the parting from her, GOD be praised!"

And the star was shining.

Thus the child came to be an old man, and his once smooth face was wrinkled, and his steps were slow and feeble, and his back was bent. And one night as he lay upon his bed, his children standing round, he cried, as he had cried so long ago:

"I see the star!"

They whispered one another "He is dying."

And he said, "I am. My age is falling from me like a garment, and I move towards the star as a child. And O, my Father, now I thank thee that it has so often opened, to receive those dear ones who await me!"

And the star was shining; and it shines upon his grave.

1896

MY FELLOW TRAVELLERS

Mary Angela Dickens

As with Julian Hawthorne trying to establish himself in the wake of his father, it seemed impossible for any of Dickens's children to follow a literary career. They established themselves in other ways. Kate (1839–1929), who had married Charles Collins, became better known after her second marriage as the artist Kate Perugini. Henry (1849–1933) became a barrister and a judge and was knighted in 1922. Several left England completely. Walter (1841–1863) joined the army and went to India in 1857 where he died a few years later. Francis (1844–1886) also went to India just after his brother died and joined the Bengal Mounted Police. He later went to Canada and joined the Mounties. Alfred (1845–1912) emigrated to Australia where he was followed soon after by the youngest child Edward (1852–1902). Sydney (1847–1872) joined the navy and died at sea. That leaves the two eldest children who stayed at home, Charles Jr (1837–1896), usually called Charley, and Mary (1838–1896), known as Mamie. Mamie never married and stayed with her father about whom she wrote several reminiscences.

Charley was the one who wanted to be a writer, but his father urged him to train for business. He had a good education, including attending Eton. He entered banking, then thought he might become a tea merchant. In 1861 he married Elisabeth Evans, daughter of Frederick Evans, the partner in Bradbury & Evans who had published Dickens's Household Words. *Charley became a paper manufacturer and printer but that failed and he was declared bankrupt. Dickens took him under his wing as sub-editor of* All the

Year Round, *and he continued as publisher after his father's death until the magazine ceased in March 1895. Charles, Jr, died the following year, virtually penniless, leaving his widow and children in straitened circumstances.*

The literary gene had skipped a generation. Charles and Elisabeth's eldest child, Mary Angela Dickens (1862–1948), became a noted sensationalist novelist much in the vein of Wilkie Collins. Together with her sister, Ethel, who earned a living as a "typewriter girl", typing up manuscripts for such authors as J. M. Barrie and George Bernard Shaw, Mary succeeded in pulling the family out of the financial mire in which their father had left them. Her work includes the sinister Prisoners of Silence *(1895) where a family is riddled by secrets and* Against the Tide *(1897) which continues her grandfather's obsession with illness and disease. On occasion she turned to the weird tale.*

The room was the sitting-room of a ladies' residential-flat. There were two people in it—a woman and a girl—ensconced in easy chairs, one on either side of the fire. The woman was the owner of the flat, and the girl had come up with her from the general dining-room after dinner, for coffee and conversation. Coffee was over, and upon the conversation one of those silences had fallen sometimes created by known and accepted differences of opinion. The girl was leaning forward, gazing into the fire. She had straight features, redeemed from insignificance by the keen intelligence of their expression; but this intelligence, in its turn, was rendered almost repellant by the exceeding hardness of its practicality. She looked pale and tired, as a girl clerk is wont to do in the evening.

The woman also looked weary, as though she, too, had done a hard day's work. But in everything else the two countenances were sharply contrasted. The woman's was a strong face, and one that five-and-forty years of life might easily have rendered grim, but its dominant characteristic was a steady gentleness. The irregular features spoke not merely to intelligence, but to shrewd, well-developed brain power. She was leaning back in her chair, looking absently before her, when the girl spoke suddenly.

"Miss Lanyon," she said, "I don't understand you. You are so clever! You ought to be a materialist pure and simple. Your books are splendidly up to date in some ways, and yet there is always that sad, old-fashioned, semi-Christian crank in them."

Apparently Miss Lanyon knew of something less offensive beneath the aggressive opinionativeness of the girlish personality, for she answered with an odd little smile. Her voice was brisk, and her utterance quick and decided.

"It's a great affliction to find oneself old-fashioned in these days," she said. "It is very kind of you not to despise me wholesale, Frances. As to materialism—well, I thought with you once upon a time. Ten years ago I fancy I should have satisfied you, altogether; and very little you would have liked me, if you did but know it."

The girl answered with a quick exclamation.

"You have been a materialist, then!" she exclaimed. "And you gave up certainty for all these vague theories? Well, I must say that astonishes me!"

"I am glad to hear that you are capable of astonishment," was the quick, quaintly-uttered rejoinder. Then Miss Lanyon paused. She glanced at her companion's face, and spoke impulsively.

"I don't imagine it will make the slightest impression on you," she said. "Second-hand experiences are never of the faintest use. But I will tell you of something that happened to me ten years ago. Mind, I don't say that my present opinions, whatever they may be, are the direct outcome of that experience. Never mind, now, how opinions develop; you'll know some day. It simply showed me that materialism, at any rate, wouldn't do—that there was a vast tract of country which it failed to take into account. Would you like to hear about it?"

Hardly waiting for the girl's quick assent, leaning back in her chair with something about her whole figure, even in the uncertain light of the shaded lamp, a trifle tense, Miss Lanyon began to speak again.

"Ten years ago," she said, "I had not taken to writing books, and was a mistress in the High School at Norwich. I am not an imaginative woman, and in those days I held all the views most eminently qualified to stultifying such a quality. A woman devoid of any spiritual sense, without faith, and without romance, is very seldom a pleasant creature. I was a conspicuously unpleasant specimen of the type, I imagine—that is to say, I was as hard and self-satisfied as the most advanced woman need wish to be.

"It was the middle of the Christmas term. I had come up to town, on a Saturday afternoon, on business, and was returning to Norwich on Sunday evening. My train was to leave Liverpool Street at 6.15, and my brother, at whose house I had been staying, considered it his duty to go with me to the station.

"We had no time to spare when we reached Liverpool Street. I had a return ticket, and only a handbag by way of luggage, and we went straight through to the platform. I was travelling first-class—a favourite extravagance of mine in those days—and we walked up the train to look for a carriage. As it was Sunday night, few people were travelling; but, on the other hand, few first-class compartments were provided. We looked into several, only to find that my favourite corners facing the engine were occupied, until we had almost reached the top of the train. The third carriage for the engine was a first, but I had noticed two or three people, after glancing into it, hesitate, and then pass on down the train. Consequently, I was not surprised to see my brother, who was a few steps in front of me, pass it also, almost without looking in. I was very much surprised, however, when I passed it myself, to see that it was absolutely empty. I stopped, and called to my brother.

"'Where are your eyes, Edward?' I said. 'This carriage is just the thing. It's empty.'

"He turned back with a kind of vague dissatisfaction on his face.

"'Is it?' he said. 'Oh, I suppose it's all right then.'

"I had opened the door by that time, and, as he still hesitated, I got in. I did not take the corner nearest the door by which I had entered, as one naturally does, but I went instinctively, and without thinking about it, to the other end. I put down my book and umbrella on the seat there, and then my brother got in with my bag. He made no comment on my choice of a seat, and got out again rather quickly.

"'Awfully stuffy carriage,' he said.

"A scathing reply was on the tip of my tongue, when I became aware of the approach of a porter with foot-warmers, and directed his attention to him.

"'Put one in here,' I said. 'The further end.'

"The man did so. He paused a moment, and then put another tin into the carriage, close to the open door.

"'I suppose he thinks that you are going, too.' I remarked to Edward, as the man moved away.

"He answered rather absently.

"'Yes, I suppose so,' he said. 'Are you quite sure—'

"The ringing of the bell interrupted him, and in another moment the train was moving slowly out of the station. I arranged my possessions to my liking, tucked myself in my rug, and took up the book with which I intended to beguile the time, looking forward to a truly pleasant journey.

"My book was one in which I had expected to be considerably interested, and I was rather annoyed when it gradually dawned upon me that it was not absorbing my attention in the least. I hardly seemed to take in, or to care to take in, what I read, and a feeling of vague dissatisfaction, utterly objectless and unreasonable, was stealing in and poisoning my contentment. Certainly, the weather was disagreeable. The wind was rising as we got out into the country, and it howled and shrieked about the train as it pursued its rapid way.

But I am not usually affected by such influences, and it surprised me considerably to think that the contrast between the clamour outside and the dead stillness within the carriage should have the power to distract me. I found myself growing actually restless at last, and I thought it was time to concentrate my attention forcibly on my book. I made myself thoroughly comfortable, turning away from the empty carriage towards the window by which I was sitting, and propping one elbow on the ledge.

"I suppose I made myself too comfortable, for I went to sleep. I woke suddenly, opening my eyes with a full consciousness of my surroundings, and, as I did so, I was amazed to think that I must have slept for some time. I was in exactly the same position as that in which I had settled myself to read, and my eyes had opened directly upon the window. The train was evidently passing through some kind of cutting, and in the window the other end of the compartment was distinctly reflected. It was that which the reflection showed me that made me realize how heavily I must have been sleeping, for it witnessed to the fact that we must have stopped, unknown to me, at a station. The carriage, as pictured in the window, was no longer occupied only by myself. In the corner seats, on either side of the other door, were reflected the figures of a man and a woman.

"I did not turn round, partly through that curious notion of courtesy which dictates the ignoring of one's fellow-travellers, partly because there was something rather interesting about the appearance of these particular people, and I was idly pleased to be able to study them by means of their reflections, without being guilty of actually staring at them.

"The corner seat obliquely facing me was occupied by the man. He was reading the newspaper, and only his forehead and the outline of his head were visible to me. He had taken off his hat, and his hair appeared to be fair and crisply curling. His figure was well made, and his pose spoke to self-possession and determination. There was, indeed, something almost excessively determined in the touch with which his hand held his paper. He was a gentleman, evidently, well appointed in every particular.

"It is difficult to account for the impression conveyed by appearance only—especially by an appearance seen mostly as a reflection—but it was equally obvious to me that his companion belonged to a somewhat lower social grade. She was a girl of about nineteen, very tenderly and prettily made. The profile was charming; the small, delicately-cut features were full of expression. But there was a strained, painfully anxious look about them now, as she leaned forward, apparently talking eagerly to the man, and I found myself regretting that the noise of the train, and the shrieking of the wind—which had increased extraordinarily—should prevent my catching even the faintest sound of her voice. Arguing from something unusually dainty about her attire, from something essentially un-English about her face, and from the rapid and plentiful gestures with which she emphasized her speech, I settled in my own mind that she was French.

"I was watching her with a sense of growing fascination, when the conditions outside suddenly changed. The window ceased to act as a reflector. In place of the picture at which I had been looking the lights of a station flashed, and the train came to a standstill.

"The carriage had grown bitterly cold, and at the same time there was something curiously oppressive about the atmosphere. The door on my side opened on to the platform and I sprang up—still without looking round—and let down the window with an irresistible impulse. I accounted to myself for the haste with which I had moved by looking eagerly for a porter with fresh foot-warmers. No such person was visible, but nevertheless, I did not draw in my head again. The groups of people moving to and fro had a singular attraction for me, and I stood there, at the window, in spite of the cold—which affected me less now that the window was open than it had done when it was shut—until the train began to move again. I sat down in my corner, pulled up the window, and then turned, for the first time since I had become aware of their presence, towards my fellow-travellers.

"The corner seats were vacant! They were no longer there!

"My first feeling, as I realized I was alone, was one of blank unreasoning astonishment. It is by no means usual for a train so to run into a station that passengers can get out from either side of a carriage. Moreover, not the slightest sound of their departure had reached my ears as I stood at the window. My astonishment subsided, however. I accepted the practical explanation of the matter which alone presented itself to me, and proceeded to compose myself once more to the enjoyment of my solitude.

"But, for the first time in my life, solitude failed to make itself congenial to me. The brief interval of companionship—as conveyed by the contemplation of the reflection of my fellow-travellers—had apparently demoralized me. A singular realization of the isolation of my position, shut in there alone, and moving rapidly through the darkness, presented itself to me. The personality of those same fellow-travellers, also, had impressed me altogether unduly. It was not only that I could not forget them; I found myself dwelling on them. The girl's face came between me and the book I was reading; the man's callous indifference to her evident pleading oppressed me strangely. Vague sentences, the sense of which invariably eluded me as I tried to grasp them, kept floating through my mind, and I knew that I was trying to construct the drift of her words—those words of which I had not caught the faintest murmur. So completely possessed was I with the thought of the two that it did not strike me as being strange, when I gradually became aware of that singular feeling which everyone has experienced—the feeling that I was not alone. But I was distinctly surprised when I realized that the feeling was becoming curiously distasteful to me.

"It was absolutely still in the carriage, and, after the cheery bustle of the station, the quiet jarred on me. The beat and rumble of the train seemed to come from a long way off, shutting in the island of dead silence, of which I was the centre. I lifted my eyes from my book, on which they had been mechanically fixed, and looked about me. The dim lamp cast the usual depressing light over the usual accessories of a first-class carriage. Opposite me were the three empty places, divided by the regulation cushioned arms. On the side on which I sat were two more empty places. Between the two seats at the other end lay the unused foot-warmer. It chimed in too aptly with my weird sense of unseen fellow-travellers, and pinching myself slightly, I turned with a sharp movement of self-contempt, to look out of the window at my side.

"I looked once more, not out into a dimly discerned landscape, but into a clear-cut reflection of the carriage in which I sat. And there, reflected back with ghastly distinctness—reflected back as sitting in those seats which I had seen the instant before to be empty—were my fellow-travellers."

Miss Lanyon paused. She was looking straight before her, her hands clenched tightly round the arms of her chair. Every trace of colour had died out of her strong face, and she went on in a slow, harsh voice.

"You think you know what it is to be cold, Frances," she said. "You don't. You had better pray that you never may! It is to feel yourself gradually losing all human sensation; to feel that where there should be glowing, moving blood there is motionless ice; to feel that the very atmosphere about you is not the atmosphere of every day, warm with the breath of your fellow creatures, but something rarefied until its chill is agony. It comes about slowly—very, very slowly. First, your heart ceases to beat—dies, and grows cold within you. Then the same cold spreads, little by little, until your every limb is frozen, and you can neither move nor breathe. I have felt cold only once in my life. I felt it then. I sat in my place, spellbound, gazing at the reflection of that which I knew possessed no actual form, and the train swayed and jarred on its rushing way through the night.

"The position of the two figures had altered slightly. The man had laid down his paper, and his face was fully visible to me. It was the handsome face of a man of about thirty-five, blasé and sensual in expression, and with a suggestion of cruelty about its lines. All its worst points were evidently accentuated at the moment. The brows were heavily contracted, and the mouth was very hard. The wind had dropped, suddenly. The throbbing beat of the train went on, rapid, monotonous, unceasing. There was absolute silence in the carriage. No external sounds came between my sense of hearing and the sound of a voice. But, though I saw that he was speaking, I heard nothing.

"He was speaking sharply and decisively—that I saw. The girl was listening to him, her eyes fixed on his face, one hand pressed against her heart. It was her left hand, and ungloved, and I saw that it was ringless. Almost before he stopped she had broken again into speech. She was evidently dissenting from what he had said, trembling from head to foot with the vehemence of her emotion. Demonstrating, denying, pleading, the quivering passion threatening every moment to break through the difficult restraint of her expression, she lifted one small hand with a tremulous gesture, and, pushing the hair from her forehead, looked feverishly round the carriage. Her face was turned towards me, and I saw her eyes. Deep and dark, half wild, and desperate. I met them full, reflected in the glass, and in the same instant my own natural life, frozen and dead within me, seemed to be replaced by another. A burning, craving desire swelled up in me. I was shaken from head to foot by such an intensity of emotion as I had never known—as was utterly foreign to my temperament. And as I sat there, conscious with a ghastly double consciousness of my own rigid, spellbound figure I knew that my agony of mind belonged not to me, but to her—to the girl reflected in the glass before me.

"She paused at last in her rapid speech, and such a sick hunger of hope and fear rose in my heart as almost choked me, while she waited, leaning rather forward, for his answer. There was a moment's pause. The wind shrieked and wailed, and my eyes burned in their sockets as I strained them upon the window. Then, without a word, the man took up his newspaper again.

"On the instant the girl started to her feet, tearing the newspaper from his hands, and facing him, her slender figure tense with fury. A passionate sense of intolerable wrong, of treachery and deceit, culminating in unendurable cruelty, was burning her brain to fire, and I watched, my very life seeming to beat in her frenzied, impulsive movements. Speaking wildly, almost incoherently, she lifted her hands to the throat of her dress, and drew out a little bit of ribbon, on which was strung a ring—a wedding ring. She dragged it off, snapping the ribbon like cotton, and thrust the ring into its place on her finger, stretching out her left hand—the hand now of a wife—to him, as she did so, with a gesture which was superb in its agony and appeal. He did not move or speak; he was watching her with a heavy, lowering face; and as I looked from her to him I thought that if I had been free to talk or feel I should have felt a shock of fear.

"Then, as suddenly as it had risen, her form died away. Before I realized the change, she had fallen on her knees on the carriage floor, catching his hand in hers in such utter self-abandonment as I had never before conceived. I had heard of supplication, but I had never known what it meant until I shared the prayer which that unhappy girl raised to the man at whose feet she knelt.

"It was only for a moment. He drew his hand deliberately away, and, looking down into her upturned face, spoke one short sentence. For a moment the reflected figure of the girl knelt on there, motionless. Then she rose. She stood for an instant in silence, and then began to speak, slowly. He had driven her beyond the limits of endurance to defiance. She told him what she intended to do. I don't know what it was—I have never known—but I felt her meaning, then, as clearly as though I had heard her words. She drew from the bosom of her dress papers which she showed him as ocular demonstration of her intention, replacing them quietly. As she spoke I saw his face change. I saw the lines about his mouth contract. His hand moved rapidly to his breast pocket, the bright steel of a revolver flashed in the lamplight, and as I shrieked out in insane warning, the blackness of night passed across the reflection and I saw no more.

"The wind moaned, the throbbing beat of the train went on and on, and I sat there paralysed, staring straight before me, with burning, starting eyes. The darkness into which they looked was awful to me— the darkness which bid horror unspeakable. But the dimly-lighted carriage, on the other hand, was infinitely more awful. I dared not look round. The fearful conviction with which I was penetrated, that if I did so I should see nothing, was even more hideous to me than the ghastly companionship of which I was dimly conscious. The wild emotion of the past few moments had died out utterly. No feeling but one of sick, intolerable horror was alive in me as I waited, never turning my eyes, for what I knew would come.

"Many lifetimes of frozen suspense seemed to elapse, and then, suddenly, and without any warning—as the necessary external conditions recurred—the reflection was visible again.

"I had known what I should see. I had thought that I was numbed to any further sense of horror. But as my eyes rested on the dreadful stillness of that girlish figure, huddled limply on the seat—beside me, as it were—I knew that I had been mistaken. At first I saw that figure only. My head was growing giddy, and I was on the verge of losing consciousness, when a stealthy movement in the reflection shocked me back to life. The man, who had been withdrawn out of range of the reflector, came back into the picture.

"He was white to the lips, and the evil determination of his face was hideous to see. I felt myself shrink and cower in my corner as though I were trying to hide from his wicked eyes. He stood still, and drew out his watch. Stepping with a care intolerable in its ghastly significance, he passed the motionless body, and going to the window, let it down and looked out. Then he pulled it up again, and began to move about with quick, decisive movements. He took down his Gladstone from the rack, and unstrapped a second rug. Without an instant's pause, he lifted the heavy, inanimate form, and placed it carefully in the corner. With the same rapid, callous movements, he drew from the dead girl's dress the papers with which she had threatened him. One rug he arranged about her so as to give the impression of a sleeping figure; the other he flung on the floor at her feet, where it looked as though it had slipped from her knees. He put on his hat, and took his bag in his hand.

"By this time I knew that we were slackening speed, slackening it slowly, and with the deliberation incidental to arrival at a large station.

I felt that in a moment more the reflection must cease. We were going slower and slower. I saw the man put his hand on the handle of the door, turn it, and stand waiting. I saw him jump out, and then—the lights of a station once more, and the train at a standstill.

"I was released. I knew nothing else. An insane desire to see that cruel deed avenged, to bring down justice on the doer, literally possessed me. I rushed across the carriage, flung open the door, and clutching at the first person I saw, entreated him wildly to stop the murderer, to fetch a doctor, not to let him go. I was vaguely aware of a circle of bewildered faces about me. I heard my voice rise to a hoarse cry, and then I fainted."

Miss Lanyon's voice ceased abruptly, and there was an interval of dead silence. She had spoken in a low, vibrating voice, the very intense restraint of which witnessed, as no words could have done, to the strength of her feelings. Her breath was coming thick and short. The girl who had listened to her was very still; her fingers were clenched tightly together in her lap, and she was rather pale. It was Miss Lanyon who spoke first.

"That's all," she said. "Don't take the trouble to comment, Frances. I know all the stock observations as to optical delusions, overstrung nerves, and dreams. Only I myself can realize the awful reality of that ghastly experience. I don't expect to convey it to anyone else."

"Did you ever find out—did you ever hear of any reason?" The girl's voice was low and awestruck. The manner with which Miss Lanyon had told her story had affected even her self-assured practicality.

There was a moment's pause, and then Miss Lanyon said, hoarsely:

"I found out, with infinite difficulty, that the dead body of a girl, shot through the heart, had been taken out of the train which reached Norwich at that same time in the evening, on the same day of the same month two years before. I heard that no clue to her identity had ever been discovered, and that her murderer had never been traced. And I heard that she had been found in the carriage occupying the same position on the train as that in which I had travelled from London—the third from the engine."

A low, inarticulate exclamation broke from the girl, and then she was silent again. She was evidently making a valiant stand against the impression made on her, when she said, with rather uncertain assurance:

"It's a most curious story, Miss Lanyon, and I'm immensely grateful to you for telling it me. All the same. I don't see—"

Miss Lanyon interrupted her brusquely.

"No," she said. "But I did see. That is just the difference."

1965

TO REACH THE SEA

Monica Dickens

The more prodigious literary gene, and for that matter the acting gene, was passed down through Dickens's barrister son, Henry Fielding Dickens. Charles Dickens loved the theatre and performing perhaps more than he loved writing. Through Henry's children Enid and Gerald, Charles became the great-grandfather and great-great-grandfather of at least four actors, as well as the great-great grandfather of the author Lucinda Hawksley.

But it is through Henry's second child and eldest son, Henry Charles Dickens (1878–1966), who had followed in his father's footsteps as a barrister, that we can trace the supernatural bloodline. Monica Dickens (1915–1992) was the second of Henry's five children, and was thus the great-granddaughter of Charles Dickens. She seems to have inherited so much of his spirit: a love of the theatre (in her case, ballet); a compassion for her fellow humans (she was an early supporter of the Samaritans and opened the first branch in the United States); as well as a love of animals—she was a supporter of the RSPCA and had a particular passion for horses, which feature in many of her books. Having failed at drama school and as a society debutante, Monica decided to enter domestic service, working as a cook and servant, which inspired her first book One Pair of Hands *(1939), whilst during the War she worked as a nurse, recounted in* One Pair of Feet *(1942). Her first novel,* Mariana *(1940) is set during the War and focuses on a lonely woman's struggle for survival. Most of Monica's novels were best sellers and her children's books endeared her to generations of young readers.*

Amongst them is the series which began with The Messenger *(1985) where a young girl is befriended by a magical horse that can take her through time and space to help innocent and deprived people. The series continued with* Ballad of Favour *(1985),* Cry of a Seagull *(1986) and* The Haunting of Bellamy 4 *(1986).*

Monica wrote the occasional ghost story including an update of her forebear's famous story as "A Modern Christmas Carol" (1975), and the following haunting tale.

It cost $250. When Jane Barlow took courage to question the price, M. Marmaduc, who had made it, said, "I am an artist, Madame, a very sensitive man. Is Madam trying to say it is not worth it?"

And it was worth it. She wore the wig that evening—blue-black, shining, superb. The party was a little depressing, so when someone said, "I've been admiring your hair all evening," she took off the wig, for a joke, and things were gayer. Then she put it on again and presently asked her husband to take her home, because the gaiety had evaporated.

She loved the wig. It sat on a stand like Marie Antoinette's severed head, and when she wore it she saw women look at her as she came into a room, and she could see them wondering: Is it or isn't it? Either way they were envious.

Before long, however, the wig began to worry her. It didn't look right any more; there was too much of it, and her face looked small. She took it back to M. Marmaduc and told him, "I think it needs redressing. There's something wrong with it."

"I am an artist, Madame—there can be nothing wrong." But when she called for it a week later, he admitted, "I think it is a finished creation, but there was a little too much hair. I have take a soupçon off here, a flick off here—it is now perfect."

Jane wore it that night, and it was perfect. "Like living hair," John said. John was not her husband, but the man she wished she had met first. "It pales and narrows your face to a kind of tragic beauty."

Jane laughed, because they must never look as if they were talking seriously in corners; but she did feel a little tragic. They had agreed to be gay and sophisticated about their situation, but tonight it seemed to be closing in on her. Her husband looked at her admiringly across the room, but she felt afraid.

Jane came home after a month's holiday, not caring that her hair was a wreck from the sun and sea, because the wig was waiting. But the very first time she wore it, it seemed wrong again. She set it in pin curls on the severed head, left it for a week, then tried it on late at night after her husband was asleep. She sat in front of her dressing table, staring with dark strange eyes at the white face dwarfed by the glorious mass of black hair.

There was no doubt about it, absolutely no doubt at all. *The wig was growing.*

She snatched it off and put it quickly back on the dummy head in the box. It was her imagination. It must be. She left it on the shelf for three weeks; then one night, with a beating heart, she put it on again.

I am going mad, she thought. In a panic, she took scissors and hacked at the hair, gathering up the fallen bits in newspaper and running down to burn them in the furnace.

The wig was unwearable now, lopsidedly chopped. She wept, the uncontrollable sobs shaking her long after she had stuffed the box back on the shelf and gone brokenly to bed.

"Why do you never wear that expensive wig?" her husband asked, and John said, irked by her moodiness when they met in the discreetly shadowed bar, "Don't let yourself go, Janey. Put on that gorgeous wig again, and sparkle."

She went to another hairdresser, not M. Marmaduc, and had her hair deepened in colour and teased into a huge frame for her nervous white face, and asked her husband, "How does the wig look?" For no one must ever know she could not wear it.

She would not look at it. Every time she opened the closet, her eyes flew to the tall box on the shelf. Her hands went up, impulsively, but she forced them down.

She waited another two months. When her husband was away, she took down the box and opened it.

It was not a shock. It was with a sigh of submissive recognition that she saw that the hair had grown at least two inches—uneven, ragged at the ends, but well below her ears when she put the wig on.

She went out and walked about the streets for half the night, not knowing where she went, knowing only that she was looking for something she would never find.

Many nights in the following months, when her husband was asleep, she would put on the growing wig and slip out of the house to wander through the streets, across the bridges, along the river wall, the long unkempt black hair shrouding her back and shoulders and half veiling her face.

They found her in the river, one cold dawn, her own hair strung like seaweed across her dead face. A boy digging for bait found the wig caught under a jetty, its long hair floating out in the murky water to try to reach the sea...

"It will cost Madame two hundred and fifty dollars."

"All right," said the customer. "But where does the hair come from?"

"Northern Italy. I used to get beautiful black hair from Sicily, but I will not buy from that salesman any more. He told me, Madame, about a girl—the young bride of a rich old man. When the old man found her with her lover, he knifed the boy and threw the body from a boat into the sea. Then he cut off all his wife's long black hair, the way they did in the war, for fraternizing.

"The young bride walked out into the sea, crazy with sorrow, looking for her lover. The salesman bought the hair. What a pig. How could I buy any more from such a brute? I am an artist, Madame, a very sensitive man."

1972

THE SECRET ONES

Mary Danby

Monica Dickens had an elder sister, Doris (1915–1998) who likewise had gone into domestic service. In 1934 Doris married Denys Danby, a veterinary surgeon and Mary (b. 1941) was their second child, and thus Charles Dickens's great-great-granddaughter. Her own novels began with A Single Girl *(1972) where a young girl faces a future after her fiancé is killed in Vietnam. She worked as an editor at Fontana Books taking over their* Fontana Book of Great Horror Stories *from the Fifth Volume (1970) and editing it through to the Seventeenth in 1984. She also continued the* Armada Ghost Book, *aimed at younger readers, from the Third Volume (1970) to the Fifteenth (1983) and edited several other anthologies including three volumes of the* Nightmares *series (1983–5) and two volumes of* Frighteners *(1974–6). She contributed stories of her own to most of these volumes, sufficient that Johnny Mains was able to compile a collection of her work as* Party Pieces *(2012). Mary moved on from writing books and stories to creating games. These included a series of* Famous Five Adventure Game Books, *based on the books by Enid Blyton, plus several board and card games including* Screamin' Genie, Telepathy *and, not surprisingly,* The Dickens Game.*

The following story has echoes of one of Dickens's Nurse's Stories.

The husband, the wife and the wife's sister arrived by boat one fear-grey dawn. Nobody saw them as they sidled down the gangplank and hurried nervously to the shelter of a deserted warehouse. They had been many days without food, hidden and afraid in the lurching hold, huddling for warmth in the relentless dark. And as the sun rose behind the cranes and girders of the quayside, they blinked uncertainly and trembled in the unaccustomed chill of an east wind that sought out their hiding place with no mercy.

Towards the perimeter of the dockyard they could see a large rubbish tip, a pile of jagged, glinting metal stuck fast in a foundation of broken crates and rotting food. A haunt of things that slid and crawled. The foraging ground for scavengers.

When the wife's sister complained of hunger, the husband went bravely forth, as was his duty, to search for food. But he had not been long gone when there was a sound of heavy boots outside the warehouse. The wife's sister froze, her eyes and ears alert to danger, while the wife curled up in despair on a heap of old sacks in the corner and made quiet crying noises. But the boots moved on, and soon the husband was back with a blackened cabbage and a large hunk of mousy bread. The three of them fell ravenously on these trophies, though the husband was watchful for the wife, even allowing her the greater part of his own share in his anxiety that she should not go short. Then, their hunger pains blunted by the feast, they slept, burrowing under the sacks to protect themselves from discovery by intruders.

When night came, they continued their travels, leaving the dockyard as silently as they had entered it. Not knowing which road to take, they crossed the countryside by field and farm, yard and garden, until they could no longer smell the rich sea-salt in the air. Now they found themselves surrounded on all sides by tall buildings, rows and rows of them, staring down in disapproval at their illicit presence. Everywhere they went, they were turned away. Sometimes it was a dog, barking his hostility from the prison bars of a garden gate, and as night fell away to day, people hustled them from their doorsteps with cries of "Dirty beggars!" and "Stinking rats!"

The husband, the wife and the wife's sister had not expected this. They were the last members of a vast family to make the journey and were disheartened to find the land of their dreams to be one of hate, not plenty. Indeed, if it had not been for a distant cousin, who met them by chance as they turned sadly seawards, they might have left the shores for good. As it was, the cousin knew a place where they could stay, and they followed him to a row of large, terraced houses in the centre of the town, where he showed them a broken window and the steps to a high attic. Here, beneath dusty beams, they found many others of their kind, the secret ones, hiding from the light and plotting the day when they could descend into the town and claim their ancient rights.

For a while, the husband, the wife and the wife's sister made their home in this heaving ghetto, venturing out only after sunset and returning in fear lest they should find their places on the grey floorboards taken by others. On one such night, the wife's sister arrived back to discover a heap of dirty bedding in her corner and began a fight with her neighbour. They clawed at each other in the darkness, shrieking and cursing, until the husband saw fit to step between them and restore brittle calm. That night the wife again made her crying noises and the husband was moved to seek for them a better way of life.

He found it the next morning, when the other occupants of the attic were slumbering away the daylight hours. At the foot of the wall separating them from the next house there was a loose brick, and by noon the husband had made a hole large enough for his family to slip through. There was no sound as they made their escape, and the partition was replaced so efficiently that no clues to their route of departure could encourage others to come after them.

The husband, the wife and the wife's sister looked with satisfaction upon their new dwelling-place. There was a window in the rafters through which the sun sent dusty beams to fade the unwanted rugs and chaircovers. Old portraits stared with lashless eyes across the trunks and cases which lay in hills of abandon like fallen monuments. The wife's sister ran blithely to a fly-blown mirror and postured in solitary glee, while the wife pressed close to the husband and breathed her silent gratitude.

Then voices came, and they huddled in the darkest place behind a tall wardrobe, not understanding the language, yet feeling that communion of terror known only to the oppressed, the ones whose safety lies in the shadows. But there was no menace in the voices, and though they came frighteningly close and brought footsteps that shook the boards and echoed among the rafters, they went away without causing harm. When the voices had gone, the husband looked out to see a large doll's house standing in the centre of the attic.

It wasn't new. They could see that. The brick-red paper was peeling around the window and the chimney swayed inanely over the roof. But it was new to the three, and they were lost in admiration for several round-eyed minutes, exclaiming over the tiny doors and the small people who lived within. But the husband was aware of something more serious nagging for his attention. Something that made his head turn from the doll's house to that part of the attic where he had last heard voices.

What the husband then saw was to prove the saving of their perilous existence. A door in the wall, which earlier he had pushed against and found immovable, now hung ajar, showing the way to a flight of ill-kept stairs. A brief reconnaissance made it clear that this was the route to the main part of the house. And in the house there was sure to be a kitchen. In the kitchen, food. When the husband returned with his message of hope, four dark eyes turned to him, shiny with joy. It was only a matter of hours now to salvation.

The day lingered on and at last gave way to night. The sounds from the house grew spasmodic. When the last door had clicked shut, the husband, the wife and the wife's sister went exploring. There were four rooms on the top landing: a bathroom and three bedrooms. From one of these bedrooms came a faint cry, as from a lost child, and the wife stopped to listen, her head bent wistfully to one side.

At the foot of the main staircase was a carpeted hall, from which branched two pleasant rooms with drawn curtains and glowing grates. The wife's sister would have stayed to warm herself, had not the husband hurried her along to the kitchen. Here they found food in great quantity: a new loaf of bread on the table, fresh cheese wrapped in a cloth. Some of it they ate on the spot, grabbing uncouthly in their eagerness to settle the days' old hunger pains. The rest of it was smuggled back to the attic, to be gloated over at leisure and nibbled at in the waking hours.

For three days the feasting continued—at night, the forays to the kitchen quarters, by day the lingering over delicious morsels. The wife became fat, and too lazy to move from her bed of rugs. The wife's sister made greedy eyes at the husband and snatched before his uncomplaining eyes the last crumbs.

On one of the nocturnal expeditions, there had been a bedroom door left open, and a low light could be seen burning at the bedside of a child. The husband, the wife and the wife's sister stole softly into the room and stood silently to watch the restless sleeping of an angel-girl. She tossed her silvery-gold hair across the pillow, her unseeing eyes searching through dreams of pain, her small, pale hands clutching at the sheets as if to clasp at life itself. Three faces turned away, each remote in its emotion, yet joined in common sympathy.

That night there was no fighting over scraps, no fierce words to disrupt the harmony of thought. That night they took turns to listen at the top of the stairs.

In the morning, the wife's sister heard noises from below and reported to the others that a visitor had called on the angel-girl—a small, hunched man who carried a black bag. After he left, there were sounds of weeping and sighing, and the three in the attic exchanged anxious glances, alert for the disturbance they could feel waiting on the air.

It came after dark, when the husband, the wife and the wife's sister were sneaking down the attic stairs in search of food. First, there was a loud cry from the child, then hurrying, slippered feet crossed to her room. There was a wail of anguish, followed by a moan of manly pain, then an unholy quiet. Into the silence came strangled sobs, and a murmuring of prayer, as the husband, the wife and the wife's sister peered with shifting eyes through the doorway of death.

The child could have been sleeping quietly, had not her eyes been so horribly open, her hands so terribly fixed in supplication. A man and a woman, kneeling in sorrow at her side, were unaware of the three shuffling figures who stood like paid mourners at the door, seeing all but the faces of parental grief. And so the scene was frozen, captive in that timeless night, as five bent heads paid homage to a lost angel.

In the morning, two grey-faced men came to lift the girl into a narrow box and carry her downstairs. Candles were lit and flowers arrived to flaunt their gaudiness against the black crêpe of tragedy. The man and the woman kept watch all day among the candles and left them burning when they supported each other upstairs to their long night of wakeful rest.

When the house was quiet, the husband, the wife and the wife's sister entered the room of peace. They gazed upon the white face and its border of pale hair, and then, in common consent, and in accordance with the customs of their race, they performed their ceremony of last rites.

It was a long ceremony, and they were still about their task when dawn stole upon the house and forced wan slivers of light between the curtains of the front room. There was still much to do, and the husband, the wife and the wife's sister worked earnestly to complete their business before day and its attendant dangers were upon them.

It was the wife's sister who heard voices in the hall, and she it was who chose to push the husband behind the door and edge him around it to safety when the two men with tall hats and grey faces came to attend to their client. Not until they had gained the attic stairs did the husband realize that the wife was not with them, but by then he could do nothing at all.

The two men had picked up the coffin-lid from where it lay propped against the wall, and were advancing on the coffin to hide for all time the sweet face of the child. They did not see, before they banged down the lid, the movement from beneath the shroud. Nor did they see the wife look up in terror, a piece of flesh held motionless between her yellow teeth as she watched the lid descending.

But upstairs in the attic, the wife's sister preened her whiskers in satisfaction before she sidled over to the husband and rubbed her fur against his twitching nose.

The Pangborn Family

When Georgia Harriet Wood married her cousin Harry Leroy Pangborn in 1894 it united two venerable colonial families. The Pangborns came originally from the village of Pangbourne in Berkshire, and David Pangborn (1615–1638) emigrated to New Haven, Connecticut in the 1630s. The Wood side of the family can trace its origins back to Edward Wood (1598–1642) who emigrated from Norwich in Norfolk to Charlestown, Massachusetts in 1640.

Both sides of the family had military connections. Georgia's great-grandfather Enos Wood (1761–1851) fought in the American War of Independence whilst her father-in-law Zebina Kellogg Pangborn (1829–1902) served briefly as a paymaster in the American Civil War and later as an instructor at a military school. It is through him that the literary gene descends. He became a journalist and newspaper proprietor and married Georgia's aunt, Harriet, in 1854. Their eldest son, Frederic Werden Pangborn (1855–1934) became a journalist and writer, amongst his books being *The Silent Maid* (1903), a medieval fantasy of a lord of the castle bewitched by a fey young girl. Zebina's youngest son, Harry, who married Georgia Wood, had also been a journalist, working on his father's newspapers, becoming a lawyer from 1902–1915 before returning to newspaper work as an editor and critic. The Wood bloodline brought both a talent for craftsmanship and a keen eye for money. Enos's son Arunah was a cabinet maker and his son, George (Georgia's father) trained as a lawyer and became a land agent and speculator.

1914

THE SUBSTITUTE

Georgia Wood Pangborn

Georgia Wood Pangborn (1872–1955) kept herself to herself. I can find no interviews with her, no contemporary studies, and nothing beyond which she chose to reveal in her fiction. Even her children, Mary and Edgar, would not speak of her. Jessica Amanda Salmonson, who compiled the only collection of Pangborn's weird tales, The Wind at Midnight *(1999), knew her daughter Mary, but realized it was forbidden territory to ask anything about her mother. Georgia was the youngest daughter by far of George Hazen Wood and Mary Prentice. Her mother was nearly forty when she was born and her eldest sister was already seventeen. Her three elder sisters were all artistic and, so far as I can tell, none of them married. After Georgia married in 1894 and moved out of the household, her mother continued to live with her other daughters after her husband died in 1898. I can't help but sense a feeling of estrangement between Georgia and her mother and sisters, a feeling that comes across in many of her stories—a sense of remoteness between a mother and her children. It was not until twelve years after her marriage that Georgia's daughter, Mary, was born. Perhaps there were still-births prior to this—I have no idea—but to read her fiction, especially her supernatural stories, is to create a picture of a woman who found it difficult to be a loving mother in the physical world but who yearned to be in the spiritual. She had already turned to writing before Mary was born. Her first and only novel,* Roman Biznet *(1902), opens with dark deeds by a father, escaping with his son, having buried his daughter whom he had just beaten to death. The eponymous hero is of mixed-race descent and the novel explores the two sides of his character that emerge from these bloodlines. It is a harrowing novel but may have been of therapeutic value so that Georgia had no need to write again at that length. Nevertheless, her stories being full of thoughts of death, suicide and madness makes one wonder just what kind of early life she had led. Over the next twenty years or so she produced many first-class stories and poems and then, around 1926, stopped. Had the need to write ceased by then, or did she have other commitments, perhaps looking after her husband who died of throat cancer in 1934? She lived another twenty years, dying at the age of 85, taking her secrets with her. The stories, perhaps, reveal all.*

The day's heat, for a time made endurable by a small breeze, had been weighed down toward evening by a thunderous humidity. Only along the line of the beach it was tolerable. Miss Marston had sat so long over her coffee that the room was now in twilight, but she had intercepted by a fretful gesture the maid who would have turned on the light. Her dining-room windows overlooked the water. Fifty feet below she could see the blurred figures of people on the beach, and could hear their voices at intervals, among them the piping staccato of Mrs Van Duyne's convalescent children, allowed to stay up and be active in the cool of the evening to atone for the languor of the afternoon. Now and then the fretful cry of an ailing baby overrode the other voices. But the babies that were sent to Mrs Van Duyne always got well. That was her very wonderful business—making them well.

The heat was like a presence—a thing of definite substance that could be touched. Like a drug, too, making the senses strange, distorting distance and time. Although her eyes were upon the ocean, where the foam appeared and vanished dimly in long lines, lit only a little way out by the lights at the pier-head, it was the dark campus of her college town that Anna Marston's vision beheld, and the unsteady foam-crests of the waves were girls in white dresses, long rows of them coming and going within the obscurity of the trees.

"I am thirty-two," said Miss Marston aloud, and for that reason thought more keenly about when she was twenty-two. The same heavy air had folded in the evening of her Commencement Day, yet the girls had not seemed to mind.

"I suppose we had plenty of other things to think about," said she.

For a while she had gone about the campus with them, singing and laughing, and then, like this, had come to her window-seat to think; to decide, finally, *not* to marry Willis.

"And Mary Hannaford came in—Mary Hannaford—to show me her ring. I told her she was silly!"

Miss Marston moved restlessly.

Matters long ago forgotten will upon occasion freakishly insist upon remembrance, approaching suddenly, like the surprise of a familiar face in a crowded street. A dream plucks us by the sleeve, and we turn to see a childish countenance which has no more right than our own to inextinguishable youth. Or again, a word or a bar of music causes the barrier of years to fall as though it had never been, and we are in gardens that were dust years and years ago. Having once returned, these revenants keep us company for a while.

"I don't see why I should keep on thinking of Mary Hannaford," said Miss Marston, and went on thinking about Mary Hannaford—that perhaps she had not been silly, after all, but rather sensible to marry instead of keeping sulkily to something she called an "ideal," as Anna Marston had done.

"I wish—" said Miss Marston, vaguely, then frowned as the cry of the sick baby came up from the beach.

"Children—" said she; yet her tone, though troubled, was not exactly that of annoyance. Annoyance does not make the eyes wet.

She struck her clenched hand into her open palm, then lay back, drowsily inert in attitude, except that her underlip was caught between her teeth and her forehead was wrinkled with discontent.

She knew that the maids had slipped out for their walk on the beach. They had passed in their black-and-white, giggling, to the bluff stairs, and their squeals of joy at their release had reached her as soon as they were out of sight. She was alone, therefore. Yet she did not feel as if she were alone; not that there seemed to be another presence in the house, but the house itself had changed. Girls—so many!—went in light-footed haste through the halls. The room in which she sat was no longer a conventional dining-room. The walls, hidden in shadow, were garishly sprinkled with photographs and college pennants; the cushions of the window-seats were bright with college colors, and in a moment more Mary Hannaford would come in, wanting to talk under cover of the darkness about how happy she was, how fortunate above all other girls in the world. Mary Hannaford again!

Some one spoke her name. She sat up quickly and was aware of the indistinct pallor of a face.

It was by the voice, however, rather than by anything she saw that she recognized her visitor.

"Why, Mary Hannaford!" said she. "I haven't seen you for ten years! And I've been thinking of you all day."

The figure came forward swiftly and seated itself at the other end of the window-seat. Anna sank back, her sudden rousing having caused that odd vertigo which is common enough in times of great heat. She could not have said whether for an instant her hand touched that of her guest or not.

When the dizziness had passed, Mary was speaking. She sat with her knees drawn up and her hands clasped about them in the attitude Anna so well remembered.

"It's ever so long since I stopped being Mary Hannaford. I'm Mary Barclay, you know."

"Of course. You were the first of our set to go. How romantic we all felt about it! But you stopped writing after the babies came. All girls do. That's what turns us old maids so sour—at least, partly. But do tell me! Have you a cottage here? And how did you find me?"

Mary Barclay appeared to be looking down at the beach. She did not answer her friend's eager queries.

Anna Marston leaned forward and regarded her anxiously.

"Aren't you feeling fit? You seem so pale."

"Oh, quite!"

Anna reached toward the electric button, but Mary Barclay's hand intervened, protesting.

"We don't want lights, do we? Don't you remember how we always liked to talk in the dark like this?"

"Well," laughed Anna, "I'd just as soon you didn't see my wrinkles yet. *You* look just the same, except that you haven't any color. You had the reddest cheeks in the class."

"And you didn't marry, after all," said Mary Barclay, slowly.

"No," admitted Anna, rather fretfully. "The right man wouldn't have me."

"That is like you. You'd never make a second choice. Not that I think it's wise of you."

From the beach the baby's cry rose again, weak, fretful, insistent. Anna Marston fidgeted.

"One of Mrs Van Duyne's patients. Of course I know the children there are all right, but sometimes I wish they weren't quite so near. That's a marasmus baby that came today. Its parents are very rich people. She's keeping the children on the beach late this evening for the coolness. Think," she broke out suddenly—"think what this day has been for the babies in the tenements! If it has been bad here, what must it have been there!"

"Yes," said Mary Barclay. "It is very bad in the city just now." She was looking steadily down toward the beach.

Anna waited for a moment, then asked timidly, "Aren't you going to tell me something about yourself and your family?"

Ten years is a long time in which to know nothing of a friend—time enough for tragedies which will not bear discussing.

"Calvin died three years ago," said Mary Barclay, after a silence.

"I didn't know," said Anna, softly.

"Three years ago. Benny was a year old then. There—wasn't anything. We had been living on his salary. Death—we had forgotten there was such a thing. I found work. You know I had a sort of cleverness about clothes. I found fashion work that paid pretty well, only… they weren't very strong babies. They had to have the best, or—or they wouldn't stay, you know. Until now—they've stayed."

"They are well now, then?"

"They are well now."

Anna rose with an exclamation and walked up and down.

"Then I envy you. What a full life! Working—and for your own children. Lucky woman! In spite of your sorrow, lucky, lucky woman! Look at me. What good am I? I started out being my father's companion and secretary. It did very well for a time. Then he married again, and I took my mother's fortune and went my own way—clubs, municipal reform, every galvanic imitation of life I could find. I've been so desperate at times—"

"I know," said Mary Barclay.

"How can you know?"

Anna halted in her pacing to stare at her friend through the obscurity.

"That was partly why I came over here," said Mary Barclay, in an odd, still voice. "I had to come, anyway, to see my babies. I had to do that," she repeated.

"Your babies? At Mrs Van Duyne's? But you said they were well now."

"Yes," said Mary Barclay, "She knows how to keep them well. The right air and food. There is so much to know. It isn't simple. If I'd tried to keep them in the city—" She shook her head. "Calvin and I always agreed that if we could only bring them safely through the first five years they would be as strong as anybody's children. Their brains are ahead of their bodies. But they aren't weaklings! If they had been—weaklings don't get anything out of life worth staying for. I—shouldn't have been able to come here tonight if they hadn't been worth while. But, you see, I know now—better than I did before—what they are."

She broke off with a cry, yet when Anna would have drawn her arms about her she evaded her like a mist.

"Envy me," moaned Mary Barclay, "but pity me, too!"

Recovering herself quickly, she leaned forward and spoke rapidly: "What becomes of children when fathers and mothers die? Sometimes things turn out all right, I know. It isn't always the same as when parent birds are shot and the nestlings starve. But sometimes it's like that. When there are no relatives to take them, and no money has been left for their support—

"What happens when a little girl is left without a mother to tell her about growing up? And then children are always so—themselves. One child is never like another, yet people who don't know try to treat them all alike.

"My little Martha! She never tells when her heart is broken or she has a pain and is really sick. She just gets cross, and you have to guess. She is apt to be rather naughty anyway. I've had to be patient—very.

And, oh, such strange big thoughts as she thinks! And she can suffer, too! And then Benny; I suppose it was his sickness that—It was too much. Mrs Van Duyne saved him. He was dying when I took him there. She saved him, but—I didn't take care of Martha right when Benny was sick, and so she began to be sick, too. What could I do? So I've let her have them. Anything less than the best wouldn't do, you see. I sold things—all I could—and went to work to earn money to pay her. Perhaps I worked a little too hard. I thought, I suppose, that so long as I was doing it for them nothing could beat me. Well, what's done is done. They laugh and have red cheeks. But—"

She rose and looked down at her friend, then out of the window.

"The nurses are bringing them in from the beach to go to bed. They are very sweet when they are going to bed. Shall we meet them?"

They stepped from the window to the porch, Mary Barclay going lightly ahead. Her dress, of some indefinite color which mingled with that of the sand, made her almost invisible.

There was a long flight of steps leading from the bluff down to the beach. From its summit the slow footsteps of the nurses and children and their mingled voices were audible before their heads came into sight.

One rather fat and sleepy voice counted the steps incorrectly: "One, two, free, seventeen, a hundred—I got up first!"

The pioneer appeared abruptly on all-fours—something of a wounded veteran by his bandaged head, but cheerful. Terrible warfare he had been through, coming out of it with flags flying and glory redounding to the surgeon first, but to Mrs Van Duyne with even honor. He bore the proud title of Double Mastoid. Death had been close at his heels; Pain unspeakable had held him very tight in her terrible arms for a long time. Silence had threatened, too: no more kind voices, no music—but all those ogres had been sent to the right-about, far away now from a fat little boy. Already he was forgetting that anything had been wrong.

"I got up quicker'n anybody," he crowed.

Then appeared a white cap, somewhat awry, and strong, kerchiefed shoulders. A young face bent over a tiny sleeping creature on an air-cushion carried steadily and lightly. This was little Marasmus, the latest recruit, and his attendant.

Then came just a plain feeding-case, whose mother didn't dare take him back for fear that she and he would go and do the same wicked things over again just as soon as his Auntie Van Duyne's back was turned. He was sleeping like a cherub. Nothing whatever the matter with *him*! He was one of Mrs Van Duyne's "Results," said to have been once the duplicate of little Marasmus, but now the kind of person that tired-eyed physicians wag their heads over gloatingly and poke in the ribs—*not* with a stethoscope—and call "Old Top" in a companionable way, as if they respected him for having done something rather fine all on his own responsibility. He had had about a year of it, and Mrs Van Duyne was going to hang on to him as long as she could, for she had her own opinion of mothers. Often and often they had undone her fine work just as she had everything going nicely. They never knew anything whatever of their children's inwardness; clothes and hair were as far as they could go. She had all that wonderful hidden territory mapped out. She didn't believe in raw milk very much, for one thing, and she did believe in a few other things which—well, she got results, anyway. Look at "Old Top"!

After him came two children, hand-in-hand; and these, Anna knew at once, were Mary's two. She would have known even without the long trembling sigh that breathed past her ear. The little girl looked so like Mary! She was about six, Anna judged, and her hair was twisted in a little knob on top of her head for coolness' sake—a fashion of hair-dressing for very little girls which, more than another, perhaps, brings a lump into the throat. Is it because of its sweet caricature of maturity, as though both the promise and the menace of the years were revealed in those lines? Or is it that the curve of the back of the neck shown in this way is so lovely that it has a spiritual significance, like the odor of the first grass in spring or the color of evening sky through trees?

She walked with a rather conceited air, her gait indicating a lofty scorn of the Double Mastoid's claim to be a pioneer. She made it very evident that *she* could come up one foot after another, just like all other grown-ups, and she did it with a swagger, to render as obvious as possible her superiority in age, strength, and wisdom over the little boy at her side, who could do no better than one step at a time, and even so had to touch his hand to the tread now and then.

They were thin children, but thin like elves—not with the sadness and languor of sickness. And their faces in the twilight had a lambent quality, their eyes a liquid brightness. One felt that if the whim took them they might easily thrust forth gauzy wings and suddenly sail away with other night creatures.

In their conversation there was a pleasing breadth of impossibility that showed them to be as yet little acquainted with the restrictions of mortal life.

"I'm going to be an engineer when I grow up," stated the boy, "but I'm not going to be a man. I'm going to be a mother. My name isn't Benny."

"What is your name?" the girl asked, without surprise.

"I'm Nelly."

"Well, then, I won't be Martha. I'll be Rosie, and you're my little sister." She was in a kindly mood, which might not last. Only so long as the current of her dream flowed smoothly would Martha be good. The interruption came quickly.

"No, I'm your *big* sister. I'm not little at all. Auntie Van Duyne says I'm getting bigger every day."

"All right, then; I sha'n't play with you," quoth Martha, crisply, and stalked ahead, as naughty as her mother had described. And then Anna saw Mary, who had silently left her side, stoop over and apparently whisper softly to the cross little face surmounted by its wisp of topknot. Martha stopped, finger in mouth, to kick the sand with her toe and look with sidelong friendliness at Benny as he arrived, panting. Then they went on, once more in amity, their short arms stretched about each other's waists. And the mother kept beside them, still whispering in their ears and kissing them. Yet—they did not turn to her or answer.

"I hope mother'll bring us some paints," Martha was saying as they passed beyond hearing.

"If she does, I'll make her a picture of an engine," Benny joyfully planned.

"Mary!" called Anna. She was surprised to feel that she was trembling, not that she was in any way afraid. She could not have said what had so shaken her. No longer seeing her friend, she laughed and said aloud, "Oh, she must have gone into the house ahead of them."

A slower step was now coming up the bluff stairs, and there appeared a figure in professional white, strong and purposeful, but for the moment rather weary and thoughtful.

Miss Marston stepped forward.

"Good evening, Mrs Van Duyne. I was coming over to see the Barclay children."

The troubled face was crossed by a flash of joyful surprise and relief.

"Oh, do you know them? I'm so thankful. I wish I'd known before. I've been nearly frantic. Of course, then, you know—"

She took a twist of yellow paper from her belt and handed it to Anna Marston, who did not open it, but trembled very much as she looked at Mrs Van Duyne, in whose fine, wise eyes the tears glittered and brimmed over, unheeded. Tears were something which in Mrs Van Duyne's code were a matter to be disregarded, like any other physical weakness in a person who never allowed herself to be sick.

"I haven't told them, of course. I shall put it off—as long as I possibly can. She worked herself to death—" She broke off with a burst of that kindly anger to which the very good and just are so easily stirred. "Her heart wasn't strong, and the heat finished her. The telegram came this afternoon. I can't tell you how glad I am to find out you are her friend. So far as I can make out she had no relatives. I"—she spread out her hands with a sort of desperation—"I do what I can."

Anna had heard tales enough to know that "what I can" meant an amazing amount of work without return in money, that it meant great kindliness, of which advantage was often taken by weak and selfish people. Not that Mrs Van Duyne ever told. Nevertheless, it had got about that one of the babies had never paid its board since it was a month old, yet you could not have guessed which was the delinquent by any difference between its care and that of "Old Top" or little Marasmus, for example, whose parents came and went in limousines loaded down with all sorts of expensive, foolish toys, whose wardrobes were all silken-fine, and who, when they grew up, would be very high and mighty folk indeed. Old Top, certainly; Marasmus, in all probability—though that was going to be pretty brisk and delicate work for a while.

"Since you are a friend," went on Mrs Van Duyne, "perhaps you can tell me what to do. I'm not talking about the immediate present.

They—well, they are here, and they are dear children, though that little Martha is certainly a handful." She half laughed through her tears. "But there is so much future... What about the years and years?"

Anna Marston was still shaking as though through the heat an icy wind had blown upon her. Once more she was aware of Mary Barclay—vividly aware—but this time it was not with her physical eyes that she seemed to see her. There was no further illusion—if it had been illusion—of that indistinct figure bending above those little, unconscious heads, touching them, kissing them, enveloping them, like a bird hovering over its nest.

Instead there was, as it were, an inward vision. She and Mary Barclay were again face to face, but it was not in any way a pitiful entreaty for charity which she read in her friend's eyes. Rather it was a command.

"Dear Mrs Van Duyne," said Anna, trying to bring her voice under control, "Mary Barclay knows that I am ready to take her place. She knows I—I want them—both of them—more than anything else in the world."

The first sigh of the coming coolness breathed past them from the sea. It was like the long breath of one who, after great restlessness, turns at last to sleep.

1965

WOGGLEBEAST

Edgar Pangborn

Although Edgar Pangborn (1909–1976) was the younger of Georgia's two children he was the first to turn to writing. His initial passion, though, was for music and he got as far as studying it at the New England Conservatory of Music in 1927 but for some reason did not graduate. He turned to farming. His love for both music and the natural world is evident in much of his fiction. He experimented with writing a murder-mystery novel, A-100 (1930), which appeared under the alias Bruce Harrison. A few years after this he sold a batch of crime stories to Street & Smith's Detective Story Magazine, *and these appeared as by Neil Ryder. After his military service during the Second World War he returned to writing but this time in the science-fiction field, emerging with the classic friendly alien story "Angel's Egg" (1951). Pangborn enjoyed writing about aliens amongst us. It was central to his novel* A Mirror for Observers *(1954) where Martians are in hiding on Earth, helping humans to develop. That novel won the short-lived International Fantasy Award. An earlier novel* West of the Sun *(1953) has humans attempting to colonize an inhospitable planet. He is best known for his stories set in a post-apocalyptic world exploring how humanity strives to recover and rebuild itself. The first novel,* Davy *(1964) is set about three centuries after an atomic war, but later books consider different periods, such as* The Judgement of Eve *(1966),* The Company of Glory *(1975) and various stories collected as* Still I Persist in Wondering *(1978). What was evident from this series and from most of his other writings is that Pangborn believed the best of mankind—after often exploring the worst—and he became regarded as one of the most genuine of humanist writers. I can't help but wonder how much was influenced by his upbringing—which, alas, remains silent.*

Molly trotted the two blocks from the supermarket with a roasting chicken for Sunday. Her round blue eyes were tranced with planning. Paper skirts on the drumsticks, toothpick legs for the olives; the raw carrots Danny liked could be cut in funny shapes. Then cold cuts for Sunday supper, and the bones could be boiled up for soup on Sunday evening while they looked at the T.V. or had a game of checkers.

Molly McManus enjoyed the rest of the Friday. She polished the living-room floor of the little house and put up two pairs of fresh curtains. Thanks to her planning ahead, she had time for a nice visit with Mrs Perlman next door who was going to have still another baby. She remembered to quit humming when Danny got home because it sometimes got on his nerves—a foreman in an explosive plant cannot have nerves. But she continued humming inside. At dinner she had a pickle-animal. That's easy—you take a pickled onion for the head, slices of gherkin for the body, and the usual legs made out of toothpicks. Danny chuckled and admired it. Molly went to bed happy, folded up in gratitude against his weary bulk, and slept a while in peace.

He was tired, but over the weekend he could rest. Molly worried about his weight. He had no bay window, but there was a hint of it. Bags were showing under his mild gray eyes, and the eyes would redden if he forgot to put on his reading glasses. His step had grown heavy so gradually, one almost forgot how light on his feet he used to be. It seemed to Molly they ought to give him an office job. She woke for an hour or so in the night, thinking about that, watching the rosy reflection of a traffic light glow, die and glow again on the bedroom ceiling. He'd earned an office job. He ought to go straight up there and *tell* them.

And she was oppressed also that night by a special familiar loneliness in her arms. She counted to eight a dozen times or so, synchronizing it with Danny's peaceful snoring, and murmured a prayer which had become little more than a wistful habit. She was forty-one; to have a child at this date would *need* a miracle.

Sunday was good, as planned. Rest had cleared away most of Danny's fatigue—in fact on Saturday he'd taken out his stamp collection and got her to admiring it, which happened only on his best days. Then at Sunday dinner-time, glorious juices rushed out of the chicken at the poke of Danny's carving knife, and the whole apartment wallowed in the golden-brown smell. Stuffed and sleepy-faced, Danny let out a hole in his belt, and Molly pretended not to notice—she was not slim herself. The afternoon darkened with February snow that would make driving unpleasant, so instead of taking off for the movies they worked on a crossword puzzle until Danny fell asleep trying to think of a Norse god. By evening they were ready for cold cuts. Molly McManus sat up after Danny got tired of watching T.V. and went to bed, to boil out the chicken bones and mend one of his shirts. In spite of the way everything encouraged you to do it, Molly hated wasting things. It seemed a little wicked as well as silly...

It crouched on the kitchen table where it had fallen, or jumped, from the strainer full of other bones. Its thin arms reached toward Molly McManus as if in a bow or a supplication, and it looked like a Wogglebeast. "Why, the poor thing!" said Molly, and as she held out her finger toward its narrow friendly head it seemed to her that the Wogglebeast sat back on its sort-of legs and shook itself slightly—anyway there was a spatter of soup drops on the table-top that didn't necessarily come from the strainer.

She hated to disturb it. She dumped the other bones in the garbage and put away the soup, but let the kitchen table alone. She was always up before Danny to get his breakfast, and it wasn't as if they had cockroaches or ants. She slipped into bed thinking some about the Wogglebeast but more about Danny.

In her drowsiness she had left a few other things untidied; her sewing-basket, for instance, sitting with its lid off beside the genuine antique rocker in the kitchen. It had come from the old country with her grandmother, a basket of sweet-scented woven grass, the dry gold of it soft with age. When she got up early Monday morning she found the Wogglebeast nestled in this basket, and started to take it out, but although it didn't draw back, it seemed to her that it shook—not its head exactly.

She placed the basket in the back of the silver drawer, leaving the drawer open a crack for air, until Danny had gone to work. Not that he would be unfriendly or unkind at all, but on work-day mornings he could not be quite with her; he never ignored her, but he had to be somehow arranging his thoughts and feelings for the trials and responsibilities of the day. She could see it happening, and help only by letting her alone. And also he was allergic to a number of things, cats and dogs for instance. And if she mentioned the Wogglebeast he might feel he had to do something about it. So—so anyway evening would be time enough.

During the day she made room at the back of the bottom bureau drawer for the Wogglebeast's basket. It was convenient; she could trot up to the bedroom from time to time to see if the little fellow needed anything. She offered it bread-crumbs, cornmeal, a few other things, but evidently it didn't need to eat, which was perhaps only natural. The bureau drawer remained open until she heard Danny drive into the garage, and as she was closing it she resolved to tell him. It really wasn't right or fair, not to.

But there had been a near-disaster at the plant. One of Danny's own crew had been careless, inexcusably careless—the man had to be fired. The whole episode was still oppressing Danny McManus like the brushing of black wings, and it was no time to be telling him about anything unusual.

Tuesday night some of the same trouble hung about him. He was grumbling that it was his own fault for not having trained the offender better.

Wednesday he was just tired out, falling asleep in his armchair, face collapsed above the drooped newspaper, defenseless and—well, not young.

By Thursday night Molly was beginning to feel a certain weight of guilt. If she spoke of the Wogglebeast Danny would rightly wonder why she hadn't done so sooner. Besides, it was acting very cooperative, the decent thing, always snug and quiet in the basket a bit before Danny was due home, although that Thursday it had been following her all over the house.

She thought Friday that it would have liked to go with her to the supermarket. But clearly the Wogglebeast itself knew that this couldn't be. It wasn't begging at all, just wistful, and when she got home it was waiting cheerfully in the kitchen and wagging—not its tail, exactly...

That afternoon she felt too lazy for the usual housework, and nearly drowsed off in the antique rocker, thinking a good deal about her grandmother, and how the old soul used to go on and on sometimes about the old country, talking high but soft like a small wind in the chimney, the way her dry laughter now and then would be like the sparks of a comfortable burning log. Until—oh, maybe drowsing for sure—Molly heard her own self saying a few foolish things to the Wogglebeast that was resting in her arms: "It's not as if I ever thought you was a wishing thing exactly, only thinking to myself I am and talking like it might be to myself, but it's best we won't tell Danny at all, you wouldn't know the things he'd do. Too bad we haven't a child, too bad he won't be squaring off and *telling* them to give him office work the way he's earned it and could have it at the drop of a word—but it's only you can't help your mind running on it sometimes, and all..."

That night Danny desired her, like a young man but not heedless, and in the good quiet afterward Molly got up her courage to say a few little things about asking for office work, and though he wouldn't say yes or no he was peaceful and thoughtful about it, not annoyed at all. Once or twice, in the heavy darkness after Danny had fallen asleep, she heard in the bureau drawer a tiny sigh not quite a grunt, very much like the noise a cat will make after turning around three times and settling down in a basket.

It wasn't until Easter Week that Danny found the Wogglebeast. He was already out of sorts, late for work, hunting a missing sock and getting mad instead of putting on another pair, and flinging himself in bullnecked impatience at all the bureau drawers, one foot in an untied shoe and the other bare entirely with all his toes angry. The Wogglebeast had been trying to hide under a brassiere. "Oh, that," Molly said—"oh, that, the little thing looked so much like a something, and wouldn't I be the one to go on playing with dolls at my age, see, the little legs he has and all?" The Wogglebeast never moved while Danny held it up; she was certain of that.

He put it back in the drawer. Not a word. He took another pair of socks. No word, no smile. He could be like that, and often it meant nothing except that he was puzzled. After he had gone Molly just made it to the bathroom, dizzy and sick.

Good and sick, but why? Surely his finding the Wogglebeast hadn't upset her that much. Something wrong with breakfast?—of course not. Unbelieving, merely touching the idea like a dab of cloud that was certain to float away, Molly counted days. How foolish can you get? And yet several times that day she studied her familiar round not-so-pretty face in the mirror, and something in her insisted that it was rather pretty. Softer anyhow, and brighter. A different look.

Two days later she walked to the doctor's office, almost furtively, as if she hadn't as good a right as anybody to a rabbit test and all that.

The test said yes.

The doctor said other things beside yes, having known her fifteen years. It puzzled her that behind his professional cheerfulness he was obviously not pleased. When she called it a miracle the best he could offer was a one-sided smile and another string of cautions and good advice. It didn't matter. The choirs sang; her thoughts ran up and down a swaying bridge of rainbows all day long.

It was after the doctor's telephone call saying the test was positive and delivering the first batch of those cautions, that she found the Wogglebeast had emptied her sewing-basket, and collected treasures of its own there: an empty spool, a bit of tinfoil, an eraser worked loose from the end of a pencil—nothing of course that anybody else was going to want or that Danny would miss. Molly didn't mind at all, especially when she noticed how it was watching her with the jokesharing gleam in—well, not its eyes exactly...

Danny was not told of the miracle until they were in bed, their faces in darkness. By then Molly was enough used to the idea so that she could quiet his anxiety a little and help him into a precarious but genuine happiness. It occurred to her as she was drifting into sleep, himself holding her as if she were spun glass, that it was going to be simpler now to arrange about Danny's relations with the Wogglebeast. You have to humor a pregnant woman and allow her all sorts of quirks.

She told Dorothy Perlman the next day—on the phone, and casually she thought, but Mrs Perlman came over immediately under full sail, pouring forth advice, suggestions, consolation, sustaining anecdotes, offering a massive shoulder to cry on and restless until it was used. Her first had scared Nathan all to pieces, she said, and even scared her a little, but when the time came it simply popped. Like *that*.

Molly McManus liked people. She was on the silly edge of telling Dorothy about the Wogglebeast, but some hint of a gray disturbance over there in the bureau drawer behind Dorothy's back, like the lifting of a worried—oh, not head exactly—made Molly feel that it might not be just the best idea.

It's not that there's anything *wrong* with a Wogglebeast. Just all that pesky explaining you'd have to do.

It happened that Danny was so obsessed with the miracle he had no mind for anything else. Molly fell into the habit of leaving the bottom drawer more widely open. The Wogglebeast clearly enjoyed that, but took no unreasonable advantages of it. It did sometimes slip out of its basket when Danny was home, but carefully, and only if he happened to be in another room—well, once, one Sunday afternoon when Molly supposed Danny was taking a nap, she did hear the abrupt thump of his feet on the bedroom floor, and the beginning of an exclamation: "B' Je—" but nothing else happened. Maybe she imagined it.

One evening in August, shortly before their two weeks' vacation in Atlantic City, Danny talked with her more searchingly than he usually did. He wanted a reassurance that she was happy—not in the future with the baby and all, but in the here and now. "Why, Danny, I am, you know I am. I bet you went to bother the doctor again today."

"Oh, for the sake of argument I did. Everything is fine, he says, and what else would he say if you went to him running a mortal fever with two busted legs?"

Molly herself knew that nothing could possibly go wrong—miracles don't. But it takes more than aspirin to get a husband through these things; from the bureau drawer came now and then a tiny sigh.

That night she woke in the small hours and noticed the Wogglebeast hesitant and forlorn on the bedroom rug. Danny was sound asleep. She held away a corner of the bed-covers so it could climb up if it wanted to, and as she went back to sleep she felt against her shoulder the dry wiggle of—not its legs, exactly.

And the next day Danny came home announcing that, as he put it himself, he was letting them kick him upstairs from foreman to supervisor. Not office work exactly, he explained to Molly's excited questions, but something like it. "And so glory be to God you won't be messing around so much with the nasty stuff all day long?"

"It'll be like that," he said rather carefully. "I told them, I said, I've been foreman a long time, and now I must be thinking about the heir of The McManus and so forth."

The Wogglebeast was well-behaved at Atlantic City. Molly had been uneasy about its smothery journey in a suitcase, but it took no harm. She had a little trouble in her mind about the hotel chambermaid, but solved it by admiring a very large handbag in a shop window, which Danny immediately bought for her; it had a compartment where the Wogglebeast was perfectly happy, and even made a sort of game out of covering itself with facial tissues and what not.

They stayed apart from the crowds, and watched the sea and the long changes of the sky. On other vacations they had often gone about with friends, in a round of parties and picnics and nonsense. She had no wish for that this time, and Danny found it natural.

One day on the beach she said, hardly heeding the way her talk was going: "I wish you'd known my grandmother, Danny. She died when I was twelve, you know, and it was like the milkweed down drying up to a little whiteness and blowing away. O the stories she used to tell, and me with my mouth open and a wind going through my wits if I had any! She told once how they came and carried her away, the Little People she meant, and you had to believe her, the way she had of telling it, how she fell asleep in a meadow on Midsummer's Night, and she eleven years old, and they came for her, and didn't they set her to ride on a milk-white pony and it went straight underground with her into their dwelling? The hollow at the foot of an oak it was, and there they fed her cakes and honey and made things out of sticks and leaves that would walk and speak and play the violin. And then I'd ask her, 'Grandmother, didn't you bring some of them home, the stick things that walked and made music?' She'd always say, 'I did and all, Molly, but you'll remember this was seventy-eighty-ninety years ago, they'd be dust now, and anyhow they couldn't come away with me from the old country...'"

Snow was falling again when Molly's pains began, rather too soon. In between them, when Danny was telephoning to the hospital, Molly petted the Wogglebeast and tried to explain how it must be quiet a few days in its basket and not worry about anything, anything at all. It was always difficult to decide just how much it understood; but it did seem to be smiling, not with its mouth exactly...

When Molly came out of the anesthetic, one of the nurses was saying like a litany: "You're doing just fine, Mrs McManus, just fine." Well, sure, she knew she was. Daniel was the beginning of a world. She looked with tolerant affection on the busy doctor and nurses, a little sorry for them because they had nothing as wonderful as she did.

So far as the doctor and nurses were aware, the baby was ten yards away in another room, where another doctor had given up trying to make it live. So far as they could see, there was no reason why Mrs McManus should hold her left arm curved like that. No reason why, torn and fading as she was, she should look so extravagantly happy. When the internal hemorrhage passed the point of no return they were still trying.

Danny happened on the sewing-basket a while after he came home, and sagged on the bed poking vaguely at it, wondering with some part of his numb mind what had happened to the old dry chicken-bone she had fancied so much. It didn't matter. There was nothing in the basket now but some kind of gray powder, and bits of miscellaneous trash—a spool, a scrap of tinfoil, never mind all that. There had always been something about Molly to make you think of a little girl playing with dolls. The strangest part of it was that you went on living. He sat drooping, considering this, the sewing-basket forgotten in his hands, watching the snow gently fall.

1984

MY NAME IS SAMANTHA

Mary C. Pangborn

As with her brother, Mary Candace Pangborn (1907–2003) was home tutored and I wonder how much of that experience is reflected in the attitude of Samantha to her mother in this story. Mary subsequently studied at Yale University and graduated with a Ph.D. in biochemistry. She holds an important place in the history of medicine way outside anything she produced in fantasy and weird fiction. In 1941, while working at the New York State Department of Health, she succeeded in isolating a pure form of the antigen cardiolipin (which she named) as an agent in detecting syphilis. She published several academic papers on the subject from 1942 onwards, and in 1949 she received the highest of six Harold J. Fisher Memorial Awards, offered to state employees for outstanding and distinguished service. She later wrote that "during a lifetime as a supposedly hard-headed biochemist, writing remained a secret vice." My suspicious mind makes me wonder whether before her retirement she may have written some fiction under a pseudonym, as her brother had. Her first fiction under her own name appeared in 1979 when she was already in her seventies and she continued to write almost into her nineties. With her passing we say farewell to the literary branch of the Pangborns.

Dear Editor, Sir or Madam: I don't know if this is the proper way to write to you, but I hope you'll read it anyway. Because if you can't help me, I don't know who can. All I want is to put an advertisement in your magazine, but I have to tell you about it so you will see it's an emergency.

I guess I'm supposed to say who I am. My name is Samantha Allenby. I don't know where Mama got "Samantha" unless she somehow knew it was a right name for a witch. Funnily enough, the kids at school don't laugh at it, they think it's groovy. Little do they know.

Mama began when I was quite small telling me about the witch things, how you're born that way, like it or not. You can choose whether to use the Power, she said, but you can't choose not to have it. I said it wasn't fair, what if I don't want to be a witch? And she got awfully mad, spitting and sputtering about people being too lazy or cowardly to use their gifts. Can I help it if I'd rather be a regular person and have fun?

O.K., I know that's silly, you don't have to tell me.

Usually there's only one in a family, she said, and it's mostly the girls that get it, because of the chromosomes. We haven't had that in school yet, I tried looking it up in the books but it was sort of hard going. In the old days, when they didn't know about chromosomes, they said witches got their power from the devil, or some such bullshit, so they burned them. It was pretty scary, the way Mama told it, so I asked her—I had to—"They don't do that now?" She said,

"No," and then twisted her mouth sideways and said, "Not exactly. But there has never been a human society where it was safe to be different. Never was, never will be! And you'd better not forget it."

When she gets angry-fierce like that, hating the whole world, you don't know how much to believe. And if you try asking questions, you only get more of the same. So I can't be sure I'm not doing something wrong, or even dangerous, writing to you about this. I can't help it, if that's the way it is, I've got to do it anyway.

Mama says she knew I was the one as soon as I was born, but when I tried to find out how she could tell, she threw up her hands and said, "You just *know*." But you have to be grown up before you really have the Power; you have to be fourteen at least, she said, and I can't wait that long. I've got to have help *now*.

I can do a few things already. There was one awful time, when I got mad at my kid sister Lollie. She's O.K., though if you want my opinion she's a bit babyish for an eight-year-old. Still, I ought not to have told her I was going to turn her into a frog. She didn't change, of course, but she thought she had; she sat scrunched up with her eyes popping and couldn't talk, horrible, and I couldn't get her to come back. Mama fixed her, and then gave me the most ghastly spanking I ever had, all the time telling me about the worse things she could be doing to me, and she said: "Never, never, never use a spell you cannot undo!"

She said that.

Later, when she'd cooled off some, I asked her why we learn the black-magic spells if they must never be used, and she said it was like a doctor studying diseases. To unmake the evil if you had to. That makes sense, I guess. But I can't see how it's any excuse for what she did.

I'm doing this wrong, trying to say everything at once. I only got a C in English, Miss Stimson said I didn't organize my material well enough. *Organize*: that's a very big word in school, like *adjust* and *cooperate*—I don't do so well at those, either. But I've got to stick to the point now. I have to tell you about Daddy and the path.

I'm the only one who dares go on the path in the woods now. Lollie whimpers and won't even turn her head to look at the trees when we have supper on the lawn. I don't know whether she knows what happened and is pretending not to; I can't always tell, with Lollie. She cries a lot since they took Mama away, and I guess I can't blame her for that.

As for Aunt Grace, she says it's too prickly and dark in there, she doesn't want to spoil her nylons. She can't admit there's anything to be scared about, because she doesn't believe Mama is a witch. She's always known it, of course, her own sister, but at the same time she *doesn't* know. If you can picture how *that* works. She says we've got to be Sensible and Realize what Really happened. That Daddy ran away with Ellen Wilson. I ask you! That's what she calls a "sensible explanation"? So you can see it's no use asking for help from *her*.

Well, you need to know about the woods. It's only a little patch of trees in the place where the road bends between our house and the next. It seems like forest when you step into it because it's thick and dark the way old pine trees get, spiky dead branches at the bottom that scratch at you, but lovely if you can slip between them, the sweet smell and the quiet, and the cushiony feel of pine needles under your feet. Daddy said it wasn't old forest, merely a field that had been let grow up to pine, sometime back when the people around here were farmers, because it was too rough and stony to be worth plowing. He always wanted to get in there and cut out the dead branches to make a place to walk, but it wasn't our land.

Then the Wilsons bought the next house beyond the trees, a dreamy old place that had been empty for a while, so the pine woods belonged to them.

They were old people—I mean really old, with white hair—Mr Wilson was retired, he'd been a professor of history. Mrs Wilson was a sweet granny-type old lady, nice quiet voice, none of that yaketa-yaketa that makes your ears feel like they want to fold shut. We did a lot of neighborly visiting, Mama and Mrs Wilson swapping recipes, and I'm telling you Mrs Wilson's cookies were out of this world. Every other Sunday we'd go up to their house and sit around drinking *tea*. I'm not kidding. It sounds boring, but it wasn't, because Mr Wilson talked the way his house looked, so full of books you'd wonder how they had room for the furniture. Then, after we'd finished the tea, Mr Wilson would get out the brandy bottle and he and Daddy would have their drinks. Mrs Wilson would say, "Well, just a tiny snort," making it sound like a big deal, and he'd give her about two swallows in a doll-sized glass. Mama of course couldn't touch liquor, and after the first time Mr Wilson remembered not to ask her.

And we talked about making a path through the woods before Ellen ever came, so that shows you she had nothing to do with it. Nothing ever, except Mama thinking what she did.

It was Daddy who thought of the path, sitting forward with his hands on his knees, the way he does, most chairs not being quite big enough for him—square and sunburned and all happied-up at the idea of an outdoor job. No one would think to look at Daddy that he works in an accountant's office. Forestry, you'd say, or maybe a sea captain. He said, "That could be a lovely piece of woods, Mr Wilson, if we'd just clear some of the deadwood out so you could walk under the trees."

Mr Wilson said, "What fun! A path to my good neighbor's house." Kind of twinkling over it, slow and brooding, warming up. "What could be better?"

Even Mama thought it was a good idea, that first day. So tiny she always looked beside Daddy, tiny and sharp-edged, her hair as black as the darkness under the pine trees; she had a shiny look to her when she was happy, though I don't suppose anyone ever called her pretty. The air sort of twanged all around her. Sometimes she could be a lot of fun. Some people think I look like her. I don't know about that, seems to me I mostly look like myself.

Anyway, it turned into a real Project for the summer, Daddy doing most of the work of course, swinging the ax and singing, but Mr Wilson came and helped, calling himself old and feeble but acting pretty spry. There was a lot of scrabbly work to do, hauling the brush away to make neat piles. Lollie honestly worked hard dragging off branches—we kept at it even when it got hot and scratchy—and pretty soon Daddy began letting me use the hatchet, after he'd watched to make sure I could be trusted with it. That made me feel good.

Mrs Wilson would bring down a big jug of lemonade for us, and we'd sit on the pine needles and drink it and admire our work. Actually, it took only a few days to make a good path so you could walk from one house to the other without ever going out on the road. We put bends in it, even where we didn't have to, so you couldn't stand at one end and look all the way to the other; that way it was dark and mysterious, like real deep forest. Lovely. Maybe we shouldn't have done that. But I don't suppose it made any difference.

It was Daddy's clever planning that set the line of the path far enough in so there were thick trees hiding it from the road. You could hear cars go past, but you could scarcely see them. Lollie loved that. "It's our secret!" she said, and Daddy laughed his big laugh and rumpled her hair as if she'd been a boy (she didn't like that, though). "We haven't any dark secrets," Daddy said, and Mr Wilson came right back at him: "Speak for yourself, young fellow!" We all thought that was just too hilarious. You couldn't imagine anyone more innocent than Mr Wilson.

We were still happy then.

But even before Ellen came, Mama had started to take against the path. A Project like that isn't ever finished, that's the best part of it, you can always find something more to do. After we had the path fixed, there was a lot of clearing needed so you could go in among the trees. It seemed Mama didn't mind having Lollie and me out there during the day, so long as we'd finish whatever jobs she'd given us first. But then when Daddy got home, he'd be working with us, and again after supper until it got too dark. And any weekend when the weather was good. No reason Mama couldn't have been out there with us, sharing the fun, but no. She'd stand at the end of the path where it came out on our lawn and holler for Daddy to come and help her with something in the house, carrying laundry baskets or fixing a drippy faucet or bringing in fireplace wood, something, anything, and usually he'd shrug and go do what she wanted, but sometimes he wouldn't. One evening we heard their voices going on and on after we'd gone up to bed; Mama said—I heard it clear as clear—"If you like your woods so much better than the house, why don't you stay there?" And Daddy laughed and said, "Swell idea! Come on, honeycomb, let's have us a night out—" and he started pulling the blankets off the bed. She wouldn't, she got madder than ever and made him put the blankets all back. But the next day everything seemed to be all right, all as usual.

Then Ellen Wilson came to visit her parents, and they invited us all to meet her.

It was a regular picnic: they had one of those tables with benches, but you could sit on the grass if you'd rather, and Ellen came over and sat with Lollie and me, easy as pie, smiling hello. We liked her right away. Lollie says she's pretty; I don't know, I didn't have to think whether she was or not, only that I liked looking at her. Not silly-pretty like those shiny magazine ads that *teeth* at you, no, she had a real *face*.

They set up the picnic table right at the entrance to the path, at their end, so every time we'd eat there it was a celebration of the path. Mr Wilson had one of those charcoal grills, you had to wait for your hamburgers while the charcoal got ready, but they tasted all the better when you got them. Mrs Wilson would sit back and twinkle, sort of laughing at Mr Wilson playing with his toy. They were like that, it was one of the good things about being with them, the way they could keep poking fun at each other without sticking any pins in, both getting a kick out of it. They used to make me feel that maybe growing up and even getting old wouldn't necessarily be all bad. Anyway, you have plenty of other time to live through before you get like that, don't you?

Well, I started to tell you about Ellen.

She had only a two-week vacation. She was studying at one of the big universities, archaeology, all about Indians; she got real excited and sparkled-up talking about it, when she saw we honestly wanted to listen. The way she told it, the Indians go way back beyond history, and you can find out things about that old time by digging up the places where they used to live, to see what's left. That's what she was going to be doing the rest of the summer, going on a "dig," she called it, out West somewhere, and it was extra-special for her because the man she's going to marry was going, too. (I put that in to help show you how wrong Mama was about Ellen.)

I thought maybe I could do some digging like that; it sounded pretty interesting, like being in a detective story and a hiking trip and a science lab all at once. She didn't laugh or tease or say how much I'd have to study in books first (I knew *that* much!)—she just looked thoughtful and said, "Sure, why not?"

So we liked her a lot, and Daddy did, too, why wouldn't he? And we were all having fun those two weeks, mostly just hanging around and talking and poking in the woods, at first we didn't notice that Mama wasn't joining it. She was terribly polite to Ellen, and maybe that ought to 've warned us, because there's a kind of politeness that's worse than yelling. I guess we were so used to Mama being sometimes peculiar, we hadn't ever thought she could be peculiar like *that*.

Ellen loved the path, loved it the right way, not oo-ah-ing or yattering how-lovely and so on, no, she walked slow, looking and smelling, breathing it in, without splattering a lot of words. Daddy was with us, and he said, "This is only part of it, come see where we cleared the rest of the woods," and they went off the path. And that was absolutely the only time they ever went off together, I know this, and there was nothing secret about it, they weren't even out of sight, merely poking about under the trees a little way off. For maybe as much as ten minutes. But Mama saw them.

She was standing halfway down the path, watching them, when Lollie and I went down toward the house, and her face had that stony-set look it sometimes gets, there's nothing you can do then except try to keep out of her way. But she smoothed it off so quick when she saw us, we thought we might have been mistaken.

There were two more good days, when nothing happened.

The afternoon of the day before Ellen was to leave, the Wilsons had a sort of good-bye party at the picnic table. Not a regular party, more of a sit-around; you don't really celebrate people's going away, even when you know they are going to something they are happy about. Cookies and lemonade, it was hot enough so the cold lemonade tasted wonderful, and everything would have been fine except that Mama wouldn't come. She told me to tell Mrs Wilson she had a headache. I did, and Mrs Wilson gave me a sort of funny look. I got the point: a headache is a sort of code between ladies, meaning I-don't-want-to-come-and-I-won't. Makes me wonder what you could say if you really did have a headache.

We'd finished the lemonade by the time Daddy got home. We heard him come up the path, whistling *Londonderry Air*—whenever he felt good he'd whistle some extra-sad tune like that. He stood around for a while, joshing Ellen about being in such a hurry to meet her boyfriend on that trip to their dig, and then he said, "Better not be late for supper," and started back. We were all pretending we weren't saying good-bye, we'd see Ellen again in the morning, though we knew she was leaving early. Some kinds of pretending are a big help, so long as everybody joins in. But Lollie wouldn't pretend; she'd worked up a real pash on Ellen, and all at once she went charging up to her and kissed her, and then went running off down the path, kind of hiccuping—ran right past Daddy and on home. I said the only thing I could think of, "Guess you'll have to come see us again, Ellen," and she said, "You better believe it." Then I went, too. I was walking a few steps behind Daddy when he came to the place you can't see around, and he went around the bend.

I went on, and saw Mama standing at the entrance to the path, paying no attention to Lollie grabbing at her. For maybe two seconds there was a sort of fire-haze in the air in front of her; she was moving her hands and twisting her face, her mouth working, but no words you could hear. Then she put up both hands flat, like pushing at something, and went away into the house.

Lollie and I said together: "Where's Daddy?"

I said, "He went around the bend just ahead of me," and Lollie said, "He never came." We looked at each other, and then we looked off different ways. Went on into the house, not wanting to, not daring to do anything else. Mama was setting three places for supper.

I was trying to tell myself it was a joke, he was hiding to tease us, and I sneaked out after supper and ran up the path hollering for him to come out. Nothing. Then I tried to go off the path under the trees, and I couldn't.

I guess I knew then, but I tried not to. Next morning all the way downstairs I told myself, "He'll be there eating breakfast, like always." He wasn't. So I nipped out and went up the path again. Mama never said anything, didn't try to stop me.

I told myself it was only that I'd been scared last night, of course I could go off the path into the trees. But no. It wasn't like a wall in the way, or anything pushing at me, only my feet kept going up and down without moving anywhere, stuck in the same place. And nothing to see except it was maybe darker than usual under the trees, and no bird noises. Nothing. I did call once, I said, "Daddy, it's Samantha, come back!" but my voice sounded so awful, making a noise all by itself in that empty place, I couldn't do it again.

It was late that afternoon when Lollie finally asked: "When is Daddy coming back?" Mama was rolling out piecrust. She sort of tossed her head and tightened her mouth and said, "When I get good and ready to let him," and snapped her mouth shut on it. Then she said, "Sometimes you have to give them a right sharp lesson."

I wanted to say, "It isn't any *them*, it's Daddy, and anyway what did he do wrong?" Didn't have the nerve. Didn't say anything. We didn't have much appetite for that pie, but the funny thing is, the pie was all right. I don't know what that proves, maybe that things don't fit together the way you might expect.

Next day was the worst, because that was when I heard him.

I thought maybe the magic would wear off by itself, would last only just so long, so I made another try at getting off the path. Same as before—I couldn't. Then there was a crashing of branches, breaking and ripping noises, though I couldn't see a whiff of motion anywhere. And I heard his voice, just once, but clear as anything: *"For God's sake, let me out!"*

I yelled back, I don't know what I said, and tried once more to push in, couldn't do it. I knew he didn't hear me. And then everything was quiet again, but the quiet was ten times worse now, because I *knew*.

I go up the path every day now, but I've never heard him again.

I went back down to the house and said, "Mama, *please*—?"

She looked at me as though she wondered how I came to be there, finally got me in focus. She said, "Well, we'll see." And that night I told Lollie, halfway believing it, "He'll be back tomorrow."

So the next morning I went up the path and just sat, waiting. And was still there when Lollie came running after me, too scared to cry and not making any sense; she kept saying "Mama—" and pulling at me to come.

Mama was sitting on the floor in front of the fireplace, a big fire roaring—in July! She had pushed the furniture out of the way so she could spread a mess of things on the floor. Things I'd never seen before, shells and stones and bits of wood with carving on, and a couple of old beat-up books—witch-things, or had been, but they were all dead. I could tell. She was weaving her hands over them, muttering and chanting, now and then she'd throw something into the fire and stop to push her hands through her hair. Her face was wild, twisted out of shape, *old*—hair all straggled and lank, falling into her eyes; she looked—oh, I shouldn't say it, but it's what other people mean when they say "looks like a witch."

And of course I knew what was wrong. She had been trying to unmake the black spell that held Daddy in the woods, and she couldn't do it.

I don't know how to explain this: if the Power is in a place, you can feel it, I mean I *can*. It was there, at first, a feeble sort of glow, but as we came into the room it sputtered and went out. And Mama didn't seem to know; she kept on trying, a minute or so longer. Then she made a dead sort of noise and started pushing all her bits and pieces from the floor into the fire. Sat there, not even crying, head down on her knees, rocking back and forth, rocking, rocking.

I said, "Mama, it's Samantha, I'm here," but she didn't hear me.

I told Lollie to run up to the Wilsons' for help, tell them Mama was sick. And then I just stood there. I guess I figured if she started setting things on fire, I could anyway put it out. She didn't, she only sat there, rocking. And then I knew she really had loved Daddy in her way, whatever her way was, even if she didn't know any better than to be jealous. And now she knew she had spoiled everything and couldn't unspoil it. I don't know what could be worse than that.

There isn't much to tell about the bad days that came next. The Wilsons sending for Aunt Grace. People coming to take Mama away to the crazy hospital.—Oh, I know you aren't supposed to call them crazies, and of course it *does* matter what words you use, nobody has to tell *me* that. Words are magic.

Anyway, there she is.

Aunt Grace is O.K., I guess, but I can't talk to her, she's too sensible. We should be grateful to her, it can't be any fun for her to come here and look after us. I could have done all the housekeeping and cooking, of course, but it wouldn't have been any use to say so, and I suppose you do have to have grown-ups around for driving the car and getting money out of the bank and stuff like that. And telling the neighbors where to get off, when they come nosying around trying to figure out what happened. Aunt Grace is good at that, she can use so many words to tell people nothing at all, it's almost fun to listen.

But meanwhile nothing is getting better. Daddy is still in the woods. And Mama in that hospital.

Aunt Grace went there to see her once, and came back saying it was no use. She won't let us go. Says: "If she knew, she wouldn't want you to see her like that. Not talking, not recognizing anyone, just sitting there. My own sister!" She thinks Mama won't ever get better. But that's because she doesn't understand about magic.

I can't explain how I know, but I *do* know that if we could get the black spell off and set Daddy free, Mama would come back, too. Maybe not the way she was, but back with us.—No, please don't think I'm silly enough to expect things to go back the way they were, before, when we were happy. They never do, do they? How do I know what will happen? I only know I can't leave it the way it is.

So now I'm asking you to put an ad in your magazine for a witch. She must be at least a third-degree witch—fourth would be better—anyway, strong enough to take off a black spell. Maybe you even know someone like that, right off, without advertising—I mean, I know most of the things you print are made-up stories, but still, you might. Anyway, tell her I haven't any money to pay her, but I'll work it off, I'll be her apprentice, as long as she likes, even after I get old enough to have the Power. She can tell, if you let her read all this, that I could do it, anything she wants. Anything.

And if she happens to be young and nice-looking, tell her she'll have to disguise herself when she goes to the hospital to see Mama. She'll understand about that.

But it must be soon, because the Wilsons are selling their house and moving away. Poor Mr Wilson had a stroke or something, they have to go where he can be taken care of more easily. So someone else will own the woods. And I heard Aunt Grace talking to Mrs Hall down the road, she says the people who want to buy the land are going to tear out the woods and build new houses, a development. And you see, if Daddy hasn't gotten out before that—well, it's not like being merely lost in the woods, the magic has put him *into* the trees, somehow, so if they start setting their machines at the trees, I just don't know *what* would happen to him.

Maybe you think they couldn't touch those trees? Just because a person can't walk in there?

You can't really suppose black magic would keep off bulldozers.

So I can't wait. Won't somebody please help me?

The Aiken Family

From Ebenezer Akin (1761–1836), as the name was then spelled, we can trace two collateral lines that reunited when Conrad Aiken's parents married. His father, William Aiken (1864–1901) a prominent physician in Savannah, Georgia, was the great-grandson of Ebenezer through his son, Jonathan (1800–1879), whilst his mother, Anna Potter (1864–1901), was the great-granddaughter through Ebenezer's daughter Anna (1790–1837). The Akins were of Scottish descent, from Aberdeen. David Akin (1635–1668?) emigrated with his wife Mary to Portsmouth, Rhode Island, in 1663. John (1663–1746) grew to be a sea captain and in 1692 acquired land in Old Dartmouth, Massachusetts where his son, Elihu (1720–1794) became a shipwright. John had been imprisoned for failing to pay over taxes that he had collected for the Court of Massachusetts which was a sign of his growing revolutionary sympathy. The Akin family became involved in harrying British ships. In 1778 Elihu expelled three English loyalists from the town. The British Redcoats descended upon Dartmouth and destroyed all Elihu's properties, including the shipyard. Elihu moved to another house owned by the Akin family which still stands today, called the Elihu Akin house. Alas, Elihu was financially ruined and died in poverty a few years later.

The Akins continued to fight in the American War of Independence. One of Elihu's sons, Jonathan (1753–1813), was imprisoned twice, once by the English and once by the French. After the War the family rebuilt the shipbuilding business but also turned to farming. Elihu's great-grandson, William Lyman Aiken (1821–1893)—the name had now mutated—was recorded by the *New York Times* as "a teacher of exceptional ability". His son, William Ford Aiken, became a noted ophthalmological surgeon.

The collateral family line saw Elihu Akin's granddaughter, Anna, marry into the Potter family. Her husband, William Potter (1784–1870) was a farmer and a Quaker in Dartmouth, Massachusetts. His ancestor, Nathaniel Potter (1613–1644) had emigrated to Rhode Island from London in 1638. Anna's son was the Rev. William James Potter (1829–1893) who had parted from Quakerism to more orthodox religion as a Unitarian minister, but then broke away from orthodoxy to form the Free Religious Association, which accepted scientific advances like Darwin's theory. His sermons became much loved and were issued in book form. Young Conrad Aiken, Potter's grandson, and whose middle name was Potter, wrote his own sermons in imitation. Thus, the literary germ was born.

1932

SILENT SNOW, SECRET SNOW

Conrad Aiken

On the morning of 27 February 1901 eleven-year-old Conrad Aiken (1889–1973), heard his parents arguing followed by two shots. He went to his parents' bedroom to find that his father had murdered his mother and then killed himself. Conrad had the presence of mind to walk to the local police station and report the incident. To say that it changed his life completely is to put it mildly. He was never the same again. He and his three siblings were sent to be looked after with different families. Conrad went to his paternal aunt, Emma Tillinghurst and her husband William, whilst the three younger children went to his mother's cousin, Louise Spooner. Although he was well looked after, Conrad later remarked that "I never felt I had a home." His uncle William was a librarian and young Aiken read voraciously. At school he edited the school magazine which contained his early writings. He went to Harvard where he became close friends with T. S. Eliot. Aiken became something of a restless traveller, with his first trip to England in 1908. He settled in England in 1921 with his first wife Jessie McDonald but returned to Harvard as a tutor in 1928, thereafter commuting between England and America for several years. He had an affair and suggested bringing his new lady back to England and living with Jessie "a trois". Jessie would have none of that and divorced him in 1930, promptly marrying one of his closest friends, Martin Armstrong. Aiken married his second wife and settled back in America. That marriage lasted only seven years and in 1937 he married a third time. They returned to England, living in Rye, until the outbreak of War saw them return to America.

His first book of poems, Earth Triumphant, was published in 1914 and it was as a poet that he established himself, winning a Pulitzer Prize for Selected Poems in 1930 and becoming the United States Poet Laureate from 1950–52. Aiken wrote many short stories, rarely turning to novel length works, but when he did, the results are often chilling, such as King Coffin (1935) where he enters the mind of an egotistical psychopath intent on committing the perfect murder. Aiken had occasional mood swings and could become dangerously irascible like his father, a problem he confronted in what he called an "autobiographical narrative", Ushant (1952). Fascinated by psychology and the workings of the mind he considered his own mental state in several stories, including the following.

Just why it should have happened, or why it should have happened just when it did, he could not, of course, possibly have said; nor perhaps would it even have occurred to him to ask. The thing was above all a secret, something to be preciously concealed from Mother and Father; and to that very fact it owed an enormous part of its deliciousness. It was like a peculiarly beautiful trinket to be carried unmentioned in one's trouser-pocket,—a rare stamp, an old coin, a few tiny gold links found trodden out of shape on the path in the park, a pebble of carnelian, a sea shell distinguishable from all others by an unusual spot or stripe,—and, as if it were any one of these, he carried around with him everywhere a warm and persistent and increasingly beautiful sense of possession. Nor was it only a sense of possession—it was also a sense of protection. It was as if, in some delightful way, his secret gave him a fortress, a wall behind which he could retreat into heavenly seclusion. This was almost the first thing he had noticed about it—apart from the oddness of the thing itself—and it was this that now again, for the fiftieth time, occurred to him, as he sat in the little schoolroom. It was the half hour for geography. Miss Buell was revolving with one finger, slowly, a huge terrestrial globe which had been placed on her desk. The green and yellow continents passed and repassed, questions were asked and answered, and now the little girl in front of him, Deirdre, who had a funny little constellation of freckles on the back of her neck, exactly like the Big Dipper, was standing up and telling Miss Buell that the equator was the line that ran round the middle.

Miss Buell's face, which was old and greyish and kindly, with grey stiff curls beside the cheeks, and eyes that swam very brightly, like little minnows, behind thick glasses, wrinkled itself into a complication of amusements.

"Ah! I see. The earth is wearing a belt, or a sash. Or someone drew a line round it!"

"Oh no—not that—I mean—"

In the general laughter, he did not share, or only a very little. He was thinking about the Arctic and Antarctic regions, which of course, on the globe, were white. Miss Buell was now telling them about the tropics, the jungles, the steamy heat of equatorial swamps, where the birds and butterflies, and even the snakes, were like living jewels. As he listened to these things, he was already, with a pleasant sense of half-effort, putting his secret between himself and the words. Was it really an effort at all? For effort implied something voluntary, and perhaps even something one did not especially want; whereas this was distinctly pleasant, and came almost of its own accord. All he needed to do was to think of that morning, the first one, and then of all the others—

But it was all so absurdly simple! It had amounted to so little. It was nothing, just an idea—and just why it should have become so wonderful, so permanent, was a mystery—a very pleasant one, to be sure, but also, in an amusing way, foolish. However, without ceasing to listen to Miss Buell, who had now moved up to the north temperate zones, he deliberately invited his memory of the first morning. It was only a moment or two after he had waked up—or perhaps the moment itself. But was there, to be exact, an exact moment? Was one awake all at once? or was it gradual? Anyway, it was after he had stretched a lazy hand up towards the headrail, and yawned, and then relaxed again among his warm covers, all the more grateful on a December morning, that the thing had happened. Suddenly, for no reason, he had thought of the postman, he remembered the postman. Perhaps there was nothing so odd in that. After all, he heard the postman almost every morning in his life—his heavy boots could be heard clumping round the corner at the top of the little cobbled hill-street, and then, progressively nearer, progressively louder, the double knock at each door, the crossings and re-crossings of the street, till finally the clumsy steps came stumbling across to the very door, and the tremendous knock came which shook the house itself.

(Miss Buell was saying "Vast wheat-growing areas in North America and Siberia."

Deirdre had for the moment placed her left hand across the back of her neck.)

But on this particular morning, the first morning, as he lay there with his eyes closed, he had for some reason *waited* for the postman. He wanted to hear him come round the corner. And that was precisely the joke—he never did. He never came. He never had come—*round the corner*—again. For when at last the steps *were* heard, they had already, he was quite sure, come a little down the hill, to the first house; and even so, the steps were curiously different—they were softer, they had a new secrecy about them, they were muffled and indistinct; and while the rhythm of them was the same, it now said a new thing—it said peace, it said remoteness, it said cold, it said sleep. And he had understood the situation at once—nothing could have seemed simpler—there had been snow in the night, such as all winter he had been longing for; and it was this which had rendered the postman's first footsteps inaudible, and the later ones faint. Of course! How lovely! And even now it must be snowing—it was going to be a snowy day—the long white ragged lines were drifting and sifting across the street, across the faces of the old houses, whispering and hushing, making little triangles of white in the corners between cobblestones, seething a little when the wind blew them over the ground to a drifted corner; and so it would be all day, getting deeper and deeper and silenter and silenter.

(Miss Buell was saying "Land of perpetual snow.") All this time, of course (while he lay in bed), he had kept his eyes closed, listening to the nearer progress of the postman, the muffled footsteps thumping and slipping on the snow-sheathed cobbles; and all the other sounds—the double knocks, a frosty far-off voice or two, a bell ringing thinly and softly as if under a sheet of ice—had the same slightly abstracted quality, as if removed by one degree from actuality—as if everything in the world had been insulated by snow. But when at last, pleased, he opened his eyes, and turned them towards the window, to see for himself this long-desired and now so clearly imagined miracle—what he saw instead was brilliant sunlight on a roof; and when, astonished, he jumped out of bed and stared down into the street, expecting to see the cobbles obliterated by the snow, he saw nothing but the bare bright cobbles themselves.

Queer, the effect this extraordinary surprise had had upon him—all the following morning he had kept with him a sense as of snow falling about him, a secret screen of new snow between himself and the world. If he had not dreamed such a thing—and how could he have dreamed it while awake?—how else could one explain it? In any case, the delusion had been so vivid as to affect his entire behaviour. He could not now remember whether it was on the first or the second morning—or was it even the third?—that his mother had drawn attention to some oddness in his manner.

"But my darling—" she had said at the breakfast table—"what has come over you? You don't seem to be listening..."

And how often that very thing had happened since!

(Miss Buell was now asking if anyone knew the difference between the North Pole and the Magnetic Pole. Deirdre was holding up her flickering brown hand, and he could see the four white dimples that marked the knuckles.)

Perhaps it hadn't been either the second or third morning—or even the fourth or fifth. How could he be sure? How could he be sure just when the delicious *progress* had become clear? Just when it had really *begun*? The intervals weren't very precise... All he now knew was, that at some point or other—perhaps the second day, perhaps the sixth—he had noticed that the presence of the snow was a little more insistent, the sound of it clearer; and, conversely, the sound of the postman's footsteps more indistinct. Not only could he not hear the steps come round the corner, he could not even hear them at the first house. It was below the first house that he heard them; and then, a few days later, it was below the second house that he heard them; and a few days later again, below the third. Gradually, gradually, the snow was becoming heavier, the sound of its seething louder, the cobblestones more and more muffled. When he found, each morning, on going to the window, after the ritual of listening, that the roofs and cobbles were as bare as ever, it made no difference. This was, after all, only what he had expected. It was even what pleased him, what rewarded him: the thing was his own, belonged to no one else. No one else knew about it, not even his mother and father. There, outside, were the bare cobbles; and here, inside, was the snow. Snow growing heavier each day, muffling the world, hiding the ugly, and deadening increasingly—above all—the steps of the postman.

"But my darling—" she had said at the luncheon table—"what has come over you? You don't seem to listen when people speak to you. That's the third time I've asked you to pass your plate..."

How was one to explain this to Mother? or to Father? There was, of course, nothing to be done about it: nothing. All one could do was to laugh embarrassedly, pretend to be a little ashamed, apologize, and take a sudden and somewhat disingenuous interest in what was being done or said. The cat had stayed out all night. He had a curious swelling on his left cheek—perhaps somebody had kicked him, or a stone had struck him. Mrs Kempton was or was not coming to tea. The house was going to be house cleaned, or "turned out," on Wednesday instead of Friday. A new lamp was provided for his evening work—perhaps it was eyestrain which accounted for this new and so peculiar vagueness of his—Mother was looking at him with amusement as she said this, but with something else as well. A new lamp? A new lamp. Yes Mother, No Mother, Yes Mother. School is going very well. The geometry is very easy. The history is very dull. The geography is very interesting—particularly when it takes one to the North Pole. Why the North Pole? Oh, well, it would be fun to be an explorer. Another Peary or Scott or Shackleton. And then abruptly he found his interest in the talk at an end, stared at the pudding on his plate, listened, waited, and began once more—ah how heavenly, too, the first beginnings—to hear or feel—for could he actually hear it?—the silent snow, the secret snow.

(Miss Buell was telling them about the search for the Northwest Passage, about Hendrik Hudson, the *Half Moon*.)

This had been, indeed, the only distressing feature of the new experience: the fact that it so increasingly had brought him into a kind of mute misunderstanding, or even conflict, with his father and mother. It was as if he were trying to lead a double life. On the one hand he had to be Paul Hasleman, and keep up the appearance of being that person—dress, wash, and answer intelligently when spoken to—; on the other, he had to explore this new world which had been opened to him. Nor could there be the slightest doubt—not the slightest—that the new world was the profounder and more wonderful of the two. It was irresistible. It was miraculous. Its beauty was simply beyond anything—beyond speech as beyond thought—utterly incommunicable. But how then, between the two worlds, of which he was thus constantly aware, was he to keep a balance? One must get up, one must go to breakfast, one must talk with Mother, go to school, do one's lessons—and, in all this, try not to appear too much of a fool. But if all the while one was also trying to extract the full deliciousness of another and quite separate existence, one which could not easily (if at all) be spoken of—how was one to manage? How was one to explain? Would it be safe to explain? Would it be absurd? Would it merely mean that he would get into some obscure kind of trouble?

These thoughts came and went, came and went, as softly and secretly as the snow; they were not precisely a disturbance, perhaps they were even a pleasure; he liked to have them; their presence was something almost palpable, something he could stroke with his hand, without closing his eyes, and without ceasing to see Miss Buell and the schoolroom and the globe and the freckles on Deirdre's neck; nevertheless he did in a sense cease to see, or to see the obvious external world, and substituted for this vision the vision of snow, the sound of snow, and the slow, almost soundless, approach of the postman. Yesterday, it had been only at the sixth house that the postman had become audible; the snow was much deeper now, it was falling more swiftly and heavily, the sound of its seething was more distinct, more soothing, more persistent. And this morning, it had been—as nearly as he could figure—just above the seventh house—perhaps only a step or two above: at most, he had heard two or three footsteps before the knock had sounded... And with each such narrowing of the sphere, each nearer approach of the limit at which the postman was first audible, it was odd how sharply was increased the amount of illusion which had to be carried into the ordinary business of daily life. Each day, it was harder to get out of bed, to go to the window, to look out at the—as always—perfectly empty and snowless street. Each day it was more difficult to go through the perfunctory motions of greeting Mother and Father at breakfast, to reply to their questions, to put his books together and go to school. And at school, how extraordinarily hard to conduct with success simultaneously the public life and the life that was secret. There were times when he longed—positively ached—to tell everyone about it—to burst out with it—only to be checked almost at once by a far-off feeling as of some faint absurdity which was inherent in it—but *was* it absurd?—and more importantly by a sense of mysterious power in his very secrecy. Yes: it must be kept secret. That, more and more, became clear. At whatever cost to himself, whatever pain to others—

(Miss Buell looked straight at him, smiling, and said, "Perhaps we'll ask Paul. I'm sure Paul will come out of his day-dream long enough to be able to tell us. Won't you, Paul." He rose slowly from his chair, resting one hand on the brightly varnished desk, and deliberately stared through the snow towards the blackboard. It was an effort, but it was amusing to make it. "Yes," he said slowly, "it was what we now call the Hudson River. This he thought to be the Northwest Passage. He was disappointed." He sat down again, and as he did so Deirdre half turned in her chair and gave him a shy smile, of approval and admiration.)

At whatever pain to others.

This part of it was very puzzling, very puzzling. Mother was very nice, and so was Father. Yes, that was all true enough. He wanted to be nice to them, to tell them everything—and yet, was it really wrong of him to want to have a secret place of his own?

At bedtime, the night before, Mother had said, "If this goes on, my lad, we'll have to see a doctor, we will! We can't have our boy—" But what was it she had said? "Live in another world"? "Live so far away"? The word "far" had been in it, he was sure, and then Mother had taken up a magazine again and laughed a little, but with an expression which wasn't mirthful, He had felt sorry for her...

The bell rang for dismissal. The sound came to him through long curved parallels of falling snow. He saw Deirdre rise, and had himself risen almost as soon—but not quite as soon—as she.

II

On the walk homeward, which was timeless, it pleased him to see through the accompaniment, or counterpoint, of snow, the items of mere externality on his way. There were many kinds of brick in the sidewalks, and laid in many kinds of pattern. The garden walls too were various, some of wooden palings, some of plaster, some of stone. Twigs of bushes leaned over the walls: the little hard green winter-buds of lilac, on grey stems, sheathed and fat; other branches very thin and fine and black and desiccated. Dirty sparrows huddled in the bushes, as dull in color as dead fruit left in leafless trees. A single starling creaked on a weather vane. In the gutter, beside a drain, was a scrap of torn and dirty newspaper, caught in a little delta of filth: the word ECZEMA appeared in large capitals, and below it was a letter from Mrs Amelia D. Cravath, 2100 Pine Street, Fort

Worth, Texas, to the effect that after being a sufferer for years she had been cured by Caley's Ointment. In the little delta, beside the fan-shaped and deeply runnelled continent of brown mud, were lost twigs, descended from their parent trees, dead matches, a rusty horse-chestnut burr, a small concentration of sparkling gravel on the lip of the sewer, a fragment of egg-shell, a streak of yellow sawdust which had been wet and now was dry and congealed, a brown pebble, and a broken feather. Further on was a cement sidewalk, ruled into geometrical parallelograms, with a brass inlay at one end commemorating the contractors who had laid it, and, halfway across, an irregular and random series of dog-tracks, immortalized in synthetic stone. He knew these well, and always stepped on them; to cover the little hollows with his own foot had always been a queer pleasure; today he did it once more, but perfunctorily and detachedly, all the while thinking of something else. That was a dog, a long time ago, who had made a mistake and walked on the cement while it was still wet. He had probably wagged his tail, but that hadn't been recorded. Now, Paul Hasleman, aged twelve, on his way home from school, crossed the same river, which in the meantime had frozen into rock. Homeward through the snow, the snow falling in bright sunshine. Homeward?

Then came the gateway with the two posts surmounted by egg-shaped stones which had been cunningly balanced on their ends, as if by Columbus, and mortared in the very act of balance: a source of perpetual wonder. On the brick wall just beyond, the letter H had been stenciled, presumably for some purpose. H? H.

The green hydrant, with a little green-painted chain attached to the brass screw-cap.

The elm tree, with the great grey wound in the bark, kidney-shaped, into which he always put his hand—to feel the cold but living wood. The injury, he had been sure, was due to the gnawings of a tethered horse. But now it deserved only a passing palm, a merely tolerant eye. There were more important things. Miracles. Beyond the thoughts of trees, mere elms. Beyond the thoughts of sidewalks, mere stone, mere brick, mere cement. Beyond the thoughts even of his own shoes, which trod these sidewalks obediently, bearing a burden—far above—of elaborate mystery. He watched them. They were not very well polished; he had neglected them, for a very good reason: they were one of the many parts of the increasing difficulty of the daily return to daily life, the morning struggle. To get up, having at last opened one's eyes, to go to the window, and discover no snow, to wash, to dress, to descend the curving stairs to breakfast—

At whatever pain to others, nevertheless, one must persevere in severance, since the incommunicability of the experience demanded it. It was desirable of course to be kind to Mother and Father, especially as they seemed to be worried, but it was also desirable to be resolute. If they should decide—as appeared likely—to consult the doctor, Doctor Howells, and have Paul inspected, his heart listened to through a kind of dictaphone, his lungs, his stomach—well, that was all right. He would go through with it. He would give them answer for question, too—perhaps such answers as they hadn't expected? No. That would never do. For the secret world must, at all costs, be preserved.

The bird-house in the apple-tree was empty—it was the wrong time of year for wrens. The little round black door had lost its pleasure. The wrens were enjoying other houses, other nests, remoter trees. But this too was a notion which he only vaguely and grazingly entertained—as if, for the moment, he merely touched an edge of it; there was something further on, which was already assuming a sharper importance; something which already teased at the corners of his eyes, teasing also at the corner of his mind. It was funny to think that he so wanted this, so awaited it—and yet found himself enjoying this momentary dalliance with the bird-house, as if for a quite deliberate postponement and enhancement of the approaching pleasure. He was aware of his delay, of his smiling and detached and now almost uncomprehending gaze at the little bird-house; he knew what he was going to look at next: it was his own little cobbled hill-street, his own house, the little river at the bottom of the hill, the grocer's shop with the cardboard man in the window—and now, thinking of all this, he turned his head, still smiling, and looking quickly right and left through the snow-laden sunlight.

And the mist of snow, as he had foreseen, was still on it—a ghost of snow falling in the bright sunlight, softly and steadily floating and turning and pausing, soundlessly meeting the snow that covered, as with a transparent mirage, the bare bright cobbles. He loved it—he stood still and loved it. Its beauty was paralyzing—beyond all words, all experience, all dream. No fairy-story he had ever read could be compared with it—none had ever given him this extraordinary combination of ethereal loveliness with a something else, unnameable, which was just faintly and deliciously terrifying. What was this thing? As he thought of it, he looked upward toward his own bedroom window, which was open—and it was as if he looked straight into the room and saw himself lying half awake in his bed. There he was—at this very instant he was still perhaps actually there—more truly there than standing here at the edge of the cobbled hill-street, with one hand lifted to shade his eyes against the snow-sun. Had he indeed ever left his room, in all this time? since that very first morning? Was the whole progress still being enacted there, was it still the same morning, and himself not yet wholly awake? And even now, had the postman not yet come round the corner?...

This idea amused him, and automatically, as he thought of it, he turned his head and looked toward the top of the hill. There was, of course, nothing there—nothing and no one. The street was empty and quiet. And all the more because of its emptiness it occurred to him to count the houses—a thing which, oddly enough, he hadn't before thought of doing. Of course, he had known there weren't many—many, that is, on his own side of the street, which were the ones that figured in the postman's progress—but nevertheless it came to him as something of a shock to find that there were precisely *six,* above his own house—his own house was the seventh.

Six!

Astonished, he looked at his own house—looked at the door, on which was the number thirteen—and then realized that the whole thing was exactly and logically and absurdly what he ought to have known. Just the same, the realization gave him abruptly, and even a little frighteningly, a sense of hurry. He was being hurried—he was being rushed. For—he knit his brows—he couldn't be mistaken—it was just above the *seventh* house, his own house, that the postman had first been audible this very morning. But in that case—in that case— did it mean that tomorrow he would hear nothing? The knock he had heard must have been the knock of their own door. Did it mean—and this was an idea which gave him a really extraordinary feeling of surprise—that he would never hear the postman again?—that tomorrow morning the postman would already have passed the house, in a snow by then so deep as to render his footsteps completely inaudible? That he would have made his approach down the snow-filled street so soundlessly, so secretly, that he, Paul Hasleman, there lying in bed, would not have waked in time, or, waking, would have heard nothing?

But how could that be? Unless even the knocker should be muffled in the snow—frozen tight, perhaps?... But in that case—

A vague feeling of disappointment came over him; a vague sadness, as if he felt himself deprived of something which he had long looked forward to, something much prized. After all this, all this beautiful progress, the slow delicious advance of the postman through the silent and secret snow, the knock creeping closer each day, and the footsteps nearer, the audible compass of the world thus daily narrowed, narrowed, narrowed, as the snow soothingly and beautifully encroached and deepened, after all this, was he to be defrauded of the one thing he had so wanted—to be able to count, as it were, the last two or three solemn footsteps, as they finally approached his own door? Was it all going to happen, at the end, so suddenly? or indeed, had it already happened? with no slow and subtle gradations of menace, in which he could luxuriate?

He gazed upward again, toward his own window which flashed in the sun: and this time almost with a feeling that it would be better if he *were* still in bed, in that room; for in that case this must still be the first morning, and there would be six more mornings to come—or, for that matter, seven or eight or nine—how could he be sure?—or even more.

III

After supper, the inquisition began. He stood before the doctor, under the lamp, and submitted silently to the usual thumpings and tappings.

"Now will you please say 'Ah!'?"

"An!"

"Now again please, if you don't mind."

"An."

"Say it slowly, and hold it if you can—"

"Ah-h-h-h-h-h—"

"Good."

How silly all this was. As if it had anything to do with his throat! Or his heart or lungs!

Relaxing his mouth, of which the corners, after all this absurd stretching, felt uncomfortable, he avoided the doctor's eyes, and stared towards the fireplace, past his mother's feet (in grey slippers) which projected from the green chair, and his father's feet (in brown slippers) which stood neatly side by side on the hearth rug.

"Hm. There is certainly nothing wrong there...?"

He felt the doctor's eyes fixed upon him, and, as if merely to be polite, returned the look, but with a feeling of justifiable evasiveness.

"Now, young man, tell me,—do you feel all right?"

"Yes, sir, quite all right."

"No headaches? no dizziness?"

"No, I don't think so."

"Let me see. Let's get a book, if you don't mind—yes, thank you, that will do splendidly—and now, Paul, if you'll just read it, holding it as you would normally hold it—"

He took the book and read:

"And another praise have I to tell for this the city our mother, the gift of a great god, a glory of the land most high; the might of horses, the might of young horses, the might of the sea... For thou, son of Cronus, our lord Poseidon, hast throned herein this pride, since in these roads first thou didst show forth the curb that cures the rage of steeds. And the shapely oar, apt to men's hands, hath a wondrous speed on the brine, following the hundred-footed Nereids... O land that art praised above all lands, now is it for thee to make those bright praises seen in deeds."

He stopped, tentatively, and lowered the heavy book.

"No—as I thought—there is certainly no superficial sign of eyestrain."

Silence thronged the room, and he was aware of the focused scrutiny of the three people who confronted him.

"We could have his eyes examined—but I believe it is something else."

"What could it be?" This was his father's voice.

"It's only this curious absent-mindedness—" This was his mother's voice.

In the presence of the doctor, they both seemed irritatingly apologetic.

"I believe it is something else. Now Paul—I would like very much to ask you a question or two. You will answer them, won't you—you know I'm an old, old friend of yours, eh? That's right!..."

His back was thumped twice by the doctor's fat fist,—then the doctor was grinning at him with false amiability, while with one finger-nail he was scratching the top button of his waistcoat. Beyond the doctor's shoulder was the fire, the fingers of flame making light prestidigitation against the sooty fireback, the soft sound of their random flutter the only sound.

"I would like to know—is there anything that worries you?"

The doctor was again smiling, his eyelids low against the little black pupils, in each of which was a tiny white bead of light. Why answer him? why answer him at all? "At whatever pain to others"—but it was all a nuisance, this necessity for resistance, this necessity for attention: it was as if one had been stood up on a brilliantly lighted stage, under a great round blaze of spotlight; as if one were merely a trained seal, or a performing dog, or a fish, dipped out of an aquarium and held up by the tail. It would serve them right if he were merely to bark or growl. And meanwhile, to miss these last few precious hours, these hours of which each minute was more beautiful than the last, more menacing—? He still looked, as if from a great distance, at the beads of light in the doctor's eyes, at the fixed false smile, and then, beyond, once more at his mother's slippers, his father's slippers, the soft flutter of the fire. Even here, even amongst these hostile presences, and in this arranged light, he could see the snow, he could hear it—it was in the corners of the room, where the shadow was deepest, under the sofa, behind the half-opened door which led to the dining-room. It was gentler here, softer, its seethe the quietest of whispers, as if, in deference to a drawing-room, it had quite deliberately put on its "manners"; it kept itself out of sight, obliterated itself, but distinctly with an air of saying, "Ah, but just wait! Wait till we are alone together! Then I will begin to tell you something new! Something white! something cold! something sleepy! something of cease, and peace, and the long bright curve of space! Tell them to go away. Banish them. Refuse to speak. Leave them, go upstairs to your room, turn out the light and get into bed—I will go with you, I will be waiting for you, I will tell you a better story than Little Kay of the Skates, or The Snow Ghost—I will surround your bed, I will close the windows, pile a deep drift against the door, so that none will ever again be able to enter. Speak to them!..." It seemed as if the little hissing voice came from a slow white spiral of falling flakes in the corner by the front window—but he could not be sure. He felt himself smiling, then, and said to the doctor, but without looking at him, looking beyond him still—"Oh no, I think not—"

"But are you sure, my boy?"

His father's voice came softly and coldly then—the familiar voice of silken warning...

"You needn't answer at once, Paul—remember we're trying to help you—think it over and be quite sure, won't you?"

He felt himself smiling again, at the notion of being quite sure. What a joke! As if he weren't so sure that reassurance was no longer necessary, and all this cross-examination a ridiculous farce, a grotesque parody! What could they know about it? these gross intelligences, these humdrum minds so bound to the usual, the ordinary? Impossible to tell them about it! Why, even now, even now, with the proof so abundant, so formidable, so imminent, so appallingly present here in this very room, could they believe it?—could even his mother believe it? No—it was only too plain that if anything were said about it, the merest hint given, they would be incredulous—they would laugh—they would say "Absurd!"—think things about him which weren't true...

"Why no, I'm not worried—why should I be?"

He looked then straight at the doctor's low-lidded eyes, looked from one of them to the other, from one bead of light to the other, and gave a little laugh.

The doctor seemed to be disconcerted by this. He drew back in his chair, resting a fat white hand on either knee. The smile faded slowly from his face.

"Well, Paul!" he said, and paused gravely, "I'm afraid you don't take this quite seriously enough. I think you perhaps don't quite realize—don't quite realize—" He took a deep quick breath, and turned, as if helplessly, at a loss for words, to the others. But Mother and Father were both silent—no help was forthcoming.

"You must surely know, be aware, that you have not been quite yourself, of late? don't you know that?..."

It was amusing to watch the doctor's renewed attempt at a smile, a queer disorganized look, as of confidential embarrassment.

"I feel all right, sir," he said, and again gave the little laugh.

"And we're trying to help you." The doctor's tone sharpened.

"Yes sir, I know. But why? I'm all right. I'm just *thinking,* that's all."

His mother made a quick movement forward, resting a hand on the back of the doctor's chair.

"Thinking?" she said. "But my dear, about what?"

This was a direct challenge—and would have to be directly met. But before he met it, he looked again into the corner by the door, as if for reassurance. He smiled again at what he saw, at what he heard. The little spiral was still there, still softly whirling, like the ghost of a white kitten chasing the ghost of a white tail, and making as it did so the faintest of whispers. It was all right! If only he could remain firm, everything was going to be all right.

"Oh, about anything, about nothing,—*you* know the way you do!"

"You mean—day-dreaming?"

"Oh, no—thinking!"

"But thinking about what?"

"Anything."

He laughed a third time—but this time, happening to glance upward towards his mother's face, he was appalled at the effect his laughter seemed to have upon her. Her mouth had opened in an expression of horror... This was too bad! Unfortunate! He had known it would cause pain, of course—but he hadn't expected it to be quite so bad as this. Perhaps—perhaps if he just gave them a tiny gleaming hint—?

"About the snow," he said.

"What on earth!" This was his father's voice. The brown slippers came a step nearer on the hearthrug.

"But my dear, what do you mean!" This was his mother's voice.

The doctor merely stared.

"Just *snow* that's all. I like to think about it."

"Tell us about it, my boy."

"But that's all it is. There's nothing to tell. *You* know what snow is?"

This he said almost angrily, for he felt that they were trying to corner him. He turned sideways so as no longer to face the doctor, and the better to see the inch of blackness between the window-sill and the lowered curtain,—the cold inch of beckoning and delicious night. At once he felt better, more assured.

"Mother—can I go to bed, now, please? I've got a headache."

"But I thought you said—"

"It's just come. It's all these questions—! Can I, mother?"

"You can go as soon as the doctor has finished."

"Don't you think this thing ought to be gone into thoroughly, and now?" This was Father's voice. The brown slippers again came a step nearer, the voice was the well-known "punishment" voice, resonant and cruel.

"Oh, what's the use, Norman—"

Quite suddenly, everyone was silent. And without precisely facing them, nevertheless he was aware that all three of them were watching him with an extraordinary intensity—staring hard at him—as if he had done something monstrous, or was himself some kind of monster. He could hear the soft irregular flutter of the flames; the cluck-click-cluck-click of the clock; far and faint, two sudden spurts of laughter from the kitchen, as quickly cut off as begun; a murmur of water in the pipes; and then, the silence seemed to deepen, to spread out, to become worldlong and worldwide, to become timeless and shapeless, and to center inevitably and rightly, with a slow and sleepy but enormous concentration of all power, on the beginning of a new sound. What this new sound was going to be, he knew perfectly well. It might begin with a hiss, but it would end with a roar—there was no time to lose—he must escape. It mustn't happen here—Without another word, he turned and ran up the stairs.

IV

Not a moment too soon. The darkness was coming in long white waves. A prolonged sibilance filled the night—a great seamless seethe of wild influence went abruptly across it—a cold low humming shook the windows. He shut the door and flung off his clothes in the dark. The bare black floor was like a little raft tossed in waves of snow, almost overwhelmed, washed under whitely, up again, smothered in curled billows of feather. The snow was laughing: it spoke from all sides at once: it pressed closer to him as he ran and jumped exulting into his bed.

"Listen to us!" it said. "Listen! We have come to tell you the story we told you about. You remember? Lie down. Shut your eyes, now—you will no longer see much—in this white darkness who could see, or want to see? We will take the place of everything... Listen—"

A beautiful varying dance of snow began at the front of the room, came forward and then retreated, flattened out toward the floor, then rose fountain-like to the ceiling, swayed, recruited itself from a new stream of flakes which poured laughing in through the humming window, advanced again, lifted long white arms. It said peace, it said remoteness, it said cold—it said—

But then a gash of horrible light fell brutally across the room from the opening door—the snow drew back hissing—something alien had come into the room—something hostile. This thing rushed at him, clutched at him, shook him—and he was not merely horrified, he was filled with such a loathing as he had never known. What was this? this cruel disturbance? this act of anger and hate? It was as if he had to reach up a hand toward another world for any understanding of it,—an effort of which he was only barely capable.

But of that other world he still remembered just enough to know the exorcizing words. They tore themselves from his other life suddenly—

"Mother! Mother! Go away! I hate you!"

And with that effort, everything was solved, everything became all right: the seamless hiss advanced once more, the long white wavering lines rose and fell like enormous whispering sea-waves, the whisper becoming louder, the laughter more numerous.

"Listen!" it said. "We'll tell you the last, the most beautiful and secret story—shut your eyes—it is a very small story—a story that gets smaller and smaller—it comes inward instead of opening like a flower—it is a flower becoming a seed—a little cold seed—do you hear? we are leaning closer to you—"

The hiss was now becoming a roar—the whole world was a vast moving screen of snow—but even now it said peace, it said remoteness, it said cold, it said sleep.

1932

THE PIPE-SMOKER

Martin Armstrong

Conrad Aiken and Martin Armstrong had been friends since they'd met in Florence in 1911 and he had become supportive of Aiken's wife Jessie when Conrad met another woman back in the States. Jessie divorced Conrad and married Martin. He became a wonderful stepfather to the three children, John, Jane and Joan.

Martin Donisthorpe Armstrong (1882–1974) was a Geordie, Newcastle born-and-bred. His father, Charles Armstrong (1850–1923), was an architect whilst on his mother's side he was descended from wool merchants. Martin had no desire to follow either vocation. Of greater literary significance was his maternal grandmother, Elizabeth Wordsworth (1821–1881) who was a cousin of the more famous William Wordsworth. Armstrong followed Wordsworth's passion for observing the world about him and he excelled as a poet—one of the so-called Georgian Poets who thrived in the reign of George V and who included Robert Graves, Rupert Brooke and Walter de la Mare. Armstrong's first book of poetry, Exodus, *appeared in 1912 and though several more volumes appeared he also embraced the short story and had a fascination for the fantastic and absurd. His first such collection was* The Puppet Show *(1922), which includes several perceptive fables reflecting the vicissitudes of life. His fantasies and weird tales were collected in* The Bazaar *(1924),* The Fiery Dive *(1929) and* General Buntop's Miracle *(1934). In all these stories we find unusual things happening to normal people, but we also find the author using his skills of perception to open our awareness to a strangeness we might otherwise miss. Nowhere is this more potent than in the following story, set in a house where Armstrong once lived.*

I don't usually mind walking in rain, but on this occasion the rain was coming down in torrents and I still had ten miles to go. That was why I stopped at the first house, a house about a mile from the village ahead of me, and looked over the garden gate. The house didn't look promising, for I saw at once that it was empty. All the windows were shut, and not one of them had a blind or a curtain. Through one on the ground floor I saw bare walls, a bare mantelpiece, and an empty grate. The garden, too, was wild, the beds full of weeds: you would hardly have known it for a garden but for the fence, the vestiges of straight paths, and the lilac-bushes which were in full bloom and sent showers of water to the grass every time the wind tossed them.

You can imagine, then, that I was surprised when a man strolled out from the lilacs and came slowly towards me down the path. What was surprising was not merely that he was there, but that he was strolling aimlessly about, bareheaded and without a mackintosh, in the drenching rain. He was rather a fat man and dressed as a clergyman, grey-haired, bald, cleanshaven, with that swollen-headed and over-intense look which one sees in portraits of William Blake. I noticed at once how his arms hung limply at his sides. His clothes and—what made him still stranger—his face, were streaming with water! He didn't seem to be in the least aware of the rain. But I was. It was beginning to trickle through my hair and down my neck, and I said:

"Excuse me, sir, but may I come in and shelter?"

He started and raised puzzled eyes to mine. "Shelter?" he said.

"Yes," I replied, "from the rain."

"Ah, from the rain. Yes, sir, by all means. Pray come in."

I opened the garden gate and followed him down a path towards the front door, where he stood aside with a slight bow to let me pass in first. "I fear you won't find it very comfortable," he said when we were in the hall. "However, come in, sir; in here, first door on the left."

The room, which was a large one with a bow-window divided into five lights, was empty, except for a deal table and bench and a smaller table in a corner near the door with an unlighted lamp on it.

"Pray sit down, sir," he said, pointing to the bench with another slight bow. There was an old-fashioned politeness in his manner and language. He himself did not sit down, but walked to the window and stood looking out at the streaming garden, his arms still hanging idly at his sides.

"Apparently you don't mind rain as much as I do, sir," I said, in an attempt to be amiable.

He turned round, and I had the impression that he could not turn his head and so had to turn his whole body in order to look at me.

"No, oh, no!" he replied. "Not at all. In point of fact, I hadn't observed it till you pointed it out."

"But you must be very wet," I said. "Wouldn't it be wiser to change?"

"To change?" His gaze became searching and suspicious at the question.

"To change your wet clothes."

"Change my clothes?" he said. "Oh, no! Oh, dear me, no, sir! If they're wet, doubtless they'll dry in the course of time. It isn't raining in here, I take it?"

I looked at his face. He really was asking for information. "No," I replied, "it isn't raining in here, thank goodness."

"I fear I can't offer you anything," he said politely. "A woman comes from the village in the morning and evening, but meanwhile I'm quite helpless," He opened and closed his hanging hands. "Unless," he added, "you would care to go to the kitchen and make yourself a cup of tea, if you understand such things."

I refused, but asked leave to smoke a cigarette.

"Pray do," he said. "I fear I have none to offer you. The other, my predecessor, used to smoke cigarettes, but I'm a pipe-smoker." He brought a pipe and pouch from his pocket; it was a relief to see him use his arms and hands.

When we had both lit up, I spoke again; I was conscious all the while that the responsibility for conversation was mine; that, if I had not spoken, my strange host would have made no attempt to break the silence, but would simply have stood with his arms at his sides looking straight in front of him either at the garden or at me.

I glanced round the bare room. "You're just moving in, I suppose?" I said.

"Moving in?" He shifted slightly and turned his intense, uncomfortable gaze on me again.

"Moving into this house, I mean."

"Oh, no," he said. "Oh, dear me, no, sir. I've been here for several years; or, rather, I myself have been here for nearly a year, and the other, my predecessor, was here for five years before that. Yes, it must be seven months now since he passed away. No doubt, sir"—a melancholy, wistful smile unexpectedly transformed his face—"no doubt you won't believe me—Mrs Bellows wouldn't—when I tell you I've been here only seven months, there or thereabouts."

"If you say so, sir," I replied, "why should I disbelieve you?"

He took a few steps towards me and lifted his right hand. Reluctantly I took it, a thick, limp, cold hand that gave me an unpleasant thrill. "Thank you, sir," he said; "thank you. You're the first, absolutely the first...!"

I dropped the hand and he did not finish the phrase. He had fallen, apparently, into a reverie. Then he began again. "No doubt all would have been well if only my... that is, my predecessor's old cousin, had not left him this house. He was better off where he was. He was a clergyman, you know." He opened his hands, exhibiting himself. "These are his clothes."

Again he absented himself, fell into a reverie, while his body in its clergyman's clothes stood before me. Suddenly he asked me: "Do you believe in confession?"

"In confession?" I said. "You mean in the religious sense of the term?"

He took a step closer. He was almost touching me now. "What I mean is," he said, lowering his voice and looking at me intensely, "do you believe that to confess, to confess a sin or a... crime, brings relief?"

What was he going to tell me? I should have liked to say "No," to discourage any confession from the poor old creature, but he had put his question so appealingly that I could not find it in my heart to repulse him. "Yes," I said, "I think that by speaking of it one can often rid oneself of a weight on the mind."

"You have been so sympathetic, sir," he said with one of his polite bows, "that I feel tempted to trespass...!" He lifted one of his heavy hands in a perfunctory gesture and dropped it again. "Would you have the patience to listen?"

He stood beside me as if he had been a tailor's dummy that had been placed there. His leg touched my knee. I felt strongly repelled by his closeness. "Won't you sit down there?" I said, pointing to the other end of the bench on which I was sitting. "I should find it easier to listen."

He turned his body and gazed earnestly at the bench, then sat down on it, facing me, a leg on either side of it, leaning towards me. He was about to speak, but he checked himself and glanced at the window and the door. Then he took his pipe from his mouth and laid it on the table, and his eyes returned to me. "My secret, my terrible secret," he said, "is that I'm a murderer."

His statement horrified me, as well it might; and yet, I think, it hardly surprised me. His extreme strangeness had prepared me, to some extent, for something rather grim. I caught my breath and stared at him, and he, with horror in his eyes, stared back at me. He seemed to be waiting for me to speak, but at first I could not speak. What, in the name of sanity, could I say? What I did say at last was something fantastically inadequate. "And this," I said, "weighs on your mind?"

"It haunts me," he said, suddenly clenching his heavy, limp hands that lay on the bench in front of him. "Would you have the patience...?"

I nodded. "Tell me about it," I said.

"If it hadn't been for the legacy of this house," he began, "nothing would have happened. The other, my predecessor, would have stayed in his Rectory, and I... I should never have come on the scene at all. Although it must be confessed that he, my predecessor, was not happy in his Rectory. He met with unfriendliness, suspicion. That was why he first came to this house—just as a trial, you see. It was bequeathed to him empty: simply the house—no furniture, no money—and he came and put in one or two things—this table, this bench, a few kitchen things, a folding bed upstairs. He wanted, you see, to try it, first. Its remoteness appealed to him, but he wanted to be sure about it in other ways. Some houses, you see, are safe, and some are not, and he wanted to make sure that this was a safe house before moving into it." He paused and then said very earnestly: "Let me advise you, my friend, always to do that when you contemplate moving into a strange house, because some houses are very unsafe."

I nodded. "Quite so!" I said. "Damp walls, bad drainage, and so on."

He shook his head. "No," he said, "not that. Something much more serious than that. I mean the spirit of the house. Don't you feel"—his gaze grew more piercing than ever—"that this is a dangerous house?"

I shrugged my shoulders. "Empty houses are always a little queer," I said.

He reflected on this statement. "And you have noticed," he inquired at last, "the queerness of this one?"

I did, as he asked me the question, feel that the house was queer; but it was *his* queerness, I knew well enough, and the grim suggestiveness of his talk, that made it so, and I replied, "Not queerer than other empty houses, sir."

He gazed at me incredulously. "Strange!" he said. "Strange that you shouldn't feel it. Though it's true that... that the other, my predecessor, didn't feel it at first. Even this room—for this room sir, is the dangerous room—didn't seem strange to him at first; no, even in spite of a very peculiar thing about it."

If it had been fine, I should have ended the conversation and left him, for the old man's talk and manner were making me feel more and more uncomfortable. But it was not fine: it was raining as hard as ever and was becoming very dark. Evidently we were in for a thunderstorm.

The old man got up from the bench. "I think I can show you, now," he said, "the peculiar thing about the room. It is visible only after dark, but I think it is dark enough now."

He went to the little table in the corner and began to light the lamp. When it was alight and he had replaced the frosted-glass globe, he brought it to the larger table and set it down on my left. "Now," he said to me, "sit square to the table."

I did so. Before me across the bare room was the curtainless five-lighted bow-window.

"You are sitting now," he said, laying a heavy hand on my shoulder, "where the other, my predecessor, used to sit and take his meals."

I could not restrain a start, nor resist the impulse to turn and face him. It made me uneasy to have him standing over me, behind me, out of sight. He appeared surprised. "Pray don't be alarmed, sir," he said, "but turn back and tell me what you see."

I obeyed. "I see the window," I said.

"Is that all?" he asked.

I stared at the window. "No," I said. "I also see five reflections of myself, one in each light of the window."

"Just so," said the old man; "just so! That is what the other saw when he took his meals alone. He saw the five other selves each eating its lonely meal. When he poured out some water, each of them poured out water; when he lit a cigarette, each of them lit a cigarette."

"Of course," I said. "And that alarmed your friend, the clergyman?"

"The Reverend James Baxter," said the old man; "that was his name. Be sure not to forget it, my friend; and if people ask you who lives here, remember to say the Reverend James Baxter. Nobody knows, you see, that... that...!"

"Nobody knows what you told me. I understand."

"Exactly!" he said, suddenly dropping his voice. "Nobody knows. Not a soul. You're the first person I've mentioned it to."

"And you've had no inquiries?" I asked. "This Mr Baxter was not missed?"

He shook his head. "No," he said. "Even Mrs Bellows, who looked after him from the start, is not aware of what happened."

I turned round and faced him incredulously. "Not aware, you mean to say...?"

"Not aware that I'm not he. You see," he explained, "we were very much alike. Quite remarkably so! I can show you a photograph of him before you go and you'll see for yourself."

I now decided that, rain or no rain, I would go; there did not seem much reason, beyond the rain, for my staying. I stood up. "Well, sir," I said, "I can only hope that you will benefit of having relieved your mind of your... secret."

The old gentleman became very much agitated. He clasped and unclasped his two limp hands. "Oh, but you must not go yet. You haven't heard half of it. You haven't heard how it happened. I had hoped, sir—you have been so kind—that you'd have the patience and the kindness to...!"

I sat down again on the bench. "By all means," I said, "if you have more to say."

"I had just told you, hadn't I," the old gentleman went on, "that I... that the other... that my predecessor used to sit here at his meals and see his five other selves mimicking him? When he lit his cigarette he saw five other cigarettes lighted simultaneously."

"Naturally," I said.

"Yes, naturally," said the old man; "it was all perfectly natural, as you say; perfectly natural till one night, one terrible night." He stopped and stared at me with horror in his eyes.

"And then?" I said.

"Then a strange, a dreadful thing happened. When he, my predecessor, had lit his cigarette, watching those other selves, as he always did, he saw that one of them, the one on the extreme left, had lit, not a cigarette, but a pipe."

I burst out laughing. "Oh, come, come, sir!"

The old man wrung his hands in agitation. "It is comic, I know," he said, "but it is also terrible. What would you have thought if you had actually *seen* it yourself? Wouldn't you have thought it terrible? Wouldn't you have been appalled?"

"Yes," I said, "if it had actually happened. If I had really seen such a thing, of course I should."

"Well," said the old man, "it *did* happen. There was no possible mistake about it. It was appalling, ghastly." There was as much horror in his voice as if he had actually seen the thing himself.

"But, my dear sir," I said to him, "you have only the word of this Mr... Mr Baxter for it."

He stared at me, his eyes blazing with conviction. "I *know* it happened," he said; "I know it much more certainly than if I had seen it. Listen. The thing went on for five days: on five successive evenings my predecessor watched in horror for the thing to right itself."

But why didn't he go—leave the house?" I asked.

"He daren't," said the old man in a strained whisper. "He daren't go: he *had* to stay and see for certain that the thing had righted itself."

"And it didn't?"

"On the sixth night," said the old man with bated breath, "the fifth reflection, the one that had broken away from obedience, had gone."

"Gone?"

"Yes, gone from the window. My predecessor sat gazing in terror at the blank pane and the other four stared back in terror into this room. He glanced from the empty pane to them and they stared back at him, or at something behind him, with horror in their eyes. Then he began to choke... to choke," gasped the old man, himself almost choking, "to choke, because hands were round his throat, clutching, throttling him."

"You mean that the hands were the hands of the fifth?" I asked, and it was only my horror at the old man's horror that prevented my smiling cynically.

"Yes," he hissed, and he held out his thick, heavy hands, gazing at me with staring eyes. "Yes. *My* hands!"

For the first time I was really terrified. We stared speechless at one another, he still gasping and wheezing. Then, hoping to soothe him, I said as calmly as I could: "I see; so you were the fifth reflection?"

He pointed to his pipe on the table. "Yes," he gasped; "I, the pipe-smoker."

I stood up; my impulse was to hurry to the door. But some scruple held me there still, a feeling that it would be inhuman to leave him alone, a prey to his horrible fantasy; and, with a vague idea of bringing him to his senses, of easing his tortured mind, I asked, "And what did you do with the body?"

He caught his breath, a shudder distorted his face, and, clenching his two extended hands, he began to beat his breast convulsively. "*This*," he shouted in a voice of agony, "*this* is the body."

1982

OLD FILLIKIN

Joan Aiken

Conrad Aiken and Jessie McDonald had three children, John (1913–1990), Jane (1917–2009) and Joan (1924–2004), all of whom became writers. John preferred science fiction, selling a series to the British New Worlds *magazine in 1947, following the conflict between a colonized world around Alpha Centauri and invaders from Earth. The series had been drafted as a novel but was split for the magazine. It was later reconstructed as* World Well Lost *(1970). As a career, though, Aiken was a biochemist and writing was little more than a hobby. Jane, who wrote as Jane Aiken Hodge after her marriage to historian Alan Hodge in 1947, turned mostly to historical fiction, with many stories set in the Regency period so beloved of Georgette Heyer whose biography she wrote:* The Private World of Georgette Heyer *(1984). She also wrote a biography of Jane Austen, entitled* Only a Novel *(1972). Her many historical novels began with* Marry in Haste *(1961), the story of a loveless marriage set in Napoleonic Europe.*

The youngest of the three siblings was Joan, and the only one born in England. Her passion was for fantasy and the supernatural and many of her books were written for children—she had sold her first stories to BBC radio for Children's Hour *in 1944. Story collections for younger readers include* All You've Ever Wanted *(1953),* More Than You've Bargained For *(1955),* A Necklace of Raindrops *(1968),* A Small Pinch of Weather *(1969) and* The Last Slice of Rainbow *(1985), whilst stories for older readers were collected in* The Windscreen Weepers *(1969) with a final collection assembled by her daughter,* The People in the Castle, *published in 2016. Joan is probably best known for her alternate world series that began with* The Wolves of Willoughby Chase *(1962), but in a prodigious writing career she produced over a hundred works including crime and historical novels, taking a leaf from her sister's book with* Jane Fairfax *(1990), a novel drawn from Jane Austen's* Emma. *She was awarded an MBE in 1999 for services to children's literature.*

When I corresponded with Joan in the 1970s and 1980s I asked her the extent to which her writing was influenced by her father and her response is of relevance to this volume:

> You ask about being the daughter of a noted American poet. Obviously this did influence me and so did the fact that my father put me on to reading writers such as Fitz-James O'Brien, Poe, and the poems of Vachel Lindsay. But I was equally or even more influenced by my English stepfather, Martin Armstrong, with whom I actually spent most of my childhood.

Nor should we forget the influence of her mother, Jessie, who home-tutored Joan and read to her a wide range of stories. This stimulated Joan's imagination. As her daughter Lizzie remembered in 2009, her mother was "...aware of the power of stories to heal or distract, to uplift and encourage [and] she used her gift to pass them on..."

Truly a gift to us all.

Miss Evans, the maths teacher, had thick white skin, pocked like a nutmeg-grater; her lips were pale and thick, often puffed out with annoyance; her thick hair was the drab colour of old straw that has gone musty; and her eyes, behind thick glass lenses, stared angrily at Timothy.

"Timothy, how often have I *told* you," she said. "You have *got* to show your working. Even if these were the right answers—which they are not—I should give you no marks for them, because no working is shown. How, may I ask, did you arrive at this answer?"

Her felt-tip pen made two angry red circles on the page. All Timothy's neat layout—and the problems were tidily and beautifully set out, at least—all that neat arrangement had been spoiled by a forest of furious red X's, underlinings, and crossings-out, that went from top to bottom of the page, with a big W for Wrong beside each answer. The page was horrible now—like a scarred face, like a wrecked garden. Timothy could hardly bear to look at it.

"Well? How did you get that answer? Do you *understand* what I'm asking you?"

The trouble was that when she asked him a sharp question like that, in her flat, loud voice, with its aggressive north-country vowels—*an*swer, *ask*, with a short a as in grab or bash—he felt as if she were hammering little sharp nails into his brain. At once all his wits completely deserted him, the inside of his head was a blank numbness, empty and echoing like a hollow pot, as if his intelligence had escaped through the holes she had hammered.

"I don't know," he faltered.

"You *don't know*? How can you not *know*? You must have got those answers *some*how! Or do you just put down any figures that come into your head? If you'd got them *right*, I'd assume you'd copied the answers from somebody else's book—but it's quite plain you didn't do that."

She stared at him in frustrated annoyance, her eyes pinpointed like screw-tips behind the thick glass.

Of course he would not be such a fool as to copy someone else's book. He hardly ever got a sum right. If he had a whole series correct, it would be grounds for instant suspicion.

"Well, as you have this whole set wrong—plainly you haven't grasped the principle at all—I'll just have to set you a new lot. Here—you can start at the beginning of Chapter VIII, page 64, and go as far as page 70."

His heart sank horribly. They were all the same kind—the kind he particularly hated—pages and pages of them. It would take him the whole weekend—and now, late on Friday evening—for she had kept him after class—he was already losing precious time.

"Do you understand? Are you following me? I'd better explain the principle again."

And she was off, explaining; her gravelly voice went on and on, about brackets, bases, logarithms, sines, cosines, goodness knows what, but now, thank heaven, his mind was set free, she was not asking questions, and so he could let his thoughts sail off on a string, like a kite flying higher and higher...

"Well?" she snapped. "Have you got it now?"

"Yes—I think so."

"What have I been saying?"

He looked at her dumbly.

But just then a merciful bell began to ring, for the boarders' supper.

"I've got to go," he gasped, "or I'll miss my bus."

Miss Evans unwillingly gave in.

"Oh, very well. Run along. But you'll *have* to learn this, you know—you'll never pass exams, never get *any*where, unless you do. Even farmers need maths. Don't think I enjoy trying to force it into your thick head—it's no pleasure to *me* to have to spend time going over it all again and again."

He was gathering his books together—the fat, ink-stained grey textbook, the glossy blue new one, the rough notebook, the green exercise book filled with angry red corrections—horrible things, he loathed the very sight and feel of them. If only he could throw them down the well, burn them, never open them again. Some day he would be free of them.

He hurried out, ran down the steps, tore across the school courtyard. The bus was still waiting beyond the gate; with immense relief he bounded into it and flung himself down on the prickly moquette seat.

If only he could blot Miss Evans and the hateful maths out of his mind for two days; if only he could sit out under the big walnut tree in the orchard, and just draw and draw and let his mind fly like a kite, and think of nothing at all but what picture was going to take shape under his pencil, and in what colours, later, he would paint it; but now that plan was spoiled, he would have to work at those horrible problems for hours and hours, with his mind jammed among them, like a mouse caught in some diabolical machinery that it didn't invent, and doesn't begin to understand.

The bus stopped at a corner by a bridge, and he got out, climbed a fence, and walked across fields to get to the farm where he lived.

There was a way round by a cart track, the way the postman came, but it took longer. The fields smelt of warm hay, and the farmyard of dry earth, and cattle-cake, and milk, and tractor-oil; a rooster crowed in the orchard, and some ducks quacked close at hand; all these were homely, comforting, familiar things, but now they had no power to comfort him; they were like helpless friends holding out their hands to him as he was dragged away to prison.

"These are *rules*, can't you see?" Miss Evans had stormed at him. "You have to learn them."

"Why?" he wanted to ask. "Who made those rules? How can you be certain they were right? Why do you turn upside down and multiply? Why isn't there any square root of minus one?"

But he never had the courage to ask that kind of question.

Next morning he went out and sat with his books in the orchard, under the big walnut, by the old well. It would have been easier to concentrate indoors, to work on the kitchen table, but the weather was so warm and still that he couldn't bear not to be out of doors. Soon the frosts would begin; already the walnut leaves, yellow as butter, were starting to drift down, and the squashy walnut rinds littered the dry grass and stained his bare feet brown. The nights were drawing in.

For some reason he remembered a hymn his granny used to say to him:

"Every morning the red sun
Rises warm and bright,
But the evening soon comes on
And the dark cold night."

The words had frightened him, he could not say why.

He tried to buckle his mind to his work. "If $r \geq 4$, r weighings can deal with $2r-1$ loads—" but his thoughts trickled away like a river in sand. He had been dreaming about his grandmother who had died two years ago. In his dream they had been here, in the orchard, but it was winter, thick grey frost all over the grass, a fur of frost on every branch and twig and grass-blade. Granny had come out of the house with her old zinc pail to get water from the well.

"Tap water's no good to you," she always used to say. "Never drink water that's passed through metal pipes, it'll line your innards with tin, you'll end up clinking like a moneybox. Besides, tap water's full of those floorides and kloorides and wrigglers they put in it—letting on as it's for your good—hah! I'd not pay a penny for a hundred gallons of the stuff. Well water's served me all my life long, and it'll go on doing. Got some taste to it—not like that nasty flat stuff."

"I'll wind up the bucket for you, Granny," he said, and took hold of the heavy well-handle.

"That's me boy! One hundred and eight turns."

"A hundred and eight is nine twelves. Nine tens are ninety, nine elevens are ninety-nine, nine twelves are a hundred and eight."

"Only in your book, lovie. In mine it's different. We have different ones!"

An ironic smile curved her mouth, she stood with arms folded over her clean blue-and-white print overall while he wound and counted. Eighty-nine, ninety, ninety-one, ninety-two...

When he had the dripping, double-cone-shaped well bucket at the top, and was going to tilt it, so as to fill her small pail, she had exclaimed, "Well, look who's come up with it! Old Fillikin!"

And that, for some reason, had frightened him so much that he had not dared look into the bucket but dropped it so that it went clattering back into the well and he woke up.

This seemed odd, remembering the dream in daylight, for he had loved his grandmother dearly. His own mother had died when he was two, and granny had always looked after him. She had been kind, impatient, talkative, always ready with an apple, a hug, a slice of bread-and-dripping if he was hungry or hurt himself. She was full of unexpected ideas, and odd information.

"Husterloo's the wood where Reynard the fox keeps his treasure. If we could find that, *I* could stop knitting, and *you* could stop thinking. You think too much, for a boy your age.

"The letter N is a wriggling eel. His name is No one, and his number is Nine.

"Kings always die standing up, and that's the way I mean to die."

She had, too, standing in the doorway, shouting after the postman, "If you don't bring me a letter tomorrow, I'll write your name on a leaf, and shut it in a drawer!"

Some people had thought she was a witch, because she talked to herself such a lot, but Timothy found nothing strange about her; he had never been in the least frightened of her.

"Who were you talking to, Granny?" he would say, if he came into the kitchen when she was rattling off one of her monologues.

"I was talking to Old Fillikin," she always answered, just as, when he asked, "What's for dinner, Granny?" she invariably said, "Surprise pie with pickled questions."

"Who's Old Fillikin?" he asked once, and she said, "Old Fillikin's my friend. My familiar friend. Every man has a friend in his sleeve."

"Have I got one, Granny?"

"Of course you have, love. Draw his picture, call him by his name, and he'll come out."

Now, sitting by the well, in the warm, hazy sunshine, Timothy began to wonder what Old Fillikin, Granny's familiar friend, would have looked like, if he had existed. The idea was, for some reason, not quite comfortable, and he tried to turn his mind back to his maths problem.

"R weighings can deal with 2r–1 loads..." but somehow the image of Old Fillikin would keep sneaking back among his thoughts, and, almost without noticing that he did so, he began to doodle in his rough notebook.

Old Fillikin fairly leapt out of the page: every stroke, every touch of the point, filled him in more swiftly and definitely. Old Fillikin was a kind of hairy frog; he looked soft and squashy to the touch—like a rotten pear, or a damp eiderdown—but he had claws too, and a mouthful of needle-sharp teeth. His eyes were very shrewd—they were a bit like Granny's eyes—but there was a sad, lost look about them too, as there had been about Granny's; as if she were used to being misunderstood. Old Fillikin was not a creature that you would want to meet in a narrow high-banked lane, with dusk falling. At first Timothy was not certain of his size. Was he as big as an apple, so that he could float, bobbing, in a bucket drawn up from a well, or was he, perhaps, about the size of Bella the Tamworth sow? The pencil answered that question, sketching in a gate behind Old Fillikin, which showed that he was at least two feet high.

"Ugh!" said Timothy, quite upset at his own creation, and he tore out the page from his notebook, scrumpled it up, and dropped it down the well.

$$\frac{dy}{dx} = \lim_{dx \to 0} \frac{f(x+dx) - f(x)}{x}$$

"*Numbers!*" he remembered Granny scoffing, years ago, when he was hopelessly bogged down in his seven-times table. "Some people think they can manage everything by numbers. As if they were set in the ground like bricks!"

"How do you mean, Granny?"

"As if you daren't slip through between!"

"But how *can* you slip between them, Granny? There's nothing between one and two—except one-and-a-half."

"You think there's only one lot of numbers?"

"Of course! One, two, three, four, five, six, seven, eight, nine, ten. Or in French," he said grandly, "it's un, deux, trois—"

"Hah!" she said. "Numbers are just a set of rules that some bone-head made up. They're just the fence he built to keep fools from falling over the edge."

"What edge?"

"Oh, go and fetch me a bunch of parsley from the garden!"

That was her way of shutting him up when she'd had enough. She liked long spells by herself, did Granny, though she was always pleased to see him again when he came back.

"The arrow → tends to a given value as a limit..."

"Timothy!" called his father. "Aunt Di says it's lunchtime."

"Okay! Coming!"

"Did I see you drop a bit of paper down the well just now?"

"Yes, I did," he admitted, rather ashamed.

"Well, don't! Just because we don't drink the water doesn't mean that well can be used as a rubbish dump. After dinner you go and fish it out."

"Sorry, Dad."

During the meal his father and Aunt Di were talking about a local court case: a man who had encouraged, indeed trained his dog to go next door and harass the neighbours, bite their children and dig holes in their flowerbeds. The court had ordered the dog to be destroyed. Aunt Di, a dog-lover, was indignant about this.

"It wasn't the dog's fault! It was the owner. They should have had *him* destroyed—or sent him to prison!"

"If I had a dog," thought Timothy, "I could train it to go and wake Miss Evans every night by barking under her window, so that she'd fall asleep in class. Or it could get in through her cat-flap and pull her out of bed..."

"Wake up, boy, you're half asleep," said his father. "It's all that mooning over schoolbooks, if you ask me. You'd better come and help me cart feed this afternoon."

"I've got to finish my maths first. There's still loads to do."

"They give them too much homework, if you ask *me*," said Aunt Di. "Addles their minds."

"Well, you get that bit of paper out of the well, anyway," said his father.

He could see it, glimmering white, down below; it had caught on top of the bucket, which still hung there, though nobody used it. He had quite a struggle to wind it up—the handle badly needed oiling, and shrieked at every turn. At last, leaning down, he was able to grab the crumpled sheet; then he let go of the handle, which whirled round crazily as the bucket rattled down again.

But, strangely enough, the crumpled sheet was blank. Timothy felt half relieved, half disappointed; he had been curious to see if his drawing of Old Fillikin was as nasty as he had remembered. Could he have crumpled up the wrong sheet? But no other had a picture on it. At last he decided that the damp atmosphere in the well must have faded the pencil marks. The paper felt cold, soft, and pulpy—rather unpleasant. He carried it indoors and poked it into the kitchen coal-stove.

Then he did another hour's work indoors, scrambling through the problems somehow, anyhow. Miss Evans would be angry again, they were certain to be wrong—but, for heaven's sake, he couldn't spend the whole of Saturday at the horrible task. He checked the results, where it was possible to do so, on his little pocket calculator; blessed, useful little thing, it came up with the results so humbly and willingly, flashing out solutions far faster than his mind could. Farmers need maths too, he remembered Miss Evans saying; but when I'm a farmer, he resolved, I shall have a computer to do all those jobs, and I'll just keep to the practical work.

Then he was free, and his father let him drive the tractor, which of course was illegal, but he had been doing it since he was ten and drove better than Kenny the cowman. "You can't keep all the laws," his father said. "Some just have to be broken. All farmers' sons drive tractors. Law's simply a system invented to protect fools," as Granny had said about the numbers.

That night Timothy dreamed that Old Fillikin came up out of the well and went hopping and flopping away across the fields in the direction of Markhurst Green, where Miss Evans lived. Timothy followed, in his dream, and saw the ungainly, yet agile creature clamber in through the cat-flap. "*Don't!* Oh, please, *don't!*" he tried to call. "I didn't mean—I never meant *that*—"

He could hear the flip-flop as it went up the stairs, and he woke himself, screaming, in a tangle of sheet and blanket.

On Sunday night the dream was even worse. That night he took his little calculator to bed with him, and made it work out the nine-times table until there were no more places on the screen.

Then he recited Granny's hymn: "Every morning the red sun, Rises warm and bright, But the evening soon comes on, and the dark cold night."

"If only I could stop my mind working," he thought. He remembered Granny saying, "If we could find Reynard's treasure in Husterloo wood, *I* could stop knitting, and you could stop thinking."

He remembered her saying, "Kings die standing, that's the way I mean to die."

At last he fell into a light, troubled sleep.

On Mondays, maths was the first period, an hour and a half. He had been dreading it, but in another way he was desperately anxious to see Miss Evans, to make sure that she was all right. In his second dream, Old Fillikin had pushed through her bedroom door, which stood ajar, and hopped across the floor. Then there had been a kind of silence filled with little fumbling sounds; then a most blood-curdling scream—like the well-handle, as the bucket rattled down.

It was only a dream, Timothy kept telling himself as he rode to school on the bus; nothing but a dream.

But the maths class was taken by Mr Gillespie. Miss Evans, they heard, had not come in. And, later, the school grapevine passed along the news. Miss Evans had suffered a heart attack last night; died before she could be taken to hospital.

When he got off the bus that evening and began to cross the dusk-filled fields towards home, Timothy walked faster than usual, and looked warily about him.

Where—he could not help wondering—was Old Fillikin now?

STORY SOURCES

The following gives the first publication details for each story and the sources used.

"Krantz's Narrative" by Frederick Marryat first appeared in *New Monthly Magazine*, July 1839 as chapter 39 of *The Phantom Ship*. Published in book form in *The Phantom Ship* (Colburn, 1839).

"The Haunted Nursery" by Florence Marryat first appeared in *Once a Week* in 1886 (issue not traced) and was syndicated elsewhere including the *Ballarat Star* (20 March–3 April 1886) and *Frank Leslie's Popular Monthly* (May 1886). Not published in book form.

"The Watcher" by J. Sheridan Le Fanu first appeared in *Dublin University Magazine*, November 1847 and was first collected in *Ghost Stories and Tales of Mystery* (James McGlashan, 1851). It was slightly revised and retitled "The Familiar" in *In a Glass Darkly* (Richard Bentley, 1872).

"What It Meant" by Rhoda Broughton first appeared in *Temple Bar*, September 1881 and was included as an Appendix in *Rhoda Broughton: Profile of a Novelist* by Marilyn Wood (Paul Watkins, 1993). It was collected in *Rhoda Broughton's Ghost Stories*, edited by Marilyn Wood (Paul Watkins, 1995).

"Fran Nan's Story" by Sarah LeFanu. First published in *Uncertainties, Volume 1*, edited by Brian J. Showers (Swan River Press, 2016).

"Young Goodman Brown" by Nathaniel Hawthorne. First published in *New England Magazine*, April 1835 and collected in *Mosses from an Old Manse* (Wiley & Putnam, 1846).

"The Mysterious Case of My Friend Browne" by Julian Hawthorne. First published in *Harper's New Monthly Magazine*, January 1872 and collected in *The Rose of Death*, edited by Jessica Amanda Salmonson (Ash-Tree Press, 1997).

"Unawares" by Hildegarde Hawthorne. First published in *New England Magazine*, December 1908 and collected in *Faded Garden*, edited by Jessica Amanda Salmonson (The Strange Company, 1985).

"A Child's Dream of a Star" by Charles Dickens. First published in *Household Words*, 6 April 1850 and collected in *Reprinted Pieces* (Chapman & Hall, 1861).

"My Fellow Travellers" by Mary Angela Dickens. First published in *The Gentlewoman*, 19 December 1896 and collected in *Unveiled and Other Stories* (Digby, Long & Co, 1906).

"To Reach the Sea" by Monica Dickens. First published in *Ellery Queen's Mystery Magazine*, September 1965 and collected in *The Fifth Fontana Book of Great Horror Stories* edited by Mary Danby (Fontana, 1970).

"The Secret Ones" by Mary Danby. First published in *The Seventh Fontana Book of Great Horror Stories* edited by Mary Danby (Fontana, 1972) and collected in *Party Pieces* (Noose & Gibbet, 2012).

"The Substitute" by Georgia Wood Pangborn. First published in *Harper's Magazine*, December 1914 and collected in *The Wind at Midnight*, edited by Jessica Amanda Salmonson (Ash-Tree Press, 1999).

"Wogglebeast" by Edgar Pangborn. First published in *The Magazine of Fantasy & Science Fiction*, January 1965 and collected in *Good Neighbors and Other Strangers* (Macmillan, 1972).

"My Name is Samantha" by Mary C. Pangborn. First published in *The Magazine of Fantasy & Science Fiction*, January 1984.

"Silent Snow, Secret Snow" by Conrad Aiken. First published in *The Virginia Quarterly Review*, October 1932 and collected in *Among the Lost People* (Scribner's, 1934).

STORY SOURCES

"The Pipe-Smoker" by Martin Armstrong. First published in *The Fortnightly Review*, October 1932 and collected in *General Buntop's Miracle* (Gollancz, 1934).

"Old Fillikin" by Joan Aiken. First published in *Ghost After Ghost* edited by Aidan Chambers (Kestrel, 1982) and collected in *A Whisper in the Night* (Gollancz, 1982).

For more Tales of the Weird titles
visit the British Library Shop (shop.bl.uk)

We welcome any suggestions, corrections or feedback you may have, and will aim to respond to all items addressed to the following:

The Editor (Tales of the Weird), British Library Publishing,
The British Library, 96 Euston Road, London NW1 2DB

We also welcome enquiries through our Twitter account, @BL_Publishing.